The BRAHMINS

The BRAHMINS

Eileen Lottman

DELACORTE PRESS/NEW YORK

Published by
Delacorte Press
1 Dag Hammarskjold Plaza
New York, N.Y. 10017

Manufactured in the United States of America

First printing

Designed by MaryJane DiMassi

Library of Congress Cataloging in Publication Data

Lottman, Eileen.
The Brahmins.

I. Title.
PS3562.079B7   813'.54   82-2353
ISBN 0-440-00313-X   AACR2

*This novel is dedicated to
the warm and happy memories given
to me by two people who loved Boston:
Betty Worden and David (Modisette) Ford.*

THE
STAFFORD-PORTER
LINEAGE

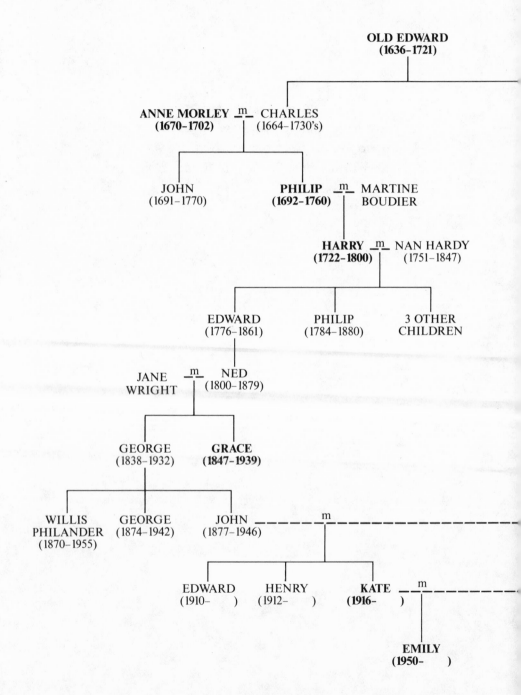

OLD EDWARD
(1636–1721)

ANNE MORLEY _m_ CHARLES
(1670–1702) (1664–1730's)

JOHN   **PHILIP** _m_ MARTINE
(1691–1770)   **(1692–1760)** BOUDIER

HARRY _m_ NAN HARDY
(1722–1800) (1751–1847)

EDWARD   PHILIP   3 OTHER
(1776–1861)   (1784–1880)   CHILDREN

JANE _m_ NED
WRIGHT (1800–1879)

GEORGE   **GRACE**
(1838–1932)   **(1847–1939)**

WILLIS   GEORGE   JOHN _m_
PHILANDER   (1874–1942)   (1877–1946)
(1870–1955)

EDWARD   HENRY   **KATE** _m_
(1910–   )   (1912–   )   **(1916–   )**

EMILY
(1950–   )

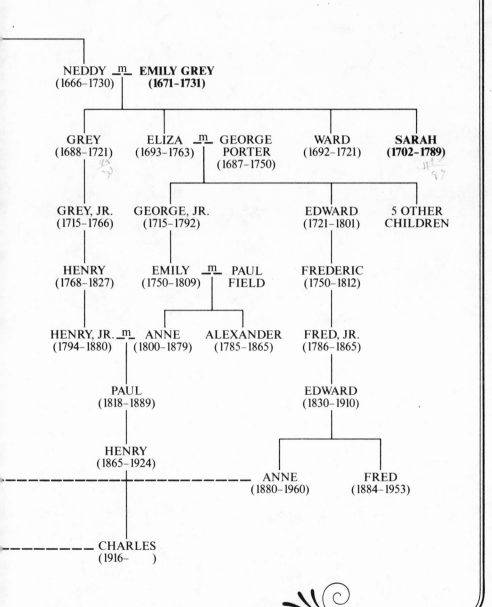

NEDDY _m_ **EMILY GREY**
(1666–1730) **(1671–1731)**

GREY
(1688–1721)

ELIZA _m_ GEORGE
(1693–1763) PORTER
(1687–1750)

WARD
(1692–1721)

SARAH
(1702–1789)

GREY, JR.
(1715–1766)

GEORGE, JR.
(1715–1792)

EDWARD
(1721–1801)

5 OTHER
CHILDREN

HENRY
(1768–1827)

EMILY _m_ PAUL
(1750–1809) FIELD

FREDERIC
(1750–1812)

HENRY, JR. _m_ ANNE
(1794–1880) (1800–1879)

ALEXANDER
(1785–1865)

FRED, JR.
(1786–1865)

PAUL
(1818–1889)

EDWARD
(1830–1910)

HENRY
(1865–1924)

ANNE
(1880–1960)

FRED
(1884–1953)

CHARLES
(1916–   )

1918: KATE

Kate Stafford's earliest memory was of her great-aunt Grace setting the nursery tablecloth on fire. The famous artist had come up to have a look at young Kate and had put her black cigar behind her back so that the heavy odor wouldn't go right up the baby's nose. After all, Grace Stafford was a sensitive person, internationally acclaimed for her delicacy of feeling and genius for expressing emotions on canvas. But as the 300-pound woman bent over to inspect her small relative, the cigar caught the edge of the lace cloth and a flame leaped up behind the stout, black-trousered backside. Kate, who was two and a half, said nothing, although her eyes went very round. Her great-aunt Grace assumed the child to be struck dumb with awe at the presence of her own handsome figure; later she would amend her first impression and decide that the girl was not quite bright. After all, even a two-year-old should be able to shout, "Fire," when it sees one. The fact was that Kate was already so bored it didn't surprise her at all to see the wicked witch go up in smoke, exactly as predicted in the storybooks. Everything was predictable on Beacon Hill.

Part
ONE

Chapter One

1927: KATE

Kate was so scared she thought that the leaping of her heart might be visible through her starched white middy, and that was why the man on the opposite side of the aisle kept lowering his *Transcript* to peek at her. His large, flat, watery eyes seemed to curve around his temples like a toad's. He gave Kate the willies.

The train lurched and racketed and clattered in the night as it rushed headlong away from Boston. Out there, beyond her own eerily transparent reflection, she could see occasional pinpricks of light. When the steam whistle shrieked suddenly at a crossing, she felt her bones jump inside her skin. The man across the aisle crunched his newspaper down and peered over at her like a giant fish coming up to the surface to have a look-see. This made Kate sit up very straight in her seat and let her Stafford chin jut out.

She thought about moving away, to another seat, but she didn't want to call attention. The kindly-looking porter came through her car every once in a while, to announce the next stop or offer to sell cigarettes and candy bars. He looked down at her as if she needed something but he didn't quite know what. There were only two or three other passengers in this car, and most of the little shaded lamps had been turned out. Behind her, she adjudged from the dim ghostly reflection in her window, there were only two little pools of yellow light in the entire swaying, clattering, lonesome car besides her own.

It was her old bugaboo, the dark. Maybe it had been a mistake to travel by night, not because of her childish fear of the dark, of course, but because people might think it odd for an eleven-year-old girl to be traveling alone at night all the way from Boston to New York. It might have been more intelligent, she thought, and it certainly would have been safer, if she had figured out a way to run away during the daylight hours.

But the Lone Eagle had made his solitary journey by night as well as day. And if she didn't face up to real danger and test her courage to its limits, she wouldn't be worthy of him.

Kate Stafford was exceptionally well educated for a girl her age, being a Boston girl, and she had inherited a keen native intelligence from a line of extraordinary ancestors. She was not really so naïve as to think that Charles A. Lindbergh would be impressed with her daring to be out alone after dark, to leave her home without anyone's knowledge, and to walk all the way to Back Bay Station and buy a ticket and go off to New York all by herself. Of course not. These things were nothing except to her. It was a private test, and here she was. She had proved to herself that she had courage, and now . . .

There was a sudden choking, strangulated sound close behind her, a knife plunged into a human throat. Kate was too well brought up to turn around, but her eyes stared back hugely at her from the window, and her palpitating heart seemed to stop. The gruesome sound was followed by a gurgling intake of breath, as if the victim were drowning in his own blood. Kate felt sick to her stomach. The train lurched and screamed in the night and kept rushing heedlessly onward. There was a smaller, more intimate whistling sound now, with sighing undertones, the last gasp of the dying man, she knew it. She stared at her own face in the dark glass: bulging eyes; mouth hanging open in a horrified and most unladylike way. Right through her own image she could see the man across the aisle, reading the *Transcript* as if he had heard nothing. Out there, the darkness and the unknown countryside.

The throat-ripping sound came again, with something unmistakably like one of old Beadie's snoring noises when he was asleep on the rug and having one of his basset hound dreams. Kate realized that she had just heard her first human snore.

She couldn't understand how people could actually sleep in public, but she thought she'd probably better try it herself. The train would get to New York City very early in the morning, and it was to be the most important day of her life.

She reached up to pull the little chain on her lamp and immediately regretted it. The reflection of her face in the window stood out more sharply. It was her old nightmare, the incubus that invaded your body and took over while you slept. Kate reached up and pulled the lamp on again and settled herself as best she could with her too-thin, too-pointy Stafford chin straight ahead, not wanting to turn toward either the window or the man.

She read too much, that was her trouble. One of her nurses had told her that way back when she was only four, and even though her entire family scoffed at such nonsense (pointing out at the same time that one must always be considerate of the innocent belief in folk-myths which servants often hold), she had worried about it. That night, she remembered, her brother Edward had come up to her sitting room (still called the nursery in those days) with quotations from Francis Bacon and Henry Thoreau and one of the Lowells about reading maketh the whole man and so forth. Her father had told her that boring story about how their family had been one of the original founders of the Athenaeum and other libraries where even the public could read freely. But it had been Annie Malone who had sat with Kate when she had nightmares from reading *The Prisoner of Zenda,* and Annie was the one who rocked her for hours while she sobbed over the fate of *Black Beauty.* In the back of her mind, Kate still reserved the possibility that Annie had been right; she used it now as a kind of litany to ward off threats of nightmares. You read too much; that's all it is, my girl.

She breathed a name to herself: Lindy. It seemed to her then that all her failing courage leaped back into her being with that magical word. But what if he didn't care for that nickname? The popular press had given it to him, and her father always said that while the free press was necessary, one should never believe what was printed there.

Charles, she almost said aloud. Charles. No, she had a cousin named Charles whose bland face inserted itself between her and the memorized vision of the tall, shy aviator with the leather helmet and white scarf.

Lindy and Kate. There was only a fourteen-year difference in their ages; maybe that seemed important to some people, who thought of her as a child. But he would understand. The Lone Eagle would be the one person in the entire world to see beyond the child's body she was trapped in, to see the *person* underneath. And in a few years the age difference would mean nothing, and everyone would say, "Well, they were right, Lindy and Kate, and we were wrong. They are so obviously and eternally perfect together after all."

She hadn't quite thought out exactly what she would do when she reached New York City. Surely it would be simple enough to find out where he was staying. He was the hero of the day, and anyone would be able to tell her where to find him. And when she did . . . she would have to think of a way to let him know who she was. His future wife.

Her thoughts insisted on hazing over just there. It happened every time she tried to imagine exactly what would have to transpire in order for him to recognize his destiny in her brown eyes. Something would happen, and he would say, startled, "Why, she is so much like me!" and then he would take her with him wherever he went. They would never be separated. She would be with him on his next flight—she wouldn't be the least bit afraid to fly over the ocean—and if he faltered, she'd be there to keep his spirits up. He had said he had been lonely, but no more would he have to suffer from this terrible thing. Kate herself had never exactly been lonely, but she was sure she understood what it must be like. It must have been awful for him, but now, together, they could do anything in the world, anything, and he would never be lonely again. They would fly together; he would teach her how. And she would have things to teach him, too: She was very good at history, and poetry, and seeing inside the hearts of others. Once he knew her, he would see that they were fated for each other, like Cathy and Heathcliff. She didn't even care if he didn't want to marry her, she thought daringly as the train took a jolt that made her come wide-awake.

The man with the toad eyes had turned out his lamp and was apparently sleeping, his head thrown back against the dark outline of the seat. But she knew that he was still watching her, with the peripheral vision possible with such eyes. Insects had them and saw six images at once of the same object. Kate shuddered, closed her own eyes, and tried to go back to her daydream.

If Lindy didn't want to marry her, she would understand perfectly. The fact was that eleven really was too young to get married, probably even in New York. It would be just as nice if they could be pals, really special-and-forever pals, friends with a closeness and understanding all others must envy. They wouldn't have to "do it" then; it would be a pure and perfect relationship.

Every novel I've ever loved starts with someone leaving home, she thought, and oddly comforted, she felt herself drifting toward sleep. The train barreled on through the night, and dawn broke along the eastern shore, a hot, sunny June day. Kate felt the warmth and sunlight against her eyelids, but she slept soundly through the slowing of the engines, the screeching of the whistles, and the clinging and chugging into the underground tunnels of the city. When the porter gently shook her arm to wake her, she was the last person still in the train, and outside her window it was as dark as ever, and she was a very scared little girl.

She stuck out her chin and held her back straight and pulled on her brown felt hat (her mother always said if you wear a good brown Boston hat, people will recognize and respect you anywhere on earth, and Kate believed it to be true) and she tightened her fist around the handkerchief that had four dollars knotted into its corner. She went out on the platform, which seemed to be belowground in a very dirty cellar. Steps led up, and on the level, still underground, Kate saw to her great relief a sign that said Women. Of course one was never, never supposed to use the facilities in a public place; but she was 250 miles from Boston, and there didn't seem to be much else to do. She knew what her mother would have done, and she thought fleetingly of her uncle's apartment at the Dorset Hotel; but one didn't run away from home and then drop in to use the facilities. This was an adventure, after all.

She only glanced in the mirror, knowing how depressing it would be. One did with what one had. She had the face and body and clothes of a very plain and proper schoolgirl from Boston, Massachusetts. Suddenly she had an urge to throw her good brown felt hat into the receptacle for dirty linen. But she had to have something on her

head, and it would have to do until Lindy could get her a helmet like
his. Then she wouldn't care what anybody said. But for now she
yanked the shapeless thing down and tugged at her garters and
smoothed her pleated skirt and walked out of the women's room to
begin her adventure. She tried to ignore her terror and a sudden longing for breakfast.

She walked slowly across the enormous cavern where people rushed
every which way and lights blinked and black men with red caps and
jackets bustled about, carrying luggage. Everyone was in a hurry,
and the noises were urgent: the booming mechanical voice constantly
repeating track numbers and times of departure, calling out the names
of cities like an insistent geography lesson; a woman sobbing out
loud as she clung to a man dressed in a black suit who carried a
suitcase bound with ropes; babies fretting everywhere; a disorderly
gang of uniformed little boys following men with signs for Camp
Wahtahotchee, some of them crying (orphans being kidnapped?);
young women in heels higher than she had ever seen and skirts that
showed their knees—more interesting people than she had ever known
in her life—and under everything a low hum of excitement and motion that was thrilling to her, and terrifying.

She saw a lighted sign that identified the information desk and
went up to inquire of the gentleman sitting there.

"I beg your pardon, sir, but would you please tell me where Mr.
Charles Lindbergh is staying? I've just arrived from Boston, and I
don't—"

"You gotta talk louder, can't hear ya."

Shouting—raising one's voice for any reason, ever—was a cardi-
nal sin just below the level of using physical force. But this was New
York City. Kate tried to speak louder, raising herself on tiptoes and
leaning toward the gentleman, who was frowning down on her and
making no effort to be pleasant.

"I asked about Mr. Lindbergh," she explained as loudly as she
could. "Do you know where he is staying in this city, please?"

"Little lady, you must be pullin' my leg. Where do ya wanna go?
Come on, I got no time for jokes. Speak up now; don't waste my
time."

Embarrassed, Kate moved back from the information desk, bumping into a woman who was waiting behind her. She apologized, but the woman refused to accept her apology and just pushed her way up to the desk.

Bewildered but undaunted, Kate looked around the whirling terminal. She caught sight of a blue-uniformed policeman. Relieved, she walked over to him and held out her hand. She was embarrassed all over again to note that her glove was soiled, and of course, she had forgotten the extra pair, as she often did. There were streaks of dark soot along the fingers. She wondered if she ought to mention it, but the policeman didn't even seem to notice that her hand was out to him. He looked down at her, but he kept his own gloved hands behind his broad back. Maybe his were soiled, too.

"Are you lost, little girl? Something wrong?"

"Yes, please, sir," she said, withdrawing her hand in some relief. She'd have to go back into the women's room and try to get the glove clean before she met Lindy. Mended gloves were a sign of sensible frugality, a quality much desired in anyone, but there is never any excuse for uncleanliness; what would he think of her for forgetting the extra pair?

"Well, then, what's the trouble?" the policeman asked, bending down a little to smile at her. He was nice, with a red face and small, even teeth. His hair under the cap seemed to be sandy-colored, like her brother Edward's. It made her feel easier.

"I want to find Mr. Charles Lindbergh, please. I thought the people in New York would know where he is staying; but the man at the information desk seems to be hard-of-hearing, and I couldn't just ask a stranger, so I'm very glad to have found you. Can you tell me, please?"

"Well, now what would you be wanting to find Lucky Lindy for, if I may ask?"

The red-cheeked policeman was still smiling, and yet Kate knew he wasn't laughing at her. She felt an immense release of tension and wanted to confide everything to him at once.

"I've come all the way from Boston to meet him," she said. As if that would explain something.

The cheerful look on his face seemed to darken with a little cloud of doubt. The policeman straightened up, and Kate could hardly hear his next words because he was now so tall and remote. He took her hand and led her gently all the way up some stairs and out of the station to the street.

She went with him willingly, of course, not that she had any choice. She only hoped he was taking her where she wanted to go.

There was a gaudy blue and white painted police car at the curbstone. He opened the door and waited politely enough for her to climb inside. Another policeman was at the driver's wheel, and he said, "What's this then?" but he smiled at her. Both men had strong Irish brogues, which Kate recognized with a kind of warm familiarity. She hadn't realized that they had Irish people in New York, too, and letting them be policemen was quite a daring and wonderful thing, she thought. That could never happen in Boston. She settled herself in the back seat of the auto.

"Where are you taking me?" she asked. "To Mr. Lindbergh?" If that were the case, she should think very hard in the next few moments about exactly how she intended to present herself to him. It was the one thing she hadn't quite figured out yet. Suddenly it loomed rather importantly.

"Well, now, I thought we'd just go along to the precinct house first," said the nice sandy-haired one, half turning in the high front seat to look back at her kindly. "We've got good coffee and doughnuts there. How about some breakfast, eh? I'll bet you haven't had yours yet. All alone in the city, are you?"

"Am I arrested?" she asked, with more curiosity than fear. "On what charge?" She knew what to say because she had read that plenty of times. What a thrilling time she was having, no matter what happened.

"My goodness, look at that!" she exclaimed, forgetting not to point in her astonishment. They were crossing a wide avenue, where there were more cars and more people than she had ever seen in her life, and they seemed to be wading through the contents of a million wastebaskets! Bits of paper were mounded like autumn leaves along the streets on both sides and scattered up and down the avenue everywhere. It looked to Kate, as the police car maneuvered slowly through the clot of traffic at the intersection, as if New York City had never heard of such a thing as a street sweeper. Both her escorts looked up and down the avenue and clucked their tongues and shook their heads at the mess, but they seemed more amused than embarrassed.

She was terribly excited. She tried to sit back like a lady, but her eagerness got the better of her manners and she found herself with her head practically out the window, peering out first one way and then the other.

"Oh, there was a grand parade yesterday for your friend Lindy," the red-cheeked policeman told her. "People throwin' every scrap of paper they could find out of all their windows, ticker tape and all, up and down the avenue clear from the Battery. It was somethin' to see all right."

"Sanitation Department is having some trouble gettin' it all cleared away," commented the other, who shifted the gears and began to inch the sedan forward across the avenue on Forty-second Street.

"But that's terrible! Why would people do a thing like that?" Kate asked.

"Why, it was a celebration, don't you see. It was beautiful, just beautiful. People wanted to show their respect. Like rose petals at a coronation, you might say."

"Like laurel leaves crowning a great conquering hero in ancient Rome," she said excitedly.

"Somethin' like that, sure. It was like the inside of a paperweight, if you ever seen one of them, with the snow falling so nice? Ah, a beautiful sight. But I'm just as glad not to be on the sanitation detail this day."

"Yes, I can understand that," she agreed, feeling very grown-up.

"Now, missy, what's your business with Mr. Lindbergh, if I may ask? Or would you rather wait to get a little food inside you first? And by the way, what about your folks? Your mama and papa know where you are, do they?"

"What time is it?" She didn't mean to be rude, but she wasn't able to answer his question directly.

"It's gettin' on to nine o'clock. Now then . . . I answered your question, how about answerin' mine?" He was half turned around in the front seat, smiling and friendly, but she had the uncomfortable feeling she was being "grilled."

"Yes, sir," she said. "My parents surely do know I'm gone by now."

"Oh, I see."

"She ran away, Mike." The driver offered his opinion without taking his eyes from the street where they were inching along. Kate thought that he should just concentrate on driving and leave the detecting to the nicer one.

"Did you run away then, dearie?" Mike asked her, and now she saw that his smile was actually kind of phony. Patronizing, because she was only a child.

She sat stiff and furious, her face turned to look out the window. She knew that she had been trapped by the third degree (well, not exactly, but they would have stopped at nothing; they were very clever, and she was a mere pawn in their clutches), trapped by a deceptively friendly face into confessing everything. Now they would send her back, probably under armed guard, maybe handcuffed to the train seat. One thing seemed depressingly certain: She and Lindy were not to meet after all.

"Here we are then."

The car had stopped in front of a red-brick building with a sign over the door proclaiming that this was Precinct 84.

Kate shrank back inside the car when they opened the door for her.

"This is a false arrest," she said as boldly as she could. "You have no grounds for arresting me."

"Now, we're certainly not arresting you, little girl . . . say, I can't keep on calling you that now; it's hardly even respectful, and you nearly a young lady at that. I do beg your pardon." He held out his hand to her, and while she was pondering the important problem of whether to tell her right name or use an alias, she took his hand and stepped out onto the running board.

"I'm afraid I didn't get the name, though," he said.

"Stafford," she answered with dignity as they mounted the steps to the station house. "Kate Stafford." Now it was out; her family would be disgraced. The consequences were too grim to think about.

They were inside the reception area of the police station. Kate looked around with great interest. It was not much different from the descriptions in the thrillers, even to the high desk at one side with an alert-looking elderly policeman sitting ramrod-straight, pencil in hand, waiting for one of his men to bring in a culprit. She was it. Despite the shame to the family, Kate felt a wonderful thrill of adventure.

"How do you spell that?" Mike was asking in a kindly voice as he led her to the high desk.

She looked at him in amazement. Perhaps he had not heard her.

"Stafford," she said clearly. "Kate Porter Stafford."

"Right," he said. "And would you be good enough to tell us how you spell it then? With an *e*?"

She stared at him. Who in the world didn't know how to spell Stafford? And where on earth would one put an *e* anyway? She couldn't believe that in New York City there were people who didn't know how to spell.

Watching carefully to make sure they weren't joking her, she spelled it out for both her "friend" and the man at the desk, who copied it out slowly into his ledger. Then she gave her address and watched them take that into account. Beacon Street evidently didn't mean a thing in New York City, not even number 4.

But within ten minutes they had telephoned to Boston. They had spoken to her father, whose voice could not be discerned from where she stood, even though she listened very hard. She heard only the precinct sergeant's voice on her end and long pauses while her father, she supposed, was doing his part of the talking. Then the elderly policeman hung up the receiver onto its hook and looked at her oddly. She recognized the look. There was definitely something about talking to a Stafford—at least one of the grown-up men of the family— that put a kind of respectful look on people's faces.

"Your father is sending someone for you," was all the policeman said.

"Yes. Thank you," she answered politely. She was resigned to her fate. She would be eleven years old for the rest of her life, stuck in this grim dependent condition, never allowed to leave Beacon Street again as long as she lived. And the people in her family usually lived very, very long lives.

The punishment for having run away would be a terrible one: death by boredom. She sighed so loudly that the desk sergeant looked over at her in alarm. But she was sitting with straight back and hands folded in her lap, waiting, resigned, on the long, narrow bench that reminded her of church.

Back at home she would have to stand for an eternity with eyes front, paying strict attention to her father's lecture on family tradition, honor, the responsibilities of enlightened wealth and social privilege. She would stare at the dark satiny mahogany of his desk, the red blotter in its etched leather holder, the gleaming silver water pitcher made by Paul Revere, the crystal inkwell and pewter ashtray, while the neatly leather-bound books tempted her attention into daydreams with their scrolled gold titles. The things her father told her would have to be iterated again and again, and she would be expected to contribute some original thoughts and considerations to prove she had paid close attention. He would listen to her, too, and she had better be thoughtful and respectful and careful about expressing herself.

Her mother would call her into her upstairs sitting room for quiet talks on manners and what was "expected" from a young lady of one of the First Families. Even her brother Edward, who should be much too busy studying for his entrance examinations for Harvard, would take time out to walk around the Common with his young sister and lecture her humorlessly about her place in the scheme of things. She wondered if her other brother, Henry, would be conscripted for moral instruction duty, too. Dear Hank, she wouldn't mind it nearly so much from him. At least he confessed to having doubts himself once in a while.

Kate rose from the bench and went over to ask the desk sergeant if she might be shown to the ladies' facilities, please. Another young policeman led her down a corridor and pointed out a door to her, then seemed prepared to stand waiting for her to come out, however long she took.

She rubbed the soot and grime out of her white gloves as best she could with the cold water from the pitcher in the tiny but clean room. She washed her face and then suddenly wondered if she was going to cry. She decided not to. She didn't want to keep that young man waiting for her all day out there in the bleak corridor.

Six days later Charles A. Lindbergh came to Boston, where he was greeted by a demonstrative gathering. There was a public ceremony of welcome at the Arena on St. Botolph's Street, with cheers and applause and speeches. When the happy citizens were at last persuaded to retire to their homes to tell their friends and families that they had seen the Lone Eagle in the flesh and heard his shy speech of gratitude for such a fine welcome, the hero was taken to the quieter confines of the Explorers Club, where a select few of the city's leading citizens raised a toast in twenty-year-old port or hundred-year-old brandy. (Such substances were considered by the members to be far beyond the provinces of the amendment prohibiting ordinary alcoholic beverages; the law was for the protection of the lower classes, who were not able to control their appetites, and had nothing to do with such men as were gathered in this great old mansion tonight, except of course, that they and their good wives had been instrumental in legislating it.) They made eloquent and heartfelt speeches in praise of the young man's courage and modesty. There were a few in this exclusively masculine company who saw danger to their own way of life in the prospect of new horizons that this young nobody had opened up with his damned daring deed. They saw signs of imminent and perhaps irreparable changes about to erupt on the world; these few wise men neither smiled nor bestirred themselves to shake his hand, but the young man did not notice.

At precisely eight o'clock the gaunt young hero was taken to the ultimate bastion of civilized conversation, quietude, and sanctuary from the common clamor: the home of Mr. John Wright Stafford, at 4 Beacon Street.

The guest list included, in addition to Mr. Lindbergh: the host's brother, Willis Philander Stafford, the present president of Harvard College, and his wife; the hostess's aunt, Grace Stafford, world-famous artist and iconoclast who wore men's clothing and at the age of eighty showed no signs of succumbing to the pressures of conventional social behavior; Grace Stafford's adopted son, Peter, who called his foster mother "Daddy" and otherwise never looked up from his plate; Dr. and Mrs. Cameron Bellmore, he being the Nobel prize winner who had discovered one of the key principles of aerodynamics which had made Mr. Lindbergh's flight possible; Senator and Mrs. Paul Porter Stafford, cousins of the host; and the two brilliant and handsome sons of the house, Edward Porter Stafford, who was seventeen, and Henry Grey Stafford, fifteen. The host's daughter, Kate, reputedly very clever, although plain, was not being allowed to join the family and guests at dinner this evening. She was being punished for some escapade or other.

"Tell me every word he uttered, and tell me how he looked and what gestures he used, and his face—tell me every single solitary detail about his face! Tell me everything you can remember, every word he said, and oh, concentrate and remember, Hank, please!"

It was very late, long after midnight. The sleeping house groaned from time to time as it shifted on its elderly haunches. Out on the second-floor landing the ormolu clock from China ticked off the minutes, hours, days, months, phases of the moon, and seasons for planting and harvesting. Otherwise, all was silent; the occupants of the great house slept privately, alone, behind closed doors with sitting rooms discreetly between.

But the two youngest had their own tradition, and they had shared the mysterious hours of the night for as long as Kate could remember. Hank was four years older, but she thought she remembered his face peering over the sides of her baby cot at her; or maybe the memory had taken root in her brain because he had told her about it many times. Hank had been fascinated by having a sister and would creep down the hall and into the nursery at night to see whether she had grown big enough yet to talk to. Brother Edward had never shared the wakefulness that kept little Henry stalking about the house alone like a silent small ghost in his long white nightgown and bare feet. He had never told anyone of his aimless vigil. By the time Henry was old enough to feel lonely in his insomniac wanderings God had presented him with a new baby sister, and he watched and waited patiently for her to grow big enough to share his secret times. It had never occurred to him to wonder if she would be a sleeper like the others or a walker like himself. By the time she was two she had proved a companion of the night.

Careful not to wake Nurse, the little boy would appear at the baby's cot and help her climb over the side. They would cross the room on tiptoes, guided by the moon through the curtains and, in winter, the glow from embers of the evening's fire banked to last as long as possible. Hand in hand, the two would creep past the sleeping servant, cross the length of the nursery past the table, the desk, the sofa and armchairs, the dollhouse their grandmother had played with, the bookcases and glass-front cabinets filled with toys and storybooks. They would walk out into the wide winding corridor, where the night-lamp flickered behind the purple etched-glass chimney of the wall sconce that was older than the house. The two of them would usually go to the boys' sitting room, where they could huddle on the window seat and look down on the silent, empty, moonlit Common. Hank would tell her stories, and she would listen; later, when she learned to talk, they shared their feelings, thoughts, and dreams in those conspiratorial hours when they believed themselves the only two people in the world who were awake. One night when Kate was six years old, she told Hank solemnly that a sleeping spell was cast over the world nightly; only they had escaped its touch, for reasons which would be clear to them "someday."

When they grew older and Nurse no longer slept so near, Hank and Kate preferred the nursery window seat, with its frayed and faded old blue cushions, to the room which Hank shared with their older, more sober-sided brother. On the night that Charles A. Lindbergh came to dine and Kate was not allowed at the table, she waited for her brother for what seemed like hours before he finally joined her there. The sheer white ninon curtains were tied back so that a stray June breeze might be tempted to turn in as it passed the open window. Out on the Common, all was still; nothing moved except the moon, and that too slowly for the eye to follow.

"Tell me," Kate urged. Hank leaned back on his side of the window seat. He was staring out as if he could see something unusual. He hadn't answered her. She thought he was probably reconstructing the evening in his orderly mind, so that he wouldn't forget any details. She appreciated that, but she was desperate to hear. She adored Hank, but sometimes he was very like their father.

"Tell," she urged again.

"He was—well, ordinary," Hank said at last. He looked up quickly to see how she reacted to that.

"Oh, Hank!" She sighed, as if she carried a heavy but long-familiar burden that she must put down very, very gently. "Hank, how can you possibly say he's ordinary when he's just done the most extraordinary thing any man has ever done in the entire history of the world! No matter how he acted or what he said, it couldn't possibly be ordinary. Shy, maybe, or . . . modest? Maybe tired, goodness knows he has reason to be tired. His public has made terrible demands on him. Maybe he is really beastly, or charming, or dull . . . although I can't see how that could be. But not ordinary, Hank. How could you come up with such a word as that for the man all the world is calling the Lone Eagle?''

Fifteen-year-old Hank was unmoved by his sister's protests. He nodded his head thoughtfully, having heard her argument, having considered it, and having decided that his first evaluation was still an accurate one.

"The fact that his accomplishment was so extraordinary is what made his conversation and his composure at the dinner table and later in the drawing room so ordinary. You must see the irony, Kate.''

"Oh. Well, I guess so. I guess I see. Well . . . tell me exactly what he said. Every word you can remember.''

The moonlight gleamed down on the polished wood floor, giving it the patina of old dead bones. Kate was trying to be mature about all this, but it still hurt worse than anything she had ever known. Her parents knew exactly how to punish her in the worst, most unforgettable way. She would bear the scars of being excluded from her own family's dinner table for the rest of her life. But in the back of her mind, as she waited for her brother to describe the evening, she knew she wasn't entirely sorry. She knew now that Mr. Lindbergh would have seen her as an ordinary eleven-year-old girl who wasn't allowed to speak until spoken to, and never, never would he have discerned who she really was underneath. He would not have recognized his fated lover . . . or whatever the lady was called in such affairs. She couldn't have borne that.

Around the next corner in her mind was the terrible knowledge that her family really did know what was best for her. She didn't have to think about that just now because, at last, Hank began to talk.

"He said that he'd never expected that a flying voyage to Paris, France, would land him in such distinguished company in Boston, Massachusetts.''

"Well, now, that's not ordinary. I think that's quite witty. What then?''

"Well, then Father said—"

"I'm not interested in what Father said. What did Mr. Charles A. Lindbergh say?"

"How can I possibly tell you one without the other?"

It was, in fact, she had to admit to herself later, as she lay in her bed waiting for sleep to come in a race with the first rays of morning, a very ordinary conversation. It just showed that such an exceptional man could be at his ease anywhere in the world. She wondered if anyone had told him that there was a very special yellow-haired daughter upstairs in the house, being kept prisoner (well, it was yellow in certain lights, at the end of summer anyway, if you looked closely through the brown). All the waiting at her open window had failed to produce Mr. Lindbergh riding across the Common to her rescue. He was staying right over there, at the Ritz Hotel; she could see its prim bulk looming above the trees on the other side of the Public Garden. Maybe she should keep the vigil . . . but she wasn't that silly. He didn't even know she existed.

In her dream she was crossing the Atlantic Ocean, but not in the brave little *Spirit of St. Louis* with the handsome hero at the controls. It seemed to be a kind of old sailing ship, creaky and smelly, and all she saw was the waves and the sky. It seemed to her that the dream voyage went on forever, and she would never get to her destination, and she didn't even know what the destination was. She was terribly bothered, not knowing, and tried to ask the funny-looking old man standing next to her at the railing, "Where are we heading? When will we arrive? What will it be like?"

But there was only endless ocean and her own impatience. She was holding something in her arms, something precious, and she was standing in moonlight. The man standing next to her didn't even know her name. He called her Emily.

When she awoke, she realized that she had been dreaming an old story she had read many times. She had had the dream before. It helped take her mind off wanting things she couldn't have.

Chapter Two

1688: EMILY

Sometimes it seemed to Emily that she had not really slept at all since marrying eight months before, but she was young and still excited by the secrets of the night; there would be time enough to rest when she was old. The bed had grown cold where he had risen from her side, and the child moved restlessly in her belly. She turned on her back and drew the quilt close to her face, peering out with drowsy, contented eyes to watch her husband as he worked. How handsome he was, and how extraordinary that he had chosen her! She wondered if she would ever accustom herself to the wonder of it.

Two candles on the easel frame illuminated his profile, and she smiled to see how far away he was already from the wild physical joys of an hour before. She knew if she spoke to him now, he would not hear her. She had learned to accept this distance and to honor it with her silence. Deep in his own vision, he bent all his energies now toward transforming the remembered line of a cheek, an eye, a hand onto the canvas with his deft brush.

How lovely it was to know such privacy, to have a bedchamber only for themselves, a door that shut, and oil lamps that could burn all night if they wished. All the seventeen years of Emily's life had been lived with her sisters and brothers all atumble on their pallets and at table, two rooms in a fisherman's cottage on the dockside, where a candle was a luxury, where chinks in the walls let in the stink and noise of the street outside.

Emily Grey had been a quiet, observing, hardworking child, knowing herself to be both plain and sensible, expecting little from life. Her mother had died in childbed when Emily was only three. Her father's two successive wives had come and spawned more damp, demanding babies, and both had died in weariness and pain, leaving Emily to cope. She took secret pride in her own strength; she had made herself a private vow that she intended to keep: She would not be one of the sad dead ladies. She would live to be as old as the oldest man in Liverpool, in all of England, in the whole world. She intended to outlive everyone. She didn't know quite why; life wasn't all that lovely, to be valued so highly, after all. But she made the vow and intended to keep it.

She thought, since she was ugly, no man would ever want her, and that fact might keep her alive all the longer.

But here she was in a fine wooden house away from the market's clatter, in a real feather bed, in a chamber with a door that shut and a gentle, loving husband who saw beauty in her.

She had caught him out one day, sketching her picture as she waited for her father's dory on the windy quay, with runny-nosed Meg in tow and a basket of cauliflowers and onions on her arm. She had called out to him, teasing, and he had advanced a bit shyly toward her, holding out the sketch for her to see. She had looked at it and was astonished.

He found her brown eyes clear and calm and intelligent, her bones well arched beneath glowing skin, and her sharp chin had gentled under his chalk to seem almost noble, the whole being a portrait of herself seen through the eyes of either a fool or a man in love. She had looked straight at him then, across the bawling Meg and the redolent onions, and found herself hoping, almost praying, that he was not a fool.

Neddy Sifford had come calling on her after that, with his nice clothes and quiet manner, and he had taken the shouts and laughter of her family in stride, looking only at her as he sat at table waiting for her to turn from her chores with the gift of her smile or a word for him. Her father said he was dreamy, but he had given his blessing

because Neddy was the younger son of Edward Sifford, who owned
two ships and had a reputation for shrewd dealing. Neddy worked
alongside his father and older brother every day, even though he
dawdled every sunrise and sunset along the dock, sketching common
people that were hardly fit subjects for a serious artist. If the boy was
daft enough to draw faces anyone could see on the street just by
looking, well, that was his business. Her father would miss Emily in
the house, but if he passed up this chance, he might have her on his
hands for the rest of her life. It was time to think about marrying
again himself.

And now it was all settled: Emily's life. She spent her days in
quiet company with her sister-in-law, Anne, sharing the easy work
of keeping this fine house—six rooms for only five people, and those
all adults—it was a pleasure to scrub the wide-beamed floors until
they shone, to polish the sturdy furniture that had been brought from
Spain on one of Old Edward's ships, to sit in comfort near a window
with real glass in it, bright with the afternoon sun, and stitch and
drink tea. And the nights, shared with the strangeness and dearness
of the slim young man who was her husband. His lovemaking was
both tender and fierce, and it was enough. When he rose from her
arms to go to his easel, she saw that he was transported into a world
of his own where she could never follow; that, too, would have to be
enough. She was content. Soon, very soon now, she would have a
child to fill her arms.

Neddy seemed not to notice that the room had gone cold. She drew
her shanks up as close as she could to her swollen body, turned over
on her side, and wrapped the folds of her nightdress around her icy
feet. The early September winds had brought a strong hint of the
winter to come down on the city; soon it would be necessary to begin
warming the bed with coals from the kitchen fire.

Drowsing, she was brought sharply back to her senses by a sudden
pounding on the door of their room. She glanced at Neddy, but he
seemed oblivious of the thundering noise, even as it was instantly
followed by his father's imperious shouts.

"Wake up! Leave off what you're doing and hear my news!"

"Neddy. Neddy!" she called across the room. He stirred himself
from his deep concentration and looked vaguely out at her, as if still

unaware of the bellowing outside their door and the rattling of the latch, but responsive to her low, urgent call.

The door burst open, banging against the inner wall. Edward Sifford stood like a giant bull with his head bent beneath the low doorframe. He was much too large a man for any normal-sized room to contain him comfortably. At nearly fifty-two his great head was topped with thick black hair, showing not a sign of gray. His face was permanently reddened from years of hard life at sea. His shoulders filled the doorway from side to side. He had built this house for himself and his sons; it was indisputably his, yet his massive presence seemed ill-fitted to its cozy dimensions. As if, in attempting to domesticate a lion, one were to place it in a tabby's cage.

Old Edward (called that since the birth of his second son and namesake, Neddy, twenty-two years before) stood there, looking at the bed, bewildered into momentary and uncharacteristic silence for a scant catch of breath. He turned to the corner where his son sat, quite naked, paintbrush poised in the air, staring back at him without shame or interest.

"Well, I'll be damned! A ripe young bride in your bed and you at that damned paint again! Just because she's on the nest doesn't mean she's not still tasty. Why, now's the time to enjoy her, you ass. She's a whole lot more than the skin and bones she was on your wedding night! My God, boy, don't tell me your brother's got at you with his pissant moralizing. Don't you keep away from this luscious piece here with any notions like that. If you think hunkering your wife is just for breeding and then it's time to lay off, I'll have a go at her myself, by God. You won't waste such a treasure under my roof—"

"Oh, hush, Edward. You'll have Neddy believing you mean it. What a terrible old man you are. What are you doing at this hour of the night? Just come from the tavern and drunk enough to roar, are you? You'll wake the roosters, and the whole city will think it's morning." But she could see, from the corner of her eye, that Neddy was beginning to tremble. She would have laughed aloud but for him.

"Woman, don't try me!" Edward boomed, his voice setting the timbers of the house to shake. "There's more at the tavern than ale and whiskey. There's men with information that can save a man's—

never mind! I've got news, very great news, and it's not the kind to keep. There's a schooner sailing on the morning tide for America, and she's called the *Sally Bow,* and we're on her. What do you think of that? Pack your warmest clothes; never mind the furnishings, no time to waste. Hie yourselves now, get going, or you'll be left, I swear it!''

As her father-in-law moved back from the doorway, Emily caught a glimpse of another figure behind him. It was Neddy's elder brother, Charles, as tall as Old Edward but lean as fish scales, shadowy in the dark alcove between the walls. Emily drew the quilt up to her chin.

"Father," Charles demanded in his most patient, long-suffering, ministerial tone, "please explain why you've wakened us all in the middle of the night like this, what craziness, is it drink? Is that it . . . are you feverish or—" Charles stopped. He stepped back into the deeper shadows, out of Emily's sight, as his father turned on him furiously.

"I'm sailing on the *Sally Bow* in the morning, and you're going with me! And you can take that mewling wife of yours along if you want to, but I certainly think you'd do better to find a savage woman to tame when we get to New England. Fresh start, that's my advice, but take her along if you want her. Now get out of my way and start hauling my good sea chests down from the warren."

He was off then, his echo hanging back, the whole house shaking with his heavy tread. Neddy sat as if paralyzed, staring at the open doorway and Charles's dim shadow still hovering there. Emily waited until Old Edward had shouted for Charles once more and the thin wraith of her brother-in-law had moved away. Then she threw back the quilt and pulled her ungainly body forward until her feet reached the cold floor.

"He means it, you know," she said, "and we'd better begin."

It was a household well tuned to obedience. Old Edward Sifford was both immovable object and irresistible force. Other men had learned that well; his sons had learned it early. His bluster and powerful physical presence galvanized the attention of everyone around him. Just his appearance in a room, public or private, even on the streets and docks or on the deck of one of his ships, was enough to hold all eyes and ears and tongues. His sons had been swept into the orbit of Edward's magnetic course like satellite moons, yet the three were very different men. Edward Sifford's sons were as iconoclastic as himself.

Both sons had labored since early childhood, apprenticed in their father's trade, learning the singular ways Old Edward pursued the competitive, cutthroat business of ships and trade. Still, Neddy followed his own obsessive dreams with brushes and canvas, and Charles found his life made tolerable and his way illuminated by God Himself. In these pursuits they were very different from their father; in the fact that they did not, would not, could not forfeit their individual directions, they resembled him exactly.

Edward Sifford's reputation as a man to be reckoned with had not come easily, nor had it come entirely within the law. He had begun as an orphan, running away from the workhouse to become a cabin boy. He had put in his time and his broad shoulders as an impressment agent, seeking out seamen in the pubs and whorehouses of Liverpool, clouting heads when necessary to get his quota, not above drugging a man's ale or worse, rounding up bodies for which sea captains and shipowners paid him by the head, bloodied or not. Edward had hoisted cargo; he had slaughtered dogs to be roasted and dried for voyages; he had shipped out as able seaman, third mate, second, and first; and finally, he had taken over as captain when the incumbent met with a mysterious and unfortunately fatal accident in the North Sea. He had lied and slashed and slaved and fought with his bare hands or any other weapon he could take hold of, and he had reached the age of fifty-two in possession of two reasonably seaworthy old frigates able to port-hop with any cargo that paid well, a fine house on dry ground, and two legitimate sons to carry on his name. They were disappointments to him. He thought them both weak, and (just as bad) they bored him.

Old Edward's salty tongue, his intolerance, his godlessness, his vast energies and impatience for getting on with life, his huge bulk, and his restless spirit had overwhelmed his sons. They were dutiful and respectful and scared to death of him.

To the old bull's unending surprise and delight, his plain and skinny daughter-in-law wasn't afraid of him; in fact, she was a match for him in wit and boldness. That she was the bride of his foolish younger son only made the surprise all the more unexpected, and therefore delicious. Old Edward and young Emily had inexplicably become each other's best friend.

It was only that Emily Grey had never been in awe of anyone in her life, and when she became Emily Sifford, there was no reason to change that she could see. She liked Old Edward, seeing in him (and wouldn't he be furious if he guessed!) a lonely man who had been disappointed by everyone he'd ever trusted. His wife had died in childbirth, leaving him with two boys to raise on his own. He'd done it, too, giving up the sea and settling down to running his various businesses from a warehouse and office on the wharf. He had refused to send the boys to a wet nurse or give them up to the care of paid servants. When accused of loving them too well to send them away, Edward had denied it angrily and shouted to all who made it their business that he was damned well going to call the tune for his only legitimate heirs to dance to.

"Do you think it's too much ale, or a nightmare of some kind?" Neddy was asking now, scratching his head with the hard tip of his paintbrush. "Why would he wake everybody up with such a wild notion—"

"Neddy," Emily said patiently, "come help me with the chest. Take that end, and we can drag it from under the bed together. It will hold all we need."

When the chest was opened before them, Emily knelt beside it and began to lift the carefully folded linens from their storage place. "The quilt will take the place of this finery," she said. "But the little christening dress takes up hardly any room, and surely one luxury can be allowed. Do hurry, Neddy! You must wrap your canvases and paints."

His eyes opened wide, startled, and a look of dismay replaced his vagueness. "Yes, yes, of course," he said. He began to gather rolls of canvases in his arms.

"Oh, my love, we can't take them all!" she said gently. "Here," she added, "you'd better put on your breeches."

"But I can't leave my work behind, can I, Em? Look, this portrait of little Meg is still unfinished . . . the sketches . . . I must spend another afternoon on John Street Wharf when the light is right, there's a fishmonger there, see, here is her face, her eyes aren't right yet, I have to—"

"Oh, my dear!" Tears sprang to Emily's eyes; the tears she would not shed for herself (never to see her father and the little ones, ever again) came readily for her husband. She held her arms open to him, letting the linens fall to the floor in a heap.

But Neddy stood apart from her, holding his breeches in one hand, his paintbrush in the other, wrestling with his bewilderment as best he could, shaking his head to clear his thoughts, unable to believe what was happening.

She stooped heavily, picked up the embroidered pillowcase she had made for her baby's cradle, folded it carefully, and set it aside. "It may be his idea of a joke, although it has no point that I can see. But even so, I'd rather be ready for a voyage that never happens than find myself in the middle of the sea without a warm shawl or a change of clothes. Come on, Neddy, you have to decide. Wouldn't it be best to take only the untouched canvases so that you'll have material for new work? We don't know if there will be such amenities available in the colonies . . . oh, Neddy, think of it! Isn't it exciting? We're going to New England! They say Boston is quite civilized . . . well, we'll find out soon enough. Hurry now, please, dearest. I'll have the chest filled before you . . . oh, the tiny rocking chair! No, there won't be room for that."

The house was fully aroused and rocking now with the echoes of Old Edward's shouts and the heavy clump of his boots as he strode back and forth, issuing orders to his sons and daughters-in-law, turning out shelves and cabinets and trunks and bellowing for them to hie themselves, the tide would not wait for them. Emily felt her heart beating wildly with the adventure. She dressed herself quickly while she continued to sort and select the goods which could be carried with them and the many—too many!—things which must be left behind.

Neddy was swept on the tide of her busyness and began finally to move about, dressing himself and then rolling the new canvases and his favorite brushes in linsey-woolsey, placing them in the chest. Soon it was filled with all it could hold. Dawn had begun to strain its cold gray rays through the real glass windows of the parlor.

"We'd better eat a hearty breakfast," she said cheerfully, and went to see about it.

She found Anne already stoking the fire, about to take the kettle out to the well.

"Isn't it exciting?" Emily said, hugging Anne's thin shoulders as she took the heavy kettle from her. "I'll do it," she said. "I feel the need of a breath of air."

"Take my shawl," Anne said, handing it to her.

"No, look at you, you're shivering. I feel strong and well and quite warm from the work of packing. The cold will be exactly what I need."

"Oh, Emily, is it really true? Are we really being taken so far from home and never to see England again?"

"But the air will be clean and pure in New England, with no coal smoke to infect the lungs! I'm sure everyone is very much healthier there. Think of it, Anne, no more grime and coughing. I'm sure it's true. Why, you'll profit from the sea journey itself, and in New England you'll be able to carry and deliver lots of babies. I'm sure of it!"

"It's true then. We are actually going, aren't we?"

"What does Charles say?"

"That his father is mad, but it is true, we're actually going. Charles says he is glad to go because there are still places in the world where people follow the will of God and live so as to drive out the devil."

"A world without the devil in it? Well, then it must be Heaven, or at least the Garden of Eden! Now, aren't we the lucky ones, Anne, to be going to such a paradise?"

She was satisfied when she had coaxed a tight, reluctant smile from her sister-in-law, and then she slipped out the door into the crisp, cold morning.

A small boy, tousled and sleepy-eyed, joined her at the well, and she offered him tuppence if he would run to the docks, find her father, and give him her message. The boy nodded, filled his bucket, and ran off toward his house, sloshing water onto the cobblestones in his haste.

Emily returned to find the others assembled at the table, with Charles impatiently awaiting her return so that he could begin the grace. She set the kettle on the fire and slipped her bulky body onto her chair, bowed her head, and listened as well as she could. Next to her, at the head of the table, Old Edward fidgeted and harrumphed noisily while Charles droned his pious monologue to God. He gave

his usual ardent thanks for the food they were about to eat, prayed
for the fertility of his wife and the faith of his father to be restored,
enumerated the many blessings for which they were all most humbly
grateful, and then began a long devotion begging the Lord to watch
over them on their perilous and possibly foolhardy journey into the
unknown, and their future lives about to be delivered unto Him . . .
suddenly Old Edward sighed loudly and reached for the bread. He
tore the end piece and began to eat. Charles pretended to ignore his
father and kept his eyes downcast, his long, thin fingers entwined,
his voice unperturbed.

The kettle sputtered and bubbled, and the bacon began to sizzle on
the fire. Charles finally came to the amen; Emily and Anne rose to
their feet to get on with the cooking, and Old Edward erupted like a
volcano too long dormant.

"This house and all that's left in it have been consigned for sale,"
he announced, "and the next ship over to Boston will bring us a fair
amount or I'll have the neck of the solicitor, well he knows that. I
may be across the world, but he knows my reach is long and I think
he won't dare cheat me. There'll be someone looking after our interests besides him anyway. Always set a watcher to watch the watcher,
boys, you hear me? I hope you've learned that much. We'll keep the
ships, and when the winter's over and the thaw comes, I'll have them
brought to Boston to be the start of our new fleet. Yes, fleet. Turn
your backs on this place and all the old ways, laws that tie a man
down so he can't do honest labor. From now on we'll look forward,
not back. Well, what do you say to that, Neddy? He's daydreaming,
of course. I'll trust to you, Emily, to see that he gets aboard, although what loss it would be if he missed the sailing, I'm sure I can't
think. Well, Charles? You're the one who's always thinking about
the next world—what do you say to the New World, first? There are
fortunes to be made out there. Fortunes . . ."

"It's a very sudden decision," Charles said.

Edward answered him curtly. "Once taken, the decision rests on
the tide. The *Sally Bow* will be the last ship to make the Atlantic
crossing before the winter closes in. If we're not on her, it would
mean waiting until spring. I see no point in sitting around and brooding on a decision already taken. Are you with me or not?"

"Do we have a choice?" Neddy asked, suddenly perking his head up.

"No!" his father roared. "By God, this is an ungrateful bunch. Stay if you want, and rot in the stink of Liverpool. Neither of you could make a living without me, and you know it. You're my only legal sons, and you'll be on that ship! And the day will come when you'll thank me. I'll tell you the truth—that it's not for you but for your sons that I'm doing this. You're both too blind and too fat-headed to see it. Give me some tea, Emily, good and black."

Oh, you've your reasons, you tough old man, but you're not telling them, Emily thought as she poured the steaming brew all around.

"I've sent a boy to bring my father here," she said quietly. "I hope he wasn't too late to find him before his boat went out."

She was immediately sorry she had spoken. The effect on Anne was like a physical blow to the already trembling pale young woman. A whimper escaped her thin lips, and she bowed her head to hide her face. Her husband gave her a glance but looked away quickly, unable or unwilling to offer her comfort.

"Oh, Anne, dear, I am sorry! But there's time to say good-bye, and think how pleased your mother will be that you're going to a healthy place. You must go and see her right now. Leave the kitchen as it is. I'll do it. Go on, Anne, hurry."

Anne looked timidly at Charles for his approval. He waited a beat, then nodded, and she seemed to melt from the table as she backed away toward the door.

"We board within the hour!" Edward warned loudly.

Anne slipped out the door.

"When is the tide?" Emily asked.

"The tide's at nine," Old Edward grunted in answer to her question.

"Surely not!" she exclaimed. "When it was at late midmorning yesterday?"

"God save me from the fisherman's daughter!" Edward shouted, and arose from the table. He stormed through the kitchen-parlor, which connected all the rooms in the house from its central square. He could be heard thundering around his bedchamber, banging and hammering his sea chests shut.

A knock sounded on the door, and Emily quickly opened it to admit her father. The boy was alongside him, small and red-nosed from running in the cold. Emily took tuppence from the pewter mug atop the cupboard and gave it to him. He was off on the run again. I must remember to take the coins, she thought, suiting the action to the thought by emptying the mug into her apron pocket.

"What's this about?" her father asked loudly. A man of the sea, father to a large brood of noisy children, he had no lower tones for society. In some ways, he reminded her of Old Edward, who was, of course, not anywhere near so gentle as her dad.

"Have a cup of tea, Pa," Emily said, but he shook his head. He's growing old, she thought suddenly, looking at him for the last time. His hair is thin and there is a gauntness in his cheeks I never noticed before. Her heart turned over in her breast as the realization hit her fully. He was nearly forty; she wouldn't be around to tend him in his old age. She wouldn't see her sisters and brothers growing up—she would never see any of them again. Even as the thought struck her through with a sharp and terrible pain, she steeled herself against it. No time for sentimentality, my girl, she said to herself briskly, as she would say a thousand and more times in her life to come.

"Calling me out from a day's work! I thought I'd find you dead or dying. Emily, don't ever do that to me again! What a fright you gave me, and now I've missed the best catch of the morning. What's this about, now?"

"We're going to New England, Pa. Now do sit down."

He did, falling heavily into the chair and staring up at her from under the folded brim of his wool cap. His mouth was open and his eyes squinted with the permanent frown that sun and brine had creased there. He said no more, but waited for an explanation. Emily poured his tea and set it down in front of him, but he paid no attention to the fragrant cup. He never took his staring, uncomprehending eyes from his daughter's face.

"If you'll excuse me, sir," Charles mumbled then, and still John Grey paid no attention. In the silence, Charles backed awkwardly out of the room. Emily looked to her husband, but Neddy was sipping disconsolately at his tea, no help at all. It did seem sometimes that men took changes much harder and slower than women. Both her dad and her husband seemed to be in shock, leaving her to cope, wouldn't you know?

"Well, Pa," she said a bit more sharply than she intended, "there's nothing for it. Old Edward has decided that we'll sail on the morning tide. What time is the out tide today, by the way?"

"Half past eleven," he answered, still staring at her as if memorizing her face.

"But Edward says we have to be aboard the ship by nine," she mused aloud. "I wonder why. Well, he's the one who decides, and there's no point in questioning him. Not yet anyway. So I'm going then, Pa."

"Will you . . . will you come and see the little ones before you go?"

"Of course I will. Of course I will, Pa. How could I go off to the other side of the world without saying good-bye and . . . but enough of that, you'll have me crying in a minute. Would you take some porridge, a bit of kipper?"

"No."

"Now don't be sad, old Dad. Think of the great adventure I'll be having!"

"I'll never see my grandchild."

"Oh, Pa!" She threw herself onto his lap, heavy belly and all, nearly toppling them both off the chair. Awkwardly, unaccustomed to caresses, he put his hands on her shoulders.

"If you don't want to go, then I say you don't have to," he said firmly. "Damn Edward Sifford, and damn the rest of them, too. You stay right home with me and your kin. Let 'em go, Emmy. Let 'em go."

"We could stay behind," Neddy spoke up suddenly, rousing himself from faraway thoughts. "We could stay."

"No," Emily said firmly, collecting herself and rising from her father's knees with a quick, light touch of her fingers to his weathered cheek. "We must go. Your place is with your father, Neddy, and mine is with you. But who would want to say no to such a grand . . . adventure?" Her throat was choked; the words came hard.

"Adventure, is it?" her father said sadly. "Well, then I'll kiss you good-bye and give you my blessing. There's no more that I can do, is there?"

"No, Pa."

"It's a long way to go."

"Yes."

"And never to see you again."

Emily was determined not to cry. She looked desperately to Neddy to say something that might lighten the terrible weight of parting.

"I'll sketch the baby on the instant he's born," he said, "and . . . and . . . we'll name him for you!"

Emily and her father stared at him, and then she burst out laughing. "Old Edward will be furious," she said. "It's wonderful! It's a wonderful idea, Neddy, isn't it, Pa? Grey Sifford, that's what he'll be. Even if he's a girl, I promise! And you'll have a portrait of him— or her—to hang over your bed, Pa. Now, what about that? Something to be glad of, a proud thing, to have a grandson bearing your name all the way across the world in America?"

"I won't have to put up with the bawling and shitting, at that," her father said, with a bit of his old twinkle. "The tea's gone cold, Em."

Within the half hour she was back at the little cottage with him and the little ones around her, hugging and kissing and making promises to send word by every packet, and beads made by the Indians, and to pray for them all, each by name, every night of her life. She put away in their larder all the dried food and preserves and flour and salt and jams she and her dad and Neddy had been able to carry from Old Edward's house.

And by nine o'clock they were aboard the *Sally Bow* and claiming their space for the long voyage in the close quarters of the passengers' cabins belowdecks.

The women's area held twenty-four pallets shelved alongside the bulkheading, one above the other until they were lined up like narrow steps to nowhere. There was a rough-hewn table running the length of the cabin between the bunks and a space deep in a low corner where chests and trunks could be kept. There were no portholes and no provisions for washing. The overhead was so low that even Anne could not stand upright. What light and air filtered into the cabin came from the small square opening through which they had descended from the deck above.

Anne dropped to her knees on the cold rough boards and buried her face in her hands. Whether she was crying or praying, Emily didn't know, not that either would do much good that she could see. Two crewmen carrying their baggage came heavily down the steep ladder, and Emily chose a place for their belongings. She selected two lower bunks near the hatchway for herself and Anne.

"Come on, dear, let's go up on deck. We'll have plenty of time down here in this gloomy place, but only a little while longer to see Liverpool!''

On deck, all was damp and drizzly, with movement everywhere, scurrying and hauling and shouting and crowding. Seeing none of the Sifford men, Emily pulled Anne along until she found a place at the dockside rail where they could stay out of the way of all the bustle, looking down at the wharf. The drizzle turned to a steady rain now, and dank fog obscured everything beyond the first row of warehouses.

"Our last sight of home," Anne murmured sadly.

"Well, it would be if we could see a damned thing," Emily agreed. She was fumbling in her reticule for a handkerchief. The rain had made her face quite wet, and for some reason her nose was stuffed up. She hoped she wasn't getting a cold or worse. Fine time to get sick, and two months away from delivering the child as well.

"Emily, you're crying!"

"What a silly thing to say, Anne, for heaven's sake. It's the rain on my face, that's all. I can't seem to find my handkerchief."

"Mine is terribly damp, but you're welcome to it."

"Thanks." Emily blew her nose loudly and made a dab at her eyes. "It's almost impossible even to see the wharf now," she said briskly.

"Emily, it's all right to cry if you want to. Sometimes it helps."

"Oh, there you are!" It was Neddy, shouldering his way toward them. "Are you all right?"

"Of course we are. Where is Charles, and your father?" Emily asked. Whatever had been creeping up inside her seemed to abate with her husband's presence. She wasn't sure whether that was because he was a comfort or because she knew how much he needed her to be strong. Either way she was grateful, having been in danger of embarrassing herself a moment before.

"My father refuses to come up on deck until after we've sailed," Neddy said. "And Charles has met a minister, a Mr. Graham, and they seem to have a lot to talk about."

"How strange of Old Edward not to want to supervise the sailing," Emily mused.

"Why? It's not his ship."

"No, of course not. But that would make no difference to him. I wonder why he's hiding. . . ."

"Hiding?"

"Well, Neddy, I didn't mean hiding, exactly. . . ."

"What are you thinking, Emily?" Anne asked quietly.

Emily laughed suddenly and lifted her long, thin face up to the good English rain. "I'm thinking," she said, linking arms with her husband and her sister-in-law, "that we'll never, never be bored with life, not as long as we're part of Old Edward Sifford's family. Not even in Boston, whatever that turns out to be like!"

Chapter Three

1688: EMILY

She stood at the rail in the moonlight, cradling her two-week-old son in her arms and rejoicing in the solitude, the clean expanse of calm sea and infinite sky. In the terrible weeks since setting sail, she had come to value fresh air and privacy more than she feared the noxious vapors of the night air.

Only the rhythmic sloshing of the waves against the *Sally Bow*'s hull broke the silence, a sound as familiar to her now as her own breathing. The November moon was cold and far away, yet its light sat gently on the sea and seemed to reflect peacefulness as far as the eye could see. Careful not to look up into the dizzying heights of the swaying masts, Emily lifted her face to inhale the briny tang of the wind, taking the pleasure of it deeply, almost defiantly, into her starved lungs.

She had not had the strength to climb up out of the airless, dank women's cabin since giving birth, and confinement had been a nightmare these long dark days and endless, sleepless nights. The storm had tossed the ship frantically for nearly a week; she had been tied to her narrow wooden shelf of a bed with rags to hold her and the helpless infant. In terror she had lain awake night and day, fearing that he would stop breathing. The longing for light and air had weighed on her so hard that her weakness had lasted much longer than it should have. Not even the whale-oil lamps could stay lit down there in the close stench of unending seasick, unwashed flesh, women's blood, and women's sighs.

Her sister-in-law, Anne, lay on her berth throughout the voyage, ill of ship's fever and seasick, unable to lift her head from the pallet. Many of the women were struck down so, and the others, more fortunate in their strength, served them as best they could. Of course, there were quarrels and tears and strange alliances, but there was some laughter, too, and a bit of song now and then.

Emily, after giving birth, had fallen into a fever and delirium. When she recovered her senses, she found that being helpless made her nearly mad with the need to move, to climb up into the wind and spray, to escape this rocking, stinking, airless tomb of women.

The baby, miraculously, suckled at her breast and did not die. Neddy and his father came down into the women's quarters to see the child, and of that Emily had only the memory of disappointment on their faces. But now, on deck, she looked down at the scabby little face in the moonlight and saw for the first time that he was beautiful. She longed for Neddy, to show him that all was well. More than well. She had survived the confinement, and their son, too, was a survivor, and moreover he was beautiful.

She could breathe again. She thanked God for the sea and the sky and the land somewhere ahead, for her own life and her son's. The moon was waxing, growing full in its wintry sky, and all the familiar stars were there, pointing the ship to a new life in a new world.

"All's well," called out the watch.

Yes, she sighed.

She held the baby close to her racing heart and laughed aloud in sheer exuberance at being alive in such a world at such a time. She lifted him close to her mist-washed face, to let him breathe the sea, defying the dangerous night vapors to harm this bright new child.

"Look, little Grey," she said aloud, "look at the beautiful sky, see the stars. . . ." The infant squirmed and mewed, and she laughed again. In a quick, impulsive motion, she loosened his swaddling enough to bare his thin little hands. The boy gulped and cried out, once, with the shock of the cold, salty air, and then he went alarmingly stiff and silent. She shook him gently. I've killed him, she thought. I've killed him. But then he gasped and gulped the air like

a starveling little bird, openmouthed—she would have sworn that her
baby laughed! She held him with a sudden surge of love deeper than
she had ever known, full of joy and gratitude and hope.

"Are you standing the watch, girl? Then we're in good hands."

"Edward! Oh, I am glad to see you. Isn't it a beautiful night!"

"Yes," her father-in-law answered, and then as if ashamed to be
caught in such an admission, his voice went gruff. "Is it well with
you?"

"Your grandson wanted to see the world." She laughed.

Old Edward peered down at the infant. "Looks a damn sight better
than when I first saw him," he grunted. "Surprised he lived, puny
little thing. He's got tough blood, though, between yours and mine,
eh?"

"And Neddy's."

"The boy may have had something to do with it, but by the life
of me, I never thought he'd know how. I'd have expected him to put
a daub of paint on his cocket and give you a picture of a baby and
never know the difference."

"What a really nasty old man you are, Edward," she said, "and
talking about your own son. Neddy's a man, and there's no one can
tell you that as surely as I, so best you believe it and stop plaguing
the poor fellow."

Edward shook his head. His massive thatch of dark hair danced
wildly as a gust swept across the deck, snapped the sails, and rippled
the waters beyond. "You're a worse tease than I am, girl, and I
suppose I must thank Neddy for bringing you to me at that. We're
getting a southerly, by God! Land soon. Not long now."

The ship tacked into the wind, and now the spray leaped over the
rail, stinging their faces. Emily wrapped the baby closely again, and
he promptly sighed and went to sleep.

"What are you doing awake at this hour, Edward?" she asked.

"Sleep is for the virtuous, and the old," he retorted. And then he
added mischievously, "Neither do you sleep, I see."

"I've been longing to catch a breath of air for weeks now," she
said. "It seems a very long voyage."

"It is that. To the other side of the world."

"You haven't answered my question. Damn! The wind is turning sharp. I have to think of the child. How I hate to climb down into that hole again!'' But she sheltered little Grey with her body against the spray and turned toward the hatchway.

"Stay," her father-in-law said gruffly, "I'll make a pallet for you to sit, out of the wind. Come into the lee, here by the galley overhang."

She followed his hulking, oddly graceful figure as he moved nimbly between the rows of lashed barrels that held the dwindling supplies of dried meat, fresh water, and flour.

"Mind the lines," Edward muttered, but he did not look back to see if she was following or turn to help her over the slippery coils of rope that caught at her skirts and hazarded her steps in the darkness. Once in the lee of the cookhouse, he stooped to fold his coat into a cushion, which he placed atop a pile of barrel staves neatly stacked for kindling. Emily sat carefully, easing the sleeping infant onto her lap.

Old Edward leaned against a winch, reaching up with one giant hand to grasp the stays to steady himself against the wind. The moon lit his features with a cold oblique light, and from her little seat low in his shadow, Emily saw that her father-in-law was truly the awesome presence that both his sons feared. Without his coat, his white shirt quickly soaked from the spray, she could see the powerful muscles of his arms and chest, and he seemed impervious to the elements.

She wondered that he wished to spend his time with her. He startled her by answering her unspoken thoughts.

"You make no judgments," he said to the wind. "You accept every man for what he is. That's a rare quality in any man, much rarer still in a woman. We have much the same spirit, you and I. That's why I tolerate your company so well."

She was silent, not knowing how to respond to a compliment so unexpected and so heartfelt.

"I walk here every night," he went on. "Sometimes I meet Mr. Graham. He's a Roundhead, but not one of those moralizing types. As cultists and purists go, he's a reasonable man. He's told me quite a lot about Boston and what to expect there."

"Yes. The women talk about what he's told them, too. They're

cheered to know their children won't be growing up as wild savages.
But they're fearful, too.''

"Women are always fearful. What has the Puritan said to frighten
them?''

"That the new governor of Massachusetts Colony is harsh and that
he's brought the Anglican worship into the very churches that were
built to keep it out. That the king's charter for the colony, which was
very liberal, has been revoked and a Mr. Mather has gone to London
to beg another. Or to demand, rather, so Mr. Graham put it. He
accompanied Mr. Mather there and comes back now with the disap-
pointing news that so far king and Parliament are insistent on punish-
ing the colonists for their unruliness. He fears there will be trouble.''

"Politics? The women talking politics! Will your sex never cease
to astonish me?''

"Oh, hush, Edward, what nonsense. Anyway, it's freedom of
worship they want, more a matter of religion than politics.''

"The same, Emily, the same. Always has been, always will be,
no matter how they try to separate the two.''

"All's well,'' called out the watch high over their heads. The eerie,
disembodied voice echoed out over the water and reverberated in the
stillness of the night.

"Keep a sharp eye for land tonight!'' Old Edward bellowed suddenly.

"Aye, aye, sir,'' came the answer.

Emily giggled. "Does he think you're the captain then? Or have
you in fact taken over the command and not thought to mention it to
me?''

"Don't be saucy,'' was the retort, but she knew from his cheerful
voice that he found the assumption not without merit. He had cap-
tained many vessels before and was surely hard put not to tell the
master of the *Sally Bow* how to run his ship.

"Edward.''

He didn't answer, waiting for her to speak further.

"Why did we leave England so abruptly?''

She was testing the limits of her father-in-law's unusually mellow
mood. But she knew her husband would never confront his father so;
there was only one way to find out and that was for her to ask out-
right. She might not get an answer, but she might.

But before Old Edward had a chance to answer, angrily or not, they heard the sounds of a man's boots approaching along the deck. In a moment a slender figure, tall and straight, appeared alongside Edward, outlined to Emily's view against the muted moon in the cape and hat of one of the Puritan cult.

"Good evening, or rather good morning, Mr. Stafford," the man said pleasantly. "Is your conscience keeping you up again? Oh . . . good morning, Mistress Stafford. I didn't see you there in the shadows at first. My apologies."

"Good morning, Mr. Graham."

"God's blessings on you and your little son. Are you well again at last? We have all prayed for you and your child."

"Thank you. I'm quite well, and my son is thriving now that he's had his first breath of good clean sea air."

"I see that you don't believe in the dangerous properties that are said to be carried in the night by the one whose element is darkness."

"Nor do you believe it, sir, or I doubt that you would be walking the deck at this hour," Emily pointed out, a bit too bluntly. Was this Puritan (fanatics, all of them, everyone knew that, although they were said to be quite well respected in the colonies) trying to tell her what to do, what to believe? He would soon learn his manners if he thought that Emily Grey Sifford was in need of guidance from him.

But Mr. Graham surprised her with a low, agreeable chuckle and a slight bow in her direction. She wished she could see his face, but the moon was at his back. Was he laughing at her? "You've found me out," he said cheerfully. "If the devil is abroad at night, then he'll have to deal with me because I'm like you—I refuse to be frightened away from enjoying the extraordinary beauty of the night."

She had never heard any man talk like that, not even Neddy, who found beauty in everything but never spoke of it in words. Here was a strange man; she would have liked to keep him talking awhile longer, but he tipped his round-brimmed hat and continued his walk along the deck.

As his footsteps receded and the night was silent again except for the ship's creaking breaths, Emily asked her father-in-law a question that would tolerate no evasions.

"Is there something you wish to tell me, Mr. Stafford?"

"You took note of that, did you?"

"It seemed a bit off, that a man like Mr. Graham, who they say was entrusted with important messages from the king to his colonies, would make a mistake in a man's name?"

"Oh, politicians do make mistakes, Em. They do. That should come as no surprise."

"Not to know the name of a man he's spent hours and, from the sound of it, whole nights gabbing with? I think not."

"Well, then you know that our family name is now Stafford. It has a good solid sound, don't you think? New life, new world, new name. Stafford. It suits, I think."

"Sifford suited."

"There is a small matter of a warrant out for a fellow by the name of Sifford," Edward admitted with a rueful laugh. "In England, of course. But I thought it best not to run the risk of being confused with that scoundrel, in the unlikely event that the little tax-collecting rats manage to sniff their way across the sea."

Emily was thoughtful and glad of the darkness that hid her grin as she realized what the old rascal was up to. So now she had the reason for the sudden departure. She remembered how Old Edward had stayed below, even while the hands were casting away and all the other passengers were at the rail, waving and watching the last of Liverpool fall behind them. Now she understood. He had been hiding. Tax evasion, was it? More likely caught red-handed with some illicit cargo, smuggling . . . or worse. How exasperating, this incorrigible old man; she wondered fondly that he had managed to stay out of prison all these years.

But all she said aloud was: "How clever you are, Edward, and thoughtful, too. We certainly wouldn't want to get into trouble just because of the coincidence at having the same name as some probably innocent man wanted by the cruel tax collectors."

"That's right, my girl. I knew you'd see it right off. You're quick, and that's the truth. You could have been a man."

"I suppose you think that's the compliment a woman most wants to hear." She sighed furiously. "Oh, well. What do you think might have happened to the man Sifford, the one wanted?"

"Oh, he just disappeared off the face of the earth or went over-

board in the night. I think his trail might lead them a bit of a chase—
there were rumors he's gone to France—but it has nothing to do with
us now.''

"Grey Stafford.''

"What's that?''

"I'm trying on my son's new name. He seems indifferent.''

Edward was looking up at the sky. "We're coming into clouds
again,'' he observed. "The watch will be over soon, and no point in
sending up another without a moon to see by. There'll be no land
sighted this night. Let's go to bed then, shall we, and up at dawn to
see Cape Cod?''

"Are we really so close then?''

"Aye. The storm put us off course, but we've righted her again
and should make up the time with this southerly coming up strong.
Come on now, and be the first up in the morning.''

"I will,'' she said eagerly. She did feel that she could sleep now.
They walked the few steps to the hatchway, and he bent to open it
for her. As she stepped down into the dark close warmth of the cabin,
she paused to whisper up to him, "Good night, Mr. Stafford.''

"Emily.''

"Yes?''

Below, women stirred and moaned in their sleep.

"The child is handsome enough.''

She smiled, not knowing if he could see her face in the shadows,
and stepped carefully backward down the steep ladder. He closed the
hatch, and she found her way to her berth, where she fell into a deep,
untroubled sleep, her son in her arms.

The old man had indeed seen her face, lit by the moon's last light
before the cloud slipped over it. Her chin was sharp and her eyes too
small, she had a plain complexion, and her hair hung dankly on her
forehead; but he was reminded of a Madonna he had once seen in
the port of Barcelona when he had last gone into a church to pray.
His young wife, Kate, had been dying then, giving birth to Neddy.
Her memory still mingled with the face of the Madonna in his mind.
Emily'll build me a fine line of sons and grandsons and heirs to come
for the rest of time, he thought, and with my blood and John Grey's,
they'll be kings in the new world. Kings, why not?

"Mr. Stafford! Sir!" The urgent call seemed to come out of the night itself, strangely choked and eerie on the wind. He looked forward and aft, saw no one.

"Up here, sir! The watch!"

He snapped his head upward to the swaying mast and saw the boy frantically waving, in peril of falling from his perch. "Good God, what is it, boy?"

"My eyes, sir, my eyes!"

"What of your eyes, boy? Shout it out then!"

"Mr. Stafford . . . I can't be sure . . . can you help?"

Without hesitation Edward grabbed the stay and swung his powerful body upward, onto the rigging and to the crosstree, as lithe as a boy himself. In a moment he was climbing the mast, feeling the powerful thrust of the wind against the timber and the canvas until he reached the crow's-nest platform where the young watch stood trembling with excitement, pointing off past the port bow. There was hardly room for the two of them on the square foot of planking. The boy was shaking like a willow tree; he grabbed onto the older man's arms. No two should be there at once; there was real danger of catapulting over; the mast swayed madly, and the deck and the sea were very far below.

"Steady," Edward said calmly. "You've seen something? Something you doubt too much to shout out then? Where away?"

"Yes, sir, aye, sir, that's just it. Over there . . . dead ahead . . . but it's not there now."

"Give me the glass."

"The clouds covered the moon just as I saw it . . . my eyes . . . I might have only thought I saw something . . . it'd be the brig at least for a false call, wouldn't it, sir?"

Edward held the spyglass to his eye with one hand, steadying himself on the rail of the perilous perch with his other. He looked toward the horizon for a long time until his sight was accustomed to the formless dark ahead. The boy bit his lips and clenched his fists and waited.

"LAND! LAND HO, DEAD AHEAD!"

Edward's shout must have raised the ghosts of sailors long dead and rotted in the sea a thousand fathoms beneath them. The boy quaked. Their little foothold swayed and creaked as it lurched from side to side, protesting the double weight.

"It's all yours, boy, all yours!" Old Edward said with a grin. He swung himself off the nest and skittered down the mast as lightly as cold drops of water dancing on a skillet. When, a scant moment later, the second mate came bounding from the wheelhouse, Edward stood on deck again, innocently peering across the water. His eyes asparkle, he stepped aside, out of the mate's path, as the officer bore hastily toward the mizzen.

"What say you?" he shouted up, and the boy answered boldly.

"Land, sir! Dead ahead!"

"If you're wrong, I'll have your hide!" the mate roared, but the boy's arm pointed with unswerving certainty toward the beclouded horizon.

"I'll have a look," the mate muttered to himself. He threw his weight up onto the crosstree.

Other passengers, roused by Edward's call, had struggled from belowdecks, and the crew scrambled out of the fo'c'sle in disarray. All rushed to the rail to peer into the rising fog. On the heels of the shouts and chatter, a low collective moan of disappointment: Nothing could be seen but a rapidly lessening field of cold Atlantic sea and a sky obscured now in lowering clouds.

Mutters arose. The watch had gone daft. He'd be thrashed for it, and no mistake. Days or weeks of the journey still lay ahead, the storm had blown them far off course, and New England was only a myth. A joke. The boy would be hanged. And quartered.

In another moment the captain strode on deck, half-dressed and pulling on his coat as the crowd made room for him to pass.

"What's this, what's this?"

"Why, your bright-eyed lad has sighted land, sir!" Edward laughed.

"The devil he has!"

From the crow's nest now came the second mate's angry shout: "I see nothing! Nothing to report, sir!"

"Change watch!" the captain shouted angrily.

"Now then, Captain, but isn't it possible that the boy saw truly before the dark closed in?" Edward asked the disgruntled master, whom he had already found to be without humor or much good sense.

"By my reckoning, Mr. Stafford, we are still three days from the first landfall," the captain answered curtly. He turned on his heel, not waiting for the mate and the erring watch to descend. The men on deck watched him go in silence.

"Now then," Edward said loudly, "my money is on the lad. A fair wager? Who will have me on?"

"I will, sir," said one of the passengers, and in an instant several men were clustered around, eager to take the bet.

"Your five guineas against my one that we all see land by the first light of day?"

"Aye." They all were willing to wager; had not the captain decreed that they were a full three days' from land? This Stafford may have been a ship's master once, but he was past his prime and not privy to the charts on this vessel. A young farmer was designated to hold the wagers, and money changed hands with increasing appetite and greed.

By morning the dunes of Cape Cod were clearly visible against the brilliant sunlit blue sky. Old Edward had gained a sizable profit and the undying loyalty of the young watch.

On the afternoon of the following day the first mate was hard put to keep her on an even keel, with so many passengers crowding the starboard rail to watch the rising landmass take shape before their eyes. The long inertia had ended, and smiles miraculously altered the faces which had been gaunt and ill these long weeks. Belowdecks there was a bustle of activity, linens taken out for airing and chests dragged forward to be repacked for the arrival.

Anne Stafford tried to rise from her pallet, but even with her sister-in-law's help, she could not find the strength to climb up to the deck.

"Tomorrow we'll stand on firm, dry land again, dear, and you can sit in a garden and walk where there are trees. We'll sleep in real beds and eat fresh meat and vegetables . . . Mr. Graham says that one can eat meat every day in Boston. You'll be fine and healthy again. The voyage is over, Anne, we're home!"

"Home."

"Yes, home. It will be home to us, and we can make of it what we wish. Mr. Graham says that the streets of Boston are clean and there is room everywhere for cows and sheep to graze and beautiful hills where one can climb and see the sweep of the harbor below.''

"I'm going to die, Emily.''

"Of course not, what nonsense. The voyage is over, and we have everything to look forward to. Yes, yes, Grey, heavens, what an appetite!'' She opened her breast to the hungry little mouth and smiled at Anne. "You're going to have children soon, I know it. You'll see, I'll wager within a year you'll—''

"I . . . don't want . . .''

"Anne!''

A tear formed in Anne's eye and made its solitary way slowly down her sunken cheek onto the thin, hard pallet.

Having used all her patience, Emily rose from her sister-in-law's side, shrugging away the sense of doom and sadness in which Anne had wrapped herself.

"Look, my greedy son has finished gobbling up his dinner and he's fast asleep,'' she said. "I'm going up onto the deck now. Would you like to try, one more time, to raise yourself and come with me? I'll help you.''

Anne's weak head moved from side to side, no.

As Emily ascended the little steps into the sun and air, she looked back briefly and smiled, although Anne was not looking at her. "It's a new world, Anne. That's what Mr. Graham calls it. The New World. What can possibly be wrong if we have a whole new world to ourselves?''

But Anne did not respond. Emily went on up to join the excited crowd on deck. There was much laughing and pointing to the virgin white dunes and pristine shoreline as the ship tacked south of the long hooked peninsula that was named for a fish.

"How is Anne?'' Neddy asked when he saw her, and she shook her head in answer: not well. Emily glanced sideways at Charles, who stood a few paces away from them, gazing out at the shore.

"If her husband asked for her, maybe she would be better,'' she said tartly, but if Charles overheard, as he was meant to, he did not respond.

Neddy was sketching the approaching coast with a minute bit of charcoal on a bit of paper. His eyes were lit with excitement, which

Emily knew came not from the prospects of the landing, but from the singular pleasure of the visions in his head and the skill in his hand.

Prayers of thanksgiving for the end of their journey, led by Mr. Graham, had been offered at the morning's first sighting of land. Even Old Edward had doffed his hat and stood aside in an attitude that might be considered respectful while the service was celebrated. Now he could be seen near the bow of the ship, in steady and earnest conversation with the Puritan. The two men could not be more different from each other, yet they had become fast friends during the long voyage, with much to talk about. Many people, and particularly Emily, wondered what common ground the minister had with the blaspheming old scoundrel, but there they were, laughing and chattering like two magpies raised in the same cage.

"What do you suppose your father and Mr. Graham find to talk about?" she couldn't help asking. But Neddy was absorbed in his drawing and didn't hear her.

Charles answered her. He moved closer as he spoke, until he was at her side, still gazing out on the hypnotic sight of land.

"I wonder if our father is benefiting from the views of Mr. Graham on the subject of gambling," he said.

"It's hardly Edward's style to listen with such eagerness to a sermon on his sins," Emily replied, laughing.

"Ah, but this is not Old Edward Sifford. This is Mr. Stafford of Boston, a new man who presents a new face—albeit a false one—to the New World."

"Charles, haven't you taken the new name for your own?"

"For now it seems I am forced to."

"Then your face, too, is false," she couldn't resist pointing out.

"Indeed."

"Oh, Charles, why must you be so stuffed up, like a great stubborn ram in need of a purgative? And so busy moralizing about your father you've no interest at all in your poor sick wife. How can you ignore her so?"

"Anne is in good hands. You're taking excellent care of her, I'm sure. The truth is that the one visit I made to the women's quarters made me sick to the point of actual vomit. It's fetid in there and no place for a man. Let her come on deck, and I will be as attentive as your husband is to you."

Oblivious of the angry dialogue, Neddy stood serenely apart with his charcoal and paper.

Emily barely controlled her fury. "Yes," she said icily to her brother-in-law, "I did hear that the men's accommodations are scented with attar of roses and violets."

"You heard wrong," Charles said without humor, still gazing away from her.

"Why are you so angry at the world, Charles?"

"It's a godless place when a man like my father can lead us all. Look how the Puritan minister listens to him and see how lightly his sins are regarded. Even with a Papist king, England is a godlier place than the one we will be forced to live in now."

"Well, we'll have you to lead us in charity and compassion, won't we? If your example is followed, just think how good the world will be then! No man ever to say a kind word to his wife, no one to laugh ever again, not even smile. I don't think I've ever seen you smile, Charles. Is that what you want of us all?"

"If that is what's needed to drive out sin, yes."

"Sin? What sin? Loving your wife? Is that a sin?"

"Whatever takes a man's love in any measure away from God is surely a sin."

"I will not argue about love with you. You know nothing of it."

"Nor would I argue God's will with a woman."

Loud laughter was heard from the two men at the prow, and Charles turned to walk away. Emily pitied him, but her natural enthusiasm for life had no patience for such a sour and gloomy presence. Not this day, surely! She wrapped her shawl more closely around herself and her son. The wind had turned bitter cold, and chunks of hard, glittering ice floated on the water, closing in on the ship, warning of the winter to come. Emily shuddered with a long chill of incipient homesickness deep in her bones. There would be no word from England for many months to come.

Gulls soared out to greet them and, circling the masts, escorted the *Sally Bow* into the harbor. Their first sight of Boston was strangely familiar: a forest of tall masts huddled against a low-lying framework of brick and timber buildings encircling a half-moon of wharves. The air was clear, and the busy waterfront slowly came into perspective. Different by a hundred years from the dingy, coal-encrusted port they had left only months before, Boston shone in the reflected rays of the sun high overhead. As they tacked in closer, they could see the countinghouses, warehouses, sail lofts, taverns, and coffeehouses of the waterfront and a tall white church steeple at the end of the street. Soon they could hear the sailors' curses and the clatter of anvils and hammers and cartwheels and the shouts of vendors. Small boats came out to guide them to their docking, and people were gathering on the wharf to greet them with shouts of welcome and pleas for news of England.

Mr. Graham was met by five unsmiling men in the same Puritan garb he wore—gray woolen capes without adornment, round hats, and high white collars. They came aboard the instant the plank was down and surrounded the minister with anxious faces.

"Mr. Mather will not return until the charter is reinstated," they heard him say to the men. "The king is adamant, but there is reason to believe much of the Parliament is on our side."

"Will they seize the throne from the Papist?" an angry voice called out from the dock as the small knot of men left the ship. The other passengers, awaiting their turns to disembark, looked to the source and saw several groups of men standing in small clusters. The owner of the angry voice was dressed in animal-skin trousers and a wolf's-fur cape; his face marked him an unmistakably ruddy Englishman, but his bearing seemed to second the worst fears of the newcomers that they would all turn into savages here.

"Are we rid of Andros?" called another man, and all eyes were on Mr. Graham and his gray-clad group.

"Not yet, friend, but soon perhaps," was the answer.

"Put William on the throne and he'll recall the governor!"

"Down with King James!" came the treasonous shout, causing the newcomers to gasp with shock.

Instantly soldiers appeared, the king's own, and they seized the shouters, cuffing them about and dragging them off.

"Well, it's a lively place and no mistake about it," Old Edward exclaimed with glee.

"The man spoke treason," Charles reminded him quietly.

"I don't know what it is they want, but it does appear they are an ungovernable lot," another passenger remarked with disdain.

As they edged their way to the landing ramp, Anne quietly collapsed into unconsciousness. Charles lifted her into his arms, and thus they first set foot in Boston: a hearty old cheater bearing trunks and boxes more than double his own weight; his elder son carrying the frail body of his sickly wife; his younger son pushing and shoving at a sea chest with rolled-up canvases under his arm; and a seventeen-year-old girl holding her firstborn to her wildly beating breast.

Chapter Four

1689: EMILY

The first winter was the hardest they had ever known. Endless snow, sometimes floating silently down from a bland, bright, sun-filled sky, more often raging wildly against the wind which shrieked and rattled through the town. The streets and houses were covered with white, and within days of the *Sally Bow*'s arrival and hasty departure for the isles, Boston Harbor froze solidly from Town Dock to Nantasket. No ships could come or go, and the citizens hunkered down in their low, narrow houses to hibernate. The new arrivals found shelter where they could, for there would be no housebuilding until the frigates could navigate the waters down from Maine with the great trees that grew so plentifully there. The Stafford family took refuge in two small, dark rooms above Mistress Abbott's Inn on King's Street. There they would wait out the long, frigid nights and spend the brief daylight hours as profitably as they could.

Their proprietress was a jolly woman, red-cheeked and enormous, with only three teeth left in her head but a ready smile and hearty laugh. Men still found her attractive, and Old Edward made no secret of his carnal interest in Mistress Abbott. She made her guests welcome in the two common rooms of the inn. From the front room the sound of boisterous men in their cups rose at all hours; in the commodious kitchen the hearth became the center of life for the women and children. While the bread baked in the great ovens, birds and game turned on their spits, and caldrons of stews, soups, and por-ridges cooked slowly from their hooks over the banked fires. The women warmed themselves, and friendships were formed.

With gossip and needlework and church services when a way could be cleared through the snow, waiting for the winter to end, the women passed the days. The men ventured out to the coffeehouses or the Town Meeting House, although business had come to a frozen hiatus along with the shipping. Only religion and the parading of the king's troops through the town seemed to continue through blizzards and snowdrifts, hail and drizzle, come what might from the Almighty. Each morning at dawn a cannon shot woke the town as the despised Governor Andros asserted his sovereignty, the red-coated soldiers pa-raded from Fort Hill to the South Battery, and the faithful made their way between the quiet houses to church.

Emily could no more bear the restrictive confines of the cheerful inn than any other place where she felt unable to move about freely. On days when the other women were grateful for the fire that warmed the kitchen, Emily sometimes would leave Grey in their care, bundle herself in shawls, and venture out to explore the streets and lanes of Boston. She was looking for the perfect site for the Staffords to build their first home. She explored the length of King's Street from the First Church to the royal barricades; she turned up narrow little lanes with grand names like Marlborough Street and School Street (where her son, she thought proudly, would one day join the chorus of voices she could hear within, reciting Latin phrases in unison) and Newbury and Stuart. She skirted the great expanse of fields and ponds and trees known as the Common Pasture and strode briskly along the waterfront lane called Charles Street, where the sea lapped from un-der its icecap at the very foot of the houses.

Ignoring the frostbite that turned her nose first red, then white, Emily trudged her way along the Neck, that narrow spit of land con-necting the peninsula of the town to the mainland. It was a forbidding place in the winter. The narrow, snow-rutted pathway was criss-crossed by the bowsprits of the ice-locked ships tied up on both sides, lying silent in the waters of Back Bay and the South Cove. Both sides of the road were barren and marshy under the ice, and there was a gallows tree standing near the infamous Inn at the Neck, from which drunken argument and bawdy songs issued forth at any hour.

But in the spring the Neck would be filled with traffic from the farms and nearby towns, with tradesmen eager to sell their produce and goods to the people of Boston. The ships would ply in and out with the inevitable excitement of arrival and departure, loading and unloading. It would be a profitable place for a business, she thought. She would tell Old Edward about it, if she could pry him loose from the plump flanks of Mistress Abbott long enough to discuss family business.

Old Edward had lost no time in gaining a foothold in the New World, and had begun to talk of politics and enterprise with impatient gusto. His sons were less inclined to share his enthusiasms, but they listened with dutiful concentration as they sat with him in the places where men conducted their affairs. They followed in his wake like two sturdy dories towed behind a full-rigged frigate in a high wind, from Mistress Abbott's Inn to the taverns, the coffeehouses, and the Town Meeting House.

Old Edward had been talking of a part interest he would buy in a schooner; it would be the beginning of a fortune to be made in the glorious, limitless new future. He talked expansively at table, never stopping the boisterous flow of boasts and promises, gibes and gestures, even as he reached out to pinch the innkeeper's plump knee.

"Privateering, now there's a splendid opportunity for a man who knows ships," he charged one midday, gesturing with his knife, scattering mashed turnip onto the plate of the man next to him. "England pays handsomely for anyone bold enough to board and confiscate a ship found wrongfully in its waters," he went on, oblivious of manners and all else but his own passions. "A shipowner can make a fair fortune as a privateer if he's got stamina and the stomach for it. Half to the king, of course, but half the bounty to the man of guts, and that's fair enough. Why, there's a Boston man who's bountied himself five thousand guineas and more in a year's time, a Mr. Cabot, I believe, or so the talk is. And legal, too. Legitimate."

"We have no ship, Father," Charles put in quietly. He was seated at the far end of the table, near the women, between two gentlemen in Puritan gray.

"Ships are easy to come by if a man knows how," Edward answered, dismissing the problem with another wave of his hand, this time without the knife in it. "Don't look on the dark side of life, my boy. I earned the price of two ships with my strong back and my two hands once, and with my sons to help me now, we'll soon have a fleet! And there's trading to be done, they tell me, for a man who knows his way to the West Indies and Africa and back."

"What trading is that, Mr. Stafford?" one of the men asked.

"Why, all kinds of goods and commodities not to be found here, taxed too high by our own mother country to be profitable. And they tell me there is a growing thirst back home for the excellent rum of Massachusetts. Do you know there are already eight distilleries in New England, making rum for export? I mean to establish a circular trade: sugar for the rum . . . sugar from the Indies, and rum to old England, that's the route."

"And Africa?"

"What about it?"

"You mentioned trade with Africa, I believe, sir."

"Oh, did I? Well, slaves, of course. Nobody's been able to domesticate the red Indians for slaves, not yet, they haven't, so there's plenty of use for African blacks, and they fetch a good price, I'm told."

"Slavery is against the law of God," his son Charles put in, almost in a whisper.

"When God makes the laws of men, I'll abide by them," his father retorted with equanimity. "In the meantime, my boy, I suggest you abide by man's laws and leave God to the ministers. Now, Mistress Abbott, what's a poor sinner to do for more of those delicious turnips? Would you ask your 'indentured servant' to bring the dish around once more, for a man who's never made a claim to be better than any other?"

"Eulalie! More turnips!" the proprietress shouted. The quiet African woman hastened with the stewpot from the hearth.

"There's a merchant named Sam Belcher with two warehouses on the street that bears his name," Neddy said in the silence that followed the slave's round about the table. "I spoke with him. He's willing to take a partner in an importing venture."

His father stared at him in astonishment. Neddy rarely spoke at all.

When he did, it was more likely to be a comment on the quality of the light that fell across a room or the structure of bone beneath a woman's cheek than a practical matter of business.

Mistress Abbott roared with laughter. "Belcher!" she shouted gleefully. "That miser, what a thief he is! You'll have your breeches stolen from off your backside if you go partners with that one!"

"It's true," one of the Puritan gentlemen agreed sadly. "Mr. Belcher sold part of his land for such a price to the town that the larger part of his lane has been renamed as an ironic tribute to his perspicacity. Belcher Lane still exists, but the main part of his lane is now called Purchase Street, in honor of the exorbitant price he charged for access."

Old Edward was delighted. He much preferred doing business with a scoundrel than a man who claimed to be honest and upright, moral and filled with brotherly love. These things did not exist in business; far better that they were dispensed with as hypocrisy, was his view on it.

"How do you know this Belcher, Neddy?" he asked.

"I . . . he has rented space to me in one of his warehouses," Neddy stammered. "I go there to paint when the light is good."

Holding her breath until her father-in-law should explode his wrath, Emily was relieved to see him smile. So if the end was to be a good business deal, he had no objections to his son's "wasting time" with his paints. She let her breath out with a sigh, gathering odd looks from the women beside her.

The biting winds turned, at last, and the snows began to slake off, thinning by mid-March to sleet and rain. The ice slowly cracked and then broke in the harbor, and one day the rich, loamy smell of good black earth rose through the running snow, slush replaced ice, and suddenly bushes of forsythia broke forth all over the town in glorious bursts of gold. Everyone strolled out and greeted each other, children ran and shouted, and the ships teemed with men readying them for the first spring voyage.

Timber arrived from Maine, a house began to take form on Charles Street, facing the sea.

Anne conceived but carried the child for only a few weeks. It was her third miscarriage, and she mourned without complaint, sadly but devotedly taking charge of active, squirmy, laughing little Grey while Emily busied herself about the construction and furnishing of the new house.

The long months of winter's inactivity, the icebound isolation, and the shrouds of snow affected Boston city in the same natural way that the frozen ground prepares itself to nurture fertile seeds. By the time of the April thaw restless energies had provided rich soil for rumors to grow and spread.

One morning a message ran through the town like magic. No one afterward could remember how or why everyone seized on the news—if news it was, and not still rumor. King James had been overthrown! Without waiting to learn the truth of it, men picked up their arms and strode in groups of two and three toward the Town House, with the women following closely after them, clutching babies and trying to subdue the schoolboys' rowdy shouts. Fueled by the balmy spring weather, the spirit caught fire in Boston that day, and within moments of the first shouts the townspeople were gathered below the arcade of the Town House. Governor Andros was there, looking down on them. In his position of superiority, closely surrounded by his red-coated guards, his haughty presence was a focus for their unrest.

"Surrender, Andros!" someone shouted, and the cry was taken up. Muskets were waved threateningly. "Hang him!" was heard from various quarters of the crowd.

"I represent the king! This is treason!" Andros retorted haughtily. "You'll all be hanged for this!"

Royal soldiers were marching in orderly files up from the harbor and the Fort Hill garrison, but suddenly the colony's own militiamen were assembling, rushing every which way from their houses in hastily half-donned uniforms. They quickly formed a staunch circle around the crowd in the street, facing out toward the approaching king's men.

"Fire! Fire on them!" the governor shouted imperiously.

A musket shot exploded with ear-shattering suddenness, and a woman's shriek was heard above the shocked, suddenly silent crowd. As the black smoke cleared, two things became quickly evident: the blast had come from a townsman's gun, and Governor Andros was no longer to be seen in the arcade above.

"You've killed him!" someone shouted in horror, but the answer came quickly and with authority in a broad Liverpudlian accent.

"No, sir, I have not!" It was Old Edward Stafford whose musket still smoked hotly. He brandished it in the air for all to see. "I fired in the air, and Andros has got away!" he shouted. "After him, and watch the dock! He'll head for his barge. Quick, the alleyway!"

The crowd surged toward the side entrance of the Town House through the leaderless troops, who gave way in confusion. But the governor had been quick. He was away, and showing rare agility and speed as he bolted, coattails flying, heading pell-mell down the winding street toward the water.

"Take the barge!" The command rang out from an unknown quarter but was instantly acted upon. The men already at the wharf leaped onto the governor's barge and threw off the confused guard. A shout of victory went up from the dockside, but Andros turned to run for the garrison house at Fort Hill, only steps from the wharf.

With Andros safely behind his thick fortress walls, there was nothing to do but disband. But the mood was angry, and satisfaction had been denied them.

"Call a meeting of the townsmen," Mr. Graham said, and the word passed quickly through the crowds. Within moments the hall was filled to overflowing; those without pews to sit upon stood along the edges, and others waited anxiously outside. The citizens' representatives conferred publicly, and news of their proceedings was quickly passed through the door and out into the streets.

Mr. Graham urged patience, pointing out that a ship would come any day with news from England. Perhaps the Parliament had persuaded the king to renew the charter of the Massachusetts Bay Colony. Perhaps it was true, as rumor was brought on a ship from the Indies a week before, that James had lost his throne to William months past, and therefore, the colonists were in the right to overthrow Andros. Perhaps, on the other hand, all present were guilty of vile treason and legally eligible for hanging for this day's action.

Others spoke. They argued hotly and coolly, reasoned with democratic fairness, and orated with passionate fervor. While the meeting proceeded, Old Edward Stafford made his way to the militiamen, who stood and sat uneasily on the governor's barge and along the wharf, awaiting orders.

Noting an officer's insignia on one fellow's coat, he sauntered alongside and struck up a conversation.

"I am Edward Stafford, shipowner and privateer," he said. "May I have the pleasure of your acquaintance, sir?"

"John Fisher, tailor," the man replied, "presently acting colonel in the Boston militia, as you see, sir."

Without seeming to, Edward nudged the colonel a bit apart from the other men, continuing the conversation on a genial, casual plane. Out of anyone's hearing, he nodded toward the wharf's promontory and said, "You mark that cannon, Mr. Fisher?"

"Yes."

"Only ten redcoats to guard it."

"The cannon points out to sea. The trouble is in the city; no doubt Andros feels secure enough from invasion by sea."

"Do you think you could take the cannon, Colonel?" Old Edward asked.

"Oh, well, ten men . . . certainly we could. But we have no need to guard the sea surely. I see no point in such an exercise. The cannon is no threat to us, Mr. Stafford. You might learn more about such tactics were you to join us in the militia. You look like a strong man, and age is no barrier."

"Yes, I was thinking of doing just that, Colonel Fisher. Every civilian envies you this day, you may be sure. Right in the thick of the action . . . but about the cannon, sir. If you were to take it, and to swing it around so that it pointed at the garrison, where our dear governor and all his troops sit trembling . . .?"

John Fisher looked at the older man with sudden respect. His eyes twinkled, and he shook Old Edward's hand and laughed, then broke away, motioned for his men to follow him, and huddled with a handful of officers to give them the plan.

Within moments, without a skirmish, they had surprised the cannon guards and sent them skittering up to join their comrades at Fort Hill, where they turned around in time to see their erstwhile weapon now swinging slowly around to point its nose at them.

When Edward turned, still wearing his canary-digesting smile on his weathered old cat face, he saw to his surprise that his daughter-in-law was a step behind him. She had heard it all.

"Commanding the militia, are you now?" she scolded, laughing.

"Don't know what you mean," he growled, striding ahead of her in the direction of the Town House.

"Was it you who told them to seize the barge, so he couldn't escape to Castle Island?" she persisted, matching her strides to his.

"Tend to your child, madam, and leave men to their affairs," he answered. He went into the hall to announce that the time was ripe to demand the governor's surrender. He explained the position of the cannon and received a standing round of cheers from almost every man in the house.

A messenger was sent to Andros, demanding his surrender. He refused. The breathless rider who returned with the arrogant answer was dispatched back to Fort Hill at once with the mission of most courteously drawing the governor's attention to the cannon pointed directly at him. Within the hour the rider returned triumphantly to the Town House, but his message was a request for time to consider.

The day wore on, with emotions alternately high and low. By midafternoon a rider had galloped across the Neck to announce that fifteen hundred citizen troops had gathered from the countryside and were waiting in Charlestown to be ferried across the Charles River to aid the Boston militia, if necessary. This word also spread into the fortress, and shortly thereafter the terms were presented to the governor: the surrender of his flagship, the *Rose*.

They waited. Five o'clock was the deadline, a full hour and a half before sunset.

At ten minutes before the hour an escort emerged from the fort, and the governor rode in stately silence up the street to the Town House. There he formally gave up command of the *Rose*. Within moments the flagship was stripped of her sails, and the governor given safe-conduct back to his mansion on the hill. From his windows he could look out on the harbor, where the symbol of his control lay at anchor helplessly bobbing with the outgoing tide.

"Self-government, that's the thing," Old Edward exclaimed at the late supper which was finally set that evening. Candles were lined up all up and down the long communal table in the kitchen of the inn, in a recklessly expensive celebration of the victory. Yet there were some at the table who did not understand, who still thought it treason and were afraid.

"Andros's authority was unlawful," he went on. "If it's true that James is no longer on the throne, then we've a new king and a new charter, too, these many months past."

"Rumor. Until we know for certain, we are bound by law—"

"The colony is not the old country," Edward retorted hotly, "and we won't be bound by tyranny in any shape or form. Legal or otherwise, say I."

"For a dickey-sam, you talk more like a Plymouth Rocker," joked a farmer who hadn't been heard to talk at table once during the long winter. Now that he was planting his own fields, and his house going up in the center of the rich, loamy land, he emerged from his winter shell like a pod shyly rising from the earth itself.

"A dickey-sam, Mr. Caldwell?" Old Edward asked quizzically.

"Why, that's the name we use for a man from Liverpool!" the farmer exclaimed. He chuckled and went on chewing his food with a satisfied shaking of his head.

"We, sir? Who, sir?"

"Why, we Boston men."

There was general laughter, for the farmer had come on the *Sally Bow* with the rest of them. The tension of the long day's insurrection was lifted, and if any had private fears about the morrow—and all did—they kept it to themselves.

Six days later official documents reached Boston attesting to King James's "abdication" and proclaiming King William and Queen Mary, both with equal bloodlines to the throne, the lawful sovereigns of England, Scotland, Ireland, and the dominions beyond the seas.

There was rejoicing, if not unanimity, in Boston. Arguments raged everywhere about the kind of charter wanted, the rules of self-government to be demanded. Men debated hotly in taverns, on street corners, in meeting halls and coffeehouses, against an undercurrent of shrill discord from diehard royalists, who viewed all such talk as treasonous.

But nothing goes unmeasured; daily life continued hard. The city was tested by a series of hardships: a killing epidemic of pox; scores of disastrous fires; a summer of drought and deadly, killing heat. Three years would pass before the Reverend Increase Mather would return with a new royal charter for Massachusetts. But babies grew and houses became homes and friends helped one another, and few ever looked backward.

Old Edward began with part interest in one of Mr. Belcher's ships and soon had another of his own, and another. He privateered and came home with roaring tales of treasures buried on an island off the coast of the Providence Plantations, of battles fought on the high seas and Spanish jewels, doubloons, and diamond-encrusted porcelain eggs with clockworks inside, stolen from the palaces of the Russians.

"Dumped overboard," he groaned, on returning from one of his voyages. "Just as I was boarding, I saw the captain pry open a cask and tip the spoils into the sea. I swear, the light from the gold and rubies and emeralds and diamonds shone for a fathom and more before they sank through the blue, blue water to the bottom. A waste, a cruel waste."

"Blue water?" Emily asked. "In the Atlantic? Is that not unusual? Where exactly did this encounter take place, Edward?"

"In the king's legal waters, of course. What do you take me for? It was blue because it was . . . it was the Gulf Stream! Women should be seen and not heard, damn it!"

"It must have been the Gulf Stream surely. And I'm equally sure that the Gulf Stream belongs to King William, and your commandeering another ship could never take place in international waters. I meant no wrong," she said, trying to sound abject. But there was a rich twinkle in her eye which her father-in-law did not fail to appreciate.

"But if it was the Caribbean, which they do say is very blue, then surely your act was piracy and not the king's honest business!" Charles, humorless but not a fool, missed little.

"It was the Gulf Stream. Mind your business," his father retorted.

"And did you kill the captain for having disposed of your bounty?" Charles asked. He sat in semidarkness, out of the lamplight, apart from the others.

Emily and Neddy and Anne, even the baby Grey, were crowded around the table, celebrating Old Edward's homecoming, eagerly listening to his exploits.

"No," the old scoundrel replied, laughing, "I would have, for a moment, but something in the man's eyes . . . I respected what he'd done, you see. . . . I wondered if I might have had the strength to do the same. A matter of principle, and damned hard. Ah, but the sight of all that bounty, falling so slowly in the water, tantalizing, out of any man's grasp . . . he did what he had to, and I respected him for it.''

"So you didn't kill him," Charles said.

"Well, it wasn't because I'd grown soft," his father retorted. Then Edward turned his attention to the splendid roast beef, and no more was said of the matter.

Charles had grown leaner and indisputably dour in the three years since their arrival in Boston. He took full charge of the family business when his father was at sea and had proved to be astute, fair-minded, and hardworking, although morose and disinclined to conversation. He had adopted the unadorned gray of the Puritan sect and spent all his waking hours either at work or at prayer. Anne spoke hardly at all anymore, even to Emily.

Neddy worked alongside his brother at the dockside office, conscientiously counting cargo and portioning out routes and dealing, with an unsuspected talent for diplomacy, with the new governor and other representatives of the Crown. Emily had fixed a special room for him at the top of the frame house on Charles Street, where he could paint. Neddy spent most of his nights there; she had learned to sleep alone. Many nights he no longer even took the time to warm his side of the bed before getting up to work. Emily lulled herself to sleep thinking of many things and sometimes, lying wakeful, she would think of Mr. Graham, the minister. One night, perhaps more than one, she wondered what his arms would feel like if they were holding her. When such thoughts came to her, she made herself get out of the warm bed (Neddy's bed, whether he chose to use it or not!), and she would kneel on the hard floor to say prayers. But most of the time Emily slept with a clear conscience, on the weariness of a full day's work.

All the profits from Edward's privateering exploits went into buying new ships until Emily, on her own, decided that money should be set aside for the future, for the house she dreamed of, and for their children to come. All one night she sat over the account books with her father-in-law, and despite his growling and fuming, she had

her way so that each arrival of a Stafford ship saw a sizable percent-
age of the take put into savings. The family fortunes grew. Within
three years the Stafford line was plying a regular route with five wholly
owned ships: from Boston, with a cargo of rum, to Africa, where the
rum was traded for slaves; to the West Indies, where the slaves were
bartered for sugar; and back to Boston, where the sugar was sold to
the rum distillers, along with the choicest, healthiest of the blacks
saved for the higher profit to be taken in that civilized city. Only one
ship of the line privateered, although that was by far a more profitable venture than mere shipping. Old Edward trusted no man but
himself to do this delicate work and render an honest accounting of
the booty taken from trespassing vessels.

Every time Edward returned from a voyage to tell tales of Captain
Kidd (a very good friend of his, he said), and plague breaking out in
the slave hold, and spear-carrying savages leaping from the beaches
of Africa to attack the ship, and voodoo practices in the Indies, he
found Emily happy to see him, Neddy politely distant, Anne more
preoccupied, and Charles more tight-lipped.

There began to be words between the father and his elder son,
bitter words. Name-calling: thievery, murder, greed; righteous hypocrite, weakling.

And one night, before the candles were lit on a lingering autumn
evening, Charles quietly announced his intention to leave Boston.

"Leave? Leave the family? Leave me? I won't have it!" Old Edward roared in disbelief.

"God has seen fit to allow my wife to conceive again, and this
time I know what I have to do. The child will survive only if I am
worthy. I'm going to Salem to join the community of God-fearing
men. Anne and I will live as God intends us."

"Crap and nonsense! It wasn't God who impregnated your wife,
and if it was, then the child should be born in a manger. What gall,
what ballocks to think you have the direct line to God! That's your
sin, boy, that's pride and wickedness, to think you're holier and purer
than other men. I've heard that children are forbidden to laugh in
Salem. They say it's a wonder that children are begotten at all in that
miserable place."

Charles answered with the gentleness that infuriated his father most.

"You talk about principle, but you can't seem to understand that I must live by the principles I believe in. I see God's will now, I see it very clearly. I've spent my life in evil ways and have much to make up for. My plan is set, Father. Anne and I will leave tomorrow."

"Forever!" Old Edward bellowed. "Don't you forget, it's forever if you go!"

His rage reverberated through the house. In the next room little Grey began to whimper in his bed. Emily couldn't go to him; her hands were holding Anne's thin, trembling shoulders in a vain attempt at comfort. Anne's head was bowed low over the plate before her; her arms were clutched together over her rising belly beneath her apron.

"Anne is not well," she said quietly to Charles. "You can't take her away to Salem in her condition. She's delicate and should be close to the doctors here in Boston."

"She will be closer to God, and He will protect her," Charles answered firmly. He pursed his lips tightly, determined to say no more.

"Go and be damned to you then," Edward shouted. He rose from his chair and swept his greatcoat off the hook behind the door. In a moment he had charged out into the gathering dark, striding toward King's Street and Mistress Abbott's Inn.

"I want to catch the light," Neddy mumbled in the silence that fell on the house after Edward had gone. He gathered up his sketching papers and threw his cape over his shoulder hastily, then followed his father's retreating figure across the pasture. For a moment Emily let herself think that Neddy might have gone after his father, to reason with him, but of course, he had not. He was heading for the sunset on the Neck, where the ships formed silhouettes against the sky.

"Oh, Anne," Emily murmured. She looked up at Charles, who had turned his back to the room and seemed to be deep in prayer against the wall cupboard. "Come with me, dear," she said. "I want to see to little Grey." She helped her sister-in-law rise from her chair, and they went into Emily's bedchamber, shutting the door between themselves and Charles.

"You must refuse to go," Emily said. "You can stay here. I'll take care of you. We all will."

"No," Anne answered wearily, sadly. "I have to go. He's my husband."

"He's become a zealot, a fanatic. You'll live like a drudge, indentured to his idea of God's will . . . they say Salem is a solemn place, where no one smiles. Oh, Emily, never to hear music again, or see people dancing, or children playing freely . . . ."

"It can't be like that," Anne assured her quickly. "I'm sure it's not. And isn't it possible that Charles will change? If he finds peace of mind, he might become more . . . more . . . he might change. . . ." She trailed off, not quite sure what she wanted to say.

"It's a damned shame!"

"Emily!"

"Yes, I know. I talk like a man, like Old Edward, swearing like a deck hand. I don't care. Edward is the only one in this family with any life in him at all. I'd rather be like him than . . . oh, Anne, isn't it hard to be a woman sometimes?"

Anne's cold, thin fingers spread across her rounded middle. She smiled wanly. "I have this," she said with shy pride. "This one will live. I know he will. I believe that Charles is right."

Emily sighed. She couldn't have said why she was so impatient with Anne's dutiful acceptance of her husband's domination. But it crossed her mind, fleetingly, that it was a lucky thing she had married Neddy and none other. He was increasingly content to lean on her in all things now, and that suited her independent temper exactly.

She bent to cover little Grey's legs with the quilt he had kicked off. He was fast asleep, his chunky little legs so uncharacteristically still that she put her hand on his chest to make sure he was breathing. Then she straightened up and smiled at Anne.

"Yes," she said, "whatever you have to do for your child, you'll do. And never regret it. There are satisfactions in being a woman, and they're great and deep. Promise to send word to me often . . . tell me how you are and if you need anything. Salem's not so far away; it's only a day's ride or less if the roads are dry, they say. I could be there quickly, if you needed me for any reason, or you could come home. Promise you'll send word, and often. Whenever a rider comes from Salem, let him bring a message from you. We mustn't let the family break apart. Our children will be cousins after all!''

Anne smiled with genuine pleasure. With a shock Emily realized that it had been many months, maybe years, since she had seen Anne happy.

"Anne!"

The smile vanished with the sound of her husband's voice calling from the other room. Anne got up and went to him immediately. Emily followed, leaving the candle lit in case little Grey awoke again. She thought it entirely possible that there might be more shouting in this house before the night was over.

But she was wrong. Neddy came home when the last ray of sun had faded from the sky, and he hurried directly to his little studio at the top of the house to fill in the colors he had just studied. Anne and Charles retired early to their bedchamber to pray and ready themselves for their journey. Emily climbed into her bed, found it cold, but decided against lifting the child from his trundle to keep her company. She lay listening for her father-in-law's tread, but he spent the night at the inn. She knew what to picture: Old Edward telling bawdy and bloody stories of his exploits at sea to anyone who'd listen and then being carried to Mistress Abbott's bed amid much hilarity by men nearly as unconscious as he was.

In the small frame house on Charles Street, where the waves sometimes reached up to the low white pickets, all was quiet.

In the morning Charles and Anne left for Salem, never to return.

Chapter Five

1692: EMILY

The house on Pemberton Square was almost finished. It would have three full stories and a great portico surrounding the entire structure, looking over wide lawns and an apple orchard. There would be real glass in every window. Neddy's studio would be open to the light from every side, and the nursery would have its own fireplace, plenty of cupboards and shelves for books and toys, and three separate sleeping chambers, for Emily was determined that this child would be a girl and that there would be another as well.

She supervised the construction almost daily, riding from Charles Street to stand for hours, despite the increasingly heavy burden of her coming child, watching each phase of the work and conferring with the architect and workmen. As her dreams were realized in the brick-by-brick structure rising on the crest of the easternmost peak of Trimountain, looking out over the sea, new ambitions swelled within her. Emily had polished her rudimentary reading skills since coming to Boston and was determined that her children would be educated in manners and scholarly achievements, able to take their places as leaders of their own times to come.

The ferocious heat of August was on the city now, and Emily was looking forward to an afternoon nap as she climbed up into the carriage to be driven home. The glass had been installed that day in the windows of the parlor and dining hall; it was satisfying to see the purplish tinge of the sun's rays reflecting through the best English glass onto her own finely sanded hardwood floors. Only a few more weeks in the little frame house by the water's edge, and then they would move from Charles Street to the fine new mansion where her second child would enter the world. It was a long way from the fetid ship's cabin where little Grey had been born four years before; it was a long way from the fisherman's cottage on the Liverpool docks where she had started life herself.

A long-distance messenger's horse stood tethered to the low pickets outside the house, sweated from a hard ride in the sun. Emily's pulse began to race: a letter from Anne! News came rarely, and she found herself uncharacteristically anxious as she hurried down from the carriage into the doorway of her house. She tried to calm herself with the firm recollection that Anne's first child had been born healthy, a son named John, nine months old already, and Anne had conceived again almost immediately. The second child might have already arrived, she told herself, good news. But wasn't it too soon? Emily scolded herself for unnecessary worry; she would know what the messenger brought soon enough. It was the heat, she told herself, that made her blood race so. She hastened through the little hallway into the kitchen, where the rider was waiting, seated on a chair, drinking loudly from a ladleful of cool pump water. The slave Maribess had fetched it for him and now stood watching suspiciously as though the strange man might try to make off with her dipper. She snatched it from him as soon as he stood up, when Emily hurried into the room.

"A letter?" she asked quickly. "From Salem?"

"Yes, ma'am," the man replied. He was raw-beef red, dripping sweat, and he seemed to be having difficulty finding her letter in the depths of his leather pouch.

Emily took it from him as rudely as Maribess had grabbed away the dipper. She motioned to the slave to give him a coin from the jar on the cupboard shelf that was hidden behind the sugar bin. She took the letter to her room, sat down heavily on her rocking chair, caught her breath, and broke open the seal.

EMILY COME HELP ME.

The handwriting was scrawled across the page, slanting crazily, ending in a black puddle of unblotted ink that ran like tears to the bottom of the page. The handwriting was unrecognizable, and she stared at it for a long moment, mesmerized by its strangeness, thinking how odd it was that Anne had not signed her name, nor punctuated the sentence, nor blotted the paper with a bit of sand. Anne had been sent to school as a child and had always taken shy pride in her writing. Emily shook herself and rose to go to the door of her bedchamber, calling out to Maribess to have the carriage made ready. She would ride to Salem at once.

She felt the baby inside her protesting the hurried movements, the oppressive heat, the panic that she felt coursing through her own veins and, therefore, surely those of the child. As quickly as she could, she packed a few essentials—a nightdress, a change of petticoat and stockings, a brush for her hair, a box of talcum powder and some salt against the heat—and tiptoed into the room where the wiry four-year-old lay sleeping. She kissed his moist brow softly and left his door ajar so that Maribess would be sure to hear him when he woke.

The ride to Salem was long, and the road, after the first few miles, quite desolated. The driver begged permission to stop at a farmhouse after two hours of steady pacing in the still-fierce late-afternoon sun.

"There might not be another house for ten miles or more," he said, wheedling in a way that set Emily's teeth on edge. This was one of Edward's men, hired in some moment of who knew what weakness or blackmail. The man was unpleasant and had obviously never had a thorough washing of his body in his life. "The horse is overheated," he went on whiningly, "and I've an ungodly thirst myself, ma'am, an honest thirst, raised by the dust, and if I may say so, you look a bit tired, Mistress Stafford, yourself. I'm thinking it's my duty to look after you, ma'am. . . ."

"It certainly is not your duty. I will look after myself. You are in my employ, Mr. Jaffe, and I have no time to waste."

"But Black Jack, ma'am . . ."

It was true, the horse had worked up a powerful sweat and must be cooled and rested if the journey could continue at any pace whatsoever.

They drew up to the house, to find the farmer and his wife almost pathetically glad to have a bit of human company. The man stopped his work in the cornfield, wiping his face with his sleeve. He pumped water into a large oak bucket and brought it into the house. His wife talked unendingly, asking for news of Boston, not stopping her words long enough for answers. She set cool milk and johnnybread before them, offered to make tea, and vowed she would kill a chicken if they would stay for the evening meal.

"Thank you," Emily answered, "but I can't stop. I'm in a very great hurry to get to Salem. My sister-in-law needs me."

"But you're in no condition for such a ride!" the farmwife exclaimed. "And we've heard so many terrible tales from that ungodly place recently. Terrible!"

"What tales?" Emily asked, alarmed.

"A traveler came four days ago, saying he was bewitched and that the devil is walking in Salem. He was running for his life, he said, and only the week before, a party of gentlemen rode from Boston to sit in judgment on women who've been accused of corrupting innocent young girls with the devil's work. Surely you've heard—"

"I don't listen to such nonsense," Emily said.

"You'd do well to listen if your sister-in-law is there. She may have been bewitched herself. Many come past this house and they stop and they tell us things. We saw with our own eyes—didn't we, John?—a man with a mark on his forehead, red and thick as a strawberry, put there by a witch's spell. And the gentlemen going to Salem, fine men, well dressed they were, and educated, not the sort to waste their time unless they had it on authority that they were going to deal with the evil one himself."

"I heard about them," Emily admitted. "But perhaps they intended to quiet such fears, rather than fire them?"

"That may be," the woman said with a wide sweep of her eyes from side to side, as if fearful of what might be lurking in her own cavelike kitchen. Then she felt compelled to offer her advice.

"That child you carry would be better off far away from that wicked place," she said, nodding sagely. "He could get the mark of the devil on him before he's even born, poor thing. You can stop here for the night and ride back to Boston first thing in the morning, before—"

"I'm grateful for your hospitality," Emily cut in firmly. "But I must be on my way. May I pay you for the excellent meal?''

"Five shillings, silver," the farmer said, holding out his hand.

"A bit high, but I suppose good advice comes higher than good fresh milk," Emily retorted. She signaled to the driver that she was ready to be helped back into the carriage.

"Jack's hardly lost his sweat," the driver complained, "and it'll soon be dark. I've heard these warnings before, Mistress Stafford. I'm a God-fearing man and won't knowingly go to the devil. Begging your pardon."

"Do you mean you refuse to take me to Salem?" Emily asked furiously.

"Aye. That's it. I refuse. Respectfully, ma'am, most respectfully. But as a freeman it's what I can do, and as a Christian it's what I must. Let me take you back to Boston, then, and not look for trouble."

They stood in the little doorway of the farmer's cottage, with the elderly couple listening and staring at them. Emily stepped out into the bright daylight and looked up at the sky, already beginning to streak with crimson. The worst heat of the day was past, and she was anxious to be under way again. She had no fear of the night, but she had no wish to test the devil's own element with her defiance either. She had no choice in the matter; why couldn't these people see that?

"The horse belongs to my husband, and the carriage as well, don't they?" she asked the driver.

"Aye. And your father-in-law, to be precise, ma'am."

"And you refuse to take me to Salem?"

The man scratched his head. "I'm a freeman," he repeated. "In your employ, mistress, but not in your servitude."

"That's true. But I intend to go on to Salem, and at once. Will you drive me or not?"

"You can't go alone in your condition," the farmwife put in.

Emily took a wool rag from the post seat and began to wipe down the horse's strong flank. She said nothing but took great care and patience with him. Black Jack stood quietly munching long grass, in the shade of an oak tree, waiting to go on. He was strong, but she hoped she could handle him.

"Help me up," she ordered the driver.

Shaking his head, the man did as he was told and stood off quickly as Emily took the reins and whip in hand.

"How will I get back to Boston?" he asked, whining again.

"The devil can take you," was her answer as she flicked the whip in the air. Black Jack started off with a sprightly gait.

Sunset, glorious and extravagant, lit the sky and the wild fields and sandy marshes all around her. An occasional salty breeze filtered across the bogs from the sea as she followed the barely discernible ruts that marked the road northward. Darkness enveloped the landscape, and the stars were brilliant above her head, with a pale, pale moon keeping its distance out in space. All was silence except for Black Jack's steady hooves carrying them forward.

The child protested with angry jabs and seemed to be stretching its growing arms and legs in every possible direction. Bouncing along the dirt path, up hills and down, through streams, and across mud-filled swamps, Emily longed for a cushion to sit on. She tried to occupy her worried mind with plans for making coach and carriage seats out of down, covered in velvet, for future rides, even if merely to cross the Common or go down Orange Street to the market at the Neck. Blue velvet, she thought. Tassels? Deliberately keeping her mind from straying to the anticipation of what she might find at her journey's end, she pushed away the ominous words of the farmwife and the superstitions of the lazy driver, the vivid picture scrawled across her memory of Anne's urgent note. Perhaps red for the cushions, she told herself deliberately. And no tassels.

The village of Marblehead was well lit with lanterns, swinging from a long row of taverns and public houses along its main street. Emily felt the first real twinges of weariness since her ride had begun long hours before. She needed to rest, but it was only a little farther to Salem, and the urgency of Anne's message propelled her onward. Soon she and Jack were on the desolate swampy plain again, with no company and no cheer but the stars. The moon had retired from the summer sky.

It was well past midnight when she approached the first farms that skirted Salem town. The road cut almost due northward through the fields and pastures of the householders; vainly she looked for lamplights in the dark huddled buildings along her way. But it seemed that everyone was abed. How would she find Anne? She had no idea.

Riding steadily, she came to a covered bridge crossing a wide dark strip of quiet water. No one guarded the bridge, and she felt a prickle of danger as she urged Jack into the dark tunnellike crossing. The bridge's wooden planking and the curved roof that protected it from rain and snow made the horse's hooves echo, to her lone ears, like a cavalry troop descending on the town. If there were no highwaymen lying in wait within the bridge's eerie hollow, surely the sounds of Black Jack's pounding shoes would rouse the city to greet her with raised muskets at the other side.

But she emerged from the crossing into silence, all the more terrifying because she had geared herself to expect anything but that. The houses were set deeply back from the road, but they were close together, lined up like sullen orphans, all costumed alike in drab, all watching without expression or greeting as a stranger rode past.

It is a Puritan place, she admonished herself, and perhaps they are opposed on principle to candles or lamps late at night. (Not Mr. Graham, the only Puritan she knew personally, of course, but he was hardly typical of his sect.) Never had she imagined a town so quiet and so dark. So hostile.

At last she saw a flicker of light, down a narrow lane, into which she turned without hesitation. As she approached, she saw that the lane ended with a flat square brick building which had a candle burning in its window. She was desperate enough and emboldened enough to alight from the carriage, to knock at the dark wood door.

Her knocking brought no answer but its own echo, a lonely sound. She pounded with both fists on the unyielding door. No one would leave a candle to burn in an empty house; if the tenants slept, surely the raps which sounded so loud to her ears would wake them. She stepped back from the door to look up at the window again and to call out.

"Please!" she shouted.

"Ease . . ." came the echo like an unending sigh in the unfriendly night.

"Hello! Please help me!"

"Me! . . ."

No answer but the mocking echo. Was everyone dead then? Had

she been foolish to scoff at tales of the devil? Cold panic shivered down her aching spine, despite the humid, airless night and the accumulated heat of her long ride. She withdrew from the ghostly house, backed across the yard to her carriage with her eyes fixed on the steady single flame of the candle at the second-floor window. As she stared, a gust (or a human breath?) extinguished the small bright flame, and all was darkness again.

The tales of witchcraft titillating the gossips and terrifying the believers back in Boston now danced through Emily's head. Salem was the devil's home these days, so they said. There was something strange and terrible happening in this place. Anne's incoherent letter had summoned her here. Her maid and driver and the good farmer and his wife along her route had tried to warn her away. They had feared for the child she carried as well as for herself. She had dismissed it all as nonsense, religious hysteria, superstition; and in this world, one was punished for such pride. As she climbed heavily up onto the high wooden seat, to set out in pursuit of someone alive and human in this grim village, she could not throw off the clammy sense of foreboding and pure, unnameable fear that coursed through her. The child stirred unceasingly now and would not rest.

She decided to make her presence known to the town, awake or asleep. "Halloo," she called out, at first tentatively and then louder as Black Jack trotted past a rather large meeting hall and a cemetery, more sleeping houses, and yet another burial ground. "Halloooo! Is anyone awake this night in Salem? Halloo, is anyone at home here?"

She had entered the town from the southwest. Although the houses were closely set here, there must be a public area, and she guessed it would lie northward. She turned Black Jack once again for the north star and rode in silence. A hill loomed ahead of her, huge and dark, beyond a wide clearing that must surely be a common pasture. From the top of that hill, she reasoned, she would see the entire settlement of Salem spread out, and if there be a light anywhere in the town, it would be visible from there.

Black Jack was tired, and she did not push him hard. Just below the hill there was another bridge to cross, a small one this time, and then they began the ascent along a winding, narrow pathway, hardly marked except for an occasional boulder set alongside the circuitous

tracks leading around and coiling upward to the summit of the hill.
The boulders had been laboriously placed there as guideposts, yet
without the moon to see by, each huge amorphous figure rose in the
silent, starlit dark to frighten her, close to her wheels before she saw
it, looming up without warning. She had to hold back a rising hysteria, the need to cry out each time one of the great rocks blocked
her view of the sky; they had the shapes of men, or worse.

The pathway took a final turn and evened onto a flat plain at the
top of the hill. She gentled the reins, to be nearly thrown from her
seat as the horse reared up on his hind legs. The carriage tipped, and
Emily had to grip the seat rails to keep from being spilled onto the
ground.

"Whoa, boy, whoa, there," she whispered.

She wiped her face with her sleeve, and then she looked about her.

Against the black sky, lit only by the constellations, eight bodies
hung lifeless, slowly turning on the thick ropes around their broken
necks. They were all women. Their long skirts cleared the ground by
inches, the feet dangled, the heads bowed as if heavy with repent-
ance; but it was silent, terrible, unredeemable death. The line of
corpses and the gallows trees supporting them were silhouetted against
the starlit blackness, and Emily's thought was: Dawn will never come
now. It will never be light again.

She stared down at the dark ground. Her eyes played a ghastly
trick, and she imagined herself standing in dark pools of blood. But
she would never truly be able to look away from the indelible sight
that had been burned into her memory a moment before.

Something moved, only a few feet away from her. The flesh on
Jack's rear flanks rippled; he whinnied with a low, strangely subdued
complaint. Emily froze.

She bit her tongue, hard, to keep from moaning in pure fear. The
movement began to take shape on the ground now; the dark viscous
shadow was a man. He was wrapped in a dark cape. He had covered
his face with a black kerchief, all except his eyes. He crouched low,
moved toward her.

"What business?" he grunted angrily.

Emily's throat was too dry for words to be dredged up. She could
only shake her head in horror. It was not a man she feared. She

welcomed human contact of any kind, even if his was the hand which had knotted the ropes around eight women's soft necks. She feared no man alive. Nor did she fear the dead, those eight women silently hanging. She knew now what she truly feared. It was something unhuman.

"What business?" the man repeated, coming close enough to put his hand on the wheel.

Black Jack whimpered, a sound she had never heard him make.

"I . . . I . . ." Emily heard herself croaking. Her mouth and throat were raw and achingly dry. "I . . . come from Boston," she managed to say, and hardly recognized her own voice. "I'm trying to find my relatives. Can you tell me, please . . . Mr. Charles Stafford . . . Anne, his wife?"

"The judge!" The man spit out the word, stepping back as if recoiling from her. "A righteous man . . . he killed my wife, you know, my Mary. There she is, that one, third from left. A silly woman. Stafford killed her, sentenced her to be hanged, wouldn't wait for the judgment of the elders. He knows best, Stafford does. I curse him and wish him eternal hellfire. Yes, and his sons to the seventh generation. And yours, if you be his kin."

"Oh, my God, no . . . what has happened here, tell me, tell me!"

"God's will has been done," the man said with resignation. "God's will. She was a silly woman, but never evil, not her. You'd better go," he said, suddenly lowering his voice to a whisper. "Go quickly, go faster than the devil if you can! There are witches here," he added conspiratorially. He bent closer to her; she leaned away from him involuntarily. The poor man was mad with grief; but madness was everywhere around her, and she feared for her own sanity.

"Witches!" he shouted loudly. "And not all dead yet. One hangs there moaning, can you hear her? It's my Mary. No one is safe now. Go, save yourself if you can."

"But . . ." It was hard, hard to force herself to stand her ground; but she had come for a purpose, and she would not give in to fear. "I must find my sister-in-law," she said. "Can you tell me, oh, please, the house of Charles Stafford and his wife? How to find my way? Please?"

"He's the one," the man said, nodding his head. He continued to hold the black kerchief to his mouth and nose. "Him and the others, big men, important men from Boston. Oh, there was a fine trial! The little girls said my Mary bewitched them. Stafford was there. He said it was God's will. He lives beyond the cemetery, next to the farm of Joshua Buffum. Stay on the main road next to the cemetery, and then turn to the left on Buffum's road. Good day, madam." After this spate of sensibility the man stepped back, bowed, and tipped his hat to her. His pale silhouette in the ghostly darkness was that of an old bent man, but his voice was young.

"God be with you," she said, not able to think of anything else to comfort this poor fellow.

"Ignorance and fear, ignorance and fear, look what they've done. There's my Mary there, third from the left, lost her shoe she has. Her little shoe fell off, and it's lying there on the ground, but I dasn't touch it. It's God's will. . . ." He fell to his knees, his wrath and madness overtaking him again in terrible racking sobs. Without thinking, Emily climbed down as quickly as her awkward bulk would allow. She touched his shoulder, to comfort him.

"Oh, my dear sir, I am so sorry . . ." she began.

He glared at her, and she saw his eyes blazing with madness. He leaped to his feet, jumping backward, away from her, and a long white bony finger jerked forth from the folds of his black cape, pointing at her, accusing.

"Go away, witch, witch! Murder! Murderrrr!" His shout became a shriek, an inhuman scream that followed her as she ran back to the carriage and as she turned Black Jack, and it followed her down along the curving path as the horse broke into a canter. She thought she could hear his anguished accusation still ringing through the silent village as she drove, according to his directions, past the cemetary and turned left on Buffum's road.

A small cottage lay behind a sparse lawn. She knocked at its low wooden door with both her fists, shouted for Anne, for Charles, for anyone! until her throat was so raw she feared to spit blood. Her cries woke a child inside; she could hear fretful whimpering and then another cry, an infant's bawl, more persistent, growing into an angry wail. But the door did not open, and there was no light from within. It seemed hours before she realized that there was another sound, a small scratching from within the thick rough fortress of the door.

"Hallo?" she called out. She put her ear against the door to listen. She heard the two babies crying, and nothing more for a long moment. Then a small, frightened voice of a woman, close to her ear, so faint that it might have been only her imagination.

"Anne? Is that you? It's Emily . . . oh, please, whoever you are, let me in. I'm tired, terribly tired. . . . Anne? It's Emily. . . ."

Slowly the door latch was opened from inside. At last the hinges creaked, and the door cracked wide enough for a wary eye to look out at her.

"Is it you, Anne? Please, let me in. I'm so terribly tired. I've been driving all day, all night. The village is so still I'm frightened. Anne?"

"Frightened. Frightened."

"Yes. It's true, Emily is frightened. Won't you let me in?"

Without seeing her, she knew that her sister-in-law had become deranged.

"Let me in, Anne," she commanded gently, in a more authoritative tone. Obediently Anne swung the door open another inch or two. Emily pushed at it slowly, and Anne melted backward, away from the door, into the dark shadows of the little house.

"Anne? Your babies are crying. Don't you hear them, dear? Shall we go in to them now? Anne? It's Emily, dear, here to help you."

"My babies. My boys. I have another boy, Emily," Anne said, recovering her wits, or seeming to. Her voice was trembling, but it was her own dear voice that Emily recognized with relief.

Quickly Anne moved past Emily in the dark interior, to slip the bolt fast in the door again. The shutters were tightly closed and barred. In the airless stench of old cooking and infants' messes, Emily realized that the usually meticulous Anne had not aired her house for days, perhaps weeks. She shuddered with a sudden bone-deep chill.

From the next room came the saddest sounds Emily had ever heard, the sobs of little babies who had given up hope of being attended to.

"Anne, light a candle. We must see to the children at once," she said sharply.

"It's no use. They are bewitched. They won't stop crying. They think I'm a witch, too," Anne answered listlessly.

"Nonsense! Now tell me where to find the candle before I stumble in the dark. Oh, here's the mantel, and . . . Anne? There's no candlestick here."

"No! He'll see. He'll see, and he'll come back. We mustn't have any light. We mustn't do anything to arouse their suspicions. That's what he wants."

"What who wants? Who are you talking about? Who are you afraid of?"

"Him."

"The devil? Is that it? Have they got to you with all this mania about the devil? Is everyone in Salem completely insane, even my good, sensible Anne?"

"No, not the—not that. *CHARLES*!" Anne growled out the name in a fierce whisper. Emily felt the chill of it course along her spine.

She stood to her full height despite a sudden stab of pain in her back that nearly made her cry out. She made herself speak clearly and forcefully, in a voice to serve notice on man and the devil and fear itself.

"I'm taking you back to Boston with me, and the babies, too, Anne Morley Stafford. Now you listen to me. You find a candle and light it and pack a few things—very few—quickly, while I tend to the children and—"

She was stopped by an abrupt, explosive pounding at the door.

"Open the bolt! Who's in there with you? Whose horse and carriage is this? Anne! Open, I say!"

For the rest of her life Emily would never be able to wipe from her memory the sounds of a woman crawling along rough-hewn floorboards on hands and knees, in such haste to obey her husband's command that she could not take the time to rise to her feet and walk in dignity.

Emily heard the long bolt pulled back and the creak of the hinges; then the pale starlight fell across the open doorway. Charles pushed his half-fainting wife aside in his eagerness to catch her at sin and witchery or God knew what.

"It's Emily, Charles," she said. She stood in the center of the sparsely furnished room, which she could see now was bereft of rugs, books, or any other amenities beyond the simplest of tables, a single bench, and a cold grate with no traces of an evening meal's having been prepared. The door closed again, and darkness bound the three in the room in an eerie intimacy. Emily could hear Charles's breathing, but no sound from Anne. The infants, too, were quiet now, worn to sleep in their despair.

Ignoring her, he crossed the room to unbolt the shutters of first one window, then the other. The light was barely sufficient for Emily to see that Anne had sunk back down onto the floor and had her face hidden in her apron as she rocked back and forth, tightly curled into herself.

"Anne is ill," she said. "I want to take her and the babies to Boston with me. We'll get her the finest doctors—"

"It's not doctors she needs," Charles said shortly, "and it's not meddling either. You're not welcome here, madam, and I'll thank you to leave at once."

"You promised," moaned Anne softly, "you promised, Emmy."

Emily went to her, knelt down clumsily with her own weight and weariness threatening to send her tumbling. "Yes, I promised," she said softly. She caressed Anne's matted hair with her hand and then straightened up painfully to face her brother-in-law.

"I'm taking them back with me, tonight," she said. "Get out of my way."

"Get out of my house," he countered. "I'm a man of some influence here, you might not know that. I'm a justice, and for weeks I've been sitting on judgment on women like you, witches, infested with the evil powers of Satan himself. I know you, Emily. It would pain me to speak out against my brother's wife. But if you're not yourself . . . I've seen many women overtaken by the powers of evil, poor souls, but they must be destroyed if the weaker, more vulnerable women and children are to survive. Your life for Anne's if you don't leave here at once. I can't answer for what other God-fearing men of Salem might conclude if they were to see my wife in this despicable state, like an animal, and you standing obscenely gloating over her. I must warn you plainly, Emily. Go, and go at once, or even I won't be able to save you!"

"You're threatening me!"

"A warning."

"A threat!"

"It may already be too late for you. But I won't have you tainting Anne with your evil. . . ."

His righteousness was absolute, inarguable. There was no point in getting angry; time for that later, Emily thought. But the babies . . . she had promised Anne to take the little ones, and that she must do.

"May . . . may I just see my nephews before I go?" she asked him, almost pleading, her manner subdued and quieted.

He wasn't fooled. "No. It's best if you go at once. You will not touch my sons."

"Go, Emmy, run away while you can!" Anne spoke up from her crumpled heap on the floor. Emily felt the baby in her womb turn restlessly, urging her to be away.

"What's going to happen to her?" she asked Charles.

"I'm trying to keep her madness secret from my fellow judges, God help me," he said. Genuine pain and sadness crossed his stern face. "I don't know whether I can save her."

"Let me take her with me," Emily urged once more, touched by what she thought she had seen in his face.

He shook his gaunt head. "There's no way I could hide her defection," he said slowly. "It would reflect badly on me if she just— disappeared."

"On you?"

"Yes. I'm a leader of this community. People look up to me, respect my judgment on such matters. If my own wife is bewitched . . . I would have to condemn her. They would expect no less from me . . . oh, for the Lord's sake, go!" he cried suddenly. "Go!"

"But it's you . . . you've done this to her yourself! It wasn't any witch who made Anne sad and frightened to the point of losing her reason. It was her God-fearing husband, wasn't it? With your own God and your own fears, and a birch twig in the night, in your own bed . . ."

He opened the door, stood waiting for her to go. He meant it. A moment ago she had seen a glimpse of Charles, a strange tender side mixed with dread and guilt; it might well be that the sight was punishable by death. She bent to kiss Anne's damp cheek. But her sister-in-law was muttering to herself now, a kind of babbling, and didn't notice Emily's farewell gesture at all.

She let Charles help her into the carriage. Before she let Black Jack have his way—he was fearfully anxious to be off and out of there, snorting and prancing despite the restraints—she tried one more time.

"Charles," she said softly, "let me take the babies with me. Anne's in no condition to care for them just now; I'll bring them back to you when she's—"

In answer, he slapped the horse's shank with the flat of his hand, and the startled stallion almost overturned all, rearing up furiously with a piercing shriek. Despite the shackles that held him, Black Jack pawed at the air and would have trampled the man who cringed back into the shadows. Emily's front-heavy body pitched forward. She lost the reins and felt herself catapulting over the fender. With a painful, reverberating crack, her head met the great flying mane of the rearing stallion; the collision shoved her back onto the hard, narrow seat. She held on for her life as Black Jack settled himself quickly and went off at a fast trot, dragging the reins and the broken tether behind him. Emily felt the baby she carried take a sickening, thumping turn-about inside her. Her head ached, and she wondered if she was going to vomit.

At the crossroads below the gallows hill, Black Jack slowed and stopped, breathing hard.

"Good fellow," she murmured. "Hold on there. Good Jack, good boy." Gentling him with her words and soothing tone, hoping she did not betray her emotions to the still-skittish horse, she climbed laboriously down from the driving seat and went forward to check the harness and find the reins again. She patted him and took comfort herself from the great wise eyes that looked back at her. "Let's go home," she whispered quietly. She climbed onto the step and the wheel and hoisted herself onto the seat, ignoring the angry kicks and punches in her belly, the beginning of a tearing pain along her lower spine.

As she lifted the reins, she looked up at the hill above her. The sky seemed to be lightening now, and she thought she saw people along the ridge of the summit, a row of figures standing against the fading stars. The mourners, if such they were, stood motionless. The only things moving in the chilling tableau were the eight corpses swaying in macabre pantomime from the gallows.

Skirting the hill, she proceeded at a good trot back along the south and west paths out of Salem to the Boston Road. The light was widening in the sky. Just at the edge of town she came toward a house that was set apart and larger than the rest, probably the home of the chief elder. She glanced up at a window as she passed under it, seeing the light reflecting a sudden movement there. She saw quite clearly the outlines of two heads, young girls with tight caps covering their hair. They were leaning out and staring down at her. Then she heard the most bloodcurdling sound of this unspeakable night.

The little girls were laughing.

She rode with her head bent in sorrow and pain, half-unconscious between agonizing jolts and bounces and convulsive cramps, never stopping, all the way back to Boston, to common sense, to life. It was high noon and her labor well under way when Black Jack pulled to a stop in front of the frame house on Charles Street. She could not hoist herself down from the driver's seat. She huddled there, waiting.

"Poor Jack," she moaned aloud, "heaving and panting and sweating like the martyr you are, bless you. Bless you. Beast or no, you're the only true Christian I've seen this night. Oh . . ." She was horrified to hear herself screaming aloud with the tearing, wrenching, blinding pain that ripped through her.

The door to the house was thrown open, and Maribess came running out. In a moment she had lifted Emily down in her good strong arms and carried her into the house.

"Take care . . . of Jack . . . he's overheated . . . he saved my life. . . ."

"Yes, yes, but you, my madam, you! I'll run to midwife. . . ."

"No time," Emily said.

"True," Maribess agreed, and set to work to deliver the child right then and there, on the kitchen floor.

Within the half hour a fiercely squalling boy was in Emily's arms. He would be named Edward; a second son, like his father, to carry on the name. He would be called Ward. He had an ugly dark red bruise, like a tiny crow, on his right cheek.

"The devil's mark!" Maribess gasped.

Emily inspected the child carefully. "It's nothing of the kind," she said with her last bit of strength. "Never let me hear that again, from you or anyone. Take the afterbirth and burn it. And then get me and this child to bed."

The mark disappeared gradually and was gone before Ward's second birthday. But no one ever forgot it or the circumstances of his birth nearly two months before his time. It was a miracle that he lived, a frail boy, often ill with coughs and fevers. He had a brittle, humorless intelligence, and he was capable of cruelty. Even as a very small boy he could make his older brother give in to him. He shied away from his mother's caresses and spent much time alone, gazing (so they said) at things no one else could see.

Chapter Six

1701: EMILY

"What I don't see," Emily said cheerfully, taking up an endless seam in the pattern of conversations that she and the Puritan minister had been having for nearly eleven years, "is how you justify in your own mind the pleasures you clearly take in material comforts. You preach self-denial and take jam in your tea. You're a terrible hypocrite, Mr. Graham," she said, smiling as she stirred in a good lump of his favorite rhubarb preserve.

"I know, I know," he agreed. He settled back into the new velvet and brocade chair which had just arrived from France and took the china cup from her hands. "I begin to suspect that perhaps God intends me to teach rather than set the example. My writings make people think on higher things, while my conduct allows my friends to indulge in the greatest charity of all, tolerance for human weakness. And you, my dearest friend, neither judge nor tolerate, which makes me believe you are a gift to me from God Himself. Although I have long since given up any hope of converting you to my way of thinking."

"Oh, you had me going last week, with your talk of eternity. I confess, my fear of it is not great enough to make me tremble and fall to my knees. As for retribution for my sins, I've no doubt I'll deserve whatever I get. And why spend this life being miserable when you might very well have to spend the rest of time that way? Have a biscuit.''

"No, thank you, Emily. But I'll have more of your intriguing philosophy.'' He laughed.

"They're your favorites, and hot from the oven, too.''

"For the sake of my waistline in this life and my soul in the next, I must say no.''

"Ah . . . the confirmed bachelor begins to take an interest in his figure. Now that is a topic of real interest. To the gossips, of course, not to me,'' she added with a sly grin. "Now let me think,'' she said, pretending to be puzzled, "which of the ladies has expressed a preference for slender men of the Puritan faith . . . ?''

"Not vanity, but health,'' he said.

She stopped smiling and peered at him sharply. "Are you ill, Samuel?'' she asked. "Is something wrong?''

The late-afternoon sun lit the front parlor in honeyed squares that fell through the high leaded windows across the tea table, brightening the fine Persian carpet and highlighting the silken cushions and the burnished wood panels of the large airy room. The sunlight turned the minister's soft short "roundhead" hair into a dark halo framing his strong, handsome face. He was still a most attractive man, despite the rough gray homespun he wore and the stern mask he often affected to curb his natural sunny smile, which softened his mouth and eyes when his thoughts strayed from seriousness.

Their friendship, shared and therefore sanctioned by Emily's father-in-law, was considered an eccentric and rather daring thing by the rest of Boston's society. The Puritans had dwindled in favor and reputation over the years and were generally regarded as a cult whose members might be sincere, might even be close to God, but were fanatic, humorless, and—worst of all—without style. Style had become a focal point around which society circled, a way of recognizing each other and excluding most. Life had become stratified; those who accumulated wealth and land and political power maintained strict vigilance against those who would have the same. Invisible but impenetrable barriers of class based on money had been erected to protect the fine houses, fleets of ships, places at the governor's table, accustomed seats in the front row of the Town Council. Friendship with religious zealots and merchants and strivers was a hazardous indulgence; one might be toppled by reaching downward into the grasping crowd.

Emily had no patience for anyone telling her she must or mustn't do this or that. It was her habit to remark often and loudly that she had no patience for society. Let them all dance around their silly unwritten rules and stringent manners; she had more important things to occupy her mind. Her tongue had grown sharp. A woman who sleeps alone in her matrimonial bed becomes dry in body and in wit as well.

She prided herself most of all on her honesty. And, being honest, she admitted (to herself) to being lonely. The company of women did not suffice, with their talk of childbed and recipes and the servant problem and new fashions in dress. Except for weekly gatherings for the playing of music, discussions of literature, and planning improvements for the town, the only benefit Emily could find from the society of females was the fine art of suppressing a yawn.

Old Edward was almost always away now, either on a long voyage or about his thriving businesses in the countinghouses and coffeehouses and Town Hall. And dear Neddy had drifted totally into his own world: days at his tall desk in the wharfside office; all his time at home spent in the third-floor garret. He was affable and polite, smiling when addressed directly, although needing to hear things twice before responding. He wore whatever clothes were laid out for him and treated his three growing children as distantly and respectfully as he did everyone else—his father, his wife, servants and slaves, tradesmen and ships' captains, the governor or his lady. No one could quarrel with Neddy Stafford; no one even took advantage of his sweet and other-worldly nature. From his hands came oil paintings of brilliant detail and surpassing beauty, into which he poured all the vitality he possessed. He was an artist, not a man. Not a husband anyway. He had not shared Emily's bed since Eliza's birth eight years before.

There was no self-pity in Emily's makeup. When she recognized her need for the company and conversation of men, she attended meetings of the Town Council. She was not, of course, allowed to speak, and she found them mostly fools anyhow, toadying to the governor. Now she attended only when Mr. Graham was scheduled to speak. His eloquence on the subject of religious freedom had more than a few times kept the colony from blazing up in riots to force the king's hand.

They talked of everything under the sun, the two of them. They were friends. It nearly sufficed.

Now she prodded him gently, in his silence. "Samuel? Is something wrong?" she asked again.

"A delegation of women came to me yesterday to point out that my frequent visits here might ruin your good name," he said quietly.

"Did they? What idiots women can be when they've nothing to do with their time. We do them a service, you and I. Think how bored they'd be with nothing to gossip about."

"It doesn't worry you?"

"Only if you are hurt. My 'good name' is of no concern to me and cannot be 'ruined' in any case, if for no other reason than the fact that I don't give a damn for their opinions. That in itself keeps their curiosity at a high pitch. They follow my style of dress and rush to join the groups I form . . . simply because I am very rich and because I don't care what they think of me. It's a paradox, but not a very interesting one. Oh, but you, dear Samuel, it's different for you. Your livelihood and your influence depend on the good opinions of others. I would not willingly be the cause of your loss of reputation. . . . More tea?"

"Yes, thank you—good heavens, what was that?"

Emily cocked her head to listen to the unholy shrieks from the floor above. "Only my son, most likely protesting some move that his brother has made at tiddledywinks. One of his rages, nothing more."

"I'm sorry," Mr. Graham said. "I should be accustomed to it, I mean . . . young Ward sometimes puts the fear of—oh, my dear Emily, I am putting both feet in my mouth today. My apologies. I'm not myself."

"Why not? You're very strange today, it's true. I wish you would tell me what's wrong!"

He didn't answer.

"You were going to say that Ward puts the fear of God in you? Or was it the devil? I know what they say about him. Do you know, it's Ward who makes me come closest to accepting your notions about such things—nine years old and still wailing like a banshee. Go ahead and say it right out. I don't mind. You know very well I prefer the truth, and the more frankly said, the better. Ward's touched by something, and that's certain.''

Mr. Graham set his cup and saucer down carefully and leaned forward to take Emily's two hands in his own. "He will surely outgrow it,'' he said, as he had said many times before.

Emily smiled a bit absently, pulled back her hands, and picked up her needlework from the basket beside her. They sat for a few moments, companions at ease with each other, without words. He still leaned forward, watching her slim white hands with the single gold ring methodically plying tiny, neat stitches through the fine linen stretched tautly around a hoop.

They were, for a moment, like portraits: contentment and peacefulness in a setting of elegance and ease. It pleased her to see herself and the minister in this setting she had created. They were in the front parlor of the finest house on Pemberton Square, seated at the little grouping of chairs near the fireplace. On the other side of the huge central hearth, opening into the kitchen area, the servants and slaves were preparing the evening meal. There were four spacious rooms on the main floor of the house, grouped around the great brick fireplace, separated by foot-thick oak doors and decorated with the widest panels which could be found in the great forests of Maine. In addition to this cozy parlor, there was another front room for formal entertaining, a dining hall with long windows opening onto the garden, and the kitchen, which ran the rear width of the house. Another wing of the house held the necessary rooms, servants' sitting room and sleeping quarters, and storage rooms.

The second floor of the house was sectioned by sturdy walls and solid doorways into bedchambers, and above that was Neddy's spacious garret with windows looking out in each direction.

Every wide-mullioned window of the entire house looked out onto a great vista: to the south and east, the narrow streets and houses of the city, with the great harbor stretching beyond; on the north and west, the Stafford gardens, orchards, grazing fields. Farther on, the governor's mansion could be glimpsed through the copse.

The house was Emily's pride. The polished floors and ceiling beams were the broadest of any house in Boston, and on the second floor the ceilings of the bedchambers rose nearly eight feet. The house was furnished with rare and mostly valuable pieces, all blended into a generous whole reflecting Emily's personal tastes. If her father-in-law returned from a journey with a Persian carpet she found too red, a China vase too large for its appointed corner, a Spanish or Portuguese armoire, a French table or German pewter not to her liking, Emily simply sold the treasure to one of her neighbors or in the marketplace, at a good profit. She found and encouraged local craftsmen in their efforts to create fine furniture, and silversmiths were beginning to turn out excellent pieces right here in the colonies. The corner cupboard in the parlor, carved and joined to her own simple design, held china and glassware designed and created in Boston itself, with a style of its own not copied from European tastes. Emily had chosen from her own mind and not the faddish ideas, and she was satisfied to see other householders beginning to follow her example.

"You're determined not to confide in me today," she said suddenly, taking the minister by surprise. Waiting for him to speak, she had been surveying her possessions, satisfying herself that her house was intact, yet she believed herself to be one who cared little for material things. Irritated at herself, she brought her full attention back to her friend and his unaccustomed silence.

"No," he said, "that's not true. Never. I was thinking . . . about Salem."

"You have news of my sister-in-law!" Emily gripped her embroidery so tightly she creased the edges. "You've heard something of Anne. Tell me then."

"She's the same. No one sees her, but the elders of the village tell me that your brother-in-law still persists in his efforts to drive the devil out of her. Poor soul! Damn! It's extremists like Charles Stafford who rouse the prejudice of intemperate men against all Puritans."

"And nothing can be done to help her. Not even you can interfere with a husband's rights, not even if he beats her regularly and keeps her a cowering prisoner in the dark and filth of an airless hovel," Emily said bitterly. "Men own their wives, and that's all there is to it."

"Yes," he said sadly.

"No man could ever own me."

"I'm certain of that," her friend agreed with a rueful smile.

"And what of my two nephews?"

"They are well, strong, and hardworking—"

"Hardworking! At nine and ten, they should be playing games."

"Yes, even the Puritans believe in games for children. But they are dutiful sons to a fanatic father." Mr. Graham fell into silence again. Emily watched him for a moment and returned her eyes to her work, determined not to speak until he revealed what was on his mind.

"It's getting late," he said finally.

She glanced up at him and said nothing.

"Emily, there is something I have to tell you."

"Well, I know it, and I wish you would get it out!"

"It's not easy to say. I'm leaving Boston."

"Leaving Boston!" she echoed stupidly. It was as if he had announced that the world was going to end with the sunset.

He stood up abruptly and came around the little table to sit near her on the divan. He took both her hands in his. She felt the strong clasp and an absurd yearning to grab onto him, to keep him there somehow. But she didn't move. She saw tiny dots of perspiration on his gentle forehead. His face was only inches from hers.

"I've asked God for guidance for months now, and I know what I have to do."

"Where will you go?" There were so many things crowding into her head to ask, to protest, to cry out, but all she said was: "Where will you go?"

"I don't know."

"But why? You are so important to this community, to your own people . . . to . . . all of us."

"Flee temptation," he said in a voice so low she could hardly understand, even though his lips formed the words clearly and she could feel his warm, sweet breath against her cheek.

He lowered his head so that she couldn't see his eyes now, only his fine profile, so familiar, so close that she longed to reach out and stroke the line along his throbbing temple, his cheekbone, his firm jaw, and his vulnerable throat, where the stiff fabric of his collar touched his skin.

She wanted to comfort him, but she clenched her hands tightly in her lap. She tried to make a joke.

"You mean because you take jam in your tea and find pleasure in a pleasant room, painting and music and—"

"Oh, stop, stop for the Lord's sake!" he cried out, from so deep a place inside himself that she knew for an instant the abyss of hopelessness that loomed for him as eternity.

His hand reached out to touch her sleeve. Through the silk she felt the heat of his flesh on her, searing-hot iron, branding her with his mark. She would feel it there all the rest of her life.

"Emily . . . Emily, oh, God, my God . . ." He was muttering her name and His over and over like an oath or a prayer, with his mouth agonizingly close to her trembling ear. His arms went around her. She had no thought but to press herself close to him, to hold and cling to him, not knowing or caring why. She was conscious only of his strength and maleness, his need, his nearness so unexpectedly imperative, the gorgeous comfort of his arms and shoulders and breast against hers, her own need to take him inside herself. She felt her body coming back to life; the long-suppressed fluids began to turn and flow deep inside her. Her open hands pressed him to her; she felt the rough texture of his jacket as an abrasive, intrusive wall between them, civilized reason and sensibility needing to be thrown off and done with.

"No, no," she whispered with all her strength, trying not to hold him even more closely as her protests escaped her lips. Trying to deny her desire, for his sake, oh, yes, for his sake . . .

"Stop, I beg you . . ." she moaned. "Oh, my dear, my love, what are we doing . . .?"

His head went down to her throat, and she felt the sweetness of his mouth against the pulse that tore from her heart up to meet him. She cradled her cheek against the strange shortness of his hair; so soft it was, so dear, like every part of him she loved . . .

When he let his arms loosen from her, she thought she might faint. The dark emptiness opened to swallow her forever; outside his embrace there was nothingness again. She stood on the edge, closed her eyes, and swayed, not caring. He held her then, gently, both hands on her shoulders, and she opened her eyes to see his eyes searching for hers, assurance and reassurance, needed and offered.

"Forgive me," he said simply, without shame.

"I want it, too," she answered.

"Yes."

"But . . . we won't, will we?" She said it sadly, as a fact, acknowledging a death. Would there be mourning, she wondered, would they each grieve privately for their unborn sin, the passion denied, or would they be secretly and separately relieved that they had won over the devil after all?

"Good-bye," he said hoarsely. His eyes were veiled now, and she wondered if they would always be so.

"I'll miss you very much," she said.

Their eyes said a good-bye of their own, and he was gone.

Two nights later, after tossing on her lonely bed for hours, Emily took her reawakened senses up to the third floor and surprised her husband at his work. She astonished him with her voluptuous caresses, and when he had finished with the just-mixed rose madder that couldn't be allowed to go dry, he stepped back to see how it would blend into the flesh tones of the portrait of their sons which he was painting (from memory, since the younger would never sit still long enough to pose), and then Neddy allowed himself to be seduced toward the narrow cot where he usually fell, exhausted, for a few hours' sleep just before dawn. Penetrating his wife's moist and eager flesh, he wondered why he himself hadn't urged this very business to occur more often. Then he began to think about the portrait and realized that a slight drop of pure vermilion might be just the thing for the mouths, at least the lower lip where the light fell. Yes it would give just the subtle hint of rosiness that was needed.

Part
TWO

Chapter Seven

1935: KATE

Kate stood impatiently at the library desk, telephone in hand, waiting for her call to be put through. She stared up idly at the "Portrait of the Artist's Young Sons," painted, of course, by the original loony-genius of the family, Edward Stafford, Jr. (1666–1730). She had always felt an affinity for the littler boy, Ward, whose face showed a sullen quality beneath the romanticized rosiness of his lips and cheeks; his elder brother, Grey, was strikingly like her own elder brother, smiling pleasantly, revealing nothing.

The painting had been hanging in the exact same place on the same wall between the two lead-mullioned windows of the library for nearly a hundred years. Kate's great-grandfather had duly noted in his journal that he had "this day, 4th May 1838, supervised the setting of the first family portrait on the wall of the library of the new house at Number Four on Beacon Street." Art historians occasionally referred to this painting and several others signed "N. Stafford" which hung in the house as priceless, meaning only that they weren't for sale. Kate yawned and straightened her seams, holding the receiver to her ear.

She finally heard the crackling static of her brother's secretary on the other end of the wire.

"Good morning, Miss Hampton. Please put my brother on the telephone."

"I'm sorry, Miss Stafford. Mr. Stafford is in conference."

"It's very important."

"Oh . . . yes, ma'am, but he asked me especially not to disturb him."

"I promise you, Miss Hampton, it will be quite all right." Good Lord, she sounded exactly like her mother! But it was useful every now and then, a bit of imperiousness, and she didn't soften her tone despite the knowledge that she was putting the working girl in a difficult position. Kate had empathy for working people and certainly didn't want to discomfit Miss Hampton. But she did need to talk to Hank. "Put him on the line, please."

"Yes, ma'am."

Kate held the telephone impatiently, listening to the distant sounds of typists clattering on their machines and voices murmuring in the background. She stared up at Ward Stafford's wicked eyes. And then Hank came on.

"Hello."

"I've found a clue to the presence of witches in the family that we overlooked before. It could be very significant."

"Kate, I'm very busy just now. Let's talk about it tonight. I'm coming home for the weekend, you know."

"I'm not talking about old Charles the Puritan, Hank. Little schoolchildren know about his being one of the Salem judges. I'm talking about the other side of the clan. I think I've uncovered something—"

"Kate, I've a client waiting and Uncle George as well. They're sitting in Uncle George's office waiting for me to finish this so-called urgent conversation. I can see them through the door, and they're not happy, Kate. How am I going to explain this crazy interruption?"

"Tell them the truth. Tell them there's a curse on the family, and it's just been traced straight back to the devil himself. Go on, try it, Hank. What've you got to lose? Listen, I've finally deciphered that old letter that Philip wrote to Sarah, after he stashed his French wife in the nuthouse and went back to England. It may be the most significant clue we've ever had! He says—listen to this *'elle a le diable en corps'*—she has the devil in her! What do you think of that! It took some work to figure out the handwriting, but that's what he wrote—"

"Yes, it sounds very interesting. I shall look forward to discussing it with you further. At the very earliest opportunity. Thank you for bringing it to my attention."

"Oh, I get it. People listening. Honestly, Hank, what do you think they're going to do? They can't fire you, you know. You're not exactly going to end up standing in line at the mission for a free bowl of soup if you . . . oh, well. But this is important, Hank. Serious scholarly research . . . Hank?"

There was a pause. Hank wouldn't hang up on her, of course. He was too well mannered and maybe even a bit intrigued—maybe even impressed. But she could feel his tension all the way from the office in Newton over the telephone wire. Should she let him, literally, off the hook? Poor Hank. Something in his genes made him worry when there was nothing in the world to worry about; she was awfully glad that particular bit of heritage had passed her by. Whoever the client was there was no danger of his getting angry enough to cause any trouble. The most important people in Boston wouldn't dream of confiding their legal secrets and problems to any firm but Stafford, Stafford & Porter. The worst that could happen to Hank would be a dressing-down, in private, from Uncle George, and the worst thing about that was the way poor old Uncle George spit when he talked.

Kate spoke quickly. "Witches, Hank, and the curse of the devil. Emily was pregnant with Ward when she made her famous ride and saw the witches hanging from the gallows, right? And then, in the very next generation, new witches' blood brought over from France, in the form of Martine Boudier. It goes all through the whole family, everywhere you turn. . . ."

"Kate, dear, I really can't talk just now."

"I'll bet we could trace the streak all the way down, through Great-aunt Grace and . . . my gosh, Hank, it could explain every single fruitcake in this family, do you realize that?"

"Yes, yes, that's very interesting. I do appreciate your research on this, ah, yes, indeed. Thank you for your help. I'll speak with you further on this tonight at the house. Well, good-bye then."

He did hang up on her then. She set the earpiece on its hook and stared up at the painting. The little boy smirked down at her. "Nerts to you," she said aloud. "If you were really cursed by the devil, why didn't you do something remarkable and awful? You know what

I think? I think the curse is that we're all doomed to be bored to death. Well, not me!'' She sighed. Talking to pictures on the wall. Terrific. She turned on the desk lamp and sat down again with the copy of her ancestor's old letter. She knew the news wasn't really hot, but it was the closest she had ever come to a revelation. She had been devoutly hoping for a revelation ever since she had learned to read.

Cousin Charles and his mother were there for dinner, which made Kate want to fidget. Charles was exactly her age, and they had played together as children; sometimes she had the impression that he still wanted to play with her, although he was too polite to make a pass, even on the many occasions when he'd been her escort for parties and dances. He was pleasant enough, and bright in his own way, but about as interesting as the pattern on the fork she kept turning in her hand, waiting for dinner to be over. Charles was so nice he even agreed to be the fourth at auction bridge with his mother and aunt and uncle, as if he could guess that Hank and Kate wanted to get off by themselves.

Hank shed his grown-up disguise as soon as they were alone. ''Okay, what gives?'' he said, imitating James Cagney and making her giggle.

''You were awfully stuffy on the phone this morning. I do apologize for interrupting important business. Really, I'm sorry. But don't you think it's fascinating? Witches from the French side as well as the English! I think I may have made a real discovery.''

''Or they've discovered you,'' he said mysteriously.

''Whew, Hank, what does that mean?''

He grinned. ''I'm not sure myself. Something like the devil finding work for idle hands—one of those good New England bromides we've been refusing to listen to all our lives. You've been spending a lot of time at the Ark, eh? I thought the senior year at Miss Christie's Classes was supposed to be very demanding?''

''Idiot stuff, Mickey Mouse busy work.'' Kate shrugged. ''What do you think, Hank? Seriously.''

''Seriously, all that stuff's been gone over before. Philip's letters especially. I don't see what's so enthralling.''

''Nobody ever paid any attention to the references to the devil, not seriously. If we were to trace that theme, all the way . . . it struck me when I really studied that phrase he used about Martine. And remembering the curse on Emily's second son, you know, the one that got born on the night they hanged the witches in Salem . . . what if we could discover a tracery of—well, what do you say to a devil's curse on the whole dang family? What do you say to that? Wouldn't it be—''

"Oh, come on, Katie! What've you been reading besides the family letters, Bram Stoker and Mary Shelley? There are no spooks or ghouls or vampires or witches in our past, just a few eccentrics at best. You're indulging in schoolgirl stuff, hon.''

"You used to get as excited as I about the mysteries and romances hiding away in the Ark. You're the one who got me started. Now you're a big grown-up lawyer and you're getting as silly as Edward and Father.''

"Well . . . maybe so, maybe so.''

It was true, very early in his life Hank had discovered the enthralling sport of digging up old wraiths and bones in the silent, almost holy temple of the marble building known as the Stafford Archives. Only members of the family and carefully screened special scholars were given access to the shelves and temperature-controlled vaults filled with journals, diaries, ships' logs, letters, manuscripts, sketches, and privately printed books by and about the various branches of the family over the past two and a half centuries. Hank had introduced his little sister to the Ark as soon as she could read, and together they had spent hundreds of winter afternoons and rainy spring and autumn days, under the benign eye of the chief archivist, Dr. Partridge, and the elderly guard, Mr. Reilly. As children they had exclaimed delightedly to each other as they discovered parts of the enduring chain of which they were the newest links. As adolescents they had dreamed of discovering secrets and mysteries no one before them had even suspected. But the great rotunda reading room and its outer chambers for quiet study held so many catalogued and bound studies and dissertations and books, authorized and unauthorized, friendly and accusing, written in florid hands, in archaic language, in code and cipher, pored over so studiously by so many serious historians, that only the most determined fantasizers could still believe there were any secrets to be found there. Kate still believed; she had thought Hank did, too. It had been their most satisfying game.

But now Hank was twenty-three, living in Newton and working in the Firm, with no time for such things. Kate, pacing through the final year of school before she was expected to go on to Radcliffe, found the Ark to be a kind of no-man's-land, a resting place between the past and the increasingly urgent idea that she might actually do something with her own life. Outside the Ark and the house on Beacon Street and the spiral staircase at Miss Christie's town house, where the girls practiced walking and saying Latin phrases, there was a depression raging, people starving and rising up to defy their oppressors (whoever they were), and she could—she would!—be a part of that.

There had been moments in the reading room, with the rose window letting down the sunlight onto the pages opened before her, when Kate had actually felt the warm breath of a great-great-great-grandmother or a long-dead cousin on the back of her neck, resurrected through words in spindly faded ink on crusty, crumbling paper preserved in glass. Hank had felt it, too. In those moments they had glimpsed the past, present, and future all at once, had understood what family meant, and marveled at the goose bumps actually raised on their young arms.

Now, disappointed at Hank's defection, she got up restlessly and walked around their two chairs. They were in the snuggery, the smallest room in the house, hidden behind the library, where the books were dog-eared instead of leather-bound and every chair had its own excellent reading light. The snuggery was cozy and private, with only one window peering down on Beacon Street through myopic diamonds of thick glass that had come from London two hundred years ago.

She sat down in the wing chair facing her brother, and wished she had the nerve to stamp her foot and shout, although of course, it wasn't Hank's fault, exactly, that he had grown up so completely, and before she was quite ready.

"I guess . . . I guess I was hoping you'd want to help research the witches' trail; round and round it goes and where it stops nobody knows . . . maybe you've got the power, Henry, maybe I have—"

"Listen, Kate," Hank said. He was looking more serious than Kate liked. "Mother and Father asked me to have a talk with you."

"Oh, that's rotten of them!" she burst out. "They know I can't resist anything you ask me to do. But I never thought you'd take their side against me. Oh, Hank, you're not, are you?"

"Of course not, Katie. Anyway, there aren't any sides. You make it sound like a great battle. They won't stand in your way. They only want—"

"What's best for me?"

"Well, yes. That's right. What's so terrible about that?"

"Only the absolute certainty that they do know what's best. Radcliffe."

"Well, isn't it?"

"Plenty of girls manage to get along very well without ever having gone to Radcliffe. Millions, in fact."

"But it wouldn't satisfy you to be one of millions, now would it?"

"Oh, Hank, I want to experience life!"

"They won't try to stop you."

"I know. It's part of their unshakable superiority. They're so sure they're right about everything they don't even have to discuss it. No pros, no cons. A Stafford can do no wrong. Well, what if I am absolutely dying to go out there and do some wrong . . . then what?"

"Poor Katie. You're looking for a fight, and nobody will give it to you. I know how you feel, really I do. Do you think I wanted to slide right from Latin to Choate to Harvard and into the Firm without even a glance at the turns in the road, the paths not taken, as the poet says . . . but hell, what's the point? When you get out there, you find that everybody wants just exactly what we've got already."

"I can't believe that everybody in the whole world wants to die of boredom on Beacon Street."

"Anyway," Hank said, cheerful again, "in a family that's got Great-aunt Grace in it, who's going to care about one more iconoclast? Or witch, if you prefer. How can you compete with her. or—"

"I know. It's not that I want to compete; I only want to be free. Free of the family and all their expectations and assumptions and goddamned understanding . . ."

"Poor Katie, you do so want to be a rebel, don't you?"

"Hank, please stop saying 'poor Katie' all the time, okay? What'd they want you to talk to me about then?"

He leaned forward across the space between their two wing chairs. In the small room the fireplace dominated the only wall space not given over to books, but of course, there was no fire. Even if it had been dead of winter, Kate and Henry would have wrapped themselves in shawls and sweaters to sit shivering rather than have lighted a fire. It was getting on to the middle of the night, sensible people were in bed, and indulgence of one's physical comforts was not well regarded in this household.

But it was early June, and there was no need for more warmth than came from their companionship itself. Hank had been living in Newton, practicing law since his graduation from Harvard Law School a year before; this was their first shared insomnia in a long time. They curled comfortably in the deep leather chairs which had been warmed and softened by three generations of Stafford bodies before them, and they talked by the light of the streetlamp that filtered through the old off-color window glass.

"Enlightened discussion," Hank began in an awesomely perfect imitation of their father's high voice (if it had been a pitch or two lower, John Wright Stafford might have been persuaded to accept the nomination to run for the U.S. Senate in '28), "is an art and skill which must be learned, honed, and—"

"Oh, stop!" Kate interrupted with a giggle. "Hank, I hear that every damn night at dinner. Don't you see, that's exactly what's wrong with us? All we do is talk about things, about people being hungry and breadlines and the unemployment and strikes and . . . sure, every point of view is considered, but nobody we know is hungry or poor. . . . I want to be part of the world. I'll even sell apples on the street!"

"Don't be daft," he answered shortly. "You have to have a Ph.D. to sell apples these days. Anyway, what about the factory? It's not fair to say the family doesn't do anything, Kate. And being poor is a childish idea. You think it would be romantic when it's anything but."

"How would you know? How would any of us know?" she said glumly.

"Well . . . don't forget the factory anyway. *Life* magazine said that Passmore was a noble experiment in ideal working conditions and raising the quality of life for the workingman and his family—"

"I know, I know, I know." She groaned. "We do our part."

"Quoting That Man in the White House isn't going to help your case around here. Isn't that the slogan for the National Recovery Act?"

"I like Mr. Roosevelt," she said, jutting her chin up and forward.

"Lots of people do," he said. "Say, would you mind if I lit a pipe?"

"When did you take up pipe smoking?" she asked curiously. "Will you let me try it?"

"Sure," he agreed. He dug into his bathrobe pocket and came up with a bulky tobacco pouch and a large, curved meerschaum.

His sister watched with interest while he filled it, tamped it just so, and carefully wrapped the tobacco in its soft binding again before lighting the pipe. It took several matches, and he almost burned his fingers twice; but soon the little room was filled with a fine, strong aroma, and the smoke was rising in a most satisfying swirl. Hank passed the pipe to Kate, and she drew on it carefully. She coughed and choked.

"Don't inhale it," he cautioned too late, pounding her on the back.

"Vile," she gasped. "Ugh!"

"Well, it's not for girls," he said. He settled back in his chair with the pipe curled in his fist, puffing on it from time to time until it went out. He didn't relight it, and they both were relieved to have the little ritual done with. The smoke lingered in the room longer than was pleasant.

"Ever tried a cigar?" she asked.

"Oh, sure." ♠

"Like it?"

"Not much. Difficult to acquire the taste."

"I hate cigars. John L. Lewis made the whole house stink the night he was here, with his big black stogie. I hope you won't acquire the taste. I think it's a low habit."

"What'd you think of him?"

"Who, Lewis? Not much. He was trying to convince Father that the workers at Passmore should be allowed to join up with the CIO. I should think John L. Lewis would have more important things to do, wouldn't you?''

"Still, it must have been an interesting discussion—"

"Boring. Boring, boring, boring, like every other evening in this house. They talked about things—oh, everybody always talks about things—but as usual, it was just talk.''

"Now, Kate, what did you want to happen? The workers coming up out of the coal mines with soot on their faces to throw a cordon around this house, to have a torchlight parade around the Common in protest against . . . against what? The Passmore experiment is wonderful for the workers. They're better off than anyone anywhere. Why on earth would they want a union? Silliest damn thing I ever heard.''

"Well . . . Mr. Lewis said that it was . . . paternalism. That eighty years of happiness and productivity under fair treatment and democratic self-government was a farce. He said as long as the company rules, the workers are not truly free.''

"And if they joined his union, they would be free?''

"Yes.''

"Do you believe that?''

"Uh . . . I don't know. I honestly don't know, Hank. But neither do you. You're living in Great-uncle Paul's house in Newton and practicing corporate law with Uncle George, and I'll bet you never feel you're missing a thing. Well, I do. I don't want to miss experiencing life the way other people do . . . oh, Hank, do you understand? Say you do even if you don't. I couldn't stand it if you were against me, too.''

"Nobody's against you, Kate.''

"I'm not saying that you're wrong for doing what you do. You know that.''

"Of course I do. That would be awfully twisted, wouldn't it?''

"I saw a movie last week, all about the Depression and how hard it is to get a job and how being poor can actually change your whole character. It made a criminal out of a very nice young man, and . . . oh, of course, it was only a story, but it made me hate myself for being rich.''

"Nothing can make a criminal out of someone if it's not in his character to begin with."

"You should have seen this movie."

"Poor Katie—oops, I'm sorry. Won't say it again. But remember the time you ran away to find Charles Lindbergh?"

"If you're saying that I live in a fantasy world, that's exactly what I'm trying to get away from. All I have are my fantasies simply because I don't know what life is really like. I'm going to get a job and my own place to live."

"A rented room?"

"Well . . . well, sure. Why not?"

"Don't let Father hear you say 'sure' like that. He'd refuse to let you go if he thought you'd come back talking slang."

"But if I don't learn to talk it, I'll stick out like a sore thumb."

"You will anyway, honey."

"Honey? Yowee, razzmatazz, where'd you pick that up? Hey, have you been mingling with the hoi polloi a bit yourself, Mr. Mystery Man? Come on, Hank, your secrets are safe with me."

"Oh, well, I go to the movies, too."

"That's all?"

"None of your beeswax, as Jean Harlow said to Franchot Tone."

"So you have a secret life, verrrry interesting. Have you a sordid little love nest somewhere, on a back street, with a platinum blond dame pining away in anticipation of your next visit, whenever it may be?"

"No, worse luck."

"Well, you can come and visit me in my rented room, how's that? Younger sister's hardly as interesting as a back street romance, but until the real thing comes along?"

"Are you really going to do that, Katie?"

"Do what?"

"Get a rented room? Share a bathroom with strangers maybe? Live with someone else's furniture . . . seriously, Kate, I just can't see it. You may run away all you like, but you'll still be a Stafford after all. That means a home and family to fall back on and a fine education, and—other things ordinary people don't have. You can pretend not to have those things, but you'll have them all the same."

"Well, does that mean I can never be human?"

"I don't know . . . maybe it's just that . . . you've already got what everyone out there is looking for. So the quest could just lead you right back here where you started."

"Bluebird of happiness, own backyard, that sort of thing?"

"Don't tell me I sound like Cousin Morley, not that, please!"

"Well, watch it, Hank. Just watch it."

"Righto."

They giggled, and then Hank said, "I think I'll have a brandy. Want one?"

Kate shook her head. "I never knew you to drink brandy before. My goodness, cigars and brandies and the next thing I know you'll be growing a mustache or some damn fool thing like that."

He bent to the carved ebony cabinet below the bookshelves. The little brass handle refused to turn.

"No use," he said. "They've locked the cellaret, and I haven't a clue where the key might be. You don't suppose it's been locked since Prohibition and nobody thought to undo it when repeal came, do you?"

"No," she answered. "It's locked against the Irish hordes, don't you know? They make quite good servants but notorious drinkers. Mother locks it for their own good. It's not the—"

Hank chimed in with her. "—money; it's the principle of the thing."

"And if the principle has been wisely invested, you need never concern yourself with the 'thing' at all."

"I never heard that part of it."

"I just made it up," she said, "natural conclusion to the world's hoariest cliché. That's h-o-a-r; yes, of course, you knew that. I'm covering up. I'm furious, actually. All this concern about the good of other people, it really makes me sick."

"How? What do you mean?"

"Well, there's no real respect, you know. None at all. We just go on thinking we know what's best for them, don't we? Oh, Hank, if I don't get out now, I'll be stuck here and be frustrated the rest of my life, like Mother, thinking I know everything—"

"Hold on a mo. Mother, frustrated? What do you mean?"

"All those Symphony committees and the Lecture Society and Luncheon Club and sitting on the board of this and the trust of that and—oh, you know. Substitutes for life experiences."

"Oh, I see. You've been reading Sigmund Freud, haven't you? A little Havelock Ellis, too?"

"So what?"

"I dimly remember being nineteen myself. All that reading, discovering what life is really about. All that righteousness—"

"Hank! Righteousness! That's exactly what I despise! Oh, hell, even you don't understand me."

"Course not, Katie. How could I understand you, you being a girl and me a grown man, but I'm trying, aren't I?"

"I . . . guess so." She felt sad. It was true, Hank had grown up and would soon become indistinguishable from the others, leaving her alone on the other side of the looking glass.

"Mother said she had no real objection to your going out on your own so long as you didn't leave Boston, of course. For some reason I found that very funny," Hank was saying.

"There, don't you see?"

"No. See what? Do you want to leave Boston?"

"No, of course not, why should I? I just want to get away from Beacon Hill and—and—and all this. But it's no good when everybody gives you permission. Wouldn't it be terrific if I had to run away in the dead of night and leave a note?"

"Didn't a certain little girl I know once try just that?"

Kate's answer was a rude yawn and a muttered apology.

"Poor Katie . . . oh, gosh, I said it again. I do see your point, though. Can't you accept us for what we are? No, I suppose not. Not yet anyway. I remember that I felt that way once, during my sophomore year it was, when I met a Jewish fellow from Chicago in one of my lecture halls. He had an interesting background, and I found myself wondering what it was like to grow up as a newcomer in this country, an outcast. . . . Oh, well, there wasn't any way I could possibly understand that, was there? Too bad, really. I liked him, but after a short while we found out we had nothing to talk about with each other."

"You are a prune, Henry."

"And you're a peach."

"Bananas."

They laughed, and Katie gave in to a more polite yawn and a good stretch. "I guess I'm not used to these late-night sessions anymore," she confessed.

They stood up and looked at each other for a moment in the light of the streetlamp dimly glowing through the break in the drapes.

"You will keep in touch with me, all the time, I mean? Don't get lost out there," he said quietly, urgently.

"With you, yes," she answered. "But I'm not coming home for Sunday suppers or anything regular like that. I really want to become—well, separate. But of course, I'll still have to keep my eye on you, just to make sure you don't get stuffy and pompous. I can see the beginnings of a very dangerous tendency creeping up. You'll need me to keep you a bit daffy."

They left the snuggery, came out into the center hall, and climbed the stairs. Near the top Henry suddenly threw one long leg over the smooth oak banister and let himself slide all the way around the curving rail to the bottom. Afraid her giggles would wake the whole house, Kate had no choice but to follow him, and with the good gray wool of her bathrobe flying wildly around her, she slid down to collapse on top of her brother in a heap on the Persian hall carpet.

"Umpfh! I think you broke my pipe!" he gasped.

"Foul old thing anyway."

"Right."

He dug into the pocket of his robe and pulled out the meerschaum, broken in two pieces where the stem met the bowl. He dug further and found a white business envelope.

"Oh, nearly forgot. Father asked me to give you this."

"What is it?"

"Don't know. Take it anyway, and let's go get some sleep."

Mounting the steps again, she opened the envelope. There were several $100 bills inside.

"I don't want this," she said, trying to hand it back to her brother.

"I shouldn't think so. Root of all evil," Hank muttered. But he wouldn't hold out his hand to take it back. He wouldn't even meet her eye, so she knew that the money was from him. She couldn't think of a way to thank him. She felt deeply, almost unbearably moved; filled with a great rush of love for Hank and for—for this old staircase, of all things, and the banister and this whole dreary old house, which was her cocoon after all. . . .

"I'll leave it on my bureau," she said.

"Oh, might as well tuck it in your sock, you never know," he answered with a wild attempt at diffidence. He bent and kissed her forehead in an extraordinary show of affection, and before she could recover from the shock, he quickly disappeared into his room. He popped his head out again. "Good night. Oh, uh . . . one other thing, not important, really. But I was thinking . . . maybe it's not just a coincidence that you've discovered witchery and yourself all at the same time," he said.

"I don't know what you mean," she whispered.

"Oh, well . . . you've got a bit of Great-aunt Grace's spirit yourself, you know. Haven't you? Mysterious as hell to me, that independence, not caring a damn for what anyone thinks. Wish I had it. Probably traces all the way back, here and there. You know what I mean. I mean, where does it come from anyway? Why not witches? Anyway, I wish I had a bit of it. Good luck, Katie. Let me know if you need anything?"

"Hank, do you really think—" But his door was softly shut between them, and she was left to ponder on it alone. Waiting for sleep, she tried to concentrate on the thrilling possibility that she might be the carrier of an ancient family curse—or blessing? But for the very first time in her whole life the past seemed remote and dead and dry compared with the future. Kate forgot about witches and tried to dream that she was an ordinary person, exactly like everyone else.

Chapter Eight

1935: KATE

The next morning the upstairs maid helped her pack her clothes. She thought there was something vaguely wrong about that; but she had no idea how to pack for herself, and there was no point in trying to stop the whirlwind force that her mother created in ordering the valises and trunk to be brought down from the storeroom, selecting shoes, underwear, tweed skirts, dresses, waists and hats and gloves, sachet and padded hangers, soap and towels, hairpins and safety pins, lace collars and the second-best pearls, milk of magnesia, cod-liver oil, talcum powder, sanitary napkins, twelve pairs of good lisle stockings in the odious brown color that had as much to do with Kate's need to leave home as any other single thing. She intended to throw the stockings away at the first opportunity (except for one pair to wear on visits home) and to buy a few pairs of the real silk, sheer kind. Flesh-colored, if she didn't lose her nerve.

Her father said good-bye at breakfast, saying he didn't see why so much fuss was being made, and he expected to see her in her place at church every Sunday morning and looked forward to the fascinating conversation he was certain her adventures would provide on the frequent occasions when she would be home for dinner. He suggested she might find this an apt time to begin keeping a journal.

Seeing the trunk and two valises lined up in the hall, waiting for the taxi (having sensibly refused to be driven to South Boston and handed out of the Daimler by Mr. Peterson in his family-retainer uniform), Kate had a moment of panic.

"Oh, Mother, don't we have any suitcases besides those?"

"What on earth do you mean?"

"They're so . . . well, look at all that brass on them, and the good leather. I mean, don't we have any that aren't so—so well made?"

"Kate, do try to make sense. I have no idea what you're talking about. Luggage is luggage. One doesn't have badly made luggage. Why would you want such a thing? One has the luggage that one has. It's not as if one went out to buy it, is it? What's wrong with Louis Vuitton's cases? They've held up admirably all these years. I can't begin to guess how many Staffords and Porters and Fieldses have taken the grand tour—and petit tours as well—with these very same cases. They'll do perfectly well. Now don't be so silly, or you'll never get along out there with working-class people. I do know quite a lot about working people, and I can tell you one thing: They don't admire silliness."

"There's the taxi. Good-bye, Mother." Kate reached up on tiptoe to kiss her mother's long, narrow face, which tasted faintly of glycerine and rosewater soap.

"Good-bye, dear. Enjoy your independence," her mother said, and if she bent at all to receive the kiss, it was imperceptible. She closed the front door before Kate was inside the taxi. No sentimentalist, Anne Stafford had a committee meeting to prepare for this afternoon.

Kate had planned this in every detail she could think of. "To the YWCA on Fourth Street, please," she said to the driver. "That's in South Boston."

"Don't I know it, don't I just," the driver answered mysteriously. He lifted the cases onto the luggage carrier and strapped them; then he handed Kate up onto the running board and into the car. Once inside she peeled off her gloves and jammed them into the pockets of her good blue coat. He tipped his cap to her and went around to the driver's seat.

She had never taken a taxi before, but she had been to South Boston twice. The first time was in 1922, when she was only six. A great ceremony at Castle Island was held to honor the two-hundredth birthday of her ancestor Harry Stafford, who had been known as the

Boston Patriot. She remembered driving through crowded streets and being stared at (they were in the old brougham; she remembered the clopping of the horses' hooves), sitting straight for hours until she ached to be allowed to move and being terrified at the sudden explosion of the cannon. She had disgraced herself by wetting her pants, but everyone ignored it. She remembered that. She smiled to herself as the taxi took her down along Washington Street to the lower end of the channel that separated Boston from South Boston.

She had come here during the previous winter, with her friend Janet Hawkesworth. The winter of 1934 had been the bitterest and coldest and longest one even the oldest residents could remember, or so they said. There had been a great deal of talking about the wretched Dickensian world over there in South Boston: scores of people, maybe even hundreds, who actually didn't have any place to live. From time to time over that winter a body was found, frozen to death in an alley or a doorway. There were long lines at the soup kitchens which had been set up through most of the charities subscribed to generously by everyone they knew. Servants from all the houses on Back Bay and the Hill and the Square had been dispatched regularly to help feed the sad-faced unemployed.

Kate and her friend Janet Hawkesworth had been reading socialist and communist tracts that winter, with mounting outrage against the unfair distribution of wealth. They had been desperately sincere in their guilt, hating their warm clothes and giving up desserts "for as long as people are starving," as Kate explained passionately when her extraordinary refusal of apple pie and hard sauce was noted. ("A worthy sentiment," her father had pointed out, "but if no one were to eat apple pie, what would become of the apple sellers?") One day Kate and Janet had dared each other into a field trip to see for themselves. Maybe there was something they could do, some way to strip themselves of wealth and privilege and share with their less fortunate comrades—how *does* one go about doing that?—and they took the Hawkesworth car because Kate wasn't positive she could trust Mr. Peterson not to tell on her. Being driven through the gray, cheerless streets in the bitter cold, the two well-meaning young ladies from Beacon Hill had to keep rubbing their scarves across the befogged windows of the limousine to peer out. (The Hawkesworth car had a heater right inside; secretly Kate agreed with her parents that this was decadent, but it was a lot more comfortable than the drafty old Daimler.) There were no people to be seen as they rode through South Boston on that mean, cold winter day, except for an occasional solitary figure hurrying along on some errand, bundled in dark clothing, head down against the wind, looking no more or less dramatically interesting than any servant one might see heading for Commonwealth Avenue to the pharmacy or market.

There were no grown men lounging about, idle, for them to be sorry for; no children in rags (thank heaven, although they had steeled themselves for such sights); no women reduced to selling their bodies to strangers on the street; no desperate characters flashing knives and worse. Hardly anyone at all. Only grim, grimy streets, lined with row after row of tenement houses, the windows of which were frequently stuffed with matted newspapers to keep out the cold (and the light!), and a feeling of emptiness and sad disillusion.

Kate and Janet hadn't said a word all the way home, and for some reason neither could explain, they never spoke of that day again. Janet gave up on socialism and communism right away, but Kate didn't. It began to dawn on her then that as long as one remained in the privileged class, one could never be truly human in the sense of sharing the common human experiences. And here she was at last, on her way to finding out about life. At last.

Now it was more than six months later, and the sun was shining and the day was balmy, and from the window of the taxi Kate saw plenty of people on the streets and sidewalks and on the stoops of buildings, women with babies in their arms, children running in circles and dashing out into the street between wagons and autos; yes, there were the men clustered here and there with nothing to do and nowhere to go, a very odd sight indeed. And yet there was a vitality and movement to the scene that set Kate's heart racing. She saw no reason for pity or guilt here, not this day. She was one of them now. It made all the difference.

She had read enough novels not to make any serious gaffes (she didn't think she made any, at any rate, and kept herself on the alert for signs that anyone might find her silly) when checking into the YWCA. She knew enough to pick up her own cases and carry them upstairs and not gasp when she saw how small and narrow and dark her quarters were. After the matron had left her alone, with a promise to send the trunk up when the "boy" got there, and the door was closed, Kate stared for a long moment at the bald light bulb that hung down on a wire in the center of the room. She'd never seen one before without a shade or some glass around it. It looked like a great jellyfish recently enough dead that you could still make out the reddish filaments inside that were its veins and organs. The light was not bright enough to read by, although it hung over the end of the little iron cot. The thin mattress was neatly covered with a rough wool blanket. Well, she thought, basic is what I want, and basic is what I've got.

It occurred to her much later, when she was already in bed with the light off, that a shade over the bulb would require a brighter wattage for the same amount of light. And that would cost more, of course. She congratulated herself silently on her first real lesson in economics, and no one had had to explain it either. She would do just fine, she knew it. As she lay in the dark waiting for sleep, she remembered that she hadn't eaten dinner. How curious, she thought, and exciting! I've missed my very first meal.

Sleep was as evasive as ever, and the uneasy sensation of lying in a strange bed in a house that was not her own, surrounded by strangers, kept Kate's eyes wide open in the darkness. Finally she sat up and pulled the string that dangled from the light bulb's socket. She almost screamed. There was an enormous black insect climbing the painted wall only inches from where her face had been a moment ago.

Kate's great-uncle Alexander Field had been a Nobel laureate biologist and had classified several prominent species of insects. There was a room in the Stafford Library filled with glass cases lined with rows and rows of Uncle Alexander Field's specimens. Kate had seen them all, even learned most of their names, but she couldn't place this one, even after her initial shock had passed at finding it at all. She found it ugly and wondered how on earth an insect had managed to find its way inside and up two flights of stairs.

She felt sorry for the creature, so far from its natural habitat, surely doomed to die of hunger and fright. She looked around the little room for a container in which she might catch the thing. She wrapped herself in her bathrobe and slid her feet into her slippers and then scooped the scurrying black insect up in both her hands. She thought of tossing it out the window, but there was nothing below except pavement and the brick façade of the building that abutted this one. The insect could no more survive there than he would if she left him on the inedible plaster of her own wall. With the thing struggling in a most repulsive way inside the closed case of her two cupped hands, Kate managed to push the door open and start down the narrow, ill-lit hallway toward the stairs.

"Hi!" a voice sang out as she passed an open door. Clouds of cigarette smoke obscured the room, but Kate made out several figures inside. Was it she whom they had hailed? She couldn't be sure. She didn't know anyone here, but it had long bothered her that she had no idea how people managed to meet each other without benefit of relatives and friends in common; maybe they just hailed each other in the night, and that was that. She hesitated outside the open door, not wanting to intrude or stare, but more mortally terrified of appearing a snob. She held her hands in front of her; the creature was struggling frantically and tickling her palms, and she was beginning to feel physically sick because she loathed the damn thing so. She stood with cupped hands and trembling chin, half smiling in case someone was watching her through the smoke and on the slight but wonderful chance that "Hi!" had been addressed to her after all.

"Whatcha got there?"

"Uh . . . ." They were speaking to her! "I've found an insect. I'm taking it back to the garden."

"Garden!" One of the figures detached herself from the haze and stood in the doorway. She was small and very pretty, wrapped in a Chinese silk kimono. Her hair was blond and curly, and she had painted her face with bright red lips and cheeks and blue on her eyelashes and lids. She was smiling at Kate, in a friendly way. "Is there a garden around here? No kidding?" she asked.

"I . . . I don't know. I just thought . . . there must be," Kate stammered. "I don't know how this thing found its way inside the building, but I thought—"

"Let's see," the young woman said. She stepped close to Kate and waited expectantly for a peep inside the rounded fingers. The insect was jumping around almost unbearably now, and Kate thought she might not be able to contain it if she opened even one finger, but the girl was so friendly and so interested that Kate did open her hands to show what was inside.

"It's just a cockroach," the girl said. She sounded disappointed. "What're you carrying a cockroach around like that for? Ecch." She shuddered, turning her face into a horrid little pout. "You nuts or somethin'? Hey, guess what she's carryin' around in her hands out here!" she called to the other occupants of the smoke-filled room.

Kate dropped the insect on the tile floor and stepped on it, hard, with her slippered foot. It gave her a deep and enormous satisfaction to feel the squish of the repulsive thing, dying, through her thin leather sole. She smiled tentatively at the blond girl, who had made the others laugh and now seemed ready to offer friendship, as if Kate had passed some kind of test or something by not getting hurt or angry.

"Come on in, why don't you?" she offered. Kate didn't hesitate. In a moment she was crowding with three other young women in the tiny room. The haziness came as much from the black Japanese lantern hung over the swaying light bulb as from the cigarettes. Introductions were made in a highly informal way.

"I'm Helen, and this is Liz; that's Roxie," the blond girl said, squeezing herself onto the bed where the others sat and lounged against dark satin pillows.

"I'm Kate Sta—Kate," she said, suddenly shy. She had to stiffen her arm to keep it from offering itself for a formal handshake. No one seemed to notice. They made room for her on the narrow bed. An overflowing ashtray with a little stork on it was balanced precariously on the coverlet. Kate hoisted herself onto the edge of the bed near the iron railing at the foot. There really was not enough room, but no one minded.

"You just move in, Katie?"

"Yes. Today."

"Got a job?"

"Not yet. I'm going to start looking first thing tomorrow morning."

"What kinda work you do?"

"Oh . . . anything. Whatever I can find. I'd appreciate any suggestions if you have them. I'm really new at this."

"Waitressing, that's all there is, if you're lucky. Unless you know how to type or something like that. Even that's not a sure thing. I'm waiting tables over at the Porter Street Tavern. You know it? Used to be a speak? Over near the park, you know, downtown. On Boylston Street. Not too bad, I guess."

"Better than the Southie Station, that's for damn sure," said the girl named Roxie. She looked older than the others and had grimy rings around her eyes, as if her makeup had smudged and just stayed there for a long time without being wiped off. Kate felt sorry for her, she looked so tired. Kate's eyes were accustomed to the smoke now and the dim, shadowy half-light.

"Where you from?" Liz asked. She lit a fresh cigarette from the burned-out end of another. All the ends in the ashtray had red gashes of lipstick on them.

"From?"

"Cut it out," the little blonde, Helen, said sharply. "Nobody has to tell if they don't want to. We all got somethin' to hide, what the hell. No questions and we'll all stay friends, right?"

Liz reached over, the cigarette in her mouth making her eyes squint against the smoke. She took an edge of Kate's gray wool bathrobe between her red fingernails. "Nice," she commented.

"Thank you."

"I just got out of jail," the older one, Roxie, said suddenly, watching for Kate's reaction.

"Well, good for you," Kate said warmly. "Welcome out."

It broke the tension which had been building in the room. Everyone laughed, and suddenly Roxie was hugging Kate and offering her a cigarette, and they all were laughing and talking at once, and she had miraculously completed the rites of passage and was a part of the group, and she didn't even know how she had done it. By the time they disbanded and headed for their separate rooms and sleep it was midnight, and Kate had three new friends, her very first sore throat from smoking Camels, and promises of help in finding a job the next day.

But only the sore throat was still there in the morning. When Kate knocked on Helen's door, there was a thump as if a pillow had been thrown against it and something which sounded indistinctly like "Go way!" muttered from inside. No sign of the other two either. Maybe six o'clock was too early for waitresses. She wished she'd thought to ask what time they should all meet. But she didn't mind waiting.

When she came down the stairs into the lobby, the night porter yawned in her face and pointed to the sign that had "Cafeteria" printed on it in small, dingy letters. She went down the dark steps to the basement and emerged in a windowless place with stained walls that had once been painted green.

There was no one at any of the oilcloth-covered tables; no one in the room at all except herself and a very fat woman wrapped in a dirty white apron, standing behind a row of steaming coffeepots and tin caldrons.

Kate sat down at a table, smiled politely toward the fat lady, and waited.

Nothing happened. The fat lady just stared at her with sleepy, uncaring eyes and then stood with her arms crossed over her grotesque bosom.

It was difficult to know what to do. Perhaps they were waiting for the serving girl to show up. Perhaps the fat lady was the cook and refused to wait on table. That would explain it. Feeling ravenously hungry, Kate was too well brought up to be short-tempered with servants. She smiled at the cook, who was just standing there and not doing anything at all that Kate could see.

Suddenly chattering could be heard in the stairwell, coming closer. Kate was greatly relieved when two other young women came into view. She wished they had been her friends from the night before (she was feeling more than a little strange and alone now), but it was a relief not to be the only one in the unfriendly room.

To her surprise the girls did not sit down but went directly to one end of the long counter, where the fat lady stood frowning. Each newcomer picked up a tray from a pile there and took flatware and napkin from bins. Then they moved along the counter and just took what they wanted and placed it on their trays. It was a buffet! Kate watched; one girl took a sticky bun, and then the fat lady poured a mug of coffee for her. The other girl had tea and a hard roll. After the fat lady had poured their coffee and tea, she went to stand by a cash register and when the girls had pushed their trays along the counter to where she stood, they gave her money, and she rang it up. Then the girls carried their trays to a table, sat down, and began to eat.

Kate rose tentatively from the table where she had been waiting. She took up a tray and slid it along until she reached the place where the fat lady stood.

"May I have coffee, please?"

She would have enjoyed cornbread and ham and scrambled eggs, but such breakfasts were already part of a different world. She could see that. She took two Parker House rolls from a cold tin bucket and kept moving along, pushing her tray. Other young women were coming into the room now, and a line started to form behind Kate. No one talked much. By the time she reached the cash register and paid her ten cents the room was filled. The coffee was bitter and weak at the same time, and the rolls were not fresh. The butter tasted very strange, too. But Kate ate the meager breakfast with good appetite and drank the terrible coffee right down to the crack at the bottom of the mug.

She saw Liz and Roxie come in and waved to them. She was certain they had seen her, but they turned to the food line without a smile or a wave at her and then took seats at a table on the other side of the room.

She pretended not to mind; but she didn't understand their rejection, and it hurt. It hurt for a long time, until it was explained to her much later: "People have this natural instinct to be friendly, but later on, when they think about it, kiddo, it's better not to open up too much. You're usually sorry if you do right at first, because sure as shootin', someone's going to want something from you, and these days you've just got to hang onto everything you've got for yourself. It's like people can't afford to be friends, any more than they can afford to eat chicken, much as they might want to. It's just hard kiddo. Nothin' personal."

The author of these thoughtful words was Rose Mallory—roommate, friend, philosopher, sometime factory worker, sometime waitress, full-time optimist and devout union member. After three days at the Y, Kate had followed a want ad to Mrs. Bundy's Boarding-house, where she asked about rooms to let. A lively young woman with red hair was running a carpet sweeper across the parlor (an agreement she had with her landlady for times when she ran a bit short of the rent money). When she heard Kate asking for a room, Rose Mallory dropped the sweeper and came over to listen un-abashedly to the conversation between the newcomer and Mrs. Bundy.

"Why not bunk in with me?" she suggested with a warm, open grin. "Okay, Mrs. B.? I've got two beds, see, one just goin' to waste, and we could cut the rent in half!"

The offer was so guileless, so cheerful and spontaneous that Kate could only agree. Sharing a room with a stranger was unthinkable, of course, but she didn't think about it, not even for an instant. Later she would be proud of her own spontaneity and eternally grateful. It was not only a furnished room Rose shared but all of her warm and generous heart. In the next months it was Rose who introduced Kate to:

boiled dinner on a one-ring gas burner;

the art of minor shoplifting, but only from big stores notorious for exploiting their workers;

inhaling Camels (advertised by athletes: "They don't take your wind");

gambling—a shared ticket in the Irish Sweepstakes ("Somebody's got to win, why not us?");

bawdy jokes and laughing out loud;

rouge and eye shadow, a curling iron, high-heeled pumps;

and Patrick Casey.

Rose would have tried to get her new friend a job at the shoe factory, but they were letting people go and threatening to close down completely, as so many other factories were doing all around them. If it weren't for Rose's membership in the union and being shop steward, too, she might not have had a job at all. As it was, she was constantly badgered and threatened, which only made her stubborn green eyes flash with the challenge of it all. Sometimes she made speeches to rally other leatherworkers around when they were scared of losing their jobs and believed the bosses' threats. "Hang on," Rose would say, "and stick together. Then there's no boss in the world can lick ya! He's lyin' if he says it's the union making the factories close down; it's his own greed because his profits aren't big enough to suit him. He's lyin' if he says he's not making profits. It's hard times for the workers and high times for the bosses, and it's our hard labor they're gettin' rich on. Hang on, everybody; they can't make it at all without us. If we stick together, we'll win.''

Kate had never witnessed such passionate speech; she had no idea that anyone could care so much, allow herself to become so—so emotional! To raise one's voice, she had been taught all her life, was to admit that reason no longer prevailed. Yet here was a young woman with no formal education, rousing whole groups of pallid and withdrawn peoples to smiles and cheers, clearly winning them to her side and to renewed energies by forgoing all the rules of debate and decorum, giving way to raw, pure emotion. For Kate, it was a revelation never to be forgotten.

With her red crinkly hair, sparky green eyes, pale skin splattered with freckles, forever joking about going to fat on the working girl's diet of beer and pasta, Rose was quick to anger and quicker to forgiveness and laughter. She was different from anyone Kate had ever known outside a wild, romantic novel. She found herself under Rose Mallory's spell and grateful for it. Rose was her clever, kind guide through the complicated and often incomprehensible world she now found herself in.

Rose had an admirer, Marco Pacelli. He owned a small, clean, but dingy restaurant in the Italian section of North Boston and had met Rose at a protest against the Sacco and Vanzetti trials. They had been ''going together'' ever since, and after eight years they were like an old married couple, except that they lived apart. Rose spent Saturday nights and all day every Sunday with Marco. But she was too independent, she said; she'd probably never marry anybody. Anyway, an Irisher like herself and a wop like him could only mean trouble for everybody if they tried to mesh, she said.

Marco went along with anything Rose wanted. That included giving her new friend Katie a job slinging hash at his Blue Grotto Café six days a week. Grateful for the chance, Kate became pretty good at it. Six days a week, the hours flew for her, chocked full of everything she had left Beacon Street to look for. It was exhilarating, exhausting, exciting. She loved Rose; she loved their cozy room with the faded, stained wallpaper and the easy chair with its springs showing through the worn upholstery; she loved Marco Pacelli and the Blue Grotto Café with its oilcloth on the tables and years of baked-in grime in the kitchen; she loved the customers who spoke Italian and gestured with their hands and left nickel tips; she even loved Mrs. Bundy's other boarders and the way they got into shouting arguments about each other's radio programs and taking too long in the bathroom. Once Mr. Lampert told Mr. Smith that he smelled bad; Mrs. Bundy had to separate the two doddering old men (who both smelled bad, if the truth be known) by rushing in from the kitchen and stepping between them, with a hot skillet in one hand and the other raised in supplication to God. Kate loved it all.

She had never told Rose much about herself, and Rose had never pried. It hadn't been intentional; at first there had been so much else to talk about. But as Kate heard Rose talking with some of her co-workers in a booth at the Blue Grotto Café, she began to feel uneasy in her mind about herself, about things she had always accepted unquestioningly. She began to see herself as the enemy.

She listened to terrible, passionately told true stories, about the inhumanly hard working conditions in factories and shops, all because of the bosses' mania for profit. And always they would wrestle with the basic problem: that owners and management didn't know how the working people really lived and what they really thought; it was a class problem, the lines could never be crossed.

The talk made Kate think about Passmore. Books and magazines used to refer to that factory town (which, she realized now, was all it ever had been) as the Noble Experiment. Passmore was supposedly an ideal workers' paradise, conceived and built and maintained by Staffords and Porters, where (to hear Staffords and Porters refer to it, at any rate) profits were secondary to the glorious personal satisfactions of knowing that one's workers were happy. Now, for the first time in her life, it occurred to Kate to wonder how the people who lived and worked in the Noble Experiment felt about it.

She had always blindly (and deafly and certainly dumbly) accepted her family's attitudes about more things than she had realized. Especially, she knew now, Passmore. Staffords and Porters really believed that their own enlightened generosity had created a brave new world, clean and modern, for the benefit of the workers themselves, who were properly grateful. Now, listening to Rose's impassioned anger, Kate squirmed in slowly dawning embarrassment as she realized that she was the Imperialist Boss, the profiteer from other people's labors, the self-appointed god who ruled other people's lives, telling them what was best for them, assuming they were stupid and unfeeling because they didn't go to Harvard, weren't born in Boston, worked with their hands. . . . She sat among the real working people and tasted the terrible knowledge of guilt, as palpable on her tongue as if she'd bitten into a sour apple.

It was impossible to put any perspective on her suddenly whirling, conflicting feelings, and so she just kept herself terribly busy and more tired than she had ever imagined it possible to be, and she and Rose always had so many fascinating things to talk about that it took a long time before she got up the nerve to tell her friend who she really was.

Rose had come dashing in at the end of a Sunday afternoon to change her clothes—she and Marco were going to a dance the mayor was throwing for the Amalgamated Clothing Workers. Kate had spent most of the day in bed, sleeping and resting and reading the Sunday funnies, and it was almost time to get dressed herself. She half sat up in her tumbled bed, with the papers all around her, and watched Rose burrowing through her dresser drawer in search of a stocking without a run in it to match the one she already had on.

Suddenly, feeling a bit like Claudette Colbert revealing her true identity as an heiress in *It Happened One Night,* stammering quite a lot and even blushing, Kate told her friend that she was one of "the" Staffords and her family lived at Number 4 Beacon Street and she was sorry she hadn't told before, but she just knew Rose would understand how much she wanted to be just a regular person—

"Well, gee, that's great, kiddo," Rose said enthusiastically. "I'm real glad to know you've got a place to go on Sundays. A family to be with, instead of wandering around the Common on your own or sittin' on a park bench or goin' to the movies alone. I guess that's why you never let me fix a blind date for you, huh? Well, it's swell, honey. I'm really kind of relieved and glad; you're lucky. Look, do you think I bulge too much in this dress? It's that goddamned ricotta cheesecake of Marco's. But he says the more there is of me, the better.'' She giggled and whirled around for Kate to judge.

Thinking it over after Rose had left, Kate began to realize that the name Stafford didn't mean what Staffords assumed it meant, not to everyone in the world. Alternating waves of embarrassment, shame, and relief swept through Kate as she got up and slowly started to dress. It was like a novel in which someone was disinherited or discovered to be illegitimate, she thought; other people's notions of who you are get stripped away, and you have to stand on your own two feet. There's freedom to be yourself, whoever you are and answerable to—my God, she could just glimpse it, not really grab hold—answerable to NO ONE. No one but yourself . . . freedom to be yourself, whoever you might turn out to be.

It was dizzying to think about. Another movie scene crossed her mind: the one in the cartoons when the bunny or mouse steps off a cliff and doesn't know it until he (or she!) looks down. Then she falls. . . .

It was time to leave for home. She was ready—good print dress, white gloves, blue snap-brim hat and brown stockings, blue shoes and handbag to match. She took a taxi to Beacon Street and presented herself in the drawing room just as the sherry was being served.

The family was fascinated by her ''adventures,'' as they called her life outside their domain. They listened attentively to the few details she was willing to parcel out to them.

''Eight dollars plus tips is a good wage for an inexperienced young girl,'' her father observed. ''Mr. Pacelli seems to be a generous enough employer.''

''I'm not sure it's quite—well, nice—for a young lady to accept gratuities for doing the work that she's agreed to do,'' her mother said thoughtfully. ''There's something rather degrading about receiving money directly from the public. As though one were a servant or somehow dependent upon the generosity of strangers for one's livelihood.''

Kate, her father, her brother Hank, and her brother Edward, and Edward's wife, Catherine, all stared at her, and she raised her Porter nose a notch higher in response, tightening her lips as if to announce tacitly that she would say no more on the subject.

"It's part of the experiment, Anne. Of course, not all the things one has to do when tasting a different way of life can be quite as pleasant as the way we do things when we're at home. Remember our wedding trip and the discomforts we endured abroad? Those things only make one appreciate home all the more. Kate will savor the value of this experience all her life, and I'm sure it will make her much kinder to servants and all who depend on her in the future."

Kate thought she remembered, when she had been small, her father making her laugh. But he never showed any signs of a sense of humor anymore, and she wondered sadly if she had made up that memory. Children can sense when grown-ups are trying to amuse them, and sometimes they laugh so as not to hurt the grown-ups' feelings . . . when you're grown-up yourself, you tend not to be so kind or ready to please.

Aunt Mole and Uncle Fred came in just then, shook hands all around, were seated and served their sherry. Aunt Mole had a real name, of course; it had been in the newspaper when she was married thirty-five years before, but no one remembered it. She had been nicknamed by an older brother while still in her crib, and the name had fitted her so perfectly that it stuck forever. She didn't seem to mind. Aunt Mole never minded anything. Most of the time she smiled, but occasionally a storm seemed to pass through the vacant lot that was her head, and she would frown and scold whoever was there for whatever offense had stirred her; then she would settle down, calm again. No one was ever anything but kind to dear Mole Porter. Her husband made very generous contributions to Symphony and Opera and all the important things.

"Kate was just telling us some very interesting stories about her work on the South Side," Anne Porter Stafford told her brother and his wife.

"Oh, yes, poor unfortunate people. I'm afraid this depression is hitting rather hard, and no sign of easing, so they say," Uncle Fred said. He was a nice man, but very like their uncle George, in that he had a habit of spitting when he talked (did two cases mean a run in the family? Kate, letting her thoughts meander in that direction, shuddered and mentally crossed herself as she'd seen Rose do to ward off bad things). One could watch the spray from his words dancing on the light that came into the drawing room through the leaded glass windows. It was a special strain of sunlight that knew its place on this side of the Hill, Kate thought: enough light to read by without having to use the electricity, but never so bright that it might fade the carpet from Persia.

"Mr. Roosevelt is going to save the country, and no one will ever be poor again," Uncle Fred said with more than a tinge of bitterness and irony. His hatred for That Man in the White House was so vehement that his more tolerant friends and relatives sometimes baited him deliberately, just to see the spume rising.

Knowing how unpleasant it could be for everyone if her brother really grew sullen (it interfered with his digestion in a way that was impossible to keep private), Kate's mother changed the subject in the subtle, deft way which was one of her most admired social accomplishments.

"The Witherspoons have sold their town house and moved to Dedham for the duration of the Depression," she said. "Halliday Witherspoon said he is contemplating writing a letter to *The New York Times* about the decline of aristocracy or some such nonsense," she announced.

"*The New York Times*? Whatever for? Why not the *Evening Transcript* so people can see it?" Uncle Fred asked, genuinely puzzled.

Suddenly Aunt Mole leaned forward and tapped her nephew Edward on the knee. She cleared her throat, and the others in the room waited politely to hear what she had to say. It was never possible to do anything but pay full and rapt attention when Aunt Mole spoke. Her windy voice would touch down like a twister, disrupting everything in its path, and then blow off, oblivious of the chaos left behind.

"If you ever go blackbirding," she advised Edward loudly, rapping him sharply on his pinstriped knee with her knuckles, "don't take the boys from the shore. Go up in the hills; they're stronger there and will fetch a better price."

There was a very long moment when no one said anything, and then Aunt Mole leaned back in her chair, quite satisfied at having imparted her wisdom, and a rather lovely, drifty smile settled back on her face.

"Now where do you think she ever got that idea?" her husband said wonderingly, not without obvious admiration for the fruitful and always creative inventions of his wife's mind and tongue. "Where in blazes—I beg your pardon, Anne," he said in an aside to his sister, and then went on without waiting for her reply. "Where do you suppose she heard that one? Must have been from her grandfather, telling tales on his father. I believe there was some rumor of his being in the slave trade. Well, now isn't that interesting?"

A tap on the sliding doors that led to the dining room was so welcome that every head (except Aunt Mole's) turned expectantly.

"Come in," Kate's mother called softly.

"Dinner is ready," the young and visibly nervous black girl told the gathering, and then she slipped back without opening the doors for them to enter.

"I've tried so many times to convince that girl she must say 'is served' instead of 'is ready,' but you see how successful I've been," Kate heard her mother saying as she took Edward's arm to lead the way. There was no hint of complaint in her tone, of course. Kate hoped the girl was safely out of hearing range.

"We must make allowances for hard times," Edward said, pompous and off the point.

Kate took Hank's arm. He winked at her to show that he understood her restlessness and her feelings of temporary alienation from all this familiar family atmosphere. But even dear Hank would have been startled to know where his sister's thoughts were at this moment. Who could imagine any sane person preferring to be in an unheated, noisy, smoke-filled auditorium draped with pathetic paper bunting and filled with unwashed laborers celebrating the working-class mayor's clever diverting of WPA funds for Boston's public transportation rather than dining with civilized, educated people in one's own tasteful, aesthetically pleasing home?

But Kate had already met Patrick Casey.

Chapter Nine

1936: KATE

"My fellow workers, my brothers in the struggle for dignity and justice, I've been asked to speak to you tonight about the great victory President Roosevelt has won on behalf of every workingman in this country—"

"How about the workingwoman?" shouted a cheerful female, if not "ladylike," voice. There were only a few people scattered here and there in the union hall; most of the folding chairs were empty. Nearly 1,000 workers had been laid off since Christmas, and it was a bitter, cold February night, with snow and sleet threatened before morning.

"Yes, don't forget the women!" a hearty male voice agreed, and others chimed in with a chuckle or two, trying to keep the spirits warm even if the body was thin and shaky.

The speaker, who had been sent from the Boston Central Labor Union to address the meeting, was a black-haired, broad-shouldered Irisher, who had a ready grin and a ready handshake and would surely go far in the Democratic party. In the meantime, he had the job of keeping the workers from losing faith in the party's broadest base, the unions. It wasn't an easy job, not these days.

"And the women, God bless 'em!" he agreed heartily now, with a laugh.

"Don't you talk down to us, young fellow. We work as hard as any man, and for half the wages more times than not. And take care of the house and kids as well!'' another, angrier voice called from the front row.

The speaker became serious, dropping his grin like a hot potato. His eyes narrowed and focused on the woman down front, and his voice grew kind and understanding and rang out clear and sure.

"The workingmen and women of this country," he said, "have, for the first time in history, achieved the recognition of their God-given right to bargain and be heard. But they must speak together, in unity and strength, and that is why the union is more important now than ever—"

"How come you can't even get thirty people out then?" called a heckler. The sparse gathering near the front of the auditorium turned around in their seats to glare at the gangly, mean-looking man in a dark overcoat who stood at the back of the hall with his collar turned up like the gangster he was.

"Because they haven't got the carfare to get here, thanks to the scum bosses!" cried the same woman who had shouted out before.

"You're carryin' names on the union lists who haven't paid dues for a year and more," the heckler went on loudly. "This ain't no representative body."

"How much did they pay you to try to break us up tonight?" the speaker called out from the stage. "We're used to your kind. If you really needed the fifty cents that bad, brother, then come and join us, and we'll all beat the filthy system that makes a decent man scab and betray his own kind."

The heckler, having the attention of all present, spit on the floor and turned his back to walk out of the auditorium. The audience now turned back to settle themselves for the rest of the evening, after the mild diversion. The speaker told them about the plans in Washington for the new Labor Relations Board and how it would give them all a voice in the courts, where it really counted. Then he introduced someone they all knew already, Patrick Casey.

Only twenty-one years old, Patrick Casey was famous in Boston for his fire-eating eloquence on behalf of those who couldn't or didn't dare speak for themselves. He had served time in jail for disrupting the peace, led walkouts, and attracted quite a following. He had spoken out against corruption in his own union, the Boot and Shoe Workers, and his thanks had been an offer of a foreman's job from his employer, which he'd turned down, and then the sack. The union itself had been about to excommunicate him, but when the newspapers wrote about how he'd been so honest and how in the long run it was that kind of thing that would make the unions live forever, they kicked out the crumbums instead and made Casey official full-time organizer. He had defied the power of a few and won the loyalty of hundreds. He was articulate, sincere, passionate, filled with rage and well-honed poison arrows, which he never hesitated to aim and let fly. Dull gatherings came to life when Patrick Casey began to talk. Even the hungriest stomachs were warmed by his energetic call to the battle against the common enemies: the rich, the privileged, the Puritans, the powerful.

Kate had heard him speak before and afterward had realized that his famous gift of speech had not been the quality which had most impressed her. In fact, she couldn't remember one thing he had said. She had listened to the tone and quality of his passion, had admired his forcefulness and the way his shabby sweater lay loosely and unsymmetrically across his frayed shirt collar. She had remembered vividly his long, thin hands gesturing in the air and his habit of pushing his sand-colored hair back from his eyes every now and then without knowing it. It was too long, as if he'd forgotten to have it cut or didn't have a mother or wife or sweetheart to do it. It had just a bit of curl to it, not a lot but enough to make you curious about how it might feel if you touched it, whether it would spring back or lie there gentled around your fingers.

This time she had promised Rose she would listen very carefully to what he said. Rose had laughed at her and promised to introduce her if she felt that way about him, although it wouldn't be a likely match with her background.

"Wouldn't we be a pretty picture?" She'd laughed. "Marco and me, and you and Patrick Casey—a wop, two mackerel-snappers, and a fine Protestant lady whose folks came over on the *Mayflower,* the four of us walking down Commonwealth Avenue singing 'There Once Was a Union Maid'?"

Thinking about that, and how she'd blushed but accepted Rose's promise of an introduction right after tonight's meeting, Kate listened to him speak and marveled at the lovely, dark, cellolike resonance of his voice coming from such a lithe and slender body.

Then she heard her own name. And to her horror and confusion she saw that Patrick Casey was pointing directly down at her from the stage.

"There she sits, in a chair much harder than her royal bottom was ever used to, her plumage of velvet and fur all laid away for the moment while she pretends to be one of us. For what purpose, do you suppose? To mock honest people, to dirty her hands with a week or two of playing at work, so she can go back to Beacon Street and be the life of the party telling all her society friends what a swell adventure she's had slumming it? And in the meantime, she's taking the very bread from the mouth of some innocent woman who desperately needs the job Miss Kate Stafford's taken up for a lark!"

He went on and on; but he seemed to be receding into a sort of invisible tunnel, growing smaller and smaller like the White Knight in Wonderland, and his voice lost its sensuous sonority, fading until, blessedly, it disappeared completely. The auditorium seemed to grow suddenly dark and cold, and Rose, sitting next to her and gripping her hand, seemed far, far away. . . . Kate slipped quietly to the floor in a dead faint.

"It was a rotten thing to do," Rose was murmuring furiously, still very far away, but Kate could hear the fury in her friend's voice. Was Rose mad at her? She hoped not; she couldn't quite remember what she had done. Something bad, awful. Her head ached. Someone was rubbing her hands. She was lying on a hard wooden floor somewhere. She could smell the dust and feel the presence of several people around her. If she opened her eyes, she would be embarrassed again, so she kept them shut. The voices began to be clearer, closer. Slowly she remembered what had happened.

"D'ya call that a fair thing to do?" Rose was saying. "Even a murderer is given the chance to defend himself before he's hung. Kate's never hurt anyone in her life. There, I think she's coming around. Kate? Hey, kiddo?"

"No harm, is it?" Kate heard Patrick Casey's voice, scornful and very, very near. "A Stafford does harm merely by being born. Living fat off the sweat of the workers, exploitin'—"

"Oh, shut up! Look at her, look what you've done. She's white as a ghost. Maybe you killed her, you and your righteousness. Where's the justice in being rotten to someone just because she's rich? She can't help it, and she's not slumming either. She works harder every day than you do, with all your talk, and never had to mop up some stranger's mess like she does a hundred times a day in the café. Yes, and dodging greasy hands aimed at her bottom the whole time, too. Here, now, Kate, you okay? Come on, can you hear me now?''

''Yes,'' she whispered. But she kept her eyes shut tightly. She couldn't look at them. She knew they were bending over her. If she had to look into Patrick Casey's eyes, she would faint again; she knew it. She wanted desperately to die.

They forced a bit of water between her lips, and she struggled to sit up and then her head cleared and she opened her eyes, and there they were—dear Rose, looking terribly worried, and dear Marco next to her, both on their knees on the cold floor of the cloakroom, and— she looked around for him. He was standing behind Marco, much farther away than he sounded. She averted her eyes when they met his.

''Are you all right now?'' Rose asked.

''I'm sorry,'' she said. ''I'm all right. I never did that before. I'm sorry.''

''You don't have to apologize. It was his fault. A lousy, rotten thing to do.''

Suddenly Patrick Casey knelt down close to her and she felt his arms around her. They were surprisingly strong for such a lean, slight man. She smelled his nearness like a rough warm blanket surrounding her. She wanted, for an instant, to wrap herself in him and hide there. But he was pulling her to her feet, helping her to a chair, holding her around the shoulders, and then she felt both his strong hands on hers. His face was so near that she had to look at him. They were the bluest eyes she had ever seen. She knew she was in love with him, and it was hopeless, horrible.

''It's my turn to apologize to you,'' he said in a shockingly soft, gentle way that melted every bone in her body. She wondered if she was going to be sick all over him. She shut her eyes and shook her head no.

''Andiamo, we go to the café,'' Marco was saying. ''I'll open the

kitchen; we'll have a cup of coffee, something, in private. It's only
a couple of blocks from here. Can she make it?''

"Sure she can. Come on then; it's a good idea," Rose said.

Patrick helped her to her feet. Someone helped her on with her
coat and tied her scarf around her head, and then they were out on
Haverhill Street with the biting cold wind and swirls of clean white
snow driving all the embarrassment and ugliness away. Kate's weakness disappeared with the impact of the cold and knowing that Patrick
Casey's arm was intertwined with hers. Marco was on her other arm,
and Rose next to him, and there they were, four abreast, young and
strong and—unbelievably—laughing! It was late at night, hardly anyone else was on the streets, and Kate was thinking exactly what she
knew Rose was thinking—two mackerel-snappers, a wop, and a
damned Protestant. She almost giggled, wondering whether Rose was
going to begin singing "There Once Was a Union Maid." Patrick's
arm felt natural and strong and warm in hers, and she cherished the
brisk moments between the union hall and the Blue Grotto Café,
thinking she might never be so happy again in her whole life.

It was cozy and secret in the Grotto kitchen, with only one dim
light and the front part of the restaurant all closed off, with the chairs
upended on the tables. They huddled around Marco's great chopping
block on stools dragged in from the front counter. Marco insisted that
only good Italian pasta could bring Kate back to perfect health (although she swore, truthfully, that she had never felt better, never),
and soon the sauce was bubbling, and the spaghetti was being pulled
from the caldron in long steaming forkfuls, and the four of them were
well into their second bottle of Marco's private stock of Chianti.

It was the oddest and the best dinner party Kate had ever known.
After the serious politics and terrible accusations, arguments, denun-
ciations, fainting, and, most momentous of all, falling secretly and
irrevocably in love with a man who had publicly stated his contempt
and loathing for her, she had found herself enjoying laughter and talk
and easy company, with hearty appetite and uncomplicated pleasure.
They were four healthy normal friends, having fun together—no different from millions of other young people in these times or any
other. They were happy, tired, a bit giddy, ebullient, sharing bits of
their life's stories with each other, bits of their lives, really.

Kate felt that she was on a plateau in time, that somehow a miraculous gift had been lent to her, a few hours of loving comradeship. It made no sense that they were talking like oldest friends, sharing memories and growing closer. Nothing made any sense, except that Patrick Casey's eyes were blue and kept searching for hers with kindness and curiosity and interest and . . . she wondered what her eyes were telling him.

"My aunt Maria Teresa saw a vision, under her bed. It was the Holy Virgin, who told her not to let Uncle Bruno sleep with her. It was their wedding night. Even when the priest told her it was her duty to have children, and never mind the Virgin, who probably meant something else, Zia Maria Teresa stuck to her guns. For forty years Uncle Bruno went around the village telling everyone she wouldn't let him near her on account of the vision. I'll tell you what else—she never swept under the bed either, not for forty years. To her it was a holy place."

"Poor Uncle Bruno." Patrick sighed when they had had their delicious laughter at the distant relative's expense.

"Oh, no," Marco said genially, lifting his glass in tribute to the memory, "all the other ladies took great pity on him. He was the best-serviced bull in Batignoglio!"

They roared with laughter.

"Families are wonderful," Rose said happily. "Do you know, one of my brothers has two wives, one on the farm and one in the city? They've known about each other for a long time, and it suits everyone just perfectly. He's in the city five days a week and goes to the farm every Saturday afternoon to drive his wife to the market and stays over Sunday. Happy as clams, all of them. Neither one of them could stand him around seven days a week, that's what I think."

"Tell them about the children," prompted Marco.

"Oh, they're all on the farm. Both his wives produce 'em, but only Sally enjoys the care of them, so that works out fine, too. I think Bob's forgotten which is which, I mean, which wife begot which kid!"

They laughed so hard that Marco choked on his cappuccino and had to be hit, hard, between the shoulders.

"I have an aunt whose son died, and they never told her. Didn't want to upset her," Kate said. "She lived for another eight years, sliding into senility because every time she asked about her son, someone would change the subject. I'm convinced they drove the poor thing batty. Although there is a certain strain of battiness all through both sides of my family."

This was not greeted by the same uproarious response that the other revelations had prompted. Kate was joltingly reminded that her family was not a laughing matter. How had she forgotten what Patrick Casey had done to her—and to her family as well? Her own disloyalty swept through her. She lowered her eyes and felt her cheeks turning red.

"I . . . I'm sorry. I guess my family's not funny."

"Just . . . well, it's kind of strange to think of people like . . . you know, wealthy people . . . with all the advantages and all . . . being just as crazy as everyone else . . ." Patrick said falteringly.

And that set them all off, Kate more than anyone. Patrick and Marco and Rose almost fell off their stools, rocking with hilarity, and Kate's cheeks were soaked with tears from laughing so hard, and none of them knew quite why it was so funny.

It was four in the morning, and Boston was totally their own, when they stood outside the stoop of Mrs. Bundy's, saying good night. The walk from the café had been a quiet, almost solemn one, still four abreast, arm in arm, strolling briskly in the predawn cold. But the laughter had run its course and the feast had ended and the dishes had been washed and dried, and soon it would be daylight, ordinary time to be shared with other people, mortals. They'd be scratching and scrambling for a taste of the warmth and joy that had come in such abundance for them that night. Everything always had to end. Kate was thinking that was the saddest thought she'd ever, ever had. She remembered something from a cynical old French novel: *"Tout passe, tout casse, tout lasse."* Everything passes, everything perishes, everything palls. Oh, no, she prayed silently as they walked, feeling the extraordinary vibrance of Patrick's nearness and the warmth of his arm along hers. Let it not be true, just this once, if You exist. But she knew she'd never done anything to merit special consideration.

"You're trembling," Patrick said. "And there's a great big tear on your cheek. Cold?"

"No." She shook her head. And he had the grace not to ask: What then?

Marco and Rose had moved off into the shadowy area behind the flight of steps leading to Mrs. Bundy's front door, where their two bodies blended together in the last lingering darkness. Patrick and Kate turned discreetly from the lovers and found themselves with nowhere to look but at each other. He was only an inch or two taller than she was. His cheeks were brick red from the cold wind, her fingers longed to lie against the smooth, taut flesh there, to trace along his cheekbone and the firm line of his jaw . . . but she clenched her hands inside her mittens, jammed into her coat pockets. She looked down at her feet in the flapping open galoshes and waited for him to say good night and good-bye, and wasn't this an odd little interlude in the middle of our real and serious no-solution war. . . ?

"You're a nice person, Kate, and I'm truly sorry for what I did," he said in a low, urgent voice, as if he'd been rehearsing it to himself for quite a while. He went on quickly, not wanting to be interrupted. Kate had no words anyway; she wanted only to listen to him.

"But it's true, what I said. Someone else needs the job you've got, needs it for life, and you don't. I'm sorry, what you've done by being a nice person is—well, you've confused me, and that's no good for me or for the cause I'm fighting. Before . . . well, before . . . I knew what side I was on, all right. Everything was clear as a bell, and now I wish you weren't such a nice person. I wish I didn't feel so . . ."

When his words trailed off to a whisper and then he just stopped helplessly and stood there in the middle of the sentence, with no more words at all (famous for his eloquence), she raised her eyes to look at him. They stood so close together their breaths mingled in the icy air, and she wondered if he was going to kiss her. She wanted it with a sense of need and urgency that coursed through her like fire set to dry kindling.

But he turned his head and then stepped back, away from her.

"You're a nice girl, but you're my enemy, don't you see?" he said, low and troubled.

"Yes. I see," she answered sadly.

"It's not you, personally . . . it's . . ."

"It's all right, I understand."

"No, you don't at all," he said, suddenly furious.

"I'll quit my job. I'll go home, where I belong. Honestly I will, Patrick. . . ."

"Well, what's that going to solve?"

"Someone else can have my job, someone who needs it. As you said. What else can I do?"

"But you don't understand, really, do you?"

Suddenly it was more than she could tolerate, and she burst out with a truthful answer, erupting from the wild melee of emotions churned in her this night. "No, I don't, you stupid Irishman! I don't understand why you're talking politics instead of kissing me!"

She turned from him and started to stamp her way up the steps to Mrs. Bundy's front door. To hell with him. He was right, she didn't belong here. She didn't understand these people, and she never would, and right now she didn't even want to. He was a clod and a— Suddenly she was whirled around, a shockingly strong hand on her arm yanking her whole body backward, pulling her rudely down the steps and into his arms before she could think of the word she wanted to describe him.

His lips were cold for an instant and then quickly warm and burning, moving hungrily against her astonished, open mouth, and her arms were around him and her body was pressing against his and their bulky woolen overcoats were in the way, but still, there was the overpowering feeling of being in the one place on earth where she truly belonged, where she fitted and felt right. The quickening of her blood deep inside her pulsed with life; all the words fled from her brain except the one: yes, yes, yes, yes, yes. . . .

His lips moved away from hers, brushed the side of her cheek gently, buried themselves urgently in her throat, her ear, her hair, came to rest with a soft sigh.

"This is crazy, it's insane, it's wrong," he moaned, still holding her tightly.

"Yes," she murmured against the cold perfection of his ear. His hair, as she had dreamed, did spring into lively, thick curls around her fingers. Her mittens fell unheeded to the sidewalk.

"Good night, all," called Rose with some amusement and astonishment from the top of the steps.

For a moment they were dazed, and then they broke apart, not quite daring to look at each other again. His hand clung for a moment to her arm and then fell away.

"Good night," everyone called. Kate went up to join Rose, and they went inside, with a last wave to Marco and Patrick, who stood watching them until they were inside the inner vestibule door.

"Well, enemy of the people, I guess you've made a conquest, all right!" Rose laughed as she led the way upstairs. She was trying to whisper, but not succeeding very well. She had drunk a lot of the vino, and her naturally cheerful spirits had been immensely lifted by the sight of Patrick and Kate embracing. Everybody should love everybody, that was Rose Mallory's philosophy of how to solve the problems of the world.

"Shhh," was all she got from Kate until they were safely inside their room. Then, leaning against the door, Kate looked at her with such eyes that Rose wondered if the girl was going to laugh, or cry, or faint again.

And all Kate knew for certain was that she missed Patrick Casey's presence with a hollow despair in every cell of her body.

"Well, you've fallen in love, haven't you? And him with you, from the looks of it," Rose said, grinning. "Well, what's so bad about that?" She turned around and shrugged out of her coat and shivered aloud. There was no heat at night, and the room was nearly as frigid as the outdoors. Rose moved quickly, to throw off all her clothes and slip into her big flannel nightgown. She had turned to leave the room to head down the hall for the bathroom when she saw that Kate hadn't stirred from the door.

"You have got it bad, haven't you? Come on, you'd better get undressed. It's been quite a night for you, kiddo, and love or no love, Marco's going to need you and expect you there making coffee and dishing out doughnuts as usual by seven. Better get what sleep you can. Come on, Katie, do your dreaming in bed!"

Kate moved away from the door, and Rose went out. It was true, she had to be at work at seven, but it was also true that some poor girl was starving, actually going without coffee at all, much less a doughnut, and maybe without a bed to sleep in, maybe hovering out there in a doorway someplace and freezing to death, because Kate Stafford from Beacon Hill was slumming and playing at being a working girl.

"Hey, now what? You still in your coat? And crying! Kate, are you sick? Come on, tell Rosie. I've got to get my beauty sleep, too, you know. Come on, 'fess up. What's the matter? Something he said? Or did? I'll bet he bites when he kisses, huh? Huh? What? Not even a smile? Oh, come on, Katie, I'm bushed. Tell me, and for Christ's sweet sake, let's get some sleep."

"I'm sorry, Rose. I've been awfully selfish."

"Well, it's not that bad. I've gone without sleep before, doesn't bother me, not as long as I'm having fun. So . . ." She bounced onto her bed, crossed her legs under the huge envelope of flowered flannel, sat with her back very straight, and waited.

"What a dear friend you are, Rose . . . I've never known anyone like you."

"Take off your coat."

"Yes."

She hung it up and moved around the room as she talked then, unbuttoning her skirt and blouse, laying them carefully on the chair, peeling off her stockings and unhooking the garter belt, bandeau, and half slip, slipping into her nightgown without even a shiver from the cold.

"I'm going to give up the job, and this room, and go back to where I belong. He was right, Rose. I'm just afraid I'll never . . ." She was appalled at the tears and blubbering that overcame her then, dissolved her so completely she couldn't say another word. It had never happened before. It was as if meeting Patrick had turned her into someone she couldn't trust, couldn't even recognize. A blob of uncontrollable emotions, idiotic and pathetic. She started to laugh at herself even while the tears poured down her cheeks and her nose ran profusely.

Rose was next to her now, trying to mop her up with an inadequate little handkerchief. They both were laughing then.

"You've really got it bad, huh? Afraid you'll never see him again?"
Kate nodded, wiped her nose.

"But you will, I'll bet a week's pay on it. A fellow like him doesn't give a girl a kiss like that one—oh, I saw it, it wasn't one of your thank-you-ma'ams, not that I'm an expert, but a woman knows. . . . You must know, too, Katie, that wasn't one of your ordinary little nice-knowin'-you-and-so-long little smackers, now, was it?

You'll see him again. Anyway, you're not deserting the movement, are you? Maybe it's true you got to be on the other side in the rotten class war . . . I dunno, maybe that part's true, I got to think about it. But hell, can't you and I still be friends even if you're living up on Beacon Street? I'm not that particular about where my pals have to flop. And neither are you, are you? Are you? Come on?''

Kate grinned back at her friend, and they hugged, and suddenly they both were very, very sleepy.

When they turned out the overhead light, they were surprised to see the room bathed in the first gray light of morning from over the chimneys of the Old South Station.

Kate wasn't the first radical Brahmin, not by two or three hundred years. It was maddening to have her politics accepted as coolly as her childish tantrums had been, her adolescent attempts to run away, her decision to leave home, her defiant return. There was apparently nothing that a Stafford could do which a Stafford (or a Porter) had not done before, in one form or another, and that was the most goddamn frustrating and enraging thing of all.

To her despair and embarrassment, she discovered that there was no way to touch the money that she thought was hers. Trust funds for every Stafford who now existed or might ever be conceived in the next ten or twelve generations had been set up by the financial-genius forefathers so that the money could never be eroded—not by the income tax, not by profligacy, not by the generous flow which would always go to charity, art, and compassion. Kate learned that she would have all her needs taken care of for the rest of her life and would never have access to the capital, the interest on the capital, the profit from investments, or the interest from the investment of the profits from the investments. . . . It was, in short, impossible for her to contribute anything in the way of hard currency to the union movement. She had only her own energy and time and intelligence to contribute. Many of the workers didn't believe that. Patrick Casey didn't.

They circled each other at meetings and tense little attempts arranged by Rose to repeat the evening at Marco's Blue Grotto, but now they were like two creatures from alien planets which had been at war since the beginning of time. They rarely spoke, and their eyes tried not to search each other out. Kate knew with cold certainty that there would never be anything between them. She would force herself, somehow, to kill every quickening of longing, every insane hope that wouldn't stay down, every rush of love that infused her whole body when the thought of him came unbidden and unwelcome to her brain.

She asked Rose never to refer to it, and when the two friends met for lunch twice a week—it was one thing Kate could afford to pay for, anyway—they spoke of everything except Patrick. Rose had been laid off from the shoe factory after all and had taken Kate's shift at the Grotto. She and Marco were trying to figure out how they could marry without being disowned by both their families. That and the falling off of union members who were losing their jobs gave them plenty to talk about. Little by little Kate was able to convince herself that she no longer thought about Patrick "that way."

Despite Patrick's denunciation of her that night in February (or perhaps only because there were so few people there), the members hadn't turned against Kate even when it was revealed that she was one of "them." Oh, a few never would trust her, they were going to remain class-prejudiced diehards all their lives; but in the main, people took Kate for what she was until she proved otherwise. Her dedicated volunteer work, loyal attendance at meetings, willingness to take on both scut work and real responsibility, sympathetic ear, and caring about every down-and-outer with a story or a grudge to tell eventually earned her election to the steering committee.

It was the proudest moment of her life, a real achievement, and she had earned it entirely on her own. (She was well aware of the irony, but amused rather than irate—a sign of maturity, she believed—when her family toasted her election by opening one of the bottles of 1870 brandy which had been a gift from Emperor Napoleon III to her grandfather for his efforts to rally world opinion against the republic.)

Patrick Casey was also on the steering committee. Sometimes, inevitably, they found themselves alone in a stuffy little meeting room or the headquarters office. They spoke civilly to each other. They spoke of union matters. They spoke of Rose and Marco. They tried to look anywhere but at each other.

One afternoon he surprised her by stopping her as she was carrying a trayful of sloppy soup bowls from the free-lunch tables to the makeshift kitchen of the Hall.

"There's something I've been wanting to say to you," he said. A dark brown strand of hair hung over her eye, and she felt greasy from head to toe. She couldn't remember the last time she'd looked in a mirror, and she knew she was a sight. But she had noticed the first tugging scents of spring in the air that morning as she'd walked to the new underground transport, and her first wild thought was to wonder if Patrick had noticed, too, and had it softened his heart? Her own heart pounded as she waited for him to go on. She stood there with the heavy tray and its sad dregs of charity soup eaten down to the last marrowbone, waiting for him to go on, but he didn't seem to notice the weight she was carrying and took his own time about going on.

"Now?" she asked.

"It's just . . . just that I want you to know I've come to respect you. I've changed my opinion, that's all. I believe that you're sincere and a traitor to your overprivileged class. I mean that as a compliment."

He was blushing, but he was looking at her.

"Thank you," she said.

"You're welcome." He turned away, finished with the terrible, onerous task he had set himself. Her disappointment was unexpectedly fierce. Now she'd have to start all over again convincing herself that she had outgrown her silly girlish crush on this impossible fellow.

She walked all the way home across South Boston and across the Dorchester Avenue bridge through the streets that turned from slum to commerce, warehouses, and docks, slums again, and busy thoroughfares with chic emporiums and larger private houses, the State House, her own house. She told herself she walked because it was spring and she wanted to smell the lilacs, but in fact, there was a terrible energy pent up inside her despite her hard work; a helpless rush of feeling that she knew would be beyond her control every time she saw him or heard his voice.

On Kneeland Street, at a little park in the middle of a crossing near the dental college, a troupe of young people were entertaining the passing crowds, hoping for a nickel or dime for their efforts. She stopped and watched them for a while. There were two mimes, one very tall and the other nearly a midget, and they made her smile.

I am attracted to him simply because it's so completely out of the question, she decided after she'd dropped a quarter in the hat and moved on. I can't have him, and that's exactly why he's irresistible. Reverse psychology, I've read all about it. If only he'd make a pass at me, I'd be certain to get over him.

Her cousin Charles kept wanting to take her places and kept hinting that he cared for her in more than a cousinly way, but Charles was a prig and a bore. Life was so goddamned perverse sometimes. Poor Rose was having her troubles, too, wanting what she couldn't have. Her priest had told her she'd be in big trouble if she married Marco, even though they both were Catholics. (And the Pope an Italian, too!) Why couldn't people love each other, or at least let each other live, Rose and Kate asked each other.

He had said he respected her. That was something.

Spring blossomed, and Boston was heartbreakingly lovely. It was hot and humid July before Patrick and Kate let down their guards and became tentative friends. It was just too hot to get worked up about anything, even love, she thought with relief. When he looked at her and talked to her now, she felt quite calm and almost in control.

One hot, airless August night, after a long meeting, he walked her home, all the way to Beacon Street—enemy territory—and stood outside the house, talking for a long time. He talked about the movement and how the workers all over the world were on the rise against oppression, how they would stand shoulder to shoulder and win their human right to live as well as anyone else. As well as any Stafford . . . although a true revolutionary wouldn't dream of taking up so much space in such sybaritic, selfish luxury. He gestured vaguely upward at the plain brick façade of her house that rose in simple elegance behind them. But then he said that Kate herself had opened his mind to the individual differences in people, and he was grateful to her.

They crossed over to the Common and sat on a bench on a shadowy path. There they tried to understand how two such different people as they could feel so comfortable with each other, so close, so understanding.

"I can't believe it, but . . . gee, it's very difficult to understand, it really is . . . I don't know how these things happen," he said.

He wasn't making any sense at all, although by some shimmering miracle, she understood exactly what he meant. But oh, she needed to hear him say the words! He was sitting with his arm bent along the back of the bench between them, as if he had his guard up. He was half turned away from her, apparently talking to the trees. In profile his face was even stronger, and she couldn't look away. She felt too far away from him, but she didn't dare move, hardly even dared breathe while she waited for him to go on talking.

She couldn't bear it.

"What things, Patrick?" she whispered.

"Oh . . . oh, you know," he said in a croaky attempt at diffidence. Then it burst out, almost a cry. "Being in love," he said.

"Yes," she murmured simply, and then he was kissing her and his arms were around her, loving her and trembling at the pleasure of holding her, and she was holding him as tightly as she could because she loved him so very much, too.

They kissed again and held each other and from time to time, kissed each other again as though they couldn't believe it could actually be sweeter each time, but it was, and then he said he would take her home and they mustn't, mustn't stay here another minute or he would start hollering out loud for sheer joy and maybe rape her in the bargain, and they laughed and kissed again and then they stood up and kissed that way, and walked back to Beacon Street with their arms around each other as tightly as they could hold and still walk, and then before they stepped onto the curb to cross the street to her house, he stopped and looked at her long and hard in the lamplight and said, "Is it totally crazy to think about getting married?"

And she said, "Oh, yes, yes, yes!" and kissed him so hard that they nearly lost their balance, and then they stopped laughing and he said, "Would you, though?" and she said, "Yes," and she went inside the house wondering how she could live through the whole night without him.

She slept soundly and dreamlessly, and in the morning she called

him to ask if it had been a dream, and he said, "Hey, I thought that
was my dream. If you had it, too, maybe it really happened!" and
they said, in the same breath at the same time, "I love you," and
agreed what a strange and unusual coincidence—a wonder, an omen—
that they had said it together like that.

He came to dinner the following week. Kate's father and mother
welcomed him as they welcomed all guests to their home, and the
evening was spent in civilized discussion of the workers' revolution,
which her father was definitely against. Kate couldn't bear the ex-
quisite weight of her secret love, her divided loyalties. She listened
to Patrick and her father agree that inherited wealth and power had
fearful responsibilities; it was the problem of defining those responsibilities which intrigued them both. "Give up the wealth, give up
the power," Patrick said calmly. "But then you give up your chance
to effect real change," Kate's father said, equally calmly.

"You're smug and superior; it's paternalistic and wrong," Kate
heard herself snapping at her father. "How can you know what's best
for someone else?"

To her horror, Patrick Casey and her father both were looking down
the table at her with nearly identical frowns on their faces.

"That clearly calls for an apology, Kate." It was her mother, to
whom manners and outward signs of respect were still more important than starvation, exploitation, or the collapse of the entire economy.

Her father and the man she loved were talking again, eager to
resume their fascinating discussion, leaving Kate out totally. As totally as her mother, who was waiting for her to apologize for a lapse
in manners as if she were a child.

"Leave me alone!" she blurted out in her mother's direction.

She heard the gasp and saw her mother's ghostly pale face, rising
at the top of a pillar of pale green silk that was too fine and too old
to rustle. Her mother murmured, "Excuse me," and left the table.
She had never done that before, never.

"Excuse me," Kate said to the two men, who didn't hear her. She
rose to go after her mother.

Anne was in her upstairs sitting room. The door was ajar. She
didn't answer Kate's knock, and Kate decided she might as well con-

tinue her round of rotten manners and walk right in. She found her
mother sitting stiff-backed on a little straight chair looking out over
the Common, far enough back from the window, of course, so she
could not be seen—as if the whole world was out there flying around
in auto-gyros with opera glasses trying to spy on her.

"Mother, I'm sorry. I came up to apologize. I was upset. I . . .
I've been upset lately. I want to tell you something, something important. Mother? Are you listening?"

Her mother turned in the chair without allowing the line of her
ramrod back and shoulders to soften. Anne Stafford's face was not
the carved stone tablet of rules that Kate knew so well from past
breaches of life's commandments. She was shocked to see how deep
her mother's anger ran. It showed clearly, and Anne had always considered showing anger one of the more serious sins. But now her eyes
were livid and her mouth was moist and her cheeks were flushed in
terrible red spots, and her words came spitting out like vicious darts
aimed at her daughter.

"You think you're in love, don't you? In love, and you think that's
all that matters! It's already made you turn on your father and on me,
hasn't it? This fine noble love of yours, I have no doubt you consider
it to be noble, rising above petty considerations of family and . . .
yes, I'll say it, why not? Class. Oh, that shocks you, my modern
democratic, radical daughter, doesn't it?"

"Only because . . . it's a word . . . he uses . . ." Kate mumbled helplessly. She was terribly confused. She tried to listen to her
mother for once. What she heard surprised her.

"You will not marry him. Do you understand why? Not because
he's Catholic; we've had Papists in this family before and managed
to survive. And it's not because he's poor or any of that nonsense. I
don't give a damn—"

It was the first time Kate ever heard her mother swear. She was so
stunned that she staggered backward a step or two and sat down,
hard, on the chaise longue. She perched on the edge, her back as
straight as her mother's, listening.

"—about his social position since he'd be elevated instantly and
you'd not be lowered one whit. Oh, I might point out that the money
would surely become a problem between you since you'd have it and
he'd be forced to use yours. He seems a proud person, and I see no

chance of happiness in that sort of situation—but that's beside the point as well. The point is that you're a Stafford.''

Anne stopped abruptly, as if having said the ultimate, there was no reason to add another word. Kate waited, but her mother turned back to stare out the window. The silence in the blue sitting room was intense. Kate longed to be back downstairs—what on earth could be happening between her men by now?—but she could no more leave this room now than she could have broken heavy chains with her bare hands. The chains were real, if not visible.

"I know I'm a Stafford," she ventured in a voice that came out maddeningly tiny. "I know that, Mother. But it's really not the same as being queen of England or something. I don't have to marry royalty, do I? What's wrong with Patrick, if not his religion or his finances or his social position? You don't know him, so how can you possibly object to him? He's got a wonderful character," she finished limply. Her mother's back was a hard audience to convince.

"Neddy Stafford's blood and determination and even his talent are part of your heritage," Anne said without turning around. Kate had to lean forward and strain her ears to hear. "His paintings are worth close to a million dollars each on the present market. Some are considered beyond price.''

"I know. What's that got to do with—"

"And you think you've got the first revolutionary in the family, you think you're so bold, don't you? You're a Stafford, Kate. There were revolutionaries in this family right here on this very ground in the war against England, and don't you forget it. Your great-great-great-grandfather, the Boston Patriot, was just as responsible for the independence of this country as Washington was, more so in the opinion of respected historians, many of whom believe George Washington was a fool and Harry Stafford the one who—"

"Mother, I'm sorry to interrupt, but I don't see what that has to do with Patrick Casey and me. This is 1936. And anyway, if our side hadn't won that war, Harry would have been shot as a traitor. You know perfectly well that there are Staffords who still consider themselves loyalists . . . Great-aunt Margaret and Uncle Daniel refuse to salute the flag and wear mourning on the Fourth of July, and what about the Staffords who went back to England and—"

"Exactly what I'm talking about," her mother said with finality.

She turned back to face Kate again. Her pale face, which had never known the softening illusion of powder or rouge, looked shockingly—to her daughter—young, warmed by unsuspected fires of emotion. Why, she was once a girl, Kate thought irrelevantly, maybe even an attractive young girl; dizzy circles of the continuum seemed to tie herself and her mother together. Kate had a sudden insight into what her mother was talking about. Young girls turning into dowagers, herself becoming her mother someday . . . her mother having once been herself, and all the other women of the Stafford and Porter and Field families, inextricably bound together by blood and chains that could never be broken—

"Listen to me. It's the sense of one's self, don't you see?" her mother was saying. "That is exactly what I am speaking about, Kate. That is my whole point. The strength that comes from knowing who you are, that is what makes us free to be what we will. Two hundred and sixty-five years of careful breeding—yes, I know what I sound like, but it is the secret of being special. Yes, special. Staffords have been Harvard presidents and artists and statesmen, and revolutionaries, too, and geniuses and industrialists, visionaries, and yes, wastrels and lunatics. . . . But it is being Stafford that makes them special. You can be anything you can be, Kate, but if you dilute the Stafford blood with unpredictable, weak, and foreign strains, you will betray all the Staffords of the past. You shall not be the one to cheapen the blood and destroy the family, Kate Stafford. I will not allow you to do that. I will have failed my own responsibility as a Porter and a Stafford if my daughter does that."

Kate was on her feet and screaming. She heard her own words shrieking out of her throat like the sound of a train whistle rushing past, far in the distance, out of control, speeding toward its own destruction. No one ever raised a voice in this house, never in this room. But Kate was shouting. She saw her mother's face, old again as it had always been . . . some remote part of Kate felt sorry for Anne Porter Stafford. But the words shrieked out.

"Your daughter! Your name and your blood and your ego, you, you, you! You don't care about me, I'm only a duty you had to produce a perfect little Stafford doll, to reflect how nicely you could bring up a proper female. I exist only to make you proud, to please you and your stuffy righteous little world on Beacon Hill! But you can't see me as a person. When I don't exactly measure up to your outdated, fascist standards of breeding and behavior, you're embarrassed, that's all you feel. I embarrass you! You don't even know I exist! You don't know what love is, not a woman's love for a man or a mother's love for her child! All you know are rules and the importance of being superior. You're an anachronism, and you don't even know it. But worst of all, you're a cold fish. A cold fish, Mother. A fine old Boston cod, dead and salted away for a thousand years, and you'll never even know it. . . ." Her voice faded away, the train gone in the night with its terribly lonely whistle silent, no more to say.

"Are you quite finished?" her mother asked coldly.

Kate nodded. She didn't look up from the Aubusson carpet which was worn from four or five generations of carefully slippered Stafford feet.

"They say that the Stafford women are sometimes blessed with the power to curse their own. Did you know that? Yes, all that nonsense about witches and curses—you never suspected that I believed in it, did you? There are many things you don't have the wit or interest to know about me, Kate. But then one never sees one's mother as— how did you put it—as a person, does one?"

Her voice was frigid; its very familiarity sent apprehensive shivers deep inside Kate. Kate wondered why she didn't turn and walk out of there. She didn't want to hear any more of her mother's words; she didn't want to stay in this room or this house another minute. Patrick was downstairs, her love, her dearest love, and together they could leave here and never come back. She would be safe and truly free, with Patrick. But he was downstairs, sharing a cigar with her father! And her mother was speaking to her, and she could never bring herself to turn her back on her mother when she was speaking, could she? She tested herself. No, she couldn't. Not a muscle would respond to her longing to do exactly that. She stood staring at the faded colors of the carpet. Her mother was saying something curious, interesting. About witches!

"If it is true, and if I have the power to bless you or curse you, then I tell you this, Kate. If you marry that man downstairs, you will never have his child. That may be a curse. It may be a blessing. It is what I wish for you."

With an almost audible snap Kate felt the lock that had held her for her lifetime break open; the invisible chains seemed to drop away. She did turn then and walked out of the room. She did not say good-bye or ask to be excused. The defiance should have turned to relief, and yet, when the door was shut between her mother and herself, Kate had the uncomfortable feeling that she was now, even now, acting exactly as her mother wished. I've got to get out of this house, she thought, blindly rushing down the stairs, if I'm to stay alive. Or I'll be salted like a cod, too. . . .

Patrick and her father were in the snuggery, warming their brandy between their palms like two cozy members of the Saturday Club. Patrick seemed to be explaining something of the rituals of the Catholic high mass, and her father was leaning slightly forward in his chair, with that keen interested expression she loved him for.

"I'm sorry to interrupt," she said. "Mother and I have had a row. I'm sorry, Father. But I want to go now, and I need Patrick to go with me."

They both stared at her, and their two faces were so nearly alike in their mixed pleasure at seeing her, annoyance at being interrupted, and difficulty in shifting attention gears to hear what she was saying that she wanted to burst out laughing. Was she about to become hysterical?

"Please," she said. It sounded very polite. It must have sounded somewhere nearly as urgent as she felt because Patrick and her father were standing and shaking hands, and then they all were in the front hall and nearing the door with the pale purple fan windows letting in about as much light as they had in prison cells; but finally they were out of there and the door was closed behind them. Kate took Patrick's hand and ran, pulling him along, across the street to the Common, along the path that cut across to the Public Garden and south. He ran with her, and she loved him for not treating the whole thing as some kind of exuberant joke. They ran seriously until they were far down Commonwealth and out of sight of the Hill. They stopped to catch their breath. Patrick waited for her to explain; he asked no questions but watched her carefully, lovingly. She knew he would run with her to the end of their strength and never ask until she was ready to tell because he truly loved her.

She leaned up and kissed him, right there on Commonwealth Avenue (their run itself had caused enough stares, but who cared? not she). He held her then, kissing her back as if they were the only two people in Eden.

"Patrick, take me someplace tonight where we can be together. All night," she said quietly.

"You're sure?"

"Oh, yes."

"Because of something that happened between you and your mother just now? Or because of you and me, and nobody else?"

She knew the right answer, the one she wanted to give, but she loved him and would not lie to him.

"She said she had the power to put a real witch's curse on us, and she hoped we would be childless. Maybe it would be a blessing instead of a curse, she said."

Patrick was shocked and showed it. Kate could see him trying to match the prosaic, dull, matronly martinet of the dining table with the vicious and exotic fairy-tale utterance. To her relief, she knew that doubting her veracity or sanity was not one of the possibilities which was occurring to him.

"And so you want to go right now and begin to prove her wrong?" he asked with a crooked little grin after a minute or two.

"Yes," she answered seriously.

Now he grinned widely and took her into his arms as if he could protect her from all doubt and unhappiness, forevermore. "It's for the wrong reasons, and you may regret it the rest of your life, but I'll not turn you down!" he fairly shouted in her ear.

"Let's go then!" She laughed.

"There's a couple of organizers spending the night in my room. Where can we go?"

"Have you got any money?"

"I'll check. Not much. Have you?"

Right there, on Commonwealth, they counted their dollars and quarters and nickels and came up with enough for a room for the night in a cheap hotel.

"You won't like it," he said ruefully. "Those places are very depressing. I wouldn't want us to run the risk of bein' sad on our first night because of someone crying next door or the paint peeling over our heads and such. Maybe we'd best wait. . . ."

"It won't matter," she reassured him in a whisper. "It won't matter. I love you. I only want to start the rest of our lives right away. It suddenly doesn't make any sense at all for us to spend another night apart. I don't care where we are, do you?"

"Let's go then."

Arms around each other, they walked all the way to Revere Beach and never even knew how far they'd gone. They laughed and smiled at everyone they met along the way and made everyone smile back to see them.

In a tacky room smelling of urine and Clorox, with an uproariously drunken party going on next door, they made love for the first time, and the second and the third, and in the morning they made love again and knew that they would never be apart anymore. They would be married right away, and they swore solemnly that they would have at least six children, not one with the Stafford chin. They almost had an argument, even while rolling in each other's arms, because Patrick said he loved her chin exactly as it was, and she said if any of their offspring inherited it, she'd drown them like kittens. Then Patrick said, and Kate agreed, that children conceived out of love as perfect as theirs could only be perfect.

The only thing that marred their first night together happened toward noon the next day, while they slept, finally, exhausted from lovemaking. A horrible nightmare crept into Kate's sleep, frightening them both awake with her hopeless, desolate sobs. She was in Patrick's arms, but she had dreamed that he was gone. She was heavily pregnant, and the child was all that was left of him. The horrible part was that in the dream she knew the child was not Patrick's at all. In the horrible dream it was not even her own but another woman's child that she carried in her womb.

Patrick held her and crooned to her, and then they made love again, and he slept while she lay awake, holding him, swearing to herself she would think only of the present and future and never again of the past.

Chapter Ten

1702: EMILY

An innocent child punished for the sin of the mother could burn in hell forever, so they said. Emily found that very difficult to believe, but she thanked God every day that she and the minister had not succumbed to their lust no matter how strong, how tempting it had been . . . and it still lingered in her mind. Then she would remind herself how lucky she was, how kind and infinitely wise the Providence that watched over her. The child could have been a bastard, sired by the Puritan to taint and forever secretly to flaw the Stafford bloodline. But how twisted and unexpected the pathways of love and lust, how curiously virtue was rewarded, after all! The minister had rekindled what she had presumed dead in herself. It had led to her sanctified marriage bed—and the child was Neddy's.

She had long given up hope of another child. This one would be her favorite, her dear, her own, her last. It was a gift from God, Emily thought to herself wryly. And well deserved, if denying the very hungers God gave you be the path to such rewards.

Both her sons and mousy little Eliza, too, had her awful chin; she hoped this one would take more after Neddy. The goodwives who were so quick with advice warned her to avoid the juice of the cranberry during her pregnancy, that its sourness would twist the infant's features. But Emily was more inclined to listen to the Indians, who, after all, had known these berries and roots and wild fruits for many generations. Maniteecha's daughter, who told fortunes and knew how to cure warts and fevers, laughed at the white women's notions and urged the drinking of cranberry juice all through the winter to avoid colds and fever. She said it would have no effect on the baby, and Emily followed this advice. It was the healthiest of all her pregnancies, and she was already thirty years old.

Ann Pollard, who kept the Horse Shoe Tavern, had given birth to her last child when she was fifty-eight, and she told Emily she had always sworn by the Indians' advice. Ann had been the very first white person to put foot on the ground where Shawmut would be settled—now that Shawmut had become the bustling metropolis of Boston, with nearly 8,000 souls, Ann Pollard at the age of eighty-two was the scandal of the town, and how she loved it. Her ribald ways and bawdy tongue had achieved the status of a civic institution. She was tolerated, with a peculiar kind of pride, where others would have been pilloried and worse. Whole congregations prayed regularly for Ann Pollard's conversion to decency and the fear of God, but still, they enjoyed the spectacle of the aged old crone swearing at the top of her lungs while she tossed a Harvard boy bodily out onto the road because he'd had a few too many ales and fired his fowling piece up the chimney.

Emily had been introduced to Ann by Mistress Abbott, who had retired from keeping the King's Street Inn where they had spent their first Boston winter. Mistress Abbott spent her days now riding around the city in her closed carriage, deploring changes and sighing for the way things used to be. She prided herself on being welcome at the finest houses on Pemberton Hill (after all, Old Edward had paid for her carriage and still settled the footman's wages every year). She would frequently persuade Emily to ride out with her, and often as not they would find themselves paying a pleasant afternoon's visit to the Horse Shoe Tavern to be regaled with Ann Pollard's wonderful, wicked stories.

Ann Pollard provided a perfect target for zealots and hypocrites alike. There were few who could not feel morally superior to Ann. Tolerating her outrageous behavior made others feel tolerant—and noble and pure in the bargain. She played her part with gusto and a tolerance for others they would have done well to emulate. Her enjoyment of earthly pleasures and happy indifference to convention had brought her five husbands, and there were plenty of good men, thirty and forty years her junior, standing in line waiting for her present spouse to make his way to heaven. No one knew how many children she had; the old lady looked ready to go another despite her balding head and wrinkled skin. She still had every tooth firmly in her head, and she walked as erect as a young peahen, and when asked, she gave all credit for her good health to six pints of ale a day and the roots and herbs of the Indian squaws.

That was good enough for Emily. She drank plenty of pressed cranberry juice all winter and never did have a cold. She drank a bit of ale as well, and it helped ease her aches and memories. In midsummer she labored for twenty hours and gave birth to a beautiful little girl. Little Sarah had a sweet disposition and Neddy's firm, rounded chin.

Emily felt all her emotions rushing forward to embrace this daughter. She remembered, with a rush of tears she couldn't seem to control, the brawling and bawling and hugging and shouting and laughing and slapping and tickling and loving of her father's brood back in the little fisherman's cottage. She would gladly have exchanged all the silks and silver, all the carpets and glass and farmland, the mahogany paneling and the view of the sea for one sticky kiss from her damp, loving Meg . . . but Meg was grown now, a mother herself twice over. For days after Sarah's birth all Emily could do was lie abed and cry helplessly and not really know why.

She had gone ahead wholeheartedly to meet this new world, bringing up her two boys in the cold and careful way of New England so that they would be strong, independent, bold, never susceptible to the irrational and debilitating winds of emotion. She had not cried at either of their births, nor at Eliza's.

The two boys were as different as sugar and salt. Sulky, silent Ward, who would materialize in a room one would have sworn was vacant, never saying a word, looking at you as if he could see your thoughts. Ward was ten years old, with the look of an old man about him, sometimes wise and sometimes very foolish. He suffered from nightmares, woke screaming to cause the entire household to tremble from the unholy sounds of this otherwise-silent child, but he would never tell what he had dreamed. A difficult child, sullen and private, unlovable. She tried. Ward would shrug when she put her hand out to touch him, as if he'd known that she did it not out of easy, natural loving but more a sense of duty, a remembrance like a footnote that Ward was her son, and still a child, perhaps in need of a caress. But he moved away from her almost absently, as if he preferred his own dark thoughts.

Grey, at fourteen, had already been to sea twice, as cabin boy and apprentice on his grandfather's ships. He was steady and dependable, quick to learn, ambitious enough to take on responsibilities beyond his age; he had little imagination and no sense of humor.

Eliza at nine was obedient, quiet, and unattractive. She cried easily. Her eyes would redden and spill over; her nose would begin to drip two yellowish rivulets onto her upper lip; her chin would quiver like an old man's beard. One could only avoid the child as much as possible and hope she would grow into a more social being by the time she left the nursery.

But this child—this minute, beautiful, serene, and intelligent infant girl—this child would be wonderful. She would find life exciting, rewarding, rich with things to laugh about and to love. In her sadness that was like a fever, Emily swore this to herself and to the baby, clutching her closely. One of her tears fell on the baby's cheek; Emily forced herself to stop crying then and begin to recover her old self again.

"Why in hell's fire anyone wants to have children is beyond my ken," her father-in-law said, by way of congratulating her on the birth of her beautiful daughter.

He was still bitter about losing Charles, although he wouldn't admit it. No word had come from Salem for years; all messengers returned with the same tale: Charles and Anne and their two sons wished nothing to do with their relatives in Boston.

"To hell with him then, and to hell with you, too!" Old Edward would storm at the innocent rider who brought the message. Then he would stomp into the dockside office, where Neddy sat dutifully hunched over account books, and rail at him for staring out at the harbor instead of keeping a close eye on the thieves and charlatans who were in their employ.

Neddy worked amiably enough alongside his father every day, coming home with the faraway expression in his eyes which meant he was already deep in his forthcoming night's work. (Sometimes after the midday meal he would start for the stairs and his studio and need to be reminded that the sun was still high in the sky and a half day's work to be done in the office.) He would take his supper, not hearing the general talk, nodding politely when addressed directly, until his family became as eager for his absence as he was to go. Up in the garret that looked out over the city and out over the harbor, he could often be heard pacing back and forth in pursuit of an elusive vision. As the years went by, Neddy had slipped more and more into the eccentric habits of a man whose mind dwelt elsewhere. He sometimes failed to recognize his wife or one of his children when passing them on the stairs. Gentle, harmless Neddy and his dreamy ways were accepted by everyone but his own father.

"If this was a civilized country, that boy would be confined to Bedlam long since," Edward grunted one evening just after Sarah's birth as he settled into the hearthside chair in Emily's chamber. He sighed and belched as the slave Garson tugged at his boots. The fire burned gently despite the oppressive August heat. It was to coddle the newborn child, of course, but the old man found its warmth a comfort, too.

"Did Neddy come home with you this evening?" Emily asked.

"We walked together from the wharf, but he never heard a goddamned word I was saying the whole time," Old Edward sputtered. "There, Garson, take them down and clean 'em, will you? Too goddamned many horses in this city; the traffic is fierce down around Dock Street and the whole commercial district. It takes forever to get where you're going, and then you come home with your boots full of manure. . . . Your husband, Emily, is good for absolutely nothing. Oh, he adds up the ledgers well enough and keeps track of the cargo and the pay, but what about the time he forgot himself and drew pictures of trees up and down the edges of the king's tax list? Trees! One of the most boring earthbound ordinary goddamn things in this world—why, you couldn't get farther from the sea if you tried. I've got important things to discuss, and no son to discuss them with. Now don't go asking me another time if your boy Grey is likely. He's young and promising, but it's too soon to tell how he'll turn out. Could go any which way.''

"Why don't you tell me what it is you're dying to discuss?'' Emily asked, her eyes dancing as she sat forward against the pillows.

Edward leaned toward her. Outlined against the fire, his whole huge body was taut and seemed ready to spring forward with enthusiasm and spirit and raw physical energy one would hardly expect in a man of sixty-five.

"The *Golden Belle* came in this afternoon from the Indies,'' he said. The excitement in his voice caught Emily, and without being aware of it, she leaned forward in an attitude much like his, listening as eagerly as he spoke.

"With news of our *Emmy*?''

"Right you are! God, if your husband had half your interest, what a business we'd have!''

"We do have a fine business, and Neddy's the only man you'd ever trust to do what he does, so be grateful for that, Edward. Now come on, what news of the *Emily S.*?''

"She's reached Jamaica with the best crop of strong young blacks yet. Our Captain Bob is the best blackbirder on the high seas, Em. By God, he swore he'd find a new safe harbor where the Africans would be unsuspecting and glad of the rum once he showed them how to use it. From what the captain of the *Golden Belle* was saying, Bob's cargo is the envy of the whole African trade, and they're offering him a bribe or two to tell where he got 'em.''

"Will he unload them all in the Indies?''

"Except for one or two of the best that we can get top price for here at home. But the sugar growers need them; they use 'em up faster than we can bring 'em over. Why? Do you need some servants for yourself? You'll have your pick of the cargo when the ship puts in at Boston, I promise.''

"No, no, it's not that. It's just . . . never mind. Foolish women's fancies. Must be the effect of having another baby. I was just thinking . . .''

"Well, go on, tell. You know I've got respect for your thinking, even when you're at your most womanish. You may be nesting, and you may be only a female; but foolish you never were nor could be. So go ahead, say what's on your mind.''

"I was thinking about those strong young blacks and wishing it didn't have to be that way. I hate slaving, taking men away from their homes and families—"

"Don't be a sentimentalist, Emily. They've no more family feelings than goats or puppy dogs."

"You wouldn't say that about Garson, or Maribess, or any of our bunch."

"They're different. Superior stock, and they've had the advantage of your civilizing influence and our example to follow. Quite a different matter, I guarantee it. The ones we pick up in the bush are wild animals. No more than oxen or, at best, a fine intelligent horse. I think you're right, Emily. Nesting has made you a bit soft. Temporarily, I hope."

"They are human, though. And we are rich enough now to be charitable. When it was a matter of our own survival, I saw it differently. Oh, the arguments I used to have with Sam Graham about slavery, you would have cheered me on then . . . but now . . . we no longer need to do this, Edward. We could give up slaving and still have enough to live comfortably—"

"When they've been traded off for the sugar, and the sugar brought home to Boston and sold to the distillers for rum, and the profits set aside for Grey's Harvard education, and Ward's (if they'll take him), and music lessons for Eliza and even this tiny little one here, when all that's been bought with the honest trading of some rum for some Africans, maybe you'll feel differently. You wouldn't want your own children to go without power or education out of sentimental feeling for some rutting animals from the jungles, would you?"

"We have more than enough, Edward. More than enough already." Suddenly Emily felt very tired, and she lay back against the pillows. Her father-in-law was lighting his pipe, puffing great black clouds of evil-smelling tobacco smoke all through the room. The baby stirred and fretted in her cradle.

"Grey will have sons someday," Old Edward said between puffs. The pipe caught, and he tossed the lit tinder back into the fire. "And Grey's sons will have sons, and they will all be Staffords. Think of that, Emily. Because of me and then because of you, there will be Staffords in the next century and even the next after that, and because of my efforts, they'll be rich, and because they're rich, they will be powerful and important men. It's no little thing," he said. The expression on his face reminded her of converts one occasionally saw in the church on a Sunday, in the grip of their newly acquired religious spirit.

"And maybe in four or six or ten generations," she said tartly, "someone named Stafford will be rich enough and powerful enough to indulge in a bit of charity or even compassion for less rich and less powerful people. Even slaves. Even black Africans. Maybe."

"I think not, Em. Sentimentality will always take second place to self-interest; that's the way of leadership and intelligence. No son of mine—" He broke off. Abruptly he leaned back against the sheltering lee of the high rounded wing of the chair.

"Grey is very much like you in many ways," she said gently, knowing his thoughts. "He loves the sea, and Maribess told me she saw him one day, in front of the looking glass, practicing to scowl exactly the way you do. She was very upset, thinks you're a bad influence."

"There, what did I tell you? They're savages and have no sense at all of what's right and wrong. Emulating me is the best thing that could happen to a boy."

Emily smiled, but her weariness was overtaking her. "I think I'd like to rest now, Edward. Your supper should be nearly ready anyway."

"But I have to talk to you. I want your opinion on the new law governing privateering. It'll affect us, Em. We've got to figure out a way around it if the Parliament settles the war against France. Do you know they've hanged a captain and four of his new crew at the Neck this week just for mistaking a Portugee for a frog ship? Hanged 'em!"

"Tomorrow, Edward. It can wait till tomorrow. It's only two days since I've given birth, and I'm still very tired."

He got up from his chair. His thick mass of hair was finally starting to lighten with intimations of age, although only here and there, slowly, reluctantly. "It's no pleasure eating alone." He was grumbling now. "I wish you'd stop having babies all the time, Emily. I trust this is the last of the lot. I miss your company when you're not there. Neddy's as good as a mizzenmast to talk to."

He walked from the room, still mumbling to himself. He is getting old, after all, she thought. I hope this family can survive without him when the time comes.

She felt terribly weary and old herself.

The infant began to fret. It was nearly dark. No breeze stirred the leaves of the tall elms that lined the square. Three other houses now adjoined the Stafford property on the crest of Pemberton Hill. The city was growing rapidly; farmland and grazing pastures were giving way to urban streets and town houses. The sprawling view from the Stafford house had become that of a city's housetops rather than a rural landscape fringed by wilderness. Emily was glad. There were still times when she missed the bustle and shouts and stinks of Liverpool.

Yes, yes, she told herself, not knowing why on earth she should be feeling so desperately low and sad, think of Liverpool and cry for your dad you'll never see again, and baby sister Meg grown and a mother herself without you to tell her the how or why . . . cry for all of that and anything that keeps you from crying for—someone else.

Sam Graham had sailed for the Caribbean islands on the very morning after he had taken her in his arms—such a very little sin!— and she had never seen him again. There had been so many things rising in her to say to him, but "It's better this way" had become her inner refrain, the cautionary air that she played over and over and over again in her brain until she thought she would go mad from it.

Little Sarah was really bawling now, squirming against her bindings and turning lobster red in her little scrunched-up face. Emily's breasts were full. She reached for the bell cord that would summon the little nursemaid, Sookie. But her hand stopped in midair.

Look at you, Em Grey, just look at you. Lying all frills and lace on the feathers of a hundred white geese, in a bed the size of the whole cottage you were born in, damned near. Too rotten rich and spoiled to get up and fetch your own bawling brat when she's hungry, got to call in an African to hoist the little creature for you.

There's no justice in a world where a twelve-year-old child is snatched from her mother and taken across the ocean so she can help another woman raise her child, Emily thought sadly. She raised herself to a sitting position, twisted her heavy hair into its accustomed knot, and swung her thin, long feet and legs over the side. She tested her strength by standing slowly, both hands holding onto the four-poster. But if there's no justice in the world, she reasoned silently and swiftly, letting her head clear of its weakness before moving farther, why, then one must take every advantage one can for oneself and one's children. The future belongs to the strong.

She walked the few feet to her child, bent to pick her up, and went to the window with the baby in her arms.

"Look, Sarah," she whispered as the little one began to suck hungrily, "that's Boston, isn't it pretty? It's your very own city. Well, I mean, it belongs to the Crown, of course, but it belongs to you, too. I think you're going to be my favorite. You've got your dad's face, even if he can't be bothered to look at it quite yet. Well, don't fret about that. As soon as you get cheekbones and shadows, he'll be sketching you and painting your portrait; you'll be the prettiest, the sweetest, the dearest . . . ."

The baby suckled and gurgled contentedly, and Emily sat on a straight chair at the window, gazing down on the graciously proportioned lawn of the square, watching the sky darken to cool the steaming city at last. Something caught her eye, a motionless figure standing half-hidden near a thicket of rosebushes at the corner. It appeared to be a young man or boy, dressed in Puritan garb, and—she leaned forward and squinted to see better in the twilight—yes, he was staring up at this house.

She stood up carefully and retreated a step back from the window, standing in the alcove with the infant at her breast. She watched the slight figure below for a long time. He did not move. There was something unsettling about a very young boy who stood so still and alone. He held his back straight and his head proud under the ridiculous high-crowned hat the Puritans affected.

Now the shadows covered the boy, but she knew he still lingered there. Little Sarah sighed deeply, brought up a noisy bit of gas, and fell asleep in Emily's arms. Her bedchamber was in darkness now; the fire already ashes. No breeze from Back Bay came to relieve the heavy summer air, even with the sun gone. But a shiver passed through her body. What was the boy doing there?

Emily turned from the window. She went carefully in the darkness to her bedside table, reached out her free hand for the steel and flint. When the spark caught the candlewick, the familiar comfort of her room bathed in the soft light made her scoff at her fears. It was not like her to act this way; childbed made one do silly things. Now she felt very tired again. She set the baby softly into her cradle and sat down upon her own bed. She reached for the bell to summon Sookie.

When the little black girl appeared shyly in the doorway, Emily gestured to her.

"Go to the window, Sookie, and look very hard out at the corner across the road, near the big clump of bushes there, and tell me if you see anything unusual."

Sookie ran to the window and threw her upper body across the wide sill, leaning on her elbows and turning her head this way and that. She stayed there for a long time.

"Well?" Emily finally called across the room to her.

Sookie obediently turned back and shook her head no.

"There might be a boy out there, a little Puritan boy. I saw him before, and I think he's still there. I want you to go out and bring him in to me. Don't be afraid. But don't take Garson with you, I don't want to frighten the boy off. Do you understand? He won't hurt you, I'm certain of that. Bring him here to me, do you understand?"

Sookie laughed out loud and nodded her head. Then she skipped from the room, and Emily lay back against the pillows to wait. Idly she wondered what had made the innocent child laugh just then, but one could never know those things. Even white girls that age giggled for no reason. The girls who had stuck their heads from the window that night in Salem . . . just gigglers, that was all.

She heard them coming up the stairs: the light pat-pat of Sookie's bare feet and the heavier, reluctant-sounding tread of sturdy shoes placed deliberately one before the other as they approached her room. They stood in the doorway. The boy was no taller than the little slave girl.

"Thank you, Sookie. You may go. Go on."

"I not scare. He scare," Sookie said proudly.

"Thank you, Sookie. You're very brave."

"He scare. I make him come."

"Yes, very good. You go and help Maribess now."

The girl was reluctant to leave her mistress alone with the stranger. "I get Mr. Staff," she offered.

"Yes, all right, that's a good idea, Sookie. Thank you. You get Mr. Stafford, bring him here."

Sookie ran from the room. The boy stood straight and proud, waiting just beyond the circle of light.

"I saw you standing out there and staring at this house," Emily said, coming directly to the point. "Will you come a little closer, please, so I can see you? And will you tell me why you are here?"

The boy stepped forward.

He had his black hat held before him, both hands clutching its wide brim. Emily nearly gasped when she saw his face clearly. He was younger than she had thought, and luminously beautiful, like a Raphael painting or one of the Michelangelo sculptures pictured in the books Neddy was always ordering from Europe. A finely drawn nose, delicate but bold; calm gray-green eyes that met her gaze levelly; mouth and throat carved from flawless marble. His complexion was nearly translucent beneath the ruddy flesh that signaled his embarrassment of the moment. His slight shoulders and scuffed shoes with broken buckles, the rough weave of his gray trousers and coat, and the weariness that rimmed those large, clear eyes with shadows only enhanced the angelic, innocent beauty of the boy. He was poor and tired, probably hungry, had come a long way and stood a long time waiting for her to summon him. That she knew at once.

"What is your name?" she asked quietly.

"Philip Stafford, ma'am," he answered. He looked directly at her as he spoke.

"Philip," she said, so choked with emotion that she could hardly speak. "Philip, I am your aunt Emily."

"Yes, ma'am."

"What has happened? Where is your mother?"

The boy looked up at her. His lower lip—not marble after all—trembled once; then he blinked rapidly. Emily opened her arms to him as she would have one of her own, but this boy stood alone, forcing back his tears.

"Anne is dead?" Emily said sadly, letting her arms fall back against the coverlet.

"Yes, ma'am."

"And your brother John? And your father? Where are they? Are they in Boston? Why are you here alone, Philip?"

"My father stays in Salem. My brother and I promised our mother we would leave that place when she no longer needed us, and we left directly the prayers were said over her grave. John has gone to sea, never to return. I am sworn not to tell the name of his ship, and I will not."

"If you are afraid of a beating, you need not be," she said wearily. "Your father's ideas of how to drive out the devil are not ours, Philip. This is a peaceful house. Did your mother tell you that? Is that why you've come here to us?"

"She said you would take us in. My brother sailed on the afternoon tide, but I . . . I have come here. If you do not want me, I will leave at once."

"How old are you, Philip? No, you don't need to tell me. I remember. You're . . . ten. Only a few weeks older than my son Ward."

"Yes, ma'am."

"Can't you call me Aunt Emily?"

"I'll try. Aunt Emily."

"You rode from Salem today then, you and your brother?"

"We walked, ma'—Aunt. We have walked for two days and most of the nights. It was very exciting. We were not afraid."

"Good. Now—"

Old Edward's swearing and stomping were the ruffles and flourishes that always announced his imminent entrance; he was on the stairs now. Emily saw stark terror in the boy's eyes, but he held his ground and showed no outward signs of fear, no particular interest in the vile sounds and threats that were coming nearer and nearer.

"That's your grandfather," she said, smiling at the boy. "He is very loud but there is nothing to fear, I promise you. Come and sit on this chair, near me. You must be very tired—"

"What the hell is going on, just when a man's about to escape the damned domestic stink of women and babies and brats for an evening's civil conversation and politicking? I'm too old to climb these goddamned stairs ten times a day—"

"I am not afraid," the boy said quietly. "But he may not lay hands on me because I am done with that for the rest of my life.''

"What's this, a little Roundhead ragamuffin? What's he doing in this house, Emily? Let's see you, boy. Too pretty for a boy. Who the hell is this, Emily? You attract babies like a turd begets flies. What the hell is going on here?''

"This is your grandson Philip,'' Emily said. On receiving a blank look, she added, ''Charles's son.''

"Charles? Charles?'' the old man repeated, stepping close to the boy and peering into his face as if he were a specimen of rock to be assayed for its value in the marketplace.

The boy looked steadily back at the giant ogre of a man, swearing and sweating, bending unpleasantly close.

"How do we know he's Charles's boy?'' Edward demanded gruffly. "Well, can he speak?'' he asked impatiently, turning to Emily as he always did when baffled or annoyed. "I don't believe it. He's probably a gypsy boy who's murdered some hapless Puritan dwarf and stolen his clothes and come here for a soft life in exchange for his lies. Where's Charles then, boy?''

"If you touch me, sir, I will kill you,'' the boy replied quietly.

"Well, there now, there's the proof!'' Edward shouted angrily. "He's no Puritan, this one. He sounds more like me at his age!''

"Well, then there's the proof,'' Emily replied shortly. She was worried about the boy, who had refused her offer to sit down and seemed to be swaying on his feet despite his defiance of the blustering old man. "Leave him alone, Edward, and let him get something to eat. He's walked all the way from Salem, day and night, and he's only a little boy, whatever else he may be.''

"What do you intend to do with him?'' Edward had backed off from the boy but kept regarding him with a leery eye.

"Feed him, of course, and give him a bed for the night.''

"You're a trusting soul. Better bed him in the stable, and lock away the silver, too.''

"I am no thief, sir,'' the boy said boldly. For an instant he stood his ground, and then his slight body slumped silently down to the floor, where he lay unconscious. The absurd black hat was still in his two hands, gripped by thin white fingers which refused to unclench, even in his swoon.

"Call Maribess, quickly, please, Edward!" Emily urged, starting to get up from her bed.

But Edward had bent and scooped the frail little figure up in one agile motion. He turned to leave, barking at Emily over his shoulder, "Stay in your bed, woman! I can't afford to have you fill this house with brats and then die on me! I'll take care of the gypsy."

The next morning, when Old Edward and Neddy had gone off to their business and the other children to the schoolhouse, Philip was brought to Emily again and settled on the bedside chair for a good long talk.

He was just as beautiful by daylight, more so because all the sad evidence of weariness and care had been lifted from his eyes and from his shoulders, or so it appeared. Maribess reported that he had eaten two great bowls full of cabbage and barley soup and then had taken on a wide rack of pig's ribs roasted to a turn, licking his fingers and saying politely that it was the first meat he'd ever tasted. Edward had bedded him down in the stable after all—the old man's compassion reached no farther than profitable, and his trust rested only with his own. The boy had yet to prove himself.

At breakfast he had stowed away half a smoked cod, a bowl of porridge with cream, and nearly a whole pot of tea along with four or five scones that went down his neat little throat as fast as Maribess could take them out of the oven. He had answered all questions politely but asked none of his own. Ward and Eliza had gotten their knuckles rapped by their grandfather for staring at the boy. Mr. Neddy smiled and said he'd like the boy for a model to draw.

After Maribess had done with her gossip report from the kitchen, Emily sent her back downstairs and settled for a chat with her nephew.

"Tell me about Anne," she said.

"My mother was mad," Philip said simply. "She screamed and beat on the door with her fists, and sometimes she would scratch from inside with her fingernails, and she cried all the time. As anyone would if kept locked in a small dark room like an animal."

"Oh, Philip . . ."

"He whipped her because he was trying to drive out the devil from her body and mind. I don't believe that's where the devil was. I don't believe in the devil at all anymore. I believe it's men who love cruelty and want to blame it on someone else.''

"You're very wise for your age," Emily said.

"I've had more than a passing acquaintance with the devil, that's all," he said. Sitting with his back like an arrow, on the edge of the chair, he shrugged his little shoulders.

"I'm glad you came to us, Philip," she said, longing to rock him and convince him, somehow, that he had no more to fear, ever.

"The elder doesn't seem glad, and it is he who will decide about me, isn't it?"

"Your father hurt him very much by leaving the family," Emily explained. "It's hard for Old Edward to forgive that. But I'll tell you a secret since you are to be part of the family from now on. Come here, and I'll whisper it to you."

Philip obediently slid from the chair until his feet reached the floor. He leaned forward warily. It was clear that no adult had ever shown simple affection to this child. Emily wondered if he would ever trust anyone at all.

"Your grandfather is all bark and hardly any bite at all!" she whispered conspiratorially. He backed off, staring at her solemnly, and she felt damned silly with that playful smile on her face. He wouldn't be an easy one.

"Ma'am?" he asked.

"I mean, you don't need to be afraid of him. Oh, plenty of people are, that's true enough. Your own father—yes, it's true. But you can be stronger than your father because you know something Charles never knew. I've told you the greatest family secret of all, Philip. Old Edward won't hurt you, not if you know that. Do you understand?"

He thought carefully before answering. She admired that in anyone; it was rare enough in grown people.

"I've vowed never to be afraid of anyone," Philip said finally. "I'll make my own way in the world."

"No, you won't, not till you're grown. You'll live here with us, and we'll make the decisions for you."

"No, thank you," he said carefully. He turned and went back to sit on the edge of the chair, facing her. "I will be grateful if you will allow me to become indentured to you. I'm strong and can work hard. Someday I will go to Harvard College. I would like to earn my way. I'm almost eleven, and with a small sum of wages for my work I can earn enough for an education by the time I'm sixteen and ready for college. That is my plan."

"Absolutely not," she said.

"Ma'am?"

"Aunt Emily."

"Yes. I don't understand?"

"You're one of us. You're not a servant, and you're not a poor relation. You're a Stafford, and you will grow up with the other Stafford children and be one of them. We will send you to Harvard if you're qualified as a scholar. The work you will do is the same as your cousins' work, and the money you earn will be invested for you as it is for them. You will inherit. Do you understand? There will be no difference between you and the others."

He thought carefully for a very long time. She watched him and waited for his decision. It was his decision, and they both knew it.

"Yes," he said finally. "That will be acceptable. I am grateful. That is the last time I will say it until I am grown and can thank you as an equal."

"Good. Now, the first thing is to get you some decent clothes. We'll have the seamstress in this very afternoon, although in the meantime, I should think you could wear something of Ward's. You're about the same size, and you can share his bedchamber, too. The two of you must become good friends. Ward needs a friend, and something tells me you do, too."

Chapter Eleven

1709: SARAH

Baby Sarah was, by some extraordinary collusion of stars, luck, and God's will, a beauty. In her face, indisputably Stafford, the stern family features were imperceptibly softened; the mouth was a hint more generous and readier to laugh; the gray eyes tilted and could turn amber or even green in certain lights. Sarah's brown hair shone like sunshine on crackling autumn wheat fields, with elusive reddish lights; it had a tendency to curl into tiny ringlets along her soft cheeks and throat.

She was quick and bright and almost always smiling. It was a source of great, gentle amusement to everyone to see how devoted the child was to her cousin Philip; she had been obsessively enamored of him, they laughed, since the very day of her birth. Only her brother Ward could resist smiling in response to the little girl's sunny presence, her earnest happiness, especially when Philip was near. Poor bilious Ward, a few weeks younger than Philip, had by the age of seventeen become a miserable, angry fellow who found no pleasures in his own or anyone else's company.

Sarah would sit for hours on the lowest step on the staircase that rose from the center room of the house, watching for Philip to come home from school. Seven years old, dressed in pristine white, her dolly in her arms, her eyes sparkling with anticipation of her idol's arrival, she could not be distracted by the teasing and tweaking of anyone—not her mother, her sister, Eliza, not her two older brothers, not even that remote and romantic figure her father. Only the object of her worship could bring the dimple to her cheek, the crow of delighted laughter. Then she would follow him everywhere about the house, chattering contentedly to her dolly in a bubbling stream of happy jabber.

He had proved to be a good-natured and hardworking boy, as pleasant as he was handsome, except when provoked by Ward. A terrible, terrifying, fathomless rage lurked deep inside Philip; his cousin's taunts or even a word or gesture from Ward had the awful power of uncapping this fury into violence. Forced to share a bed, a wood stove, a window, and the presence of each other, the two spent seven years testing the limits of self-control and civilized behavior.

A few months after Philip had taken his place in the family, terrible shouts and the sound of crashing objects against the wall woke Emily from her sleep. Rushing into the boys' room, she found the two snarling at each other from across the room, crouched like savages, each clutching an object raised in one hand. They were eleven years old, but she saw in that moment the raw power of men to kill each other—the curse of Cain, that monstrous instinct in men to invent wars. All this flashed through her mind as she swept like a mythic fury between them, a force as ardent as their own.

"Stop it! Stop!" she ordered them. She reached for the pewter candleholder which her son had raised over his head, and the boy, after a moment's hesitation, gave it over. She turned to her nephew, and from his trembling fingers she pried loose the deadly knife with which he would have killed his enemy.

She thought the whole house must come to her aid in this, but all was quiet: Neddy, of course, upstairs in his aerie, unaware of anything but his dreams of paint on canvas; the little girls fast asleep in their big feather bed, and Old Edward out carousing at the Horse Shoe, most likely. Grey was either studying or deep in sleep. No one to call upon, then.

Her instinct was to wrap the two shamefaced, unhappy boys in her arms, to put love in place of the murderous hatred she had seen. But these were men she was growing here—love and softness would not mold these two into the strong and powerful men they must become.

Her own feelings must be put away; she must think and act like a man in this moment. She alone had the burden of breaking these wild spirits, and she could not use woman's best weapon. She must think like a man now—cold and bold and unfeeling.

"Sit down," she said.

Philip, looking pale as death and shaking through his whole body, stepped backward until he came against the four-poster. Obediently he sat.

"Ward. Sit down."

Growling, red-faced, and with his hands clenched into fists, her son turned from her and went to the chair at the window. He sat down and stared at the floor.

"Look at me, both of you." She waited. Finally Ward looked at her with his surly eyes. "I don't want to know what you were fighting about. It does not matter. Do you understand that?"

Both boys nodded, slowly, their eyes on her.

"This is a civilized family, Boston is a civilized city, and you are Staffords. That is all you need to know, but it is everything. Drunkards and low sailors may fight. My father was a fisherman; he was a gentle man and a gentleman. My sons—and that includes you, Philip Stafford—will be gentlemen. Captains, not sailors, do you understand? You will grow up to lead other men. You will be rich, and that will give you power, and you must learn how to use it before it comes to you. And your sons will be greater than you, and their sons may be governors one day. That means nothing to you now, but think on it because it will mean everything when you are old enough to plant your seed rather than spew it on the bedclothes at night. There must be no occasion, ever in your lives, that will prompt you, either of you, into such wildness, such giving-way, not ever again. Now swear it to me, to each other, and to yourselves, on your word as Staffords. Go ahead. Ward, you first."

He muttered something under his breath.

"Are you ashamed to be a Stafford? Is that why we cannot hear you?"

"I swear! As my name is Stafford!" the boy shouted angrily.

"Say it calmly and proudly if you can. I mean it, Ward."

"As my name is Stafford, I swear. I'll never fight again, even with

. . . with him. But I hate him,'' the unhappy boy couldn't help adding.

"That is no one's concern but your own. Philip?''

"I swear, as a Stafford, never to fight with Ward again.''

"Never to allow your base emotions to rule your head,'' she prompted firmly.

"Never to allow my base emotions to rule my head,'' he repeated.

"Then good night,'' she said, and left them.

They could no more keep their promises than wind and water can abide peacefully together in the North Sea. But from that night on Emily interfered no more and allowed no one else to do so. No mention was made of swollen noses and bloodied faces, of noises in the night and objects crashing through windows in the maelstrom of the upstairs bedchamber. In the company of others the boys kept their silence. If little Sarah's eyes widened and teared at the sight of her beloved Philip's cuts and bruises, even she pretended to ignore all.

Sometimes in the solitude of her bed Emily lay awake and wondered what had become of the free and easy young woman she had been, quick to laughter and tolerant of weakness in others. Even her father-in-law, her old friend and confidant, was in awe of her now; when had it all happened?

Twenty years since they had stepped off the *Sally Bow* and she a fisherman's daughter with no education and hardly any sense. Boston had been mud paths and wooden frame houses, all mostly gone now through fires, replaced by stone and brick and laid out in wide avenues reaching as far as the Common Pasture and beyond, out into the Roxbury flats. Wide cobbled streets encircled daily market fairs and meandered prettily down to the busy wharves and warehouses. There was even a stone drain for sanitary purposes all down the length of Merchants Row, with talk of another to be contributed by some prominent and civic-minded citizens.

Money and power went together. Boston was the richest of Queen Anne's colonies, and her most troublesome. And the Stafford family was as important as any, with Old Edward's wealth and Emily's determination to make a place for her children in this world. The wives of their neighbors on the hill were as unprepared as she, but they had come to her from the first for leadership, which she had readily given.

The fisherman's daughter had put on fine silk shoes and become an arbiter of social rules for all to follow in the new uncharted world; only in the darkness, lying alone on her big feather bed, did she allow herself to laugh aloud at all this. In company, even if it be only a single slave, Emily's face had a stern, if not dour, expression of judgment and disapproval.

She had never wanted to be judge. How had it happened? By the abdication of others. Neddy, truly eccentric now, happy and remote up in his studio, forgetting to eat until she ordered it. Old Edward, so busy with his influence over the governor and the town's council and the amassing of more money, more ships, more power, with no time or interest for people anymore: not family, not cronies, not even women. He would die soon, she thought sadly. He was seventy-three by her reckoning, although he'd holler like a wounded bull if she ever reminded him of it. They still had their quiet moments together, mostly talking of business.

With prosperity came strangers and dangers. The Reverend Mr. Cotton Mather spoke out furiously against the liberal spirit of the city, where not only Quakers but even Baptists were being tolerated to live. In the increasing number of taverns that opened almost daily, games with painted cards were being played for high stakes; when Judge Sewall broke up a game at Edward's favorite Horse Shoe Inn, he found packs and packs of the gaudy cards strewn over his front lawn the next morning, to the amusement of many who just happened to ride by for the sight of it. (Old Edward took the credit for that escapade, much to the annoyance of his daughter-in-law, who would have been amused were it not for the example to the children.)

Adulteresses and witches were still being tried and hanged for their transgressions, but attendance at the cautionary events was lethargic and sparse. There were much more interesting things to do in Boston. The markets were bursting with goods and lively characters six days of the week; on the Common Pasture—between herds of grazing cattle and sheep on the one side, stocks and gallows trees on the other— were held flax-spinning contests and fairs with tumblers and jugglers when the weather was mild; bowling became popular, and in the winter ice skating and snowball battles filled the air with shouts and laughter. To separate themselves from the ordinary men, a club was formed, and then another, and soon all the respectable men of the city had meeting places where they could retire away from the tavern rowdies, politicians, and preachers who abounded everywhere.

As soon as the men formed their clubs, the women smartly got up their own, to read the good books as they arrived from England, to listen to music performed by experts, and occasionally to do good works among the Indians and families of the less fortunate. Life was full and exciting. There was even a weekly newspaper now, published right there in Boston, to record the uplifting events as well as the arrivals and departures of ships.

Grey finished his preparatory work and matriculated at Harvard College, across the river in Cambridge. When he was graduated, he married the quiet, near-sighted young daughter of a well-to-do lawyer who had gotten much of his fortune from representing Stafford Commission Merchants in various matters (having kept Old Edward out of prison and possibly off the gallows on more than one occasion). Edward arranged the match, pointing out to Emily that the girl's sizable dowry was a chance for the Staffords to get some of their own back. Grey took over his father's work in the firm, and with great relief Neddy retired to his studio like a bear to his winter cave, rarely to be seen again by others, even in his own household.

Ward had to plod and swear over his books to master his studies; it didn't help that such things came quickly and easily to Philip. The tension between them was a palpable presence in the house.

Grey, during his Harvard days, had commuted daily to his classes across the Charles. He had complained, along with all the other souls who had to make the crossings, of the unsafe and undependable ferries. Three boats crossed the river between Boston and Cambridge, but there were constant grumblings to the town council that the ferrymen were either drunk or asleep a large portion of the time. They missed their slips, plowed into other ships and grounded themselves on the rocky shores. They were a peril to navigation, not to mention the lives of their passengers. And their language was so notorious that many husbands refused to take their wives on crossings at all.

Seizing on this excuse, Emily decided that Ward and Philip should live in gentlemen's quarters during their college years. Separate quarters, at last. The feeling that the siege was lifted was gratifying to all except seven-year-old Sarah when the two young men received their certificates of completion from Boston Public Latin School and went off (by carriage, with all their trunks and one servant each, the long way around the Neck) to enter at Harvard College.

And to everyone's complete astonishment, sniveling little Eliza received a proposal of marriage on her sixteenth birthday, from George Porter, apprentice to an architect. A fine wedding was held, the finest Boston had yet seen, with extravagant decoration, feasting, wines, wedding gifts, and trousseau making up in part for Emily's relief at her elder daughter's having somehow attracted a sensible and respectable young man. She prevailed upon Old Edward to build a home for them, on the other side of Boston, and thoughtfully made certain it had many bedchambers, for something told her (accurately) that Eliza and George Porter would procreate obscenely.

Suddenly, all were gone now, except the littlest one, and even lively, mischievous Sarah was subdued, missing her adored Philip.

It was in Sarah that Emily saw herself—and her little sister Meg as well—with all the raw beauties and hurts she had thought well left behind in her own dead-and-gone childhood. Love burst from Sarah without inhibition; she was the only one of the children who loved hugging and kissing, loved being thrown high in the air (by Philip; the other boys and men of the house did not play childish games), and loved nestling in her mother's lap. Her full rosebud lips laughed easily and touched, deep inside Emily, bittersweet longings for what she herself might have been and was not.

Sarah's boisterous, loving nature was a throwback to memories of Liverpool and the fisherman's cottage full of the people she had loved so well. Meg, dead of childbed fever; her dad lost in a squall, years ago now; the others with their own families, their own boats, scattered in search of whatever catch life might bring them . . . Emily looked at her lovely little daughter and thought of home. Boston was as different from Liverpool as dried cod from fresh Dover sole; yet here they were, and here they must remain, even if they dried up like the very cod itself that kept Bostonians alive through the long frozen winters.

"Mother, Mistress Ann is here! I see her carriage coming. May I open the door?"

The child didn't wait for an answer but threw down her sampler and rushed down the stairs in a rush and clatter. By the time Emily could set down her own work and follow, as eager as Sarah to greet her dear old friend, there was a gust of cold air into the house and a flurry of shrieks and kisses as the little girl hurled herself into the arms of the exuberant old woman. Ann Pollard was dressed in her usual bizarre costume of reds and purples, topped with a huge bright yellow bonnet. She crushed Sarah to her in a hug that lifted the child well off her feet.

"Ann, what a tonic! You're exactly what I need today. How did you know? I swear, if you hadn't come here, I would have come to you."

"And ruin your reputation?" Ann Pollard laughed loudly. She set little Sarah on her feet, tousling her carefully brushed brown hair until it leaped up wildly to fall in curls along the child's shoulders.

"Sit down! Sit down!" Sarah begged, pulling Ann's hand to lead her to the best chair in the parlor. As soon as the old woman had plumped her great frame onto the cushions, Sarah confidently climbed onto her lap, where she was cuddled throughout the conversation that went on over her head.

"However did you guess that I'd need your company today and no one else's?" Emily marveled. "Maribess! Some tea!"

"I came to thank you for the wedding gift. Do you know, you're the only real lady in this town? Imagine, a genuine silver teapot for an old whore's seventh wedding! Or is it only six? One forgets at my age!" With that, the two women and the little girl settled into the pleasure of each other's company that comes from long understanding and mutual respect.

They were an odd threesome: the eighty-two-year-old libertine with rolls of self-indulgent flesh enclosed in bawdy silks and satin; the tired-eyed, too-thin woman of eminent respectability, her rigid spine encased in whalebone; and the ruddy little girl of breathtaking beauty cuddled in the visitor's ample lap, where she hoped to be forgotten so that she'd be allowed to stay when the talk turned womanly.

"You're a rare wonder, Ann," Emily said cheerfully, settling down for a good long talk. "I hear that your new husband is fifty years your junior and that you've dressed him in crimson velvet with gold buttons and white lace smallclothes from Madeira. Every female in New England is wondering what magic potion you've discovered and whether you'll share it.''

Ann roared and shook with laughter, nearly catapulting Sarah onto the floor as her giant breasts heaved and her great thighs divided like two halves of a goosedown coverlet weighted in the middle. Sarah turned her head away from the stale rum smell of the old woman's breath, huddling happily deep in the enormous embrace.

"Magic potion, hah!'' Ann answered when her laughter subsided. "That's what they'd like, all right. Women who turn a man away with their cold lips and preachy ways . . . and when they need a bit of loving, they think to warm him up again with a drop of magic potion in his tea. Well, I'm no witch and never have been accused of it, as well you know, Em. I'm a woman, that's all, and men seem to like that as much as I do.''

"It's true, women get bitter and cold, with the fear of having babies and the ministers preaching hellfire if you have a bit of pleasure in it—''

"You sound wistful, Em, damned downright wistful, that's the word for it. How long since your man gave you a hug and a tickle, a good long slow loving, made you feel like smiling all the day after? Go on, how long since that, Em?''

"Oh, well . . .'' Emily was flustered and reddening, much to her daughter's interest and curiosity. She had never seen her mother unsure of herself before, not in her words or her actions. What was all this about?

"Come on, love, you and I used to talk to each other, when you were a bitty little bride of nineteen—''

"Seventeen.''

"And you weren't ashamed of being a woman, and human, then. Have they got to you, those damned busy noses, with their Puritan horsepies about hell and damnation if you enjoy what God gave you to enjoy?''

"No, they haven't got to me, Ann, dear. It's just that—well, there's no one else I talk to of such things, and it's been awhile since you and I—''

"I'm not prying, Em. But you can't deny you're getting that tight and dry look that comes of needing a man's juices pumped in there. Oh, I know that look, and it saddens me to see you needy. You with this fine house and all the proper folks wanting to imitate you—oh, I hear about the Hill downtown—and healthy children and this little beauty here, but you're drying up, Em. Nothing I hate to see like I hate to see that. Look at my complexion, soft as a girl's despite the lines and wrinkles. You know what that comes from? That comes from—"

"Ann!" Emily interrupted. Then she said quickly, "Everything is fine between me and Neddy."

Even little Sarah understood that it was a lie. And that the interesting, if bewildering, subject was going to be changed, possibly into something more understandable. She felt Ann's big body shifting the weight under her.

"Well, I'm glad to hear it," Ann said. "Now, you asked about my James Henry. It's true he's only forty, but he's as raunchy as a stallion, three times a night, and he comes running back for a roll at midday as often as he can. He's a ship's chandler, you know. Does very well for himself, too. I've found true love, Emily, for the very first time in my whole life. True love! I thought I'd found it before, many a time, but I was mistaken. But now I know . . . and at my age! God has been good to me. So much for those hypocrites waiting for me to go up in hell's flames right in front of the First Church as an example to the world!"

Again Ann's huge flanks rolled and pitched with her spasms of jollity, and Sarah was relieved to see her mother's pinched face give way to warm, open, genuine laughter.

"I'm very happy for you, Ann," Emily said, reaching over to pat her friend's hand. "I'm glad you're proving all the preachers wrong. Let me give you more tea, and there are plenty of scones; do help yourself."

"My dear, I've been helping myself, with two hands, or haven't you noticed? They are delicious. Where did you get the recipe for this rhubarb jam? An Indian recipe, am I right? God, those savages know more about life than we do! If there's such a thing as a magic potion, it's in the earth, and they know—did you ever have an Indian lover? No, of course you haven't. Poor Mary Whatwashername, remember, years ago, your Mr. Mather caught her red-handed—ho-ho—with that lovely redskin of hers; she wore that mark on her clothes until she hanged herself, poor thing—''

"Sarah, go and find Sookie, and tell her to lay the fires in the bedchambers now. Run along, dear.''

Sarah snuggled deeper inside Ann's bounteous embrace and stiffened.

"No, let the child stay. What I have to tell you will go right over her head. I promise, no more jests about such things. I know, and the child surely knows, that you're the most faithful wife in Boston. Let her stay. She comforts me. I haven't had a child in my arms for too long.''

"She's only—''

"Sarah will be a woman sooner than you like to think, Emily. Leave her be.''

"Wipe the crumbs from your mouth, Sarah.''

The little girl swiped at her mouth with her sleeve. Ann Pollard laughed and jounced her affectionately. Then she caught Emily with her knowing eyes and said what she had to say.

"I know how to avoid another child, and that's what I've come to share with you,'' she announced importantly.

"Oh, Ann! You're past eighty years old. You won't have another child!''

"Don't be so sure. I was fifty-eight with my last, and I still get my monthlies.''

"You do?''

"Of course I do! But I have got a magic potion; you see the gossips aren't so wrong after all. An Indian woman gave it to me. There's plenty to share with you. Here . . .'' Ann reached for her reticule and dug inside it for a small glass bottle wrapped in linen. "Give this to your mother, darling. I can't reach that far.''

Sarah took the little vial and handed it out to her mother, who took it with a dubious look on her face.

"A drop or two of that every night before saying your prayers, if you know what I mean. It works; you can take my word for it. The red people know how to avoid large families; haven't you ever noticed that? And this is the stuff. I'm only sharing it with my best friends. Well, in truth, you're my only woman friend, Em. It works.''

Emily held the bottle in her hand, and inexplicably a tear fell on it. The drop spread in the fine linen covering as all three pairs of eyes watched it darken and widen. Emily made a hasty gesture to cover it with her palm.

''Oh, my dear!'' Ann said. She leaned forward, spilling Sarah off her lap, and held out both hands to touch Emily's. Sarah, unheeded, stood quietly watching. ''Oh, Emily, my dear! You have no need for it, is that it? How long has it been since—never mind. Come, give it back, I'll have use of it myself in time. No sense wasting it. I'd like to have a talk with that silly husband of yours—''

''No! It's not that at all. You're quite wrong, Ann. I do thank you for the potion, I shall certainly make use of it. I was just—touched, that's all. By your generous nature.''

''You need a lover, Emily. Why on earth did you let Samuel Graham go off to the Indies? Oh, well, there's no understanding the preferences of zealots, although I did think he had more man in him than most of them—''

''That's enough, Ann.''

''Eh? What's wrong?''

''I won't have any more of this conversation, that's all. Can we not talk about something else?''

''You've changed from the girl who was so eager to be alive and to feel everything. Well, I suppose we've all changed, one way or another. But it's a waste, a shame and a waste, a woman like you. Got a lot of years left, Em, you shouldn't let yourself dry up. . . .''

Emily stood up. ''It was so nice of you to visit,'' she said coolly. ''Please do drop in anytime you find yourself riding this way, Ann.''

''Not good enough for you anymore, is that it? Well, I understand. I truly do. The shame is on you, Emily Stafford, for choosing the cold proper life that makes you turn your back on old friends. Well, you're not the first to ask me to leave your house, but I never thought you'd turn so sour, not you. Help me up, will you? I'm too fat for this stiff-backed chair.''

Emily offered her hand and helped the stout old body to her feet. They walked to the door in silence, and Ann patted Sarah's cheek, bent down for a kiss, and went out, shaking her head sadly. She let her coachman lift her into the trap without looking back. The last glimpse Emily had of her friend was a whirl of purple and red taffeta against the vapid blue sky as Ann rode over the crest of the hill.

"I like her, don't you?" Sarah said. She was feeling her way tentatively, knowing something had gone wrong but not at all sure of her mother's mood.

"She's a good soul," Emily answered, too sharply. "But you needn't ever think to emulate her, Sarah, not in any way, or you'll be very, very sorry. Do you understand me?"

Sarah didn't; but she was frightened by the sadness in her mother's eyes and the tight pinch of her mother's lips, and she nodded very, very solemnly.

It was that same night when Philip came bursting into the house, on the run all the way from the ferry, to pound on Emily's door in the hours between midnight and dawn. Sarah lay in her bed in the next room, awakened by the clatter of boots on the stairs, still half in her dream about her mama having gone to fat like Ann Pollard; it was a cozy dream, and she was reluctant to give it up.

She heard her mother's bedchamber door thrown open and heard Emily cry out, "Philip!"

Sarah's body stiffened. She would have climbed right out of bed and gone to him, with the instinct of a magnet for the North Pole; but her mother's voice seemed still forbidding from the afternoon, and she waited, lying tense and listening with all her might.

Her mother's voice was muffled now. She had drawn Philip into her room, and they were speaking in low, urgent tones, which only occasionally rose loudly enough to be understood in the next room.

"Killed?"

"No, but nearly . . . horrible! Horrible! . . . Have to go away . . . have to go far away . . ."

"No! You can't leave Harvard . . . your education . . . Philip!"

Suddenly Sarah was away from her bed, pressing her body to the wall, shamelessly listening to every word.

"Philip, listen to me," her mother was pleading. "Ward has always been difficult. He can't help it. Nor can you, I understand that. Don't let it ruin your whole life. I beg you, Philip, don't let that devil win out!"

"If it's the devil I'm fighting, it's inside myself, Aunt Em. It's my own mother's madness in me, I feel it rising, and I can't control it . . . it's my own father's ragings that I hear myself shout. . . . I've got to get away; it's no good. I almost killed him tonight, Aunt Em. I almost killed Ward. . . ."

"I don't believe it."

"If the others hadn't pulled me off him, I swear he would be dead this moment. I might yet kill him another time. Please let me go. I came only to say good-bye. I couldn't leave without saying good-bye. . . ."

Sarah's eyes brimmed over with tears as she heard the deep catch in Philip's throat. There was silence on the other side of the wall for a moment. She longed to run to Philip and throw herself into his arms. Was her mother holding him close, just now, as he needed to be held? The seven-year-old cried silently on her side of the wall.

"Where will you go?"

"To London, to my brother. To work as his partner if he'll have me."

"And stay abroad, as John has? Never to come home again? I couldn't bear that, Philip. You're as dear to me as any of my own, you know that. Dearer, curse me for being an honest woman."

"You'll bear it better than if I were to murder your son."

"Don't say that."

"It's true."

Another silence. Sarah's tears stopped as she strained to hear.

"It seems I'm losing all my best friends all on this one day," Sarah heard her mother say, almost as a sigh to herself.

"Why? What do you mean? Has someone else hurt you, Aunt Em? I wouldn't for the world . . . but I have. Oh, God, I'm so sorry, so sorry. . . ."

"No, hush, Philip. You do what you must do. We all do what we must. It's hard sometimes, that's all."

"I have to go. The tide . . ."

"Yes. Bless you, Philip, for whatever my blessing is worth."

"It's what I came back for."

"Philip . . ."

"Yes."

"Sarah will miss you."

"Tell the baby to wait for me. I'll come back and marry her when she grows up!"

"Then you'd truly be my son."

"No more than I am now. Good-bye."

"Good-bye, Philip. God be with you."

Sarah slid down to the cold boards in a kind of swoon, nearly fainting with the knowledge that Philip was going away and that he would come back to marry her someday.

She heard sounds like someone crying on the other side of the wall, but that must have been her own silly mistake because her mother never cried. Her bare feet were half-frozen. She got up and walked in a daze to climb back up on the bed. She lay quietly on her back with her bright eyes ablaze, listening to the tread of his quiet steps down the stairs and out of the house.

Chapter Twelve

1721: SARAH

John Stafford had prospered since running away to sea as a strong young boy of ten, boarding a merchantman that was setting its sails to catch the afternoon tide that hot summer day in '02. Trained under his father and the other stern elders of Salem, John had grown a shell hard as a clam's and inside it an unbreakable spirit. No ship's officer, no brutal conditions, no conniving mates could elicit even a sigh from him, and no work was too hard or too filthy for his unsmiling determination. The sea air seemed to scour his musty, pent-up soul and cleanse him of the strangulating conscience and piety of home; with each blow from man or nature, John Sifford reaffirmed his freedom and renewed his vow never to return to Massachusetts.

By the time he turned eighteen he had risen to command the schooner *Bilbao*, sailing regularly between England, Spain, and the Indies. Whenever he chanced upon one of the Stafford ships, John Sifford would ask the captain to bring a message to his brother, Philip, now called Stafford, in Boston: "I prosper and hope you are the same." He was not surprised when his brother met the *Bilbao* on its return to Liverpool one day seven years after their flight from Salem. He took the lad on as ship's clerk. Together, the somber, honest John, who now gladly changed his name to Stafford for the firm's sake, and his clever and handsome younger brother found trust and opportunity. Within a very few years they were able to found a European branch of Stafford Commission Merchants in partnership with their grandfather and cousins back in Boston.

In 1721 Old Edward was eighty-five but still running the firm with undiminished vigor and voice, and he ran as much of Boston as the citizenry would let him get away with, too. But the world had outgrown his unpolished ways; shrewd enough to know it, he was too stubborn to change, and he relished his reputation as one of the colony's most colorful characters.

Men of his standing wore waistcoats and well-turned hats to business, stayed aloof from bargaining and public bickerings, spent their energies directing younger men to carry on the work. But Edward Stafford told anyone who'd listen that he, for one, had no intention of ever dying and would be damned if he'd trust any spoiled young whippersnapper who'd had life easy, even his own grandsons.

Old Edward Stafford and his sharp-tongued daughter-in-law, Emily, were two of the strongest pillars on which the commercial and social structure of Boston was building. Besides the firm, which now owned the largest fleet of merchant ships and privateering vessels that plied four continents, Old Edward had founded his own bank and his own trust company to handle his own funds and those his neighbors soon began entrusting to him, and he had purchased large tracts of wilderness all up and down the New England coastline, as well as inland to the north, west, and south of Boston.

Emily at fifty had long since given up all her girlish expectations. Good riddance to daydreams and nonsense, she knew. But when she looked long and carefully at her youngest child, sometimes a sigh could still well up from Emily's throat, surprising her with its wistful, lonely sound.

If I sigh, it's for her and not for myself, Emily would vow silently. I care for her too much and worry for her chances of ever being happy.

At nearly nineteen, Sarah was so beautiful that no one could get enough of staring and admiring and wondering at her; part of the delight was her intelligence, part her cheerfulness—but then there was her flawless, translucent skin, the dark curls, and amber green, laughing eyes. There was, of course, terrible danger in such beauty (especially in New England, some said, though they couldn't say why this was so). Speculations about Miss Sarah Stafford's future became a favorite parlor game on Pemberton Hill and on North Square. Who would be the impossibly lucky fellow to capture her in marriage? And how long could such an apparently perfect creature remain modest and unconceited? Was there any young man worthy of her, and on the other hand, would such a beauty ever be satisfied with any mortal fellow, or would she lead her future husband into bankruptcy and despair?

It was well known that Sarah Stafford had already turned down every one of the young men of her acquaintance. But even the fastest-wagging tongues couldn't say it was because her looks and her fortune gave her airs. Sarah herself told the reason, clearly enough, and it was repeated like an echoing rifle shot through the stately homes: "Why, don't you know? I'm already betrothed, to my cousin Philip!"

Philip's letters, always addressed to his aunt, came regularly during the months when ships made the crossing, with welcome news of England. He wrote almost nothing of his own life, but as the years passed, a portrait emerged, as much from what he did not say as from the rumors and gossip brought by other sources. He lived the life of a wealthy and sophisticated bachelor, immensely popular and busy with affairs both commercial and intimate. He divided his time among Barcelona, London, and Paris, mingling with royalty and politicians, men of business and women of culture. The handsome and charming young man from the colonies had become the darling of all the Continent, evidently, while contributing greatly to his family's fortunes. His reputation as a lover of many famous and infamous women crossed the Atlantic to titillate the ladies of Boston, who clicked their tongues and pursed their lips and remarked that beauty in a man can lead only to terrible, terrible trouble.

"He's only passing the time as well as he can until I'm grown enough to marry," Sarah would say, laughing when her mother sought to wake her from the foolish dream.

"A joke, a teasing remark that you overheard, to your everlasting lunacy," Emily would scold then. "You were a baby, seven years old, always making the poor boy very uncomfortable, too. He was teasing when he said he'd marry you, the kind of thing one says to show one's tolerance for a pesty child, that was all. And he said it to me, not you. Sarah, do try to be a little sensible. Sometimes I think you're as silly as your sister.''

"Yes, she is very silly, marrying a toad like George Porter. I'd rather live single than have to sleep with him every night!''

"A spinster's life is just what you deserve.''

"At least I could do what I wanted to, instead of collecting furniture and taking part in the ladies' social clubs, having to worry what the neighbors think. I don't give a hoot for anybody's opinion.''

"Opinion is one thing, and presenting yourself at the door of the poorhouse every day for your porridge is quite another.''

"Women don't have to starve just because they're not married, not anymore, Mama. Anyway, we're very rich, aren't we? Just think, someday you and I might be darling old ladies together, frightening everybody away with our terrible tempers and bad manners. Won't that be fun? Much better than marrying some walleyed pumpkin just because he's got a big house and knows how to get around a ballroom floor.''

"A woman doesn't inherit unless she's widowed, and if you persist in your silliness, you'll find one day it's too late to change your mind. Beauty doesn't last forever, Sarah. If you don't marry, you'll be forced on the charity of others, like it or not. Your brother-in-law, George Porter, might take you in . . . or he might not if it didn't suit him.''

Sarah was idly weaving the bread dough into a braided pattern of two entwining initials. She flushed now and wiped her sleeve across her forehead, leaving a pale trace of flour across the rosiness like an impish mark of defiance. But she was still smiling, as ever, with her private impenetrable faith.

"If Philip won't come back to Boston, why, then I'll go to him and remind him of his promise. There, isn't that pretty? *P* and *S,* so nicely set together that when the bread rises, the two will be well married!'' she laughed, and Emily found herself smiling, too, despite herself. Sarah was her soft spot, she knew, and no help to the girl that was.

"Stands for 'stubborn' and 'persnickety,' I guess,'' she said, turning her back so Sarah wouldn't see her smiling.

"No, for 'secret' and 'post,' '' Sarah answered serenely.

Emily left off trussing the chicken and regarded her daughter with narrowed eyes. "What's this? What are you talking about? What are you up to, miss?"

"Oh, Mama, a very polite thing, you'll be proud of my manners. I wrote a very formal, discreet invitation to my dear cousin, whom we haven't seen in so very many years, to come to my birthday ball. I reckon his answer should be arriving any day now!"

"Sarah, you didn't! Well. You've certainly inherited your grandfather's brass! That's what comes of teaching a girl to write at all, is what Old Edward would say."

"But what do you say, Mama?"

Let her be happy a little while longer, Emily thought, before she has to take her place in the world as all women must, to learn to live with pain and regret. . . .

"What I say is quit fooling with that bread and set it to rise," was her answer.

"Shall I take Father's dinner up to him?" Sarah asked.

"Yes, do. I nearly forgot about him. The poor man."

"He's painting a beautiful scene, of the harbor with the gibbet facing outward, just the bare lines of a skeleton hanging there warning the incoming sailors of the punishment for pirating. It's lovely. Eerie against the sunrise at sea, and the ships waiting to come in on the tide."

"People don't like to look at eerie pictures," Emily commented.

"Ah, but it is lovely. You ought to go up and have a look at it, Mama."

"Mr. Southy wants his portrait done and has offered your father forty guineas to do the job. But he'd rather stay in that room by himself and paint skeletons hanging on a gibbet."

"That's only a tiny part of the painting, Mama. It's mostly the sunrise and the sea and all of Boston Harbor below. It's truly lovely. And aren't we lucky that we don't need the forty guineas, so Papa can paint what makes him happy?"

Echoes of her own voice, long ago . . . Emily spoke more sharply now than she meant to. "I'll see it when it's brought down to be stored with all the other lovely pictures that have made your father happy all these years."

"I'll take him some Indian pudding. He loves that. And, Mama, can we walk up Copp's Hill for some more cornmeal this afternoon? We're running low."

"And such a fine view from the mill at the top of the hill, eh? One can see all the ships entering the harbor."

"That's true." Sarah grinned. "What a pleasant thought, Mama!"

"You have no shame at all, Sarah Stafford, and I'm at fault for letting you go on this way. Dreaming your whole life away, instead of getting on with it."

"Now, Mama, what's 'getting on with it'—breeding children? Isn't Eliza enough of a sow for you? Poor girl, she's worn out already, on the nest again for the fourth time in five years. Is that what you mean by 'getting on with it'?"

"There is such a thing as moderation."

"You should have told that to Eliza." Sarah giggled.

"Go bring your father his supper."

No letter was ever awaited so impatiently. Every Stafford vessel that came home was greeted by the owner's granddaughter, having made some excuse to be on the wharf, wondering if the good captain by any chance might be bringing a letter for her.

And one day she had it in her hand, the precious letter addressed to Mistress Sarah Stafford, in Philip's own hand.

Dearest cousin,

Your kind invitation is received here with great pleasure, having been forwarded by slow coach and packet from Liverpool to Paris, where I have been residing of late. Is it possible that my little cousin is already a woman, having reached the great age of nineteen years? Well I remember the tiny girl who brightened the days of my own youth in blessed Boston. Certainly I would not want to be absent at this great occasion of celebration on your birthday and am already in preparation for the journey. I will be bringing with me a great surprise which I hope and trust will make you and your mother and in fact all the family truly happy.

Lovingly,
Yr respectful cousin
Philip Stafford

Sarah's joy could not and would not be contained. She read and reread the letter, folding it carefully until it was nearly in shreds, carrying it in her apron pocket until the ink was nearly worn from the page, and then she pressed it reverently in her Bible, where she could read it over and over again, even in church. No one who saw the glowing cheeks and bright fiery happiness in her eyes could help being happy along with her.

Her brother Ward, now grown stout and already gouty at twenty-nine, had never forgiven his cousin for the troubles he'd had at Harvard and, indeed, all his life. He was still an unaccountably angry man, whose sole interest in life was the accumulation of money and the incessant counting of it, as overseer of the Stafford Bank of Massachusetts. "I forbid it," he announced one midday as Sarah was chattering of summer weddings and the thrill of seeing Paris, France. "I forbid it, and we'll hear no more of it!" Ward repeated. He dipped his bread into the stew, searching with it for any meat he had missed among the carrots and onions.

"Try not to be any more of an ass than you can help," his mother responded. "You've nothing to say about it. Anyway, he hasn't proposed yet. And might never," she added, with a wary eye on Sarah.

Sarah only laughed. "When are you going to take a wife, Ward? Susan Camden would have you, the silly goose."

"No more bickering," Emily ordered, and her word stood, as always. Where was Old Edward when she needed him? Having his dinner at the Horse Shoe, no doubt, and making deals for consignments of cargo in between pinching the serving maids.

"May I wear flowers in my hair for the ball?" Sarah asked now. "Blue cornflowers, they're so fine in August, and I used to make little bunches of them for Philip, do you remember? I'm sure he will remember. Oh, and Mama, won't you have a new dress made, please? For the ball?"

"Certainly not. There's nothing wrong with my blue China silk. No one's going to look at me anyway."

"Silk's too hot for August, Mama."

"Well, then you should have been born at a more convenient time. No one sensible would plan a ball in August. It's too hot for anything. Especially dancing."

"They say at the French court there is dancing every single night of the year."

"He'll regret coming back here," Ward was grunting half to himself.

"And you'll regret not holding your tongue," his mother threatened. Ward said no more and was off as soon as he had determined that there were no more oatcakes to be eaten.

The summer was unusually hot, with visible waves of humid air rising from the cobblestones, and many citizens took to wearing linen cloths over their faces to keep the fine dry dust of the lanes from their lungs. Sarah began to think of the heat as a weighted force pushing back the days so the long-awaited date could never arrive.

But finally the invitations had been delivered, and the furniture taken from the central room to make way for the ball. Tables were set up for food and drink, the floors polished and waxed, the windows scrubbed clean. Sarah's white dimity dress, with fine lace edging and a pale blue ribbon at the waist, made her feel (secretly) like a bride already when she looked at herself in the glass. All the virgins would be wearing white, of course, but she must look special, very special. A thought occurred to her that sent her running in search of Emily.

"Mama, will Papa come to the ball? Oh, he must! Can't you make him?"

"My dear, people would think they were seeing a ghost. What on earth would Neddy Stafford do in a roomful of people? He's forgotten how to talk to anyone. No, let him be."

"But Philip must speak to him! And he must announce the betrothal! He must!"

"You think it will all happen on the one night, do you? Give it time, girl."

"I've waited my whole life, Mama. This is what he's coming for, there's no need to wait any longer . . . and everyone will be there. If Philip wants to have it announced, have the banns posted that very night . . . oh, can't we, Mama? But if Papa isn't there . . ."

"Then your grandfather will have to do."

"Oh. Yes! That will be fine. I'll tell Philip to speak to Grandfather instead of Father. Will he think it strange? Oh, Mama, what if he thinks that Papa is—you know what people say, a bit—well, odd? And what if he thinks it might run in the family, and . . . oh, Mama, do you think he might feel that it's a danger, that our children might be odd? What if he decides it's too risky—''

"He's your father's nephew by blood. Whatever runs in our family runs in his as well. And if you ask me, his own father is much stranger than yours. The last I heard of Judge Charles Stafford, he was gathering up all the secular books in Salem and burning them at a public bonfire. That branch of the family has nothing much to be proud of, if you ask me.''

"Will Philip want to see his father, do you think?''

"I doubt it. Now listen to me, Sarah. You're acting very silly for a grown woman of sense. We know nothing of Philip or what he will want. He was seventeen when he left here, just a boy. And he has not proposed marriage to you. Not yet.''

"Of course not, Mama. But only because he hasn't got here yet. He wouldn't propose by letter, would he? I'm sure he has too much delicacy for that. He'll take me into the garden, and there'll be moonlight—there's to be a waxing moon that night—and we'll hear the music from the ball behind us . . . it will be very romantic, Mama. And then . . .''

"Romantic! Where do you get such ideas?''

"How did Papa propose to you? Tell!''

"On the quay in Liverpool, with the smell of fish around. It was broad daylight, and the only music was the farting of the donkeys pulling their carts along.''

"But you didn't hear it because you were so much in love!'' Sarah sighed.

"Well, if I was, look where it got me.''

On the second of August the summer doldrums set in, and scores of tall ships stood motionless and becalmed off the Cape, waiting for the wind. Boston itself seemed to be holding its breath; nothing stirred in the city now. Idlers lounged in the shade up and down the wharves and in the market stalls; the houses kept their shutters tightly closed against the deadly sun. No leaf stirred.

On the morning of the ball Sarah woke with the first rooster's crow. Tonight, she thought. Tonight all my dreams will begin to come true. There will be a wind, I can feel it coming, and it will blow Philip home to me, and he'll whirl me in his arms, and I'll be his bride by the time those crab apples turn red, I swear it.

The servants carried the sucklings and birds to the baker's ovens, and both cookstoves were going in the kitchen through the scorching heat of the day. Every once in a while one of the kitchen workers would faint and be revived, but all spirits were high. The women who came to help in the preparations for the ball laughed all day at gay Sarah, who danced and pirouetted about the house on her errands as if she were an enchanted sprite, impervious to the doldrums and the lassitude that oppressed mere mortals.

When the tables had been readied and the bread was set to cool and the kegs of rum and ale brought in and the women were having their tea before retiring to their own homes to dress, Sarah took her friend Mary Catlett out to the meadow to gather flowers for the house and the garlanding for her hair.

"Come on, Mary, I want you to whistle with me. Let's go where no one can hear."

"Whistle! I don't know how to whistle!"

"Haven't you ever tried? My brother Grey taught me. Here." And she tried to teach her friend how to make that piercing happy sound.

"What do you want to do that for?" Mary exclaimed. "It's an ugly noise, I think, and anyway, I don't believe girls should do that. I'm sure my mother would be horrified."

"It's the only way to get the ships home, don't you know that? Whistle up the wind, that's what they say."

"Oh, that! It's just a silly saying."

"Listen!"

"What? What, Sarah? I don't hear anything."

"Shhh! I can hear the sailors on all those frigates and schooners out past Provincetown, hear them? The sound of their whistling, coming right across Buzzard's Bay. They're trying to whistle up the wind, don't you hear them? Now you wouldn't dare say that sailors don't know about things like that, would you? But they need some help from this side of the wind. Come on. Do it, Mary. Like this."

Mary tried her best. But she was very nervous. Her conscience was unfailing, and it told her whistling was not a proper thing for young ladies to do.

"He's got to be here on time; he's got to," Sarah said. She stood as tall as she could, knee-deep in the cornflowers and daisies and looking out to sea. She pursed her lips again and whistled the tuneless, desperate call.

"It's hot here, and my nose is going to get all read from the sun. Is my bonnet covering it?" complained Mary.

"Mary Catlett, is that all you can think of, your nose?"

"I want to be pretty for the ball."

"You want to be pretty for John Garrett."

"Well, that makes a lot more sense than standing up here making terrible noises, trying to bring in a ship with your cousin on it, when you don't even know whether he wants to marry you or not!"

Sarah stopped whistling and stared at Mary's pouting face. Then she said, in a voice so even and calm she sounded like her mother, "They say you can always tell who your real friends are in adversity. But I don't agree with that. I think you can tell your real friends when things are going well. Those who can truly be happy for you are true friends. Other are envious and can think only meanly of another's good fortune. This is the most important and wonderful day of my life, and I refuse to be sad. Otherwise, Mary Catlett, I would be very sorry, because you are not the good friend I thought."

With dignity, tall and proud, she turned and walked through the meadow toward home, leaving Mary to scramble after her. When she caught up, Mary Catlett was astonished to find Sarah still whistling, and this time there was a tune to it, and it was a merry one.

"Are you mad at me?" Mary asked.

"No, you silly goose. Now you go on home and put on your pretty new dress, and I hope John Garrett dances every dance with you. Good-bye, Mary."

Mary watched until Sarah's jaunty bonnet disappeared into the thicket of trees bordering the Stafford orchard, and then she turned toward her own house. When she got home, she was scolded roundly for having allowed Sarah to keep her out in the sun so long. "Maybe Sarah Stafford doesn't sweat," her mother said, "but you do!" She was made to wash her whole body and rest for two full hours before dressing for the ball.

Everyone said the ball was a huge success. Sarah was danced by every young man, and she seemed her usual lively, gay self. But

Philip didn't come; no breeze stirred. The cornflowers in her hair wilted early, and she threw them out into the garden. The music and the drinking and the feasting went on and on as if they were in the French court itself; silks and brocades and fine linens and laces became stained with wine and sweat. Women retired to unloosen themselves and lie down; the older men began a game of bezique in the morning parlor; John Garrett proposed marriage to Mary Catlett (he had spoken to her father the day before, as Mary well knew), and Sarah told her friend she was truly, truly happy for her.

At two hours past midnight the great news came—Edward Stafford's indentured steward came running all the way from T-Wharf, along with representatives of some of the other firms whose owners were at the ball, to report a southeast wind rising. It was cause for a toast, and then another and another, and a great new surge of energetic dancing all around. Sarah would have kept the moment suspended in time, kept the ball going forever, if need be—certainly until dawn, or however long it took.

But the heat did not lift despite the lateness of the hour and the presence of the breeze that had begun to rustle the trees. The party was restless now, already anticipating all the ships which would dock in a few hours' time. Dancing slowed, and conversation palled; the food and wine no longer tempted. People began to signal for their carriages and make their farewells. The first rays of morning were lighting the horizon, glinting on the waters of the harbor, when the carriages began making their way from the Stafford house down and around the hill.

The guests went to their homes, to sleep if they could before going about the exciting business of the day. The wind rose steadily, and the morning proved to be cloudy and overcast. The hot spell was broken; Boston came back to life. Couriers seemed to dash about the city like ants in an anthill, bringing news from the harbor. Many people, awaiting the things that were important to them, stayed at the docks, strolling about and trying not to be impatient.

"No, you may not go to the wharf," Emily told her daughter firmly. "You will not make a spectacle of yourself, flinging your body into his arms before he's had a chance to set both feet down on land. He won't want an unbroken mule for a bride, Sarah. He's used to much better company, and you'd do well to imitate a well-brought-up young lady if you can remember anything you've been taught. Set the pies.''

"Yes, yes, you're right, Mama. Bless you, you're always right, but it's hard, waiting, waiting all the time.''

"That's why God gave that work to women. Men couldn't stand it.''

The clatter of hooves out on the street sent Sarah running to the door every little while, with Emily clucking her tongue in despair, hiding her own eagerness to see her dearest nephew again. And then, just before dusk, their own trap came around the corner, and they heard Old Edward's stentorian command to the horses, who knew where to stop without his bidding and always had.

And there they were! Emily pushed her daughter behind her and stood in the open doorway to greet them. First her father-in-law, who gave the reins to the stabler and then turned to hand down a beautiful, finely gowned young woman who was in her last months of pregnancy.

"Who's that? Why, John must be married!" Sarah gasped, peering around her mother.

"Hush. Philip! Philip, my dear, welcome home!''

Emily held out her arms to the elegant figure in the maroon waistcoat and snow white jabot, who looked as if he had just stopped out of the Grand Salon of the palace at Versailles, rather than a journey of three months at sea. Philip leaped from the carriage into his aunt's embrace and lifted her off her feet with his strong arms.

Sarah felt suddenly shy. She stood in the shadow, smoothing her apron, not knowing whether to look first at Philip or at the strange, elegant, rouged creature who stood awkwardly holding onto Old Edward's arm.

Ward was following the carriage on his roan stallion, and he pulled up now with a thick swirl of flying dust. His face was very red, and he seemed angrier than usual. "You're lucky it isn't the Sabbath,'' he called down, without humor. "You'd be put in the stocks for a public display. For God's sake, Philip, either help your wife inside the house, or take my horse and I'll do it for you!''

Sarah caught only a glimpse of Philip's fine-boned face as he

laughingly set her mother down and turned back to the fancy woman.
His wife! Surely she had heard wrong, surely it was one of Ward's
cruel and senseless jokes . . . and then she felt her mother's eyes on
her and met them and knew it was true. Emily's glance held all the
sorrow and pain that lay ahead for her daughter and a warning to be
strong. Sarah felt nothing. In a kind of trance she led them inside
and suffered Philip's greeting.

"And this is Sarah, my baby cousin, my little darling, grown into
a beauty! I've been away too long!"

"Yes," she managed to murmur.

"May I present my wife, Martine," Philip said, taking the woman's
hand and facing her to Emily. "My dearest aunt Emily."

"How do you do."

"*Enchanté* . . ." Her voice was very soft, a whisper. She was
undoubtedly terribly tired from the journey, but Sarah was not inclined to be charitable. She's whiny, Sarah thought. Whatever did he
see in her?

"My dear Martine, come and sit down. You must be tired. You
are most welcome here, of course," Emily was saying.

Traitor, Mama, Sarah swore to herself. How can you do that? She's
not . . . she can't be . . . oh, Mama, don't you abandon me, too!

"Sarah, go and tell Maribess we'll have an early supper as soon
as it's ready. Go on, Sarah, go on."

"But first, Sarah, won't you welcome your new cousin? I'm hoping you two will be great friends. Martine will need a loving friend
in this strange place, you know."

Sarah dared to meet his eyes then for a beat. She quickly looked
away. His eyes were as clear and bright as they had always been, but
they didn't see.

She curtsied quickly toward Martine. Philip's wife leaned over her
huge belly to peck Sarah's cheek. She smelled of heavy perfume and
powder. Her lips were redder than nature intended, and her breath
was not quite fresh. She was not much older than Sarah, but she
looked like a trollop. No gentlewoman would wear such paints and
scents.

"Go tell Maribess," her mother repeated, and Sarah was glad of
the chance to leave the company.

"Oh, Maribess! He's married!" she wailed, once in the safe harbor of the kitchen. There was no comfort to be found anywhere, not in the warmth of the hearth and cookstove or even in the sympathy on the slave's toothless old face.

"Now, now, no use to cry," Maribess whispered. "You had a long time on the dream. Over now. You a woman now."

"I don't want to be a woman," Sarah wailed.

"Don't blame you."

"Mama says she wants supper early, as soon as it's ready. Martine . . . Martine is tired from the journey." She practiced the name on her tongue, rolling the *r* and spitting it out.

"Yes, ma'am."

"Did you see her?"

"Oh, yes. Ver' beautiful."

"Beautiful! How can you say that! You have no taste at all, Maribess. I don't know how you can think she's beautiful."

"Mr. Philip think so, I bet."

"Ha! I don't believe it. Why, she's . . . she's vulgar, Maribess. Philip couldn't like her. She must have trapped him, that's what. Why . . . I'll bet that baby isn't even his!"

"Oh-oh. You in big trouble. You better watch out. Want to taste the gingerbread? Here."

"No. It looks awful. Too much molasses."

"Oh-oh. You letting sad make you mean. You hurt, but you better watch out. Go on back there now, and you be nice."

"Nice! Why should I be nice when everyone else is so . . . so rotten! Even Philip. I hate him!"

"Oh, sure."

"I don't know why I'm standing here in the kitchen talking to a slave! You don't understand anything."

"Maybe."

"How could he do that? He promised to marry me!"

"You still a silly child, Miss Sarah. Mr. Philip a grown man, and you still a baby."

"I know one thing. I'll never marry. Never. I swear it."

"Oh, sure. How these dumplings look to you?"

"They look lumpy if you want the God's truth. Makes me sick just to look at them."

"Oh, you mean now. I never hear you talk like that before. You growin' up to be a mean, mean woman, you don' be careful.''

"I know what I'll do. I'll go to Maniteecha's daughter and get a spell. A good spell, to undo the bad one that—that whore has put on Philip. That's what I'm going to do!''

"You end up on the gallows, girl. They hung your auntie, and they hang you, too.''

"They did not hang her. That's all you know. You are absolutely full of stupid superstitions and rumors, you silly old savage woman.''

"Go tell your mama supper ready, and tell her wash your mouth with soap, too. I never hear you talk so mean.''

The old woman gave the girl a little push toward the passageway into the main house. She watched her go and sighed with the terrible heaviness of her understanding. The slave knew what could happen when sadness turned mean.

Philip and Martine had brought all their fine French furniture with them. They planned to live in Boston, where he would take over Stafford Commission Merchants, under Old Edward's watchful but finally weary eye. When this plan was revealed, Grey sighed with relief and offered to propose his cousin in the Boston Club for Gentlemen. Ward said nothing; it was clear to everyone that he felt unjustly excluded from part of his heritage. Sarah was silent, digesting the news that Philip and Martine would be a permanent fact of life from now on. Her grandfather was crass enough to remark that silence was a rare thing for Sassy Sarah Stafford.

"Nothing to say about your cousin coming home to stay, Sally? The girl's been waiting for you to come home and marry her, Philip! Now it looks like she's going to sulk a bit. We'll not have it, young missy. Give us one of your golden smiles, eh?''

"Leave Sarah alone.''

"Now, Emily—''

"Have you ever tasted succotash before, Martine? I expect there will be something strange for you everywhere you turn for a while. I know how hard it is. But we'll all help you. Won't we, Sarah?''

"Yes, Mother. Of course.''

"Now, what is this we hear about the Whigs taking over England? Tell me everything you know about this Sir Robert Walpole, Philip. We're parched for news here, as you well know.''

"Well, Aunt Emily, it's a marvelous theory, intricate and bold. A democratic system, in which—"

"Dammit, this chicken is too damned spicy!" Old Edward roared suddenly, interrupting the conversation with an unconscionably rude shout.

Everyone stared at the old man. Without further warning, his huge head toppled forward onto the table with a dreadful thump, splattering food from his dish and overturning the gravy bowl onto Martine's lap. She wiped at her dress with her handkerchief, while the others rose from their chairs and rushed to Edward's side. He was unconscious.

They thought the fierce old heart had finally given out, but the fever came, and then the pustules and delirium. Emily refused anyone else access to the sick chamber and nursed him through the night with cold wet rags and Indian tea made from roots and herbs. But he was dead before sunrise.

The pox was everywhere. The city panicked, with the dead wagon clopping through the dark nights and citizens lying awake to listen to its rumbling, wondering where it might stop, when it might stop for them.

In the long sad vigil before Edward was taken to the Burying Ground, the shrill sounds of a woman driven by fear disturbed the hush of the mourning household. The old man lay, silent at last, on a bier in the central room, and each Stafford spent hours kneeling by his side to make the final peace and farewell to him. Above, and all through the timbers of the house, night and day, ran the constant, shrill hysteria, Martine imploring her husband in French and in English to get her away from this terrible place.

The Reverend Cotton Mather and a Dr. Boylston had devised an experiment to deal with the pox, and Emily decreed that everyone in her household, from Neddy up in his tower to the stableboy with his shovel, would abide by it. They called it inoculation; it was the radical procedure of actually putting a small dose of the pox into the veins of healthy people. Most scoffed at it, but long ago a Puritan minister had told Emily to trust the Reverend Cotton Mather's intelligence and humanity. So great was her trust that she put the lives of her entire family in his hands now. The treatment also required that no one leave the house for two full weeks. Except for the funeral, they were prisoners there, awaiting the outbreak of the sickness if it should come, avoiding others who might be carrying it.

Ward alone defied his mother's decree and Dr. Boylston's advice; he refused the injection, saying it was barbaric, even lunatic to allow the disease to be deliberately put into one's body. Ward went each day as usual to the countinghouse, and every evening he came home with a new report on the number of cases which had struck the city that day.

"Eight hundred cases, and so much for the injections. Mr. Mather will be hanged for this, when it's all over, if he isn't dead of deliberately giving himself the pox along with all the others!" Ward announced angrily one night.

"But surely there are records being kept, and surely the inoculations are proving to be helpful, or so I've heard," Philip said with keen interest.

Ward turned on him with the full rage of all the unresolved hatred of years. "It's you who brought the pox to this house and to Boston itself!" he shouted. "Judas!"

"Stop it," Emily said quietly, but there was no stopping the rage now that it was unleashed again. Ward ranted and accused, and Martine sobbed, and Philip swore he would never fight his cousin again, and Sarah listened in terror that a duel would be provoked between her brother and her beloved, and Emily kept silent as long as she was able.

Suddenly she stood, an old woman now, but ramrod-straight and awesome in her own contained fury. The shouting stopped.

"Leave this house, Ward, and stay far away. You are the devil's child and not my own."

Ward stared at her and saw that she meant it. He growled low in his throat and turned to go. From the doorway he turned and spit his final challenge to Philip.

"I'll be at the Bowsprit Tavern if you're man enough." And then he was gone. A chilling draft of air ran through the house with the slamming of the front door.

"I cause you pain whenever I show up, Aunt Emily. I'm so sorry, so deeply sorry. I never should have come back here."

"This is your home, Philip, and you are welcome always," she answered wearily. "I feel love for you and nothing but coldness for that one, my son or not. It's true. Now that Old Edward is gone, someone has to speak the truth in this house."

"Oh, Mama!" Sarah cried, going to comfort her, but Emily shrugged her away.

"I'm going to bed," she said. She took a candle and turned to the stairs, with an old woman's gait.

Just before dawn Philip tiptoed from his sleeping wife's side, prepared his pistol, and went out to meet his cousin. It was his plan to aim high and to reconcile his cousin and aunt by his own death, if necessary.

But the Bowsprit Tavern was barred and shut. He roused the proprietor, who called down from the window above that the pox had broken out that very night in the public room below. Young Ward Stafford had come in feverish and apoplectic and had fallen dead in the company of his companions, who had run for their lives to their homes. The tavern was closed until the epidemic was done with. The proprietor's wife refused to clean the mess, fearful of contracting the pox. Ward Stafford had been carted off in the dead wagon to be buried in the common grave near the pesthouse on Spectacle Island. There was no time for amenities and family sentiment in these terrifying times.

Philip broke the news to Emily at once, knocking on her chamber door to waken her. She showed no feeling. Grey proposed bribery to retrieve his brother's body for proper burial alongside Old Edward. But Emily refused. A gravestone would be set for Ward, but the grave would be empty. His body would lie forever in the pesthouse sod.

There was another victim within a few days; Grey Stafford succumbed, despite the injection, and the ground was opened for him near his grandfather. Poor Neddy was bewildered; no one was certain whether or not he understood what was happening. Emily helped him dress in proper mourning clothes, and he stood with the rest of the family over his elder son's open grave, solemn, silent, keeping his own counsel as he had done for so many years.

No one cried. Only Martine, frightened for herself and her unborn child, a stranger in a strange cold place, moaned through the perfumed handkerchief she held to her face. All else was silence except for the minister's droning eulogy and prayers. Even Grey's wife and children stood silent; the tears would come later.

Philip Stafford, supporting his swooning wife, was dressed in simple black now, and he seemed truly one of them again. His eyes searched for Emily's, to comfort his beloved aunt if comfort could be had. Instead, across the open grave his eyes met Sarah's.

All heads were bowed in prayer except those two. There passed a current between them in that one brief—and eternal—instant which would never be forgotten by either. A declaration, an acknowledgment, a depthless current of understanding so complete and irrevocable that it would change both their lives forever.

Part

THREE

Chapter Thirteen

1936-1943: KATE AND PATRICK

She was early. She didn't stop at the church door but went on down Hull Street toward the pleasant tree-shaded green of the old Copp's Hill Burying Ground. She opened the iron gate and went on inside. Kate Stafford felt a certain proprietary right, with so many of her ancestors here. Straightening her hat, she strolled past the Mather tomb and the Clarks, the Greenwoods, the Hutchinsons, and there they were, enclosed by a low railing: Edward Stafford and his younger son, Neddy; Neddy's wife, Emily; and three of their four children. All in a neat row, with simple unadorned stones, weathered and aged, but immaculate and still upright.

EDWARD STAFFORD (1636–1721)
EDWARD "NEDDY" STAFFORD (1666–1730)
AND HIS DEVOTED WIFE, EMILY (1671–1731)
GREY STAFFORD (1688–1721)
AND HIS BELOVED WIFE, MINA (1690–1758)
EDWARD STAFFORD III (1692–1721)
SARAH STAFFORD, SPINSTER (1702–1789)

Eliza, the elder daughter, was buried with her husband and his family, the Porters, at the Old Granary Burying Ground. Her shared stone had a shaft of light carved across it and an epitaph proclaiming that she had been "a good and pious wife."

Kate looked at her watch. Time for Janet Hawkesworth to finish her stint of guiding tourists through the Old North Church, that fine old traditional volunteer job for "good and pious" women of the Junior League. Kate had never questioned the value of such work before; now she felt impatient with the frivolity of it. Who cared whether tourists saw the steeple where the lanterns had hung for Paul Revere to see? There were much more important things to devote one's energies to. Even for wives, which Janet was and Kate would soon become. She would be a real working wife, not a good and pious appendage to some man's family tree.

She rose from the warm fresh lawn, brushed the back of her skirt, inspected her white gloves for grass stains, and walked back along the brick walk that divided the graves of the forefathers from those of their slaves and freedmen, who were neatly laid out on the Snowhill Street side.

Janet took her to lunch at the Union Oyster House, where she offered great sympathy and encouragement for the ordeal ahead. She admired Kate's courage in pursuing the unconventional life, envied her romance (having married her own third cousin) and trembled with her at the prospect of having to have "one of those talks" with her father.

There were some things that only a very old friend could really understand. Kate had grown away from Janet and all the old crowd, but of course, one didn't abandon all one's old friends completely. It was Janet who gave her the nerve she needed to talk to her father that evening.

In spite of the irreparable gap which had opened between herself and her mother, Kate had continued to appear, as she was expected to do, properly dressed and in control of herself, at 4 Beacon Street for dinner on a regular basis. No allusion was ever made, of course, to the passions which had been displayed: an unforgivable lapse, like having an itch in a terribly private place. Kate felt vaguely guilty for even thinking about it. She wondered if her mother thought about it. Probably not.

She had a Scotch and soda before dinner and three glasses of wine with the roast beef, ignoring her father's raised eyebrows. After dinner she went into his study, feeling wondrously calm, to tell him the plan.

"Members of this family have been married in St. Paul's since 1819, Kate," he said when she had finished. "Your great-uncle is broad-minded enough to accept your eccentric choice of husband and to perform the ceremony. It's an extraordinary concession and will have repercussions which may be exceedingly delicate for him to deal with. You know, boards of bishops or some such thing. Setting a precedent can be a very dangerous thing for a bishop, you know. Now your great-uncle is willing to do this for you, but instead of being grateful, you refuse! Really, it does seem as though you're being deliberately obstinate and rebellious. If the family can accept Patrick—a Roman Catholic!—into our bosom, I really cannot understand why you refuse to be married at St. Paul's. No one will believe that you are properly married at all if you sneak away to a judge's chamber. In fact, people might think you're ashamed of your choice . . . possibly even that you are marrying under duress, if you follow my meaning. . . ."

"Patrick and I don't believe in religious ceremonies. It would be hypocritical, Father. Please try to understand."

"You tax my understanding to the outermost limits, Kate. Isn't it enough that we're allowing this match to take place—"

"Father, I'm twenty years old. If you refused to give permission, we'd only wait a few months till my birthday and get married without it. That's the only reason you're going along with it, so let's not talk about who's being hypocritical, please."

"That's unjust, Kate, and untrue. I like Patrick. I recognize that times are changing. The Irish are here to stay, and I suppose it is inevitable that some of their blood should mix with ours . . . someday. . . . I might hope that it wouldn't be in my time, or in yours, but so be it. The Stafford line is strong enough to absorb a new strain now and then; it might even be good for us. I'm a man without prejudices, Kate. I pride myself on that, and you are well aware of it. I like Patrick. We all do. Although I must say I cannot understand his attitude toward capitalism. Or why that should interfere with the advantages we've offered him."

"He's not marrying me for any advantages."

"You delude yourselves if you think it's possible to be a Stafford—or to be married to one—without inheriting certain advantages. Don't put your heads in the sand, my dear."

"But Patrick turned down everything you offered, you and Cousin Henry and Uncle Fred and . . . didn't you all get any message from that? He doesn't want to be vice-president of the bank or groomed for head of the shipping or the railroad firm or any of that. I wish you could understand and appreciate his independence—it's so much a part of why I love him.''

"You may not believe this, my dear, but I do understand your admiration for that sort of bravado. It comes with youth. I'm sure in a few years—''

"But you don't understand anything! Patrick believes with all his heart in a classless society and in sharing the wealth and—all the things we stand in the way of. It's a great sacrifice for him to marry a Stafford, can't you see that? No, I don't suppose you ever could.''

"That is the most extraordinary thing I've ever heard! No, I don't believe I ever could see how marrying a Stafford could be a great sacrifice to any man. Does he say that?''

"No, of course not. He likes you. I can't understand it, but there it is. He likes you and Mother and Hank and even Edward.''

"Well, you see? There are things you don't understand; I'm relieved to hear you admit it. Maybe there is hope for your eventual maturation after all.''

"Oh, Father, I do love you!''

"No need to get emotional and sentimental now. You know, the Saturday Morning Club has asked me to speak on the subject of the Communist threat. I'm certain it's because I'm the only member actually privy to the workings of a true radical mind. Isn't that interesting? I intend to sit down with Patrick one evening next week to map out my speech. It's quite an advantage, in a way, to have an articulate young radical right on my own doorstep, so to speak.''

Kate sighed.

"What I'm trying to say, Kate, is that . . . well, you and Patrick have my blessing. I hope life will not be too difficult for you on the interesting path you have chosen. And of course, you can always come home. Both of you.''

Kate's eyes unexpectedly misted over. Her father cleared his throat.

"Now your trust fund, of course, will continue. There's no way you can ever touch the capital, as you know, but the income should be adequate to—''

"Patrick and I don't want it, Father. We won't touch it, not ever."

"What? By God, I believe you're actually trying to convince me that you are too young and too foolish to leave this house at all! What do you and that boy intend to live on, may I ask? Love, I suppose!"

"Patrick makes a good salary. The party pays him enough to live on. He's a very important organizer. And I'll be traveling with him, and we'll stay with other members wherever we go. We won't need to touch a penny of my money."

"And will the Communist party of America pay your bills from Stearns, and Bonwit Teller, and S. S. Pierce, and will they build a decent house for you in Milton for the hot summer months and see that you belong to a good tennis club? Will they keep you in the style to which you have been accustomed all your life? They will not, you can be sure of that."

"I don't want to live like a capitalist, Father. Not anymore. From each according to his ability to each according to his needs, that's what I believe. Why should I have all those things when other people are literally starving to death?"

"You are grinding away at my patience, Kate, and dangerously close to the end of it. Mouthing slogans is hardly appropriate for a woman and never for a Stafford. We may be parasites living on the backs of the masses, but we are also intelligent, articulate, cultured, and, above all—above all!—responsible leaders of our society, such as it is, and we do not stoop to low catchphrases and doggerel. I'm shocked and embarrassed at your silliness and can only put it down to your being a female and in love."

"Dammit, Father. For a minute there I thought we were really talking."

"I believe your mother is waiting to talk to you about some tea parties and such that she is lining up to celebrate your forthcoming visit to some anonymous justice of the peace. You have my blessing, despite all, Kate, because you are my daughter. I believe your blood and ultimate good sense will prevail. You also have your inviolable trust fund, like it or not, and I believe our little talk is concluded."

Wondering how on earth Patrick could like such a man, Kate left her father's study and went upstairs, where lists were being made and menus planned and flower arrangements considered and the serious matter of a trousseau was being debated. By calmly repeating her threat to elope, Kate managed to keep the swelling waves of social upheaval somewhere below the level of hurricane force.

Mr. and Mrs. John Wright Stafford entertained at several small teas and dinners and one modest dance, in honor of their daughter's forthcoming marriage to Mr. Patrick Michael Casey, and their friends said that the family was showing true nobility of blood and spirit by putting a brave stamp of approval on the shocking match. Others, less friendly, might have said other things, but no one of any importance listened.

The Sewing Circle was the scene of raised voices when the discussion centered on the election of Kate Stafford Casey to the exclusive group. It was traditional for a young woman to be admitted into the Circle as soon as her engagement was announced. But Mrs. Casey? Never . . . except that she was still a Stafford, no matter what name she chose to append to it, and so she was formally invited to attend a meeting—an invitation which Kate ignored. Her mother forged her name on a gracious reply, accepting the honor and responsibility. So Kate became a member, and remained so for the rest of her life.

Rose Mallory and Marco Pacelli went with Kate and Patrick to the judge's chambers in the courthouse, and afterward they celebrated with dinner at Durgin Park, which Marco insisted on paying for. They had juicy raw clams on the half shell, and then thick slabs of rare roast beef that overfilled the generous plates, and hot dark baked beans from the pot, and steaming sweet corn on the cob dripping with butter, and fresh baking powder biscuits warm from the oven, and more beer than was good for them, and then hugely mounded strawberry shortcakes with whipped cream and bright red luscious berries, and they laughed so much that the other people down the long table joined in with them, and the wedding celebration was joyous and shared with happy strangers.

It was perfect, they both agreed, as Patrick said good night on the doorstep at 4 Beacon Street. They were whispering under the lamplight, so as not to wake anyone, to preserve their little moment of being alone together, now that they were truly married.

Somehow they had promised Kate's parents that she would spend this night in her own bed, alone, in the charade of the virgin bride awaiting her wedding morning. Somehow they had agreed. They kissed each other good night and clung for a moment, and then she went inside and he walked back across Boston to his rooming house. They had their whole lives ahead of them, they assured each other and themselves.

The next morning they were married in the private chapel of the dean of St. Paul's, with just the immediate members of the family (hers) present. For the only time in his life, Patrick was glad that his parents were dead, as he stood at the Protestant altar. Then they retired to the house on Beacon Street, where the wedding party was joined by forty-five Stafford relatives for sherry and cake. At five o'clock the bride and groom were driven to the railroad station, where they boarded the train for Chicago.

Their honeymoon suite was a lower berth with a window through which they watched the world flash by. On sidings and in midwestern stations, they woke to gaze out, arms tightly around each other, thinking how snug and happy they were, how lucky, how little they deserved to be happy when the world out there was grim and gray and sad. But maybe, they told each other, and believed it, maybe their journeying through as they intended to do would make things better for everyone. The grime was on the outside of the window, and for this one night, their honeymoon night, they were happy— selfishly, marvelously happy.

Anne Stafford told a lie. It pained her to do so, but even her husband could see the necessity of it. She told a few friends, confidentially, upon being pressed for the information, that her daughter and son-in-law were taking their honeymoon in Bermuda. That was where Anne and John had gone on their honeymoon, back in '09. It probably hadn't changed a whit since then. Some things in this world have the grace not to change.

"He's a Communist, you know," she told her friends, and somehow after Anne Stafford said it, one could almost want a Communist in one's own family.

Kate and Patrick spent most of their time traveling, and when they were in Boston, they insisted on living in a rented flat in the South Boston section of town, making it impossible for them to entertain— to the disappointment of most of Kate's old friends. But generally, it was agreed, the young Caseys were truly admirable. They actually worked with unemployed men, and people who didn't even have real homes to live in, and members of unions and other dangerous societies. Boston society soon found no problem in admiring Kate and Patrick Casey while still generally condemning the Reds. No one in Boston seriously believed that these two nice young people wanted to overthrow their own class. No one knew quite what it was they were actually up to; but it was interesting fodder for endless conversations, and for that there were many who were grateful.

As for the young couple themselves, they had some troubles and some pleasures and a lot of very hard work, not ever enough sleep, and nothing in the way of luxuries. Kate found it less romantic and quite a bit less pleasant than she had anticipated, but there was pride for her every day in knowing she could do it. Things she had always taken for granted were no longer there for her to count on; she felt their absence like sticky burrs against her skin sometimes: things like indoor toilets and hot baths, balanced meals and fresh fruit, milk safe to drink, new shoes or at least new heels and soles when necessary, polite attention when someone was talking, listening to good music every now and then in a hushed concert hall in which the only odor was the occasional waft of expensive perfume, buying things that were well made instead of cheap, intelligent talk about art or anything else besides politics.

They had arguments. She accused him, sometimes, of not listening when she talked about her own expanding and often confused feelings, accused him of not really caring. He would counterattack: She was not truly dedicated to the ideals she said she would die for. He really would die for them. It struck her then that there was only one thing she would die for—him. Instead of being glad and grateful, this would make him angry. They fought, bitterly, because people who live together learn how to hurt each other. But they made up. It turned out to the relief of both of them that they did, in fact, truly love each other after all. Slowly they grew wiser about themselves and about each other. Less quick to hurt and be hurt. Tougher and smarter and—yes, inevitably—less romantic. That's the way it is. But they did love each other. She hated the fact that her father was right about some things. But he was wrong about the money. They never touched it.

After three years she was able to admit that she missed the amenities of life on Beacon Street in a fine house with servants and good art and conversation and carpets and the feeling of solid Revere silver knives and forks and spoons in her hands. But she was able to admit—and mean it—that she would rather be where she was, doing what she was doing, helping Patrick and the others organize the exploited, the downtrodden, the hopeless and poor and hungry and weary workers, rather be sleeping on lumpy smelly mattresses and drinking tap water from jam jars than sitting on Capitalist Hill living off the labor of others. Most of the time she meant it.

One night in Milwaukee she had listened with pride and love, as she always did (even if they'd had a fight), to Patrick's voice ringing across a crowded auditorium to men and women who needed to hear what he said. Kate had passed out the leaflets telling where and how to join the just-forming local, and then she had sat for two and a half hours in an airless, windowless room listening to Patrick fire up the lagging workers, while a thin, unsmiling woman blew cigarette smoke in her face. They had finally been taken to the room that was theirs for the night, and she thought: Well, there's one good thing about being this tired. I'm too exhausted to give a damn how lousy the room is. But she did loathe the sight of the little china pot under the plain iron bedstead. It meant going outside, down a flight of stairs and along the dark corridor she had seen when they came in the house, through the back door to a yard that was sure to be cluttered with parts of old jalopies and wringers from washing machines and then the squalid horrible outhouse, with a wide disease-germinating wooden seat and two holes carved in it. In a classless society, she reminded herself as she peeled off her dress and slip and pulled the green cotton nightgown over her head, in a truly free and equal world, everybody will have beautiful indoor plumbing. And then the thought struck her: Or will everybody have this instead? Which will it be, and how can we make sure we end up on the right side?

There were times when she could share such outrageous and unworthy thoughts with Patrick, and they'd laugh together until they got really silly and giggly and cuddly. But the times were harder and harder, everywhere they went, and the laughs were few now and longer between. Sometimes Kate feared, to her secret shame, that she was not serious enough. Something in her wanted to be gay and lighthearted. She tried to keep it under control.

Patrick peed in the china pot, threw his clothes on the straight-backed chair in the corner, and fell across the bed. Standing there in her nightgown and big floppy rubber galoshes with the tin buckles, Kate considered the potty for a minute, knew she never could, and sighed loudly. Then she put on her coat again, took the flashlight, and went on out.

"God damn it to hell," she was muttering as she came back inside the room a few minutes later. She shook the light dusting of snow from her hair, hung her coat on a nail inside the door, and kicked off the goddamned galoshes.

Patrick opened his sleepy eyes. "Poor baby," he murmured, "iz-zat snowing?"

"It's not that," she said crossly. "It's the curse." She jumped into the bed, and Patrick obligingly moved out of the spot he had warmed up. She snuggled against him and reached across his chest to pull the switch on the paper-covered lamp. Pale neon from a store or beanery nearby wrapped their room in cool comfortless blue. But Patrick's body was warm, and he turned to take her in his arms.

"I know," he murmured sympathetically.

"Curse," she repeated, sniffing, "that's really the name for it all right. I'll never forgive her," she swore, half to herself.

"Who?"

"My mother, of course. Who did you think?"

"What's your mother got to do with it?"

"She's the one who put a curse on us. She said we'd never have a child, and what I can't stand is for her to be right."

"Oh, come on, honey. Even your mother doesn't have that much power. But . . . don't be too sad, Kate. Maybe it's best not to bring a child into this rotten goddamned fascist world after all."

Kate rolled over and stared at him in the semidarkness. She reached out her arms to hold him tightly and buried her face in the smooth haven of his shoulder.

"I should have gone to Spain," he said after a minute.

"So you could be dragged out of a hospital and be shot like Jerry Cameron?" she whispered fiercely, holding him to her. They had just had news of their friend that day. He had been wounded at the Alcazar, and they had thought he was safe in the hospital. But the Fascists had dragged him out and lined him up with other foreign volunteers against the post office wall in Madrid and killed him.

"Before it was all lost . . . there might have been something. Men like me, staying over here where it was safe, doing a lot of talking instead of being where it might have counted. Maybe it wouldn't have all been lost if—"

"But the party ordered you to stay here. And they were right. You're much more important to the cause organizing workers than you would be getting yourself lined up against a wall and shot."

"Here, turn on your side and I'll rub your back. I know where it hurts. There, how's that? I love you, Katie. But I'm glad we're not having a child now. Hitler's going to go into Poland, I'm sure of it. He's asking for a corridor to Danzig, and they won't give it to him. He'll go in and take the whole country. Oh, God, and if there's any decency left anywhere in the world, somebody's going to have to stand up to him. What worries me is all this talk about Stalin's being willing to sign a mutual nonaggression pact with Hitler. Some of the comrades are talking about that, as if they've been asked to smooth the way for the rest of us to accept it. It worries me a lot. I couldn't stomach that, not a pact with Hitler, never. Could you?"

"Well, what could we do about it? I mean, if Stalin thinks it's the best thing—"

"I'll quit the party. I will, I swear it. If that happens."

"Patrick!" Kate sat up and stared at him. "Quit the party? I don't believe it! Everything you've worked for, everything we believe in, equality and the end of the class struggle . . . what's going to happen to that? To all of us?"

Patrick sat up and leaned away from her to reach for a Lucky from the crumpled pack on the night table. In the bluish wash of light, his face looked white and eerie. Kate cried out involuntarily, and she touched him with her fingertips to reassure herself of his warmth. He leaned against the iron bedstead, put his arm around her, and they sat together, sharing the glow of the cigarette.

"Maybe it's time to give up the party," he said quietly.

"Give it up? But it's your—our life! It's everything we believe in!"

"Not everything," he answered.

In early September, Hitler sent troops into Poland. Patrick took Kate to the house on Beacon Street, with her suitcases and paper bags full of things that wouldn't fit into the suitcases—mostly sentimental souvenirs of the places they had been and the people they had known: an album stuffed with photographs yet to be pasted in, letters from friends, mimeographed flyers advertising Patrick's appearances at rallies and meetings, copies of speeches he had made, a dried bouquet of field daisies he had picked for her one rare afternoon in Iowa, a valentine she had made for him with a bit of lace from an old discarded blouse. That was about all.

White-faced, Kate stood silently as Patrick said good-bye to her father and mother and her brothers, who had come to greet her and to see him off. The car took him to the station, where he boarded the train for Montreal. By late afternoon of the next day he called to say he was accepted as a private in the Royal Canadian Air Force.

Kate stayed silent and brooding, deliberately lonely, living for his letters, rousing herself only to deliver angry speeches to her family and all Americans for refusing to join the fight. When Pearl Harbor was attacked, she worked at the volunteer headquarters on Arlington Street long hours every day and evening. She rolled bandages, organized bond drives, oversaw the collection of scrap metal and newspapers, wrote to Patrick on V-mail stationery every day, and grew thinner and paler and more frightened as the months dragged by.

Patrick was transferred to an American Army Air Force unit, stationed somewhere in England. In August of 1943 one of her V-letters came back to her, marked with a rubber stamp that said MISSING IN ACTION across his name and APO number. Two days after her letter was returned, the War Department sent her a telegram that said her husband was missing, presumed dead. The War Department regretted deeply that Captain Casey had been shot down over the city of Bremen. He had been leading a squadron of B-17 bombers which had been highly successful in bombing the strategic target. She would receive his posthumous medal in a ceremony to be held a few weeks later.

Chapter Fourteen

1721-1734: SARAH

Standing at an open grave, Sarah experienced a moment of bitter-sweet knowledge, the abrupt end of her innocence. Her cousin Philip looked at her, and she at him and in that moment when all other heads were bowed in grief and prayer they shared recognition, shock, joy and hopelessness, discovery and loss. He loved her; they knew it in the same instant. The truth would be etched as deeply and permanently in their memories as the newly carved epitaphs in the stones around them.

She knew that her dream-filled, happy childhood had ended. Her happiness would be that memory now, of one brief moment across an open grave. She felt her buoyant spirit dying, her joy in life being lowered into the earth as surely and forever as poor dear old Grey himself. The dirt fell onto her brother's coffin. The prayers were finished. She glanced at him; he had turned his attention to his wife.

Everyone pitied Martine—swollen with child, greeted by epidemic and death in this alien place, unable to speak or understand the language. The frail Frenchwoman was holding a perfumed handkerchief to her face as she wept—for herself, Sarah thought scornfully; she's not crying for Grey, or Ward, or Old Edward, she never knew them.

Head bowed, following her mother's slow footsteps away from the gravesite on Mr. Copp's burying hill, Sarah watched Martine and Philip from the corner of her eye. He was very gentle with her; she leaned heavily on his arm. The woman was surely more to be pitied than scorned, yet the emotions Sarah felt surging through herself were not charitable.

Her face is puffy and badly rouged, her eyes too knowing, her mouth petulant; her fine Paris dress of ebony taffeta and ecru lace is out of place here. I hate her. I've never felt hate before, but I recognize it. I hate her. His child should be in my body, not that awful alien creature's. And now I shall never have a child. How will I live all the barren years ahead of me?

The family mourned. For Old Edward, and Grey, and Ward. A stone was set next to Grey's for his younger brother. No one but Ward Stafford's mother and sister and cousin ever knew that there was no body in his grave.

The season for mourning passed, with time and with the birth of a strong and healthy son to Martine. She called him Henri; Philip called him Harry. He was born on the day when the governor proclaimed the pox epidemic officially over. It was a propitious sign, all agreed, and clearly marked the time for looking ahead, never back. Black would still be worn, and no frivolities could be attended, of course; but the mood of loss and gloom was lifted with the end of the sickness and the hearty sounds of infant squalls in the house on Pemberton Hill.

Grief engraved itself permanently on Sarah's face; everyone agreed that the sad loss of her grandfather and two brothers had changed the lively beauty most drastically. She developed a nervous twitch in her left eye which often made it seem to squint, a terribly disfiguring thing in a young woman. Once known for her cheerfulness and beauty, she seemed nowadays to have a kind word for no one—and, in fact, soon became notorious for her sharp tongue and cold, contemptuous manner with the young men who would have paid her court. By the time she was twenty it was clear to all Boston that Sarah Stafford would remain a spinster all her life.

"You're jealous of poor Martine, and pettiness will ruin your life," Emily would say to her in despair. "What will become of you? You'll wither away and die alone and miserable. Is that what you want? Can't you learn to hold your tongue, to smile once in a while. You used to be so—"

"So simpy. So sweet. So stupid. I want nothing but to be left alone to my own thoughts."

"Sometimes I think that Ward's crankiness passed on at his death directly into you. You were such an amiable child, and when he died, it was as though . . . as though a body might die but the evil that lived in it—heavens, see what morbid thoughts you drive me to!"

"You're getting senile," was Sarah's cruel reply. But a personal attack always made Emily brace up and fight back, with her God-given sense of laughter.

"You're older and drier at twenty than I'll ever be," she replied. "There's the baby, waking. I'll see if I can get my senile bones up the stairs to my grandson. You ought to have a look at him one of these days. He looks just like you when he's yowling, especially if his nappy needs a change."

Despite her uncaring pose, Sarah felt a tremor of fear go through her at her mother's words. Could it be true that the old Salem witch's curse had found its way from Ward's miserable life to her own? Was she harboring some vile incubus inside herself, was the desolation she felt caused so? But if there was a cause, surely there was a cure. She would go to Maniteecha's daughter. If anyone living on this miserable earth knew how to deal with the spirits, it was that wizened old Indian crone with her mysterious eyes and hut full of stinks and brews, potions and herbal cures.

Sarah threw on her cloak and hurried from the house, ignoring her mother's call to send the wet nurse upstairs. It disgusted her that Martine could not or would not nurse her own child and that baby Harry was left to Emily's care. Emily thought of herself as the infant's grandmother, but she was not. Philip was allowing his spoiled wife to take advantage of his aunt's generous nature, Sarah thought as she climbed into the trap and ordered LeRoi to drive her to the Mohawk encampment out on the Roxbury flats.

"Come in," the old squaw beckoned from the low doorway of her hut. Had she been standing there, knowing someone would come? Did her second sight tell her who was coming, and what it was they sought? Sarah would lie because her deepest needs must stay forever secret. But she would find out from this savage woman what she needed to know. She alit from the carriage and followed the old woman inside the dark, rank-smelling room.

Maniteecha's daughter was crouching near the fire, which blazed brightly despite the mild autumn afternoon. Inside the windowless hut it was far too warm, fetid with human body smells and strange, exotic odors of cooking. A pot boiled furiously on the open hearth; the steam rose from it to fill the airless room with damp.

Maniteecha's daughter beckoned to Sarah to squat down on the blanket covering the dirt floor. The woman grinned. She was toothless. Her cheeks were smeared with streaks of dull red paint, and around her knotty throat hung a score of necklaces made from tiny colored beads patiently strung together. She wore a blanket around herself, and when she scrunched herself down, Sarah could see her gleaming copper flesh, bare of stockings or leather wrappings. The woman's feet were filthy with encrusted dust. She waited with smiling patience for Sarah to lower herself onto the blanket.

"Closer."

Obediently Sarah moved an inch or closer to the vile-smelling old woman. Maniteecha's daughter took Sarah's pale, thin hand between her own leathery fingers. One thick, hard fingernail traced both the palm and the back of the trembling hand.

"A virgin," the squaw said, grinning even wider. Her gums looked blue in the steamy half-light.

"My name is Sarah Stafford." She was testing her strength against the overpowering urge to flee. Her voice came out weak and frightened, to her own disgust.

"Oh, yes. I know. My name is Maniteecha's daughter."

"Do you have a name of your own?" Sarah asked, genuinely curious. She began to be able to breathe a bit easier, and the foul air rose in her nostrils to her brain, easing her somehow.

"Yes. But I do not tell it to you. Or to any of your tribe. Your friends have come to me many times. They seek medicine to make men love them. They pay well."

"Yes. I will pay."

"You seek medicine for love?"

"No . . . yes. Yes."

"No. You lie. I know your thoughts, Stafford daughter. Nothing is hidden from me. Don't lie."

"Then you know why I came," she said boldly. But she was frightened. This horrible old hag could read her thoughts. She felt faint. She tried to breathe deeply, but the air was stifling.

The old woman leaned toward the hearth, took a long dried reed from a basket, and lit the end of it in the fire. She waved it around her own head and then Sarah's. It smelled sweet, too sweet.

"Your body hungers for another's," the old woman said softly. She said the shocking words with such compassion that Sarah was neither embarrassed nor afraid. She felt quite under the Indian's spell, relaxed and strangely comforted. She nodded.

"But what you come to me for is not love magic. You want death magic. To poison the other, the wife. It is what you wish in your heart. That she die and you take her place."

It was not a question.

Sarah could not move her stare from the fiery eyes that held her. She did not want to accept this terrible thought, which had never entered her head, but she felt herself nodding again, slowly.

"You feel the evil now, but you hold good power inside," the old woman went on, nodding and clutching Sarah's hand. "Unopened power. Good power. Long time from now, you will make this power work over men. Not to love but to change the world. Yes, change the world! Forget murder, Stafford's daughter. You will not do murder. There is good power in you. Someday."

"But . . . there is evil in me, too?" Sarah whispered.

To her horror the old woman cackled raucously. She let Sarah's hand drop and rocked back on her haunches with grunts and whinnies of toothless mirth. Sarah was aghast. She scrambled to her feet. She looked down on the old crone, who now held up her hand, palm open.

"You pay," she said.

Sarah reached blindly into her reticule and drew out a note. She didn't look to see whether it was a pound or ten. She threw it onto the leathery palm and ran to the door of the hut. The laughter echoed after her as she ducked through the low opening into the sunshine.

All the way home, she felt cold. Cold as ice. I'll never be warm again, she thought. Warm is that stinking hut, with magic and roots and incense and things I don't understand, a crazy old Indian woman with the power to terrify. I'll never be weak and foolish again. I'll never be warm.

LeRoi told Emily, despite Sarah's warning not to. Confronted by her mother demanding to know what had transpired, Sarah told her only the last part, that the squaw had mentioned "unopened power" which would someday cause men to change the world. She scoffed as she said it, but much to her surprise her mother did not laugh.

"I do not believe that Ward was cursed," Emily said slowly. "I do not believe that the Indians have the seeing power. But I'm not such a fool as to say I know for certain that these things are impossible. The best advice I can ever give you is to be respectful of all possibilities. Never be vain enough to think you know the mind of God or even whether or not He exists."

"Or the devil?" Sarah asked.

Her mother looked at her sadly. "Yes," was all she said.

She does have fears then, Sarah thought. She is confessing to me, showing that she has weaknesses, is mortal after all. I should touch her . . . should open my arms and hold her. She has always comforted me and everyone. She was Old Edward's only real friend and has protected and comforted my poor addled father all these years. And all her children, even when we were awful . . . and Philip, she has been so much to him. What I've told her has frightened her, somehow; now my mother needs a bit of comforting herself, a touch . . .

But Sarah sat, cold as ice, and the moment passed.

Almost as though she had laid aside her armor, Emily seemed to give up her lifelong battle against troubles and pain. She was often tired now, and in the years following the terrible pox epidemic of '21, she herself succumbed to fevers and fatigue, often taking to her bed with the curtains drawn. She gave up the reins of control over the household, and the others began to rely on Sarah for order and decisions.

Philip rented a modest brick house on Beacon Street for his family. Bordering on the Common Pasture, the street was noisy and cheap; it had been called Poor House Lane until as recently as '08, when that institution was removed farther from the town's center. The constant activity in the Common and the heavy traffic all day long of vendors, entertainers, beggars, and townspeople on a multitude of errands made Beacon Street undesirable for most who could afford to live elsewhere, but Martine Stafford enjoyed looking out the window at the gaiety and life that streamed by. As for Philip, he was almost never in Boston after the first few months; he traveled nearly all the time on behalf of the family's worldwide shipping and trading business. Piracy and slaving had been given over when Old Edward had died, but there was still enough profit for all to share, invest, and still be charitable to others.

One morning Neddy Stafford was found dead in his studio, paintbrush still clutched in his hand, with an unfinished portrait of Emily as a young girl (taken from a faded old sketch pinned to the wall) half-done on his easel. They buried him in the grave that had been waiting at Copp's Hill, next to his father and his two sons.

Within the year Emily slipped quietly away in her sleep. If she protested, dying alone, no one heard her. She was sixty years old, and her life had been full and worthwhile. Everyone said so.

Grey's widow had been left with three infants, and Eliza Porter kept producing babies almost every year. Both women believed themselves to be contributing to their spinster sister's health and happiness by allowing her to care for the little ones; otherwise, how would the poor thing occupy her days? Mina and Eliza busied themselves in social duties, self-improvement, and the bringing of culture to Boston.

Philip's unhappy wife had her own dark ways of amusing herself. Her little son, Harry, learned early to flee from the smell of brandy on his mother's breath, to duck the hands of gentlemen who called on her and tried to pat his head. He ran to his aunt Sarah, who smelled of soap and talcum, liked fresh air and exercise, and never laughed at him.

It was Sarah who brought up the children, who oversaw the nannies and cooks, and who chaperoned them when they visited other homes or attended dancing classes. It was Sarah who watched them tobogganing on the hill path, Sarah who made them say their prayers at night and answered their questions and taught them their manners. Despite her oath to herself that she would go through life as a marble statue, feeling nothing, despite her tall, thin bearing and the knot of early-graying hair screwed tightly to the back of her unbending head, despite her twitchy eye, pursed lips, her silences, there was a core deep inside Sarah's stone exterior that was pure sugar water. That was a secret the children knew, one of those truths they don't even try to tell older, wiser people.

She had tried to resist him, this child who should have been her own. He looked like Philip in disturbing little glimpses now and then: a twist of his mouth; a dark curl falling just so on the nape of his neck; his eyes making her look straight into his when she would rather have looked away.

Eliza's children were growing into replicas of their parents: the girls frumpish and foolish; the boys cautious and dull. Grey's fatherless boys and the frail little girl were sweet, solemn, lacking in imagination. But Harry! That boy knew how to melt stone. As soon as he could talk, he confided in his aunt Sarah all his little secrets and private questions. He told her his jokes and thoughts and ideas; she never dismissed his childish problems, never treated him with anything less than respect despite his youth. The old maid and the little boy grew apace, loving and understanding each other. Slowly Sarah let go of her pain; slowly Harry learned to trust himself in all things.

One afternoon in April, when he was just twelve, Harry burst into Sarah's kitchen with a crumpled broadside in his hand and his face ablaze with excitement.

"A notice has gone up on the State House door—another tax on molasses!" he shouted.

"Mind your manners, Harry. Take off your hat and sit down. Here, a nice cup of tea, and I'll join you. Now, what's this?"

"The king's curtailing our trade and our distillery profits, don't you see?" he said importantly, setting his hat beside him on the bench and sliding in obediently.

"Why, yes, I do see. My mind was on something else. I have news, too."

"He's afraid we'll get too independent and not need him anymore," Harry went on. He sipped the strong hot brew she set before him.

She sat opposite. "What were you doing at the State House anyway?" she asked, trying to look stern. "It's not on the road between this house and Boston Public Latin School that I remember."

"Will you help me draft a protest?" he asked in a deliciously conspiratorial whisper.

She leaned forward and let herself smile, couldn't help it. "Of course I will. What shall we say?"

"We have to point out the political side of it. . . . Aunt Sarah! You said you have news! What is it?"

"Guess."

His finely sculpted nose—Philip's nose, exactly—began to twitch comically. His eyes danced at her as he sniffed the dulcet kitchen air with exaggerated pleasure. "Indian pudding! Sweet potatoes and . . . don't tell me . . . apple cake! A feast . . . someone's coming. Aunt Sarah, it's my father, isn't it? You always make the apple cake for him. When does he come, tonight? Tomorrow? Hooray!"

She laughed with him, hiding her own ancient, weary sadness. It was always difficult for her to see Philip, to hide the leaping of her blood (shocking in a woman thirty-one years old!) and the longings that still throbbed low in her heart. Like scars from a long-ago fever, her heartbreak should have healed and toughened and been forgotten years before this. But sometimes scar tissue is the most sensitive of all. A change in the weather—a sudden touch of summer in the air— the scent of fresh cornflowers, or the chill of early sunset might cause her terrible, unexpected pain. And always, the nearness of Philip Stafford.

She felt it in her bones, that old wariness, the need to be on guard against loving him. Sometimes she wondered if he felt it, too, if that was the reason why he spent all the long months away from Boston, away from wife and son, away from her . . . such sentimentality and nonsense! She pushed down the silliness and hoped the child never suspected it. But Harry had slipped from his bench and come around to touch her cheek with his own. His hands rested on her shoulders as he whispered in her ear. For a terrible moment she thought he might be going to comfort her.

"Aunt Sarah," he crooned, half laughing, "hadn't I better taste the cake to make sure it's right?"

She laughed out loud and shook her head at him. "And what would your father say to a cake with a bite out of it? That his son was being spoiled and his cake as well! You'd better do your lessons now, Harry. I've got more to do than sit here and jabber with you like two idle gossips."

"Then it is my father! When does he get here?"

"Tomorrow morning. He's aboard the *Emily*. The *Pride* came in today with the letter from him. Doesn't give us much time."

"A feast for my father! I have so much to tell him. I'd better compose my answer to the molasses tariff right away—there won't be time once he's here. Will you help me copy it and post it to-night?"

"Why don't you wait and get your father's thinking on it, Harry?"

"Yes, I will! That's a good idea. I'm not accustomed to having the benefit of his advice, just didn't think of it. And he'll have the latest news from London, too. Well, then I guess I'll have to work on my sums."

The expression on his face was so grim at this that it made her laugh again, and she tousled his dark hair as he set to work. Without further talk they kept each other good company, as they always did.

The entire family sat at table the next evening: Philip at the head, resplendent in the latest French fashion, which all Boston would be copying as soon as the ships were unloaded of their velvets and laces and satins and braid; and next to him his wife, Martine, her paleness hidden with rouge, her shaky hands beringed in jewels and her gown of bright blue taffeta hanging loosely on her thin frame; then George Porter and Eliza and all their brood, mannerly and quiet. At the far end of the table, facing Philip, Sarah sat with stiff back and prim lips, intent on conscientious performance of her duties as mistress of this house; at Sarah's right were Grey's widow and her three, perched like little titmice twittering and pecking at their food; then Harry, tall for his age and important, next to his father.

George Porter was asking Philip about the Molasses Act and how it would affect trade. Without being given leave to talk, Harry suddenly burst into the conversation, a young stallion rearing and snorting and unable to hold his peace.

"But trade's not the important thing!" he exclaimed impatiently, ignoring George Porter's glowering look of reproval. The Porter boys would never dare speak until spoken to. But Philip was listening to his son with interest, and so the boy went on boldly.

"England's tightening the winches to keep us under control; that's much more important than personal fortunes. The molasses our ships bring from the Indies makes us free; we can build our own economy for the colonies without help. That's what England is afraid of, that we'll become too independent. And I say we should! Break free of the Crown—"

George Porter could stand it no longer. "Outrageous!" he sputtered. "The boy is talking treason, Philip, whether you're aware of it or not. Surely we are not going to tolerate radical nonsense from the mouth of an eleven-year-old boy—"

"I'm twelve, Uncle George," Harry said politely, knowing he had his father's protection and indulgence. Philip was beaming at the boy and nodding as if something wise had been said.

"Children should be seen and not heard," George said pompously, peevishly. He cast an approving eye across his own row of orderly children, as mute and terrified as children should be.

"So you've become a politician while I've been away!" Philip said, regarding his son with real interest. "And a radical one, at that. Your uncle George is right, you know. Treason's a hanging offense still, I believe, and you are speaking treason. Are you aware of that, Harry?"

"Yes, sir."

"And it doesn't worry you? Do you hold your life so cheaply then? Or your ideals so high?"

"I'll have another glass," Martine said sharply, her accent adding slur to her already-thickened tongue. She held her empty glass up high and none too steadily. George poured it for her, and having tippled it down straightaway, she reached across the table for the flask to pour herself another. The neck of the decanter clattered against the rim of her glass as she poured. The claret spilled over onto the white damask cloth. The servant was standing by, as if the occurrence were expected; she had a towel in hand and mopped the stained cloth as unobtrusively as possible.

"There are many who feel as I do," Harry said to his father. His eyes beseeched the attention again. His mother's drunkenness at table was an overwhelming embarrassment to him. If only she would restrain herself when his father was at home . . .

"And do they speak as loudly and as bravely as you do?" Philip asked quietly.

"Some have gone underground. They don't dare speak what they feel. But they are there."

"The boy is growing up a *sauvage* . . . savage!" Martine suddenly blurted out. She leaned forward to address her husband. Her voice was shrill.

"What can you expect of a place like this, this . . . wilderness, thousands of miles from civilized people? Primitive! That is a word I have learned here. They are teaching my son to be a boor, a revolutionary . . . he will end on the gallows tree, my beautiful son who should be a count or a *maréchal*. . . . He must be taken to court, Philippe, and taught proper manners . . . you could take him . . . to better himself, his position in the world. What can one expect of a child which grows among louts and bar-bar-barians?" She belched and reached for her wineglass. "Henri must be sent to France for his education before it becomes too late. *J'insiste!*" She lapsed into French then, mumbling mostly to herself, between gulps of the wine.

Silence greeted the outburst. Embarrassed, everyone at the table looked down into his plate, except for the Porter children, who stared, and Philip, who addressed his wife quietly and not without a trace of amused detachment.

"From what I hear on the Continent, the court of Louis the Fifteenth is certainly not the place to learn civilized behavior," he said.

Sarah looked down the length of the table at him, grateful for his civility and calm. Their eyes caught each other for an instant before he looked away.

"Do tell, Philip," she heard herself urging. "We can all use some gossip that has nothing to do with politics."

His easy laugh was immediately echoed by the rest of the company, even pompous Porter, who was relieved at the change of subject.

"Well," Philip said, his eyes twinkling, "they do say that one of the king's mistresses—"

"Philip!" Eliza broke in with alarm. *"Pas devant les enfants, s'il vous plaît."*

"Yes, perhaps it is better left for the drawing room after the children have gone to bed," he agreed genially. "The customs at the court of France are not for the young, that is very true."

"Ah, oui, je comprends," Martine put in, slurring her words. She leaned forward, her arm sliding across the plate before her, oblivious of the wine stain that discolored her blue taffeta sleeve. "You make a joke to my face, that this hellhole is better than France, that the French are no good, that I do not know what is best for my son." She was crying now, and her shrill voice rose to a wail, a shriek. "I hate you, I hate all this family, all Boston and Americans!" She turned her head, leaning over so that wisps of hair escaping her combs nearly caught in the candle's flame. She was spewing her incontinent wrath at Sarah.

"It's you, bitch, who steals my son away from me! You make him to write filthy poems and letters of revolution, and you have private jokes with him, with my son. You steal my son from me!" Everyone sat stunned and appalled. Martine's shaking left hand grasped a table knife, which she clutched with whitening knuckles as she ranted on.

She turned back to her husband at the other end of the table. "Philippe, it's true. It's Sarah who does this to our Henri. She conspires with him; she ruins him. It is for spite because she hates me. Philippe, you are my hush—hush—*mari, mon mari,* stand with me against her and tell her. He is my son, mine, mine!" She began to cry, wetly, horribly.

"Martine," Sarah said calmly, "I think you had better excuse yourself and get some rest now. You're not feeling well. Hepzibah will help you to the guest room." She signaled to the waiting servant, who stepped forward to put her hands gently on Martine's shaking shoulders, to help her from the table. George Porter rose from his chair, napkin tucked into his collar.

"Yes, Martine is not well," he said. "Say good night to Aunt Martine, children. She's feeling rather ill and must—"

"No!" Martine pushed the servant away, nearly toppling her chair with the strength of her anger. "I fight for my son!"

"Well, now, Harvard is not such a bad place for an education," George went on lamely, standing there like an awkward bird, not certain whether to sit or take flight. "I myself was educated at Har—"

"I know what it is," Martine said, lowering her voice suddenly.

George sat down. "I know," she repeated. Her mouth was slack, and her eyes were unfocused; but she spoke clearly now and with the steely determination of a duelist about to make the final, lethal thrust. "My beloved husband is in love with her still," she said, flashing her glance from Philip to Sarah. "With the squinty-eyed, dried-up, ugly old spinster. Isn't it true, Philip? You are still in love with her?"

Two of the Porter children giggled in the unbearable tension. Eliza and George silenced them instantly with parental eye-threats.

Sarah could not look anywhere but at Philip.

"Yes," he said. "It is true. I have always been in love with Sarah. I am still, and I suppose I always will be. I am not sorry to say this, finally, for the first time and for all of you to hear it. It is true."

Suddenly, Martine was on her feet, her chair crashing to the floor behind her, the rage of a wounded animal on her distorted face. She was at Philip's throat with the gleaming knife in her fist, driving it into his throat.

No one noticed Grey's widow, Mina, who fainted, slipping from her seat to the floor. George Porter wrested the knife from the hysterical woman and held her with both arms behind her back. Sarah and Harry bent over Philip. Dark red blood was spilling onto his jabot and down his satin waistcoat onto the tablecloth.

"Towel," Sarah said, and Harry rushed into the kitchen to be back instantly with handfuls of towels. She stanched the wound, wrapping the thicknesses of soft flour sacking around Philip's neck until finally the redness slackened and no longer oozed through the wadding.

"Send for the doctor," Sarah said, calmly. One of her hands brushed a damp curl from Philip's cheek.

"I'll go," George Porter agreed, glad to be out of there, looking sweaty and faint himself. He patted his wife's head absently and dashed from the house. Eliza and her row of children stayed at table, munching and staring wide-eyed at the drama around them.

Philip had not lost consciousness. He leaned back with his eyes clear and steady, letting Sarah tend him. She avoided looking into his gaze.

"Hepzibah, take her upstairs. The room at the back of the house where we won't hear her. Stay with her. Give her whatever you can to calm her," Sarah ordered over her shoulder, not taking her attention from the compresses, which now were growing more pinkish, less scarlet, with each application. On the carpet from Persia, a bloody heap of discarded towels lay, slowly staining the heirloom for all future generations to see.

Martine's shrieks did not abate, although they were heard now from a distance.

When the doctor arrived, he examined Philip's wound and ordered him to be carried to bed. He was not to go home since any jostling in a carriage would be dangerous. The knife had missed the jugular, and Sarah's instinctive ministrations had been the proper thing. He helped George to half-carry Philip up to the guest chamber at the head of the stairs. Sarah and Harry followed them. Harry had his arm around his aunt's waist, and she leaned on him for their mutual comfort.

When Philip was lying in the four-poster, with George to help him undress, the doctor led Sarah and Harry from the room.

"Where's the madwoman?" he asked, already striding down the hall in the direction of Martine's screaming.

"She's only drunk," Sarah said, hastening after him.

The doctor stopped in his tracks and regarded her over his shoulder with disbelief. He only shook his head and kept on until he threw open the door of the chamber. Breaking from the servants' grasp, Martine hurled herself at the door. The doctor caught her, slapped her a stinging blow across the cheek that resounded in the air. Martine's response was an animal growl and a ducking motion with her head, as she tried to bite the doctor's hand.

"Mistress Stafford, tell my driver to ride to the asylum and send the black carriage here as quickly as possible."

"Oh, no! Surely not!" Sarah protested.

"Will you keep her here, then, with no chance of recovery? My hospital is discreet, and there she will be well tended until her lunacy passes. Here," he said to Hepzibah and the other servants, who stood terrified in the shadows of the room, "wrap her in blankets, bind her hands and feet well, swaddle her like an infant, that's the way."

He strode down the hall to tend to Philip. Sarah closed the door on Martine's wails, leaving the servants to cope. She and Harry waited outside Philip's door until the doctor came out again to assure them the wound was superficial and would soon be healed.

The black carriage had no windows. It was after midnight when it arrived at the door. Mina and the Porters and all the children had long since gone home to their own houses. There were only Sarah and Harry to stand watch while the inert, pathetically small body was carried, unconscious now, down the stairs and into the asylum wagon.

They stood in the doorway, arms around each other, until the sound of the horses and wheels on the cobblestones had faded into deep silence. The night was chilly; it was only April.

"She'll be well taken care of," Sarah said to comfort the boy as best she could.

"They'll put chains on her. She'll get madder and madder without anything to drink," he answered sadly.

"They know what's best, the doctors. We must trust that they do."

"Aunt Sarah, I think I'll have my first glass of brandy tonight. Let's go inside."

They went into the little reception room between the parlor and the dining hall. It was cozy in there. Harry took the cut glass decanter from the sideboard and poured out two round snifters. Feeling very grown-up, he handed one to his aunt.

"I'm glad my father loves you," he blurted out then, suddenly a child again.

She couldn't answer that. She hadn't let herself think about what had been said in the moment before Martine's explosion. She couldn't think about it now.

"You may sleep in the trundle in your father's room tonight, if you like," she answered instead, "to keep watch on him and be helpful if he wakes and needs anything."

Harry sipped at his brandy, sputtered, and made a wry face. "This is vile!" he muttered. He wiped his mouth, still puckered and burning. He set the glass down carefully.

"I don't much want mine either," Sarah said. "It's very late. We'd better get to our beds. Come on, Harry."

"May I stay in the small room just near my father, instead of actually with him? Do you think he will be all right without me to keep watch?"

"Yes, of course. Dr. Morris said he'd sleep through the night. But why, Harry?"

"I have to write my broadside. Against the Molasses Act," he said, reminding her a bit impatiently. Could she possibly have forgotten?

"Tonight?"

"Yes. It must circulate tomorrow, before the first tax is paid. I'll understand if you can't help me this time," he said earnestly.

"Oh. Oh, yes. All right. You're not too . . . upset?"

"No. I don't think so."

"Harry, you are a strange and a wonderful boy."

"Come on then. Let's look in on him. If he needs me, of course, I will stay with him."

She followed him up the stairs, noting again how tall he had grown and how sure his footsteps were. She shook her head as she climbed. Each person must sort out his feelings about such a night in his own way. Harry's thoughts were on politics; it was just as well. Her own were a mystery to her, and she hoped they'd stay that way.

Philip slept. A shaded candle burned on the table nearby. As they approached, his eyes opened, and he smiled to see Sarah.

"Love," he said.

"Shh," Sarah cautioned him.

"It's all right, Father. She doesn't want to talk about it, but I understand. I'm glad you love her. Are you feeling all right?"

"Harry, you're a strange boy, and wonderful."

"She said the same thing. You two think alike, do you know that?"

"Where did they take your mother?"

"To the asylum that Dr. Morris keeps."

"Poor Martine."

"Yes," Sarah murmured.

"Will they treat her well, Father?"

"Yes. If we pay well."

"Then we will."

"Of course."

"Of course."

"Good night, Father."

"Good night, Harry. You're a fine fellow, a good boy, and I'm proud of you."

"I'm proud, too, sir." With that, Harry ducked his head and left the room, to go into the little chamber where he had stayed overnight many times before.

"Good night then, Philip. Sleep well, but ring this little bell if you need anything. Your son is in the next room and I—"

"Don't go, Sarah."

"You must sleep."

"Sit here a moment. Let me look at you."

"Nothing to see. It's true, what she said. My eyes are twitchy, and I'm a dried-up old spinster."

"You're my beautiful Sarah. I told them all I love you. That I always have and always will. That's what is true, Sarah. You're very beautiful."

"Philip, don't play such games. I'm not a woman who knows how to play such games."

He propped himself up on one elbow. He whispered, "Sarah, you're trembling. Oh, my dear . . . have I hurt you so?"

"I must go."

"No."

"Yes. I must."

But she couldn't move from the touch of his hand on her arm, so gentle, a shackle she could not break. In the candle's light his eyes melted right through her. She didn't have the strength to stand. She sat on the bed, close to him, and felt that it was she, and not Martine, who should be in the lunatic asylum, a mindless creature unable to move or act or talk.

"I do love you, Sarah. Forgive me for being so late."

"Why . . . why do you torment me with this?" She whispered so low that he had to bend his head forward to hear. The bandages around his throat shone whitely. She looked, fearing they would turn pink again.

"Oh, my dear, do lie back!" she said urgently. She found the use of her hands and arms then, to push him slowly back onto the pillows.

"Lie with me," he asked her softly. "Lie with me, my dearest, only love. Come. . . ." He moved to make room for her, and it was the most natural thing in the world to let herself sink beside him, into his arms.

"You love me, too," he whispered.

"Yes."

"Oh, my dear, my own Sarah, I love you so . . . how could I have been so blind, so stupid?"

"Hush," she said, touching his beloved mouth with her fingertips. "We're all right now. We're together now, Philip. My love, my love . . ."

And slowly, gently, softly, as easy and right as the willows bending with the April wind, their mouths came together and their bodies, as it had always been meant to be.

Chapter Fifteen

1734-1765: SARAH

She woke in a strange bed for the first and only time in her life. It felt right and natural, waking beside his naked body, to the touch of his arm across her bare breasts. The first thing she saw when she opened her eyes was her whole world—Philip's eyes only inches away, closed in trusting sleep, vulnerable in her keeping.

She slipped away from his bed before he woke; it was the hardest thing she had ever done. She forced herself to rise from his warmth and the unendurable happiness of being part of him. She crept in the cold light of dawn to her own bed.

She lay rigid for a moment, knowing she must not allow herself to linger on the memory of what could never be repeated. But it was not possible to think of anything else. She got up, dressed herself, and went down to light the kitchen fires. She forced herself to think how much salt to put in the porridge, and never, never again about the astonishment of passion. Like a century plant that blooms once and once only, she must close herself against the light forever.

"Sarah?"

He stood in the doorway, rumpled and bewildered, and when she saw him, he opened his arms and she ran to them. They held each other for a moment before she broke away.

"You shouldn't be up. Your wound . . . ." she managed to say.

"It's all right. You were gone when I woke up just now. It broke my heart. . . ."

"No," she said, taking a step back, away from him.

"My love. I do love you so very much."

"It's too late for us, Philip."

"No! It can't be. Not now, not just when we've found—"

"It's morning now. The servants will be up soon. We must be sensible. Poor Martine, in the madhouse. And Harry . . ."

He stumbled to the table and sat down heavily on the bench. He put his elbows up and hid his face in his hands for an instant. Then he looked at her, not able to hide his tears.

"Oh, Philip, don't! I beg you, don't, my love. We have to be strong. I can't be, without your help."

He stood up. His white linen shirt was open; delicate curls rose from his waist to the whiteness of the bandage at his throat. She had to clench her fists behind her back to keep from reaching out to caress his firm warm flesh, tanned from the long days at sea.

"Go and finish dressing," she said. Did her voice tremble? "Then come down with the others and . . . oh, don't look at me, love! Don't look at me when anyone else is in the room."

"They know I love you."

"Adultery is a hanging offense," she said.

"Come to France with me, to England, or Spain. Anywhere, wherever you like. Come with me. We can live freely, anywhere but here. Together."

"With your wife in the madhouse and your son to grow up alone?"

"We'll take Harry with us."

"Philip, be sensible."

"How can I? How can I live without you?"

"As you've always done."

"Why won't you come with me?"

"Boston is my home. And it's Harry's home, too. He feels very strongly about political affairs here, you know. He wants to set the colonies free, nothing less. You must understand how serious the boy is."

"He's a child of twelve! He'll change many times over before he's grown. Martine might have been right about that after all, you know. He could get a fine education, at Oxford, and—"

"No, Philip. I see you don't understand about Bostonians. Harry

is a Bostonian, and so am I. We can't leave here; we both would be
fish out of water. And you and I can never marry.''

"And if you're with child?''

She stopped stirring the porridge and stared at him, the ladle slipping from her hand. Deep inside herself she felt a rich, hot, quickening at his words, a physical thing, like life itself, a lurching, flowing
protest, too urgent, too vital to be denied. Surely it could not be? So
quickly? Did one know so quickly that one had conceived? An extraordinary joy filled her body and heart and head and soul—could
that greatest miracle of all have taken place within her body?

"If we have conceived a child, then I will leave here and go with
you,'' she managed to say.

"Then I'll pray for it.''

"Oh, Mistress Stafford, you've already lit the fires, and begun the
cooking! You are earlier than I . . . sorry''

"No, Hepzibah, it's quite all right. I couldn't sleep this morning.''

"Good morning, sir. I'm pleased that you feel better.''

"Thank you, Hepzibah. I see the kettle's on the boil. Will you
make tea?''

"Oh, yes, sir. Good strong tea. Right away, Mr. Philip. And for
you, mistress?''

Sarah was shaking so, deep within herself, that she didn't trust a
cup not to rattle in its saucer. "I'll be down later,'' she said, avoiding Philip's eyes. "I have things to do upstairs.''

She knocked on Harry's door and, receiving no answer, went in.
He was gone, out circulating his broadsides around the city.

For an instant she worried that she had let the boy down. Had he
tried to wake her, as he almost always did, so that she could join
him in the stealthy predawn walk about the town, pasting up his
notices and laughing quietly together while everyone else slept? Had
Harry, not finding her, looked in on his father, to find two sleeping
figures in the bed instead of one?

Instead of the shame she knew she should feel, a sense of peace
came over her. Harry was part of her life, part of Philip. Nothing
would ever be shameful or hidden among the three of them. It was
right that Harry should know about the consummation of their love.

Philip remained in Boston for two months, longer than he had ever done. He went each day to the asylum, where he was confronted with Martine's continuing wrath. His presence did nothing to abate her ravings, and daily conferences with the doctors assured him that all was being done to calm her, the most modern medical knowledge was being put to use on her behalf, and yet they could hold out no hope for her eventual recovery. She was given all that wealth could buy: Velvet wrappings encircled the shackles that kept her from harming herself; her chamber was lined with quilts on the walls so she could not strike her head; attendant nurses stayed with her at all times; and all possible was being done to force her to eat. She screamed out for whiskey, brandy, rum, laudanum; but those were the very sources of her madness, and nothing more could be done.

Philip and Harry stayed in their own house on Beacon Street, going up the hill to take meals with Sarah and the other members of the family. It was a sad time, yet Harry's ebullient spirits could always make his father laugh, and Sarah busied herself more intensely than ever with ladies' meetings and household tasks.

And one morning she awoke with the blood starting, and she knew that it had been part of the dream, that it was not to be. The overwhelming sadness she felt was her last indulgence to herself; never again would she allow her thoughts to touch on what might have been or what had been for one mystical night. One night, out of her whole life! Put it away, shut the gates of Eden, and get on with life, she told herself.

"When do you sail again?" George asked Philip in the evening, as they sat with lit pipes out in the summer garden. The question had been asked by others, while Philip tarried in Boston through the languid early summer.

"When I am certain about Martine," he answered as he always did.

"There is no reason for you to stay any longer," Sarah said carefully, concentrating on her embroidery with serious attention.

Philip jerked his head up to stare at her across the others. The stars overhead were clear and lush, lighting their faces despite the lack of a moon that evening.

"I don't understand," he said.

"Yes. You do," she assured him, not looking up.

"What does she mean?" George asked.

"I mean that his wife is in excellent hands and all will stay the same for years to come. And that his only child fares well here," she said.

"His only child? That's a funny way of putting it," Eliza put in. Her mouth was filled with chocolate.

"But Harry is his only child," Sarah answered curtly.

"Yes. I see. Yes. There is no reason for me to neglect the business any longer. I should return to England. Soon."

"Yes," Sarah answered, more sharply than she meant to. "Soon. Right away, I should think."

"Right away," he echoed. His voice was sad and already far away.

George was still puzzling over her choice of phrase. "Well, I suppose Harry is his only child, but Liza's right, it's an odd way of putting it. Unless our Philip's dropped some bastards on the Continent that we don't know about? Hawr-hawr!"

"No," Sarah said firmly. "Our Philip has not dropped any bastards anywhere."

"Why, George, that's a shocking thing to say!" Eliza scolded.

"I apologize, dear. A jest."

"In very bad taste, George. Fit for a tavern, I should think, although I have no idea what they talk of in such places. But certainly not fit for decent company—"

"Oh, do leave off, Eliza. I said I was sorry. A slip of the tongue, spoken to Philip and not to you. In the bosom of the family, so to speak."

"But in front of me and your unmarried sister-in-law, with no regard to womanly delicacy and innocence. It is your duty to protect us from such low talk and not to bring it into the hearing of your own wife and—"

"Enough, Eliza. When will you sail then, Philip?"

During the domestic bicker between husband and wife, Philip had looked long and thoughtfully at Sarah, who finally looked up to return the gaze steadily. His disappointment was mingled with relief; that she could see, for it was her own reaction as well. There would be no child. He would leave Boston, and she would stay, the dowager spinster who led society in manners and morality, good works and cultural endeavors. Now she had two secrets from the world: Harry's politics and Philip's love. Behind her back they would pity her for never having known a man's embrace, for the twitch of her eye and her dry pinched mouth and the hauteur with which she endured loneliness. That's what the world would think. Let them think so; it suited her.

"I must see you alone for a moment," Philip whispered on the day before he was to sail. She had been very careful to avoid his company, and he had understood and kept someone else always between them. But now, as she knelt to tend the roses, with the hot sunshine on her back, the good, rich loam creeping up above her gloves to stain her sleeves, he had sought her out to say good-bye.

She looked up at him from beneath the broad brim of her sunbonnet, shading her eyes from the glare. He was so beautiful and so forlorn. She loved him. It must be the sun making her dizzy, confusing her—she couldn't remember why she was allowing him to go; she must stop him. She almost rose to her feet, to take him in her arms. But she was too weak suddenly, too sunstruck; she could only stare up at him.

"Sarah, I must have you in my arms, one more moment, please. One more—last—time. I must . . ." He spoke quietly, only the droning bees to hear him.

"Here in the garden?" she answered painfully, trying to smile. "And then directly to the Common, to be put in the stocks together?"

"I don't care. Except for you, I wouldn't care. They could never shame me for loving you. I need to kiss you, Sarah, before I go. Come to my house this afternoon, I beg you."

"No . . . oh, my darling. No. You know what would happen."

"And I'd have the excuse to stay another two months and be glad."

She laughed. "What a life we'd have. Lovemaking every time we failed to conceive and then waiting for my monthlies and the chance to try again?"

"Don't joke. I love you. I'll always love you."

"We have Martine to thank that no one remembers your declaration. Isn't that a bit of irony? And just as well."

"You'll send me away without a proper farewell?"

"Proper, Philip?"

"Why are you laughing at me?"

"Because . . . because I choose not to cry, Philip." She was still kneeling at the roses. She looked down again at the earth, the roots of the rosebush exposed now where she had carefully pried away the earth. She tried to inspect them for mealyworms, but her eyes were awash in tears that kept her from seeing clearly.

"Then good-bye," he whispered after a long moment.

"Fare you well, Philip."

"I would have liked our child."

"God knows best. Perhaps."

He was silent for so long that she finally dared look up, and found him gone. She was alone again. She forced herself to tend the roses slowly, to stay in the beating sun until she had finished her task. When she finally straightened and stood, her limbs felt tired, heavy, and old.

She dreaded his next homecoming—dreaded it, yearned for it, tried not to think of it. When, eight months later, he returned, their eyes hungrily sought each other for reassurance that their love was as strong and constant as ever. Then, oddly, a kind of peace came over them—a feeling of deep, abiding friendship, cousinship, a level of loving which a body could tolerate for all the years to come. It was as though the brief consummation of their love had been enough to enable them to move forward, at last, to another plane of caring for each other. They never again spoke of their passion, their need of each other, except for the pledge their eyes renewed each time Philip came home to Boston. *Yes, I love you and I always will; yes, I know you love me as well and as truly; no, we may not speak of it or act on it, dearest cousin.*

Martine lived for eleven years in the asylum. Every day of those long years a servant from Pemberton Square rode out to the solitary red-brick building on the Newton Road to bring broths and stews, India tea, and warm clothing to her. Her son's visits caused her to rant and rave more violently than usual, and the doctors decreed that no member of her family should visit. She died of pneumonia and was laid to rest in the Copp's Hill Burying Ground at the edge of the Stafford plot, in a grave which her husband, Philip, would someday share, provided that death did not overtake him in some foreign place.

As the years went on, Sarah found her life increasingly filled with young Harry's unbounded energies. At fifteen he entered Harvard and studied the sciences as well as letters. He went on to medical school and became a proper gentleman, enlisted in all the proper clubs under the sponsorship of his uncle George Porter or his school friends who were sons of lawyers and doctors and merchantmen as rich as his own father.

Philip's once- or twice-yearly visits to Boston were always occasions for quiet joy. Nothing passed between the two lovers that was not shared with the young man who should have been their son. Harry grew tall and strong and prosperous in his own right; Philip and Sarah were slowly aging, although not in each other's eyes. When Philip's life ended at sea on his way to them, the two he had loved so well knew that the great gift of his love would live in them, warming and protecting, for all their lives.

Set up in private practice, Harry Stafford quickly became known as the most modern surgeon and general practitioner in Boston, as well as the most stylish. Handsome and solid as the Bank of England, he could have had any young lady from the best families of Massachusetts or New York or Philadelphia, but it was his curious and idiosyncratic habit to arrive at every ball and dinner party with his spinster relative on his arm. He was genial to all, available to none. His conversation was pleasant and informed, witty and sensible, except that he refused ever to discuss politics. Claiming that his only interest in life was the practice of medicine, Boston's most eligible bachelor whiled away the years with an occasional game of cards at one of the many clubs he belonged to, or he could be found of an evening snoozing away behind the open pages of the *Evening Post*.

And after bidding his cronies or the elegant hostesses of the evening a polite good night, Harry Stafford and his spinster relative would head for home in their closed carriage, with the tall, handsome doctor at the reins. Once out of sight, the carriage would make an odd turnabout and proceed through alleyways and across the city to a secret meeting place in a barn on the road to Lexington. There they would join a handful of other activists in turning the illegal printing press, bring forth thousands of leaflets and satiric poems and bulletins and broadsides which would appear on every tree and door before daylight, urging the citizens of Massachusetts to defy the encroachments upon their God-given right to be free men. It was sedition and treason they preached. Some of their number were discovered and sent to England for trial and thence to prison.

They demanded nothing less than liberty for the colonies—revolution! They were esteemed and prominent men of the community, this group, and in touch with others in the countryside who were farmers and simpler men of the soil. Those in Boston were the literate ones, who kept the countryside alerted to their cause. They paid Josiah Quirk for the private use of his printing press under cover of night. Their output took the form of anonymous comments on public figures, suggestions for righting wrongs, exposure of immorality among the local representatives of the Crown, intimations of fraud in government business, and threats to the rights of man. On many occasions, it must be admitted, they also stooped to the airing of private grudges, being no nobler than other men because they were libertarians. (Who on earth could ever resist the temptations of a printing press, anonymity, and the eager help of others in distributing one's words?)

There were close calls. The king's troops formed the habit of dropping in at the Long Room behind Quirk's printing office, noting who went in and who came out. They questioned everyone, but no evidence was ever found to link the travelers on the Lexington Road late at night with the seditious pamphlets which continued to appear.

A hero's name was given to the leader of the anonymous radicals: the Boston Patriot. Whoever he was, there was a price on his head. His fame rose steadily among the population, in direct proportion to the frustration and ire of the governor and his troops in catching him.

There were many ingenious ways that the broadsides were carried from Quirk's barn. There were many unlikely volunteers. Sometimes the "evidence" was rumored to be transported by a woman, under her cloak, tucked inside her skirts or her hats. Sarah Stafford had been suspected but never questioned. The governor knew better than to suggest that Boston's proudest old dowager might be suspected of unsavory actions. They didn't want the whole of society rising against them.

The aging spinster with the twitching eye, whose wealth protected her from dirtying her fine shoes on the streets, whose life was a useless round of sewing bees and chatter with other old women of society, whose hats were old-fashioned and whose lips were cold and thin; Sarah Stafford, lonely old biddy in the big house on Pemberton Square, despised and feared for her sharp tongue—no one outside the faithful cadre of radical activists suspected that she was their inspiration and support.

It was Sarah Stafford who had arranged with a notorious smuggler to obtain arms during the impressment riot, hiding them under her carriage robes to distribute to the men. It was she who helped draft the plans for burning the marketplace in protest against the excise tax. It was Sarah Stafford who conceived the idea of asking all Boston citizens to put the customs officials "in Coventry," to refuse to speak with them, an act with which the people complied most heartily, partly as a lark and partly a way of showing their disdain and still remaining within the law.

The years went by with increasingly bold and clever acts of protest, yet the troops continued to patrol the streets of Boston, and the king still demanded allegiance. The lack of voice in their own destiny became more and more oppressive to the citizens, urged on by the Boston Patriot and his followers. The small group of rebels increased in number.

Sarah was sixty-three years old on the night she nearly seduced a British officer for the cause. It was the vicious spring of the Stamp Act—her own reasons for remembering that night in 1765 would have more to do with a clandestine kiss than politics.

Parliament had decreed that every document issued in the colonies, whether a newspaper, almanac, pamphlet, lease, marriage contract, or ship's bill of lading, must have affixed to it a revenue stamp, value to be arbitrarily determined by a local representative of the Crown. Even the Loyalists were outraged at this petty, tyrannical decree, and the most prominent men in all the colonies were holding meetings to determine how their protests should be framed. In the barn on the Lexington Road the men of letters were determined to use the Stamp Act to fire up merchants and mobs in real protest.

Sarah was standing guard while the men inside labored to frame their call to action. It was a windy March night, and she had wrapped herself in a cloak which covered her head and face. She sat in a wagon in the farmyard a few yards from the darkened, windowless barn. Waiting was the hardest job of all; she did it well, considering her impatient nature and her longing to be inside, where the fiery eloquence rang to the rafters. Taxation without representation, that was Harry's phrase, and it would surely inflame the people to act at last. . . . She heard hoofbeats on the road.

She picked up the reins and gentled the old farm horse to amble down the path to the gate. The horseman heard her and called out.

"Who goes there?"

"Mistress Quirk," she lied without hesitation. "And who are you?"

"Captain Grant, in His Majesty's service. You are out very late, young lady."

Young lady, indeed! She would have rapped his hands for impertinence in other circumstances. But she kept her counsel. "One of my cows has strayed," she complained in a small voice, "and without a moon I have little hope of finding her." She sighed delicately.

"Is this your farm then?"

Mr. Quirk's wife was long dead, and he had no living children. Sarah hoped the captain did not know that.

"It's my father's farm, sir." Imagine having a father alive, at her age. She kept the cloak wrapped about her face. She tried to make her voice girlish and respectful.

"Tell me, where is your father, mistress?"

"In the house, sir. Asleep. He is not well."

How could she warn the men? How could she turn the officer away from here without arousing his suspicions? At any minute the broadside might be fed into the noisy press, and the cranking begun. Surely he would hear something; all would be discovered . . .

"Would you help me search for my cow, Captain?" What a ridiculous request; she felt like a perfect idiot. But she made herself speak coyly, seductively, and hoped he would not come close enough to see her face.

"I'm on official business, Mistress Quirk. I've had a report that there are men meeting in secret somewhere around here. Have you seen or heard anything?"

She gasped aloud. "Oh, dear me, men meeting in secret! You frighten me, Captain Grant."

"I do apologize. Please don't be frightened of me. I'm here to keep the peace, and only that. It's a thankless job and a lonely one."

He was leaning from his mount to peer at her, trying to guess her age, she had no doubt. Lonely, indeed!

She sighed again. "I would invite you to the house for a good strong cup of tea," she said, "but my father is very ill, and I fear to disturb him. If he heard about men meeting around here, he would be most upset."

"There's a tavern down the road," the captain said, with an unexpected trace of shyness and a hesitating stammer which she found quite touching. They're human, like anyone else, she thought, under those red coats. And it is a lonely job he does, being hated so by the people. "Would you allow me to escort you there for a warm drink on a cold night? You'd be doing a great kindness," he finished almost inaudibly.

"A tavern! Oh, I could not!" she protested.

He recovered his military bearing at once. "Well, then I must be about my duty. I'll have to search your outbuildings, mistress. I do apologize, but—" He swung his horse around to pass her at the entrance to the path leading to the barn. Instinctively Sarah pulled her own leads to block his way with the wagon.

"Why do you keep me, mistress?" he demanded coldly.

"I . . . oh, sir! I'm afraid of alarming my father, who is near death, and," seeing that wasn't going to deter him, she added in desperation, "and I am lonely, too."

He pulled closer to her. She slunk down into her hooded cloak, as if in shyness. God help me, she prayed silently.

"A kiss then!" he said boldly. "A kiss for your sick father's sake, and I'll be off. A kiss for a lonely man on a dark and windy night, it would be an act of charity!" He tried to sound jovial. She found herself feeling very sorry for him. If he knew how old she was! A man expecting to kiss a maiden would recoil in horror from a wrinkled crone's face presented to him instead . . . blessing the clouds for covering the moon, she leaned forward.

"I have heard of soldiers who rape countrywomen on such dark, lonely roads as this," she said fearfully. She wasn't acting now, but keeping her voice low and wheedling. Her trembling was real.

"I am an officer and a gentleman," he said proudly. "You have nothing to fear from me. But the touch of a woman's lips on such a dark, bad night would be a great comfort, to speed me on my way."

The wind picked up with a wail, and she thought to her horror that she heard the press begin to crank from deep inside the barn behind her. Quickly she leaned across to him, and the officer stood in his stirrups to reach her hidden face with his lips. She felt his warm breath on her cheek and then his hand brusquely turned her chin so that their mouths could meet. He held her for a long moment, and she thought she would faint. When he finally released her, the farm-yard and all the countryside swirled around her with the howling wind.

"Tomorrow," he sang out, and then sharply turned his horse and trotted away.

Sarah sat without moving until the dizziness passed, until the hoof-beats had long faded into the night. Then she turned slowly and rode back to the barn. She dismounted from the wagon and went inside.

"There was an officer," she said.

"Sarah, why so pale? We've left you out there too long. Bob, relieve Mistress Stafford on watch, will you? Come, let me warm your hands between mine. Look, here is our paper. What do you think of it?"

"An officer?" Bob Longstreet sat on a nail keg with a huge barrel of ink between his long legs; he was mixing it with a paddle. He looked up at her, and she wanted to laugh. He had a blob of ink on the end of his long, patrician nose. He was the most cautious of all of them, with a perennially worried look. Something about the ink-stain on his nose made Sarah choke with the sudden need to laugh. Her lips tightened; her left eye began to twitch badly. "What officer? Did you recognize him? Where was he? How close did he come? What did he say? Do they suspect anything?"

"He came along the road, past the gate, and stopped there. I drove out to meet him, to stop him from coming in. A Captain Grant. I managed to turn him away. He said there was a report of men meet-ing in secret in this neighborhood. But he's gone. It's all right."

"How did you dissuade him?" Longstreet persisted.

"Reports of meetings?" Harry turned from listening to her and spoke to the others. "We should move on. Another place must be found."

"A safe house. Where will we find a safe house now? This Stamp Act will have the whole colony up in arms. No place will be safe."

"Aunt Sarah?" Harry said, questioning her with his eyes.

She nodded. She let the hood slide down from her head, although the barn was dank and chilly. The seven men gave her their full attention.

"Yes, I guess the time has come. Do you consider the house of Sarah Stafford a safe place, gentlemen?"

"Your house!"

"Surely not . . . in the center of town!"

"They would see us coming and going."

"Your reputation, Mistress Stafford!"

"Safe, surely, but if we were found there—"

"It would be the end for her and all her family."

"I'm surprised to hear such cautions at this late date," she said tartly. "Haven't we all risked everything already?"

"My aunt and I have arranged for a passageway to be dug out beneath the house on Pemberton Square. It leads to . . . well, you tell them, Henry."

"Yes, it leads to the cellar below my tavern," Henry Levitt said calmly, puffing on his odious pipe with a twinkle in his eye.

"A direct route from the Bowbell to the Stafford house? Extraordinary! Wonderful! They'll never suspect . . . what a grand joke . . . What of the workmen who have dug the tunnel? Can they be trusted: How can we move the press without suspicion . . . ?"

The questions and details of the move occupied them all most satisfyingly as the press churned out copies of the call. Shortly before dawn women and children began to appear to collect the papers for posting throughout the town and countryside. The Boston Patriot and his aunt went wearily home together; there was much to be done before the next meeting could be held.

But by the light of morning, as Sarah was preparing for bed, she looked for a long time into the shadowy reflection of a sixty-three-year-old seductress in her looking glass. Foolish and vain . . . her finger traced the wrinkles in her throat and cheeks, the deep lines radiating from her eyes and circling her mouth. A minor battle in the long war, properly unheralded, never to be noted by history. But no man could have done it.

Chapter Sixteen

1773: SARAH

She was working an intricate afghan, which should have called for her full attention. But Sarah's gnarled fingers knotted and twisted the yarn, working the hook over and under more by instinct than design. She would have to rip out the mistakes later, but that, too, was a pattern of her life, and it didn't make much difference to her anymore whether she was building or tearing down the silly thing; it was what an old woman did to pass the hours. She should have had her dinner and banked the fire by now, but she felt no more inclined to that than any other woman in Boston this night. Candles flickered and burned low in every house, keeping watchful, ever-patient vigil while the men tarried late at the meetinghouse.

A noise on the street. Sarah dropped the bulky afghan from her lap and ran to the window, forgetting her seventy-one years. She unbolted the shutter and pried it open against the bitter wind that fought her. It took all her strength to push against the blow, reminding her once again of her age and frailty. How she loathed being old! It got in the way of all the things she wanted to do. She had to step on a little footstool now to see out the same window that she had stretched easily to lean from as a girl. An icy blast of December evening struck her withered cheeks and made them tingle, a good feeling. Her bright and clear-sighted glance down North Street brought stinging tears from the cold. There was not a soul in sight.

It had probably only been the leafless old elm again, brushing its barren branches against the house, echoing and whispering to addle an old woman's mind. Not even the watchman was about, and the king's troops had stopped night patrols three years before, after the terrible massacre in front of the State House. Firing into a crowd of angry colonists had only created martyrs for the cause of independence, instead of the obedient and frightened subjects they expected. The citizens were in no mood to tolerate the presence of troops in the streets after that, and the governor had the sense to cancel night patrols.

Startled from her reverie by a swelling wave of murmurs and then shouts outside and the sound of running feet, Sarah rose from her chair, but before she could get to the door, it burst open with a wintry blast. Harry stood tall and crimson-faced with his cloak flying open behind him. He pulled the door shut and grinned at her.

"Aunt Sarah, there's going to be real action at last! Come on, help me, we've got to hurry!"

"I'm with you," she affirmed, following his wet boot tracks toward the staircase.

"Where's that old blanket that Maniteecha's granddaughter traded us for her appendectomy a few years ago . . . remember? I used to have it somewhere. And didn't I have a headband when I was a boy, with a feather or two in it?"

Sarah followed him upstairs with feet as nimble as his own, and her questions kept pace with his nonsense as he began to rummage in his wardrobe. She stood in the doorway of his chamber with her arms crossed, watching him.

"What are you doing? Feathers? What happened at the meeting-house? Will the governor send the *Dartmouth* back to England without unloading? Did he agree? What do you mean, action? What's going to happen? I hear men in the street, shouting! Harry, *what are you doing?*"

"Removing my trousers, madam. The governor's in Milton, at his country house. He doesn't think we're serious. Do we have any henna dye? I think, mixed with a bit of mud, it might do perfectly well to hide my whiteness. Ah! I knew those old leather wrappings were around here someplace. Cousin Joseph brought them to me from his travels in the interior, remember . . . years ago. Different tribes, different sort of clothing, but I suppose no one will take the time to notice tonight. . . .''

"Harry Stafford, if you don't tell me what you are doing and why you are dressing up like an Indian brave, I will burst right here on the spot. That would spoil your plans for the evening, wouldn't it? What in the Lord's name is going on?''

"Aunt Sarah, a lot of the men are dressing up like Mohawks, just to catch the watch off their guard for a moment or two, while we board and seize the cargo.''

Instantly the old lady became attentive and gleefully conspiratorial. She crossed to the bed, leaned down to pull forth a certain sea chest, opened it, and reached in to find the headband and feather carefully preserved there. She handed it to him.

"I think there's still some henna left from dying that old linen cloth for the table,'' she said. "What will you do with the tea? Not bring it ashore; that would be as bad as if the governor himself did it. It would be sure to find its way into the marketplace.''

"No, we'll dump it.''

"Harry! That's wonderful! Brilliant. Was it your idea? I'm sure it was.''

"How do you get this thing to stay in your hair?'' he asked, peering into the looking glass, holding the feather straight up from his thick curls.

"Tell me what happened. I'll run and get the dye and mud, and then you tell me everything while we finish fixing you up. Oh, what fun! I do love you, Harry, you have no idea how old and bored I'd be without you!''

"As my father often said, I am strange and wonderful.''

"I said it first!'' She laughed as she went out to fetch the things. She sent the young servant Toddy to dig wet mud from the half-frozen garden, found the henna powder, and returned to Harry's chamber in moments, out of breath. As they daubed his pale legs and arms and bare chest and shoulders and smeared his fine nose and forehead, he described the night's meeting and its outcome.

"—and then Sam Adams stood up and said, 'This meeting can do nothing more to save the country!' and then someone gave a bloodcurdling war whoop from the back of the room, and I shouted out, 'Boston Harbor a teapot tonight,' and someone else yelled, 'All to Griffin's Wharf!' and those in the meetinghouse joined with those in the street, and it was as though together we became one great cannon, ready to fire. The governor himself had lit the fuse—we sent Francis Rotch to ride to Milton to request that the *Dartmouth* be sent back to England still laden with the tea, and when word came that Hutchinson refused, it was done. I've never seen such a willing crowd, all together and for once all of a common mind. Not just the land-holders, but laborers and young boys, farmers and fishermen—the whole of the countryside is out in Boston tonight, heading for Griffin's Wharf and ready to act!''

"It's your pamphlets that have fired them up," Sarah said.

"Hurry, Aunt Sarah, get your warmest cloak, and let's be out there with the others.''

"Maybe after tonight you won't have to hide your true identity anymore,'' she muttered as she threw her long black cape over her shoulders.

"Put up your hood; it's damned cold out there,'' was his only answer.

She matched her spry steps to his long strides. The night was bitter, but the people who were filling the streets in increasing numbers seemed not to notice. Men and women and children stepped from their warm hearths and headed for the waterfront, down the three hills of Trimountain and into Milk Street and Summer Street and School Street. They were oddly quiet, with the sense of anticipation and serious purpose; neighbors nodded to each other, but few spoke, saving their energies for whatever was to come. There was a steadily mounting thunder of boots and shoes and moccasins on cobblestones and dirt, an occasional child's shout quickly hushed.

"Do you think they won't know you, Harry Stafford?'' asked a low voice coming up alongside them in the crowd.

"I'll stand and be counted with every free man alive,'' he answered. "It's not a disguise, Mr. Bolter, but a tactic to throw a bit of confusion into the watch—and any troops that might be expecting a delegation but not suspect anything from a few redskins.''

Not by nature a man of action, the 300-pound storekeeper was panting as he kept pace with Harry and Sarah, his breath visible in little puffs of grayish vapor on the night air. "The troops are all out there at Castle William, with their cannon trained on the harbor," he cautioned.

"They won't dare shoot, not with seven thousand citizens of Boston out there standing together," Sarah told him. She felt positively exhilarated, only wishing she were a man, and forty years younger, so she could be in the boarding party.

Mr. Bolter touched his hat, wished them luck, and fell back to rejoin his wife and daughters. The vanguard of the crowd surged around the corner onto the waterfront, in sight of the hundreds of tall masts bobbing alongside the wharves. A solid mass of people, moving forward, close together, murmuring like a wave that swells with an undercurrent of rising sound as it prepares to break on the shore.

Harry guided Sarah through the crowd to reach the doorway of a warehouse where she might stand protected from the wind and the dangers that could be in store. There were too many long-repressed angers, injustices to be accounted for, and the possibility of violence this night was in the very air. Other women were already pressed into the doorway; silently they made room for her.

"Wait for me, Aunt Sarah, I'll be back to take you home safely. And if not . . . ."

"Make sure you don't dawdle," she said, touching his mud-streaked face tenderly. "I'm too old to be out at night on my own."

He grinned and turned to join the other men, who were gathering at the edge of the wharf. All along the waterfront, a line of women and children stood, in their dark capes and cloaks, watching and waiting.

Three ships lay off Griffin's Wharf, low in the water with their cargo still heavy in the holds. The *Dartmouth* had been idling there for nearly three weeks, like a groaning cow long past her term, half-mired in the ice, pulling at the lines that held her in place. The other two tea ships were the *Eleanor* and the *Beaver,* lately arrived but in the same expectant condition.

Midnight had been set as the deadline for unloading the tea. Two warships had been positioned directly in the channel, broadside to the tea ships with their guns aimed at the dock. Their lanterns shone like watchful eyes. By the light of the rising December moon the ramparts of Castle William could be clearly made out, with the cannon's mouth above and the long line of red-coated musketeers pointing shoreward from below.

"Drink rum, not tea!" someone shouted from the crowd, and a great roar of laughter went up like a freshet of air after nearly stifling tension.

"Look, you can see Captain Hall on the prow of the *Dartmouth*. Come and join us, Captain!" a woman's scornful yell sounded out. Now the crowd surged forward, along the creaking boards of the old wharf, to the very edges, and others filled Pearl Street up and down on all sides.

Suddenly a motley gang of Mohawk braves leaped out of the crowd, startling the onlookers as much as the wary men aboard the tea ships. Whoops and shouts rang out as the savages swung themselves aboard, by ladder and rope, overpowering the watch and waving others to follow them. In a moment others swarmed toward the bobbing decks— men of all stripes, in cloaks and tall hats, broadcloth and homespun, ministers of the church and boys not yet full-grown, grizzled old settlers from the inland hills and cheeky sailors on a lark, austere politicians and silversmiths and blacksmiths and merchants and bankers, an army without arms, all bent on an act of treason from which there would be no return.

"They'll be turned back, they'll all be killed!" a woman cried out, but her fears were shushed by those around her. A ripple of quiet went through the crowd again as the onlookers listened for sounds that would tell them what was happening aboard the three ships.

Now only the raiders were heard, still whooping and shouting, and then the sound of ripping canvas as the tarpaulins were torn from the hatchways. And then, at last, instead of the half-anticipated noise of battle, came the gloriously welcome shout "Over the side!" and the crowd expelled one great frosty cloud of audible sighing as the first heavy tea chest went plopping into the water.

Tea . . . it was the vital warm fluid that got the blood circulating in one's body on a freezing New England morning. It was the healing potion in times of fever or sadness, the social binding for friendly converse, the necessary accompaniment to a moment's pause in the day. Tea was the satisfying finish to a meal; for some it was a substitute for soup when money was scarce. Tea was the staple without which life would be unthinkably bleak, and cold, and dry. Tea was comfort, nourishment, cordiality, hospitality, and cheer.

Plop! Another forty pounds of it hit the water. There would be no tea in Boston for the long winter days and nights to come, now. One might as well resign oneself to living without the sun . . . but if anyone on Griffin's Wharf that long and bitterly cold December night regretted the slow stains of waste which would warm the water instead of their bellies, not one would admit to it.

They listened to the laughter and shouting and huzzahs that rang from the ships' decks and echoed from the shore with encouragement every time another crate splashed into the icy brine. The people in the crowd watched and slapped each other on the backs, danced up and down as the cargo went over, chest after chest, into the harbor. From the *Beaver,* a great roar of hilarity rang out; word was quickly passed back through the multitude that one of the Mohawks, having fortified himself with enormous quantities of rum, had himself gone over the side with a resounding belly flop. His fellows pulled him up, but he got little sympathy for his half-frozen but still less than sober condition.

"Rebellion! Revolution!" an occasional shout rang out.

"To hell with the king!"

"God save the king," came the answer from another sector, "and God damn his taxes!"

Laughter vented long-smoldering angers, for the moment, and ranks closed again in the heady excitement of action. All stood behind the men on the tea ships, and yet the colony was made up of individualists, widely known to be ungovernable. If no one else could govern them, how could they possibly expect to govern themselves? And yet that was in fact what they thought they wanted. Their meetinghouses were filled day and night with argument among themselves . . . and yet here were all these thousands on this night, all of a common mind for once.

It could be done! How long the concord would last, Sarah realized, didn't really matter. This mad tea party proved that it could be done. New York and Philadelphia would follow Boston's lead, and England would know that the colonies stood together. It was Harry's dream, and it was coming true . . . .

"Three cheers for the Boston Patriot!" she heard herself shouting, as much to her own surprise as those around her. And the crowd responded with one voice.

"Hip hip hooray! Hip hip hooray! Hip hip hooray!" Despite the cold, some hats were thrown high in the air, and an answering cheer rang all down along Pearl Street and beyond the other wharves as far as could be heard.

Sarah hoped that Harry could hear and know that it was for him they cheered.

Hours went by, with the sounds of tea chests hitting the water, accompanied by shouts and cheers echoing back and forth from the ships to the crowd onshore. The sounds took on the steadying beat of a ritual. No opposition from the troops, who still aimed their muskets and cannon; the sailors aboard the vessels were apparently under orders not to resist, and the excitement had begun to pall for many, who began to drift homeward in little knots, nodding their heads and yawning, huddling against the cold they had not felt earlier. But thousands remained along the dockside to encourage and bolster the tea dumpers. The contents of three heavy ships took time to unload; no drama was without its tedious side.

"I don't trust it," a scholarly looking man was saying to another a few steps away from where Sarah stood, "it's too quiet. Why are they getting away with it so easily . . . It's worrisome."

"It may be that the king has decided to step back and let us breathe a bit."

"Oh, well, if you believe that, then perhaps you actually believe that men can change the world."

"Yes, sir, I do."

A woman's shrill voice cut in on the gentlemen: "Not men, but the women behind 'em, that's who changes things!"

The power to make men change the world, Sarah thought to herself, remembering an old Indian woman's premonition, the stench of an overheated hut, strange odors mingled with her own fear and unhappiness . . . so long ago. How desperate she had been! How she had loved Philip! He should be here; he'd be so proud of his son—but Philip was dead.

Thirteen years ago now, it was. His ship had come into the harbor and she had made his favorite apple cake and she was about to take it from the oven when Harry came home from the dockside without his father, with the unbelievable, unbearable news of his death only a day before, aboard the *Lady S*. They had brought his coffin into the house, and when she looked at him, she knew it wasn't Philip at all because her Philip never came home to Boston without that glance between them that said, "Yes, it is still true." These eyes were closed and bloodless and held no message for her. They buried him in the grave with his wife, who had died in the madhouse many years before.

Sarah went on missing Philip, but it was as though he were on one of his journeys, not dead. It was an indulgence she allowed herself. No one was the wiser. It did no harm if a foolish old woman sometimes cocked her head to listen for a footstep or dreamed of a man's embrace.

"Ah, what I'd give for one steaming cup of the damned stuff just now!" someone sighed aloud. The subdued laughter that greeted this was almost a sigh.

Plop! Splash! And voices cheering, no less enthusiastic after three hours of cold. A thousand and more still remained, watching the harbor waters fill with the bobbing chests. Out with the tide they drifted, darkening the crusts of ice that floated white against the dark water, with thick sodden tea leaves clinging like algae where some of the chests had broken open.

"They'll be sweeping it off the beaches for weeks to come," a woman commented.

"Better food for the fish than tribute to England!"

The count was sung from the deck of the *Beaver* and was passed along the crowd: "Three hundred!" Three hundred casks of tea dumped overboard. How many more before this night was done? The cold had reached the marrow of Sarah's bones. . . .

"That's the last!" the cry rang out, and now the throngs along Griffin's Wharf and Pearl Street and all along the long dockside raised a whoop of victory and exultation that must have shaken the timbers of the fortress atop Castle Island as well as the governor's very house out at Milton. Now the men were climbing down from the three empty, bobbing ships, being borne on the shoulders of the crowd.

Sarah caught sight of Harry, at last, taller than any, laughing and waving as he led the way. He had lost his headband with the feather.

At home at last, with blessed quiet and the warmth of victory as cheering in their hearts as the fire that had been kept ablaze for them, Sarah and Harry raised a toast to the citizens of Boston and the success of their "tea party." He had wiped the dye from his face and wrapped himself in a dressing gown.

They drank to the other colonies in the hope that they would stand firmly behind this radical action. And to liberty. To each other. To the hope that independence would be granted without bloodshed. That the king would see their determination and set them free.

"To my father," Harry said. "He would have been with us."

Sarah leaned back against the high wing back of her chair and sipped to Philip's memory.

"To love," Harry said.

She started to sip again, still thinking of Philip, and then she brought herself up short. She narrowed her eyes and squinted across the firelight. She knew Harry too well for any subtlety to slip past her; she was not yet senile enough or drunk enough to miss the nuance of his change in mood.

"I beg your pardon?" she said, putting her brandy glass down carefully on the side table next to her chair. To her chagrin, she hiccuped. But Harry didn't smile. He was warming his glass between his hands and staring into it.

"Harry?"

"To love," he repeated, and then he looked at her, and she saw that he was troubled.

"What's wrong, Harry? What are you trying to tell me?"

Uncharacteristically, Harry blushed.

"Good Lord! You're in love, and you're wondering how to tell me. Why, Harry!" Sarah burst out laughing. "Who's the woman? Widow Lawrence? I've seen how she looks at you. Come on, tell! It's wonderful news! Does she love you back? Who is it, Harry? It's taken you long enough. Fifty-one years old and finally in love! Well, speak up! I haven't the strength to pry it out of you, not tonight."

"Nan Hardy," he mumbled.

"Who? Who?"

"Nan Hardy!"

"Excellent, excellent! Twenty-two years old and never married, they say she's too particular! By God, she's even brighter than I thought. A lovely girl. Does she agree to marry you?"

"Yes."

"And she knows?"

"About my work in the movement? Yes."

"Good! Wonderful! Here, a toast to love indeed! And to the grandchildren I never thought I'd have!"

The word made Harry start and then grin. They raised their glasses and touched them and drank to love, to Nan Hardy, to whatever the morning might hold.

"I never liked this stuff before," Harry said, noting with a distant curiosity that he couldn't seem to speak without his words all running into each other, but not minding a bit. "But now I can see that brandy might be a passable sub-substitute for tea. All the tea is floating out to sea," he added with a deep chuckle.

"Floating out to sea," she repeated dreamily, watching the flickering firelight through the amber stuff in her glass.

"You're disgracefully drunk, Aunt Sarah," Harry admonished her.

"And you're one, too. All got up like an Indian, you old fool."

Their laughter overwhelmed them, and everything either of them tried to say dissolved into hilarious chortles as the two disreputable revolutionaries kept their vigil. When the first rays of dawn pushed at the shutters, it found the old woman, with wisps of hair fallen across her face and the distinguished doctor, with streaks of paint and mud still clinging to his cheeks, fast asleep in their chairs. Untended, the fire had miraculously refused to die but continued to burn steadily and to warm them as they took their rest.

Chapter Seventeen

1789: SARAH

The good people of Boston were rightly furious when Philadelphia was chosen as the capital of the new Confederation of States. Everyone in the world surely knew that Boston was where it had all begun, and Boston was the only truly civilized city, the hub around which all the other colonies turned; yet clever Ben Franklin (and he born right there on Milk Street in Boston!) had somehow swung it his way. Now dear Harry spent most of the year in the godforsaken wilds of Pennsylvania. He had become quite famous and was one of the elder statesmen who made up the Continental Congress, drafting a constitution and arguing about the rights of states and commonwealths under a single federal system. It was important work, of course, and Sarah and Nan were proud of him, but even with five lively young children underfoot, life was relatively dull once the war was over and it all petered down to just talk. Man talk, of course.

Sarah was very old and had lost all her teeth years before. General Washington (President now, she must remember) had taken his wooden dentures from his mouth on a visit, to show her how they worked (she thought Harry must have put him up to it). She told him they were very clever and handed them back, privately thinking how vain he was, and anyway, they were ugly. It was bad enough to be all shrunken and wizened like an old soup chicken, without paying somebody good money to carve out a jack-o'-lantern grin for your mouth. It would scare the children!

One of Harry's boys, little Philip, was as quick and handsome as his father had been, and he kept the old woman company for hours every afternoon after she became bedridden with age. He'd climb up beside her, tell her about the world as he saw it, and then she would go over his lessons with him, and tell him stories about when his father was a boy. She'd tell him about the war, too, and try to explain why so many of their neighbors and even some of their own family had stayed loyal to the king and were now living in Canada or England.

In her eighty-seventh year she decided to study Hebrew. She told anybody who was impertinent enough to ask why that it was, because she wanted to be able to greet God in His own tongue when she saw Him. The real reason was that she thought the Protestants should be more welcoming to the Jewish immigrants who were beginning to settle in Boston. She was sure they had much to teach besides the old biblical language, and she knew that if she invited one of their rabbis into her home on a regular basis, others would lose their fears and prejudices in the rush to emulate her. Or at least she hoped so. People were strange, and the richer they got, the more strangely they acted. All around her she saw people who had fled England not a generation before in search of religious freedom, or so they said, now grown fat and comfortable and looking with suspicion on others who came looking for the very same thing.

Little Philip and she studied together, stories from the Old Testament and tales of the wandering tribes of Israel. They had wonderful old books and manuscripts and scrolls spread out on Sarah's coverlet, with lovely black-inked symbols which had to be read from right to left. It was like breaking a thrilling secret code.

One afternoon, in the midst of their reading, the five-year-old asked his great-aunt Sarah a question. It was about Abraham's wife, who had had the same name as she did. But she didn't answer his question. When he touched her cheek, her head lolled over. Her eyes were open, but she wasn't able to see. There was a nice smile on her lips, though, and her mouth looked softer, not so dry and puckered. She was dead.

"Did she say anything before she lay back so quietly on the pillow, son?" Harry asked the boy gently when he arrived home for the funeral.

"Only my name," little Philip said through his tears.

Chapter Eighteen

1945: KATE

The war went on for a couple of years after Kate's letter to Patrick was returned marked MISSING IN ACTION, but she was only dimly aware of it. She couldn't buy a decent bottle of Scotch for one thing. Rum and Southern Comfort were the only pain dullers on the shelves; people would say, "Don't you know there's a war on?" when she called on the phone for delivery of Scotch, bourbon, gin, brandy. Even Lucky Strikes were dead and gone.

She kept a bottle or two of Southern Comfort in the little cabinet under her window seat. The thick, sweet stuff gave her vicious headaches and spasms of vomiting some mornings after she'd managed a couple of hours' sleep. She didn't mind; the punishment seemed just, somehow. Other than hurt and sick, she felt nothing.

At first people kept calling on the phone. Rose Mallory called often. Marco was dead, too. He had been in the infantry, a sergeant. Kate didn't want to talk to Rose. Kate's mother finally told Rose, politely, it would be better if she stopped calling. The people from the volunteer headquarters and the bond drives called, too, and friends and relatives and somebody from Washington wanting Kate to go down there and get some kind of prize to keep in a box along with Patrick's letters and the photograph of herself that had been his only possession left behind in the officers' barracks when he'd gone on his last mission. She ignored everybody and everything, just stayed curled up on the window seat against the soft worn cushions, staring out at the

Common, holding a tumblerful of Southern Comfort, sipping from it to keep the numbness from wearing off.

Dr. Hamilton came to examine her. She let him. He said she was all right physically. He said she should go ahead and grieve.

Her mother talked to her. Anne pointed out that nice girls did not drink to excess, or mourn to excess for that matter, and having made this observation, Anne Stafford was unable to comprehend why Kate went right on doing it. Her father spoke to her about Patrick's memory and how she was not showing proper respect for either her late husband or her own family.

Her brother Edward was a captain in the Navy, with his own ship and crew. He had narrowly escaped dying, they said, several times. Edward had a blue uniform with gold stripes on the sleeves and a crisp white collar and blue tie when he came home on leave. Kate had to go downstairs and join the family at dinner. Politely, no one took notice of her inability to follow the conversation.

After the war John Stafford was planning to open the last bottle of Napoleon brandy from the cellar. Some people were rumored to have hoards of hard-to-get things in their storerooms—sugar and gas and tires and cigarettes and even meat—but the Staffords and everyone they knew prided themselves on doing without. For the war effort. They didn't even use all the ration coupons they were entitled to every week. They ate cod and beans twice a week, not just on Sunday evenings.

Hank had been rejected by the Navy and the Army and even the Coast Guard. Poor Hank. It was discovered that he had a slight case of diabetes and for the rest of his life would have to inject himself with daily doses of insulin. It was a hard blow for him, but he pretended it didn't matter, and he took over the factory at Passmore as well as the bank and trust company; with his father he sat on the boards of the shipping company and the railroad as well. He and his wife kept having children and now lived in Milton, where Laura raised deformed pigmy vegetables in her victory garden.

Hank still played big brother to Kate, even though she didn't pay any more heed to him than anyone. "You're acting terribly spoiled, you know," he said to her one day, "indulging in your private grief. Whatever happened to sweet Kate who cared about everyone in the world, who had the guts to get out of Beacon Street and fight for what she believed in?''

"She died," Kate answered through the soft dim anesthetic of the booze.

"You didn't get the world the way you wanted it, so you're giving up on us," he said gently. "You've got better stuff in you than that."

"Ah, yes, the Sshtaff . . . Staff . . . Shtafford shtuff, ho-ho. Shtiff upper lip and all that shtuff. Right." She saluted him and poured herself another drink from the nearly empty bottle. Time for another trip over to Scollay Square. Nobody over there cared how much you drank or not or if there was a war on. She turned away from this righteous man standing over her. She stared out the window. The Boston Common was probably the most boring sight in the entire universe. If you looked at it long enough, enough years, you would certainly die. It was one way to go, as good as any other.

"You look like hell," Hank was saying. "When's the last time you had your hair washed?''

A snort of something like laughter rose up in her throat. She shrugged. "Funny you should ask," she said, "or did our holy mother, Annie, put you up to it, our lady of the weekly shampoo? It's all she thinks about, you know. True. War or no war—say, Hank, did you know there's a war on?—Anne Stafford has Miss Mary come every Tuesday morning, for a shampoo and pincurl. Just like she always has. All the ladies around here do. It's for the morale, don't you know. Oh, our Annie makes sure I get dragged under the faucet every Tuesday, rain or shine, death or taxes, so you've really hit on the big important thing there, Henry, old pal. I do get my hair washed, no matter what happens anywhere else in the world. Priorities, don't you know? We must keep our heads clean while others around us are losing theirs in the bombing of cities and other meaningless gestures.'' She stopped to take a long swallow of Southern Comfort.

"Oh, Katie. It's time to stop feeling sorry for yourself like this. It's been a long time, nearly two years. I miss you, Kate. When are you going to snap out of it and be yourself again?''

"Right! Snap, snap! Aren't you going to be late for a very important war profiteers' meeting or something? Go play with your trains, Hank.''

"The war's over, Kate. That's what I came to tell you. I figured you hadn't heard the news."

He left the room, left her alone. Which was exactly what she wanted to be.

It made no sense at all that she should suddenly start crying then. She had held back her tears for so long. It was hearing dear Hank say "hell" that did it: "You look like hell." He never swore, nobody in the family ever used words like that except her, and she did it only because it still shocked them. That's what made her cry.

Look where their bravissimo illusions about saving the world had got them. She and Patrick, two idiot children believing in love and marriage and comradeship and caring about the whole world and all its unfortunates. How stupid, how futile and silly they were, and Patrick had died, and it wasn't a game at all. And now the war was over and everybody would go back to being proper and selfish and normal and no one would let you think about people who were dead.

It was hours before she could stop the bone-racking sobs. She pulled herself up and went into the bathroom with its unkind, honest light. Her face was swollen and streaked with ugly scarlet scratches where she had drawn blood with her fingernails. Her eyes were hardly visible at all, little bleary puddles of salt water lurking behind puffy folds of discolored skin. Hank was right about her hair—she had locked herself in her room when Miss Mary came last week, and maybe the week before, too. She couldn't stand the thought of anyone's touching her. Now she looked at herself in the mirror and let all the self-loathing pour out. Like the flood of weeping that had overtaken her, she could not control the waves of disgust and rage that were shaking her whole body. Trembling and bent over with the agony of having to confront herself, Kate was nearly sick to her stomach at the sight of the tear-besotted, swollen, shaking, self-pitying blur.

For some reason she remembered something that had happened a long, long time before, in her room when it had been the nursery. Great-aunt Grace: "Even a two-year-old should be able to shout 'Fire,' when it sees one." Kate had remembered that all her life.

"Fire!" she whispered to her hazy reflection. "Fire!" she shouted out loud. It echoed off the flat white tiles and painted white wooden

moldings of the big high-ceilinged bathroom. "Help me, I'm on fire,"
she moaned, but there was no one to hear her.

"Help yourself," she told the mirror painfully. "Or go to hell. Go
directly to hell. Do not pass 'go.' "

Her self-indulgence had run its course. She was bored with talking
to herself and bored with staying locked inside her own morbid
thoughts and bored with hopelessness and with trying to drink herself
to death.

Stumbling, hardly able to see, eyes and head aching, she opened
the door to the bedroom and went to her closet. She threw down the
old green chenille robe that had been her only garment for days,
maybe weeks, she couldn't remember. She reached blindly into the
closet and pulled a wool dress from a hanger. Red. She dressed
quickly, not caring how it all hung together. She was so thin the
dress bunched around her waist when she tied the belt. It hung very
long, in the style of 1935 maybe, ten years old. The dress had a
history . . . so what? Everybody who had liked this dress was dead
now. It was only a dress, an old piece of cloth and nothing more. It
covered her ugliness.

She found a pair of tan leather high-heeled shoes with a strap to
go around her ankle, and she wondered when she had ever bought
such things. Probably another minor act of defiance against her mother;
surely Anne would disapprove of such silliness—sensible shoes were
the very foundation of Anne Stafford's faith. And surely she'd never
worn these on her travels with Patrick. She almost smiled to think
about such shoes attending a cell meeting or handing out leaflets on
a street corner in Wichita. . . .

Kate teetered in the shoes and wondered if she'd be able to walk
in them. The only stockings in her drawer were thick, ugly, service-
able cotton lisle in a hideous tan color. She supposed silk stockings
would be back now that the war was over, but she certainly wouldn't
have any use for extravagances like that.

She had a moment of panic as she crossed the reception hall to the
front door. What if she ran into her mother and had to answer questions? What would she say? Her mouth twitched, and she caught
herself. Imagine still being afraid of her mother. She must be thirty
years old by now, or nearly. To hell with her mother.

Kate walked east and swung onto Tremont Street. There were people everywhere; crowds were filling the sidewalks, unruly people dressed in summer clothes, all grinning and shouting and waving little flags and—there were lots of girls, and women, and they were kissing all the men in uniform that they saw. Bells and carillons rang out from every church in the city. The war was over . . . .

Kate was quickly swept along, out into the street, thronged with hysterical, shouting celebrants, all going somewhere, anywhere, they didn't seem to know or care where the swelling movement took them. Everyone seemed to need to press against others, to shout and kiss and cry and reassure themselves and each other that it was true. There was a current of life and joy in everyone. Kate let herself be pulled along.

Her wool dress was too warm for August. She had begun to perspire heavily. She thought she might faint. She realized that she must be the only one in the whole huge mob who wasn't grinning and laughing and shouting and hugging. And then, without warning, she was being kissed! She caught a blurred glimpse of the face that crushed into hers, a young boy, with red cheeks and crooked white teeth, wearing a jaunty little white sailor's cap. She wanted to reach out to him, but she was being pulled by the crowd. She wanted to turn back, to run home, to hide in her own quiet room, alone and unmolested, but there was no way to turn around. She couldn't fight against all these people.

"Hey, Mama, give us a kiss." A rude voice pushed into her ear, and a man's moist face nuzzled the back of her neck. She struggled to turn around, but there were a thousand faces all jeering and shouting and perspiring, and she couldn't know which man had done this. She wanted to find him, to talk to him. She needed urgently to know—why had he called her Mama, why had he wanted to kiss her, did he find her attractive, was she alive then?

"Kate! Kate!"

Someone in the crowd was pushing toward her, had hold of her shoulder, and then his arm was around her, guiding her out of the street. It was her cousin Charles, in his pinstriped suit and Harvard tie, saying, "Excuse me, pardon me, please, excuse me," as he made his way, with Kate, to the protection of a doorway.

"Kate, you're the last person I expected to find in this mob. Lucky I did. Are you all right?"

"Yes. Hello, Charles."

"Isn't it wonderful! Having the war over and seeing you out again all on the same day, well, it's quite a thing, isn't it? You're looking very well, Kate. . . ."

"No, I'm not, Charles, for heaven's sake. You don't have to say that. I look like hell. I've been bawling my eyes out and drinking too much, and . . . somebody kissed me a minute ago, Charles. Somebody I didn't even know. And when I turned around, he was gone, mixed up with everybody else in the crowd. It was so strange."

"Poor Kate, how awful for you. Come on, I'll see that you get home safely. Impossible to get a cab, they've blocked off the streets, and people are just going wild. But I'll take my little cousin home. Let's work our way over to Russell Street; we'll be safe there."

"But . . . no, Charles, thanks just the same. I want to celebrate, too."

"Well, let me take you to the Ritz then. I'll buy you lunch, and we'll have champagne, how's that? We'll have our own celebration. I'm so glad to see you looking so . . . I mean, out again. You've been ill a long time."

"I want to be with people. You go on, I'm perfectly all right. I think I want to stay in the streets and shout and kiss strangers. I do, Charles. I want to be like everybody else. The war is over, Charles! Isn't that wonderful?"

She leaned up to kiss him, full on the lips. Charles was so surprised that he just stared at her, and she saw in his eyes the same look that everyone in the family always had when there was mention of cousin Margaret Porter or Cousin Horace Stafford, both of whom had been safely locked up in Stafford Lawn for years. Charles clearly thought she was loony. She probably looked it, and maybe it was true.

"I'm certainly not going to abandon you to this mob, Kate. If you want to stay, I'll stay with you, and when you've had enough, I'll see you home. And . . . thank you for the kiss. It was nice."

The mob was growing and becoming more manic, with bottles of whiskey and beer being passed from mouth to mouth, and young women riding on men's shoulders and singing "Roll me over in the clover, roll me over, lay me down and do it again" and "God Bless America" and, as far as could be seen down Tremont and every street that angled from it, more and more people joining the wild street party.

"There's never been anything like this, has there, Charles?" Kate shouted as they were pushed and jostled and buoyed along.

"Certainly not in Boston!" he answered, gasping as a young woman with her pompadour in shreds leaned down from her perch atop a mailbox, reached for his hat, and grabbed it off his head. Charles watched his good straw boater go sailing over the heads of the crowd; someone caught it and tossed it again. "That was my father's," he said.

"Well, I admire your calm about it, Charles. I really do," Kate shouted. To her enormous surprise she was laughing.

"I regret that I have . . . but one hat . . . to give to my country," he panted as the crowd pulled him nearly off his feet. He was still clinging protectively to Kate's arm.

"Bravo, bully for you," she said. "Say, Charles, why aren't you in the Army anyway?"

"I was," he said. "Didn't you know? Oh, well, nothing much to be proud of. I guess the family . . . oof! pardon me . . . no, that's quite all right, my fault . . . I guess nobody talked about it much in the family. It doesn't matter."

"Well, I've been kind of out of things, you know. What happened? Tell me, Charles . . . oh, oh, oh!" The last was in response to another sailor who planted a sweet wet kiss on her cheek. She tried to smile, wondering if her mouth remembered how. She clung to Charles's arm.

"Nothing, really. I was wounded in basic training. Rather embarrassing, really. But they were good enough to give me an honorable discharge. I tried to do my part after that, in whatever way I could."

"Of course you did . . . poor Charles."

"Why 'poor Charles'?" He was honestly bewildered. They were still having to shout at each other as the crowd scooped them along toward the waterfront. Now they could hear bands playing, and guns being shot from boats on the water, and cheers.

"Well, I'm sure you wanted to be a hero, didn't you?"

"No . . . no, I don't think so. I only wanted to do my part."

"Charles . . ." She tried to stop walking, to look at him, but a very drunk young naval lieutenant singing "Heil heil, right in the Fuehrer's face" came careening against her. She had to duck her head to escape the cheerful razzberry that was part of the song, and she had to keep walking or be trampled by the mob behind. Amazingly she heard herself laugh. "This is no place to talk, Charles," she gasped. "Please . . . go on home, and let me be on my own. I want to be anonymous, can you understand that? Just for a little while . . ."

"I certainly won't leave you to the mercy of this . . . this mob!" he exclaimed.

"Charles, please."

"But . . . it's dangerous, Kate. I don't know what you're thinking of . . ."

"Goodbye, Charles!" she shouted at him, laughing, as she allowed herself to be tugged away and into the embrace of a large, burly sailor who had collected red lipstick marks all over his cheeks and chin and forehead. He kissed her, hard, and when she looked around, her cousin had fallen back into the crowd. Charles was frantic, worried-looking. When he saw that he had caught her eye, he shouted something over the heads of all the people between them. She wasn't sure, but she thought it was something about calling on her later to see if she was all right.

"Want a drink?" someone asked her, pushing a pint bottle of a brand she'd never heard of in her face.

"You bet," she answered, and took a long swallow. It was bitter and raw and set her throat on fire, and the warmth was so vital to her life that she didn't care whether or not it was true that alcohol killed germs or what stranger's lips had slobbered on this bottle. She took another good drag before handing it back. But the fellow who'd given it to her had gone on somewhere in the crowd; she kept the bottle to herself.

"Praise the Lord and pass the ammunition!" It was another sailor, this one unbearably young and rosy, smiling like his high school yearbook photo, she thought, looking vulnerable and innocent and

. . . he reached for the bottle and shocked her by putting it to his lips.

"Have you ever had a drink before?" she heard herself asking him.

The boy with the angel face had soft eyes that were brown and round and far from home. It was the first time that Kate had made eye contact with anyone for a very, very long time, and she couldn't look away.

"Hi," he said, grinning. "My name's Billy."

"I'll bet it is." She laughed.

"Well . . . what's yours?"

"Oh . . . Grace," she said. Why not? she thought. Good old Great-aunt Grace, setting the nursery on fire . . .

"Hi, Grace, how about a drink?" The boy put his arm through hers; with the press of a thousand bodies on all sides of her, she was intensely aware of one. Firm and smooth and strong he was, and no one had touched her in a very long time. She had forgotten the feeling of being on fire from a man's body, his hands, his eyes. She took the bottle from him and drained it of its last tiny drops.

"That's all we've got, Billy boy," she said, shaking her head. "All gone."

"Someone will give us some more," he said serenely. He tightened his arm through hers. "Or we could go to a bar I know. C'mon, Grace, how about it?"

"What'd you want to pick on me for? Whyn't you find a nice little girl your own age, Billy?"

"I like you, Gracie. Don't you like me?"

Kate laughed and tossed her head. "Oh, yes, I do. I surely do!"

"Well, then, come on! We got a lot of celebrating to do 'cause the war's over and Billy's not gonna die, what do you think about that? Hey! You crying? For me? For me 'cause I'm not gonna get killed?"

All she could do was nod. The tears surprised her more than they did him.

The beautiful boy maneuvered them both out of the street and over toward Scollay Square, which had gone totally berserk. The striptease parlors and the dirty bookstores and the low bars seemed to be literally dancing up and down the street; everything was movement, lights, and shouting. Kate clung to Billy's arm and descended into hell gladly, impatient to begin the crossing of the river of forgetfulness.

The door opened into a dark, long, narrow room with a bar all along one side and dim small booths on the other. It smelled of smoke and other more redolent things best left undefined. Kate had the sense that this bar was a repository for sorrows and loneliness, that on an ordinary night or day no one talked much in here. There was no mirror behind the bar. On an ordinary day all those barstools were occupied by sad and lonely drunks, lined up, facing the shelves of bottles, no one talking, no one listening. But this was V-J Day, victory over Japan, and it followed V-E Day, which had been victory in Europe, and that was the whole world—wasn't it?—and so everyone in the world was celebrating, and it was unpatriotic and unhuman not to, and so this bar was now filled with people talking to each other, just this once. A celebration. Mostly, there were sailors, no officers. There were also a few old-timers, men with red veins in their noses and shabby clothes and shaky hands. They all seemed to be grinning, and two of the old boozers were trying to sing "It's a long way to Tipperary," but they couldn't get the words out straight.

Billy led Kate to a booth occupied by a teen-age sailor who was necking with a woman in her thirties or forties, with dyed black hair and large breasts spilling half out of her dress. The woman was sprawled over the sailor's lap, so there was plenty of room for two more people in the little booth.

"Hey, Jim-o," Billy said, and, "Hey, Billy," the other answered, without taking his hand out of his friend's cleavage.

"Sit down, Grace," Billy told Kate, smiling at her as if she were the best thing that had ever happened to him. What the hell, she probably was. "Hey, Jim, this is Grace," Billy announced. Jim paid no attention. Jim's partner and pal looked up, glanced at Kate up and down, unsmilingly, and then she whispered something to Jim, pulled herself up off his lap, and straightened her skirt, and the two of them left.

Bill grinned and leaned over to Kate. "What'll you have, honey?" he asked in imitation of the big guys he must have seen in the movies.

"Southern Comfort," she said, and he grinned, pushed his little white cap back on his baby curls, and swung around on his heels in a parody of military bearing; but he kept on turning until he had done a complete about-face, and then he leaned down and kissed her, hard and sweet, at the same time gentle and insistent. His mouth lingered on hers, as if they had all the time in the world.

So quickly did her fear of the deep give way to her need that she literally became dizzy. When the boy moved away to get the drinks, Kate knew that this was her last chance to bolt, to run out of there and back to Beacon Hill and lock her door against the horrors and disturbances of this world.

"Hey, the war's over," he said when he came back to the table. He slid into the booth beside her. He put his arm around her. They clinked their glasses and drank.

"Here's to you, charming Billy," she said.

He knew someone who had a room in a house nearby. From the window they could see the masts of *Old Ironsides,* still flying an admiral's flag so that the old bastard (she knew him) could draw sea pay while eating roast beef at Durgin Park. The room reminded her of someplace she didn't want to remember, but she closed her eyes against the bare bulb hanging over the bed and reached for Billy, saying his name over and over again.

He fumbled and groaned, and it was over. She kept running her hands over his taut, smooth flesh, warm and snoring.

She didn't want to go home, but she didn't want to be there when he woke up, either. She dressed in her red wool dress and went out in the dark. The crowds had dwindled to clusters of sad drunken sailors and prostitutes here and there in the dissolute square. She went to another bar and picked up another sailor, older this time and not so pretty. He rented a room in a hotel called the Albatross. He was skilled, and for a little while she was able to forget what it was like to be alone.

Chapter Nineteen

1946-1948: KATE

Kate Stafford was acting rather badly. She refused to come down to breakfast, for one thing. When a perfectly healthy woman of thirty couldn't manage to present herself at seven in the morning, dressed and cheerful and in good appetite for the hot oatmeal and cocoa that awaited her, it was a clear sign of something seriously amiss. Kate's father was uncomfortably reminded of his cousin Margaret, whose tragic illness had first manifested itself in her refusal to come downstairs for breakfast. Her mother had found her sitting stark—well, with all her clothing removed—in her room, and of course, she had had to be taken under care from then on. Margaret had been a patient in the convalescent home for more than forty years. There had been others; in a family that goes back so far and with so many branches, a weak link, an aberration, must be expected now and then. But it was unsettling, to say the least. A second cousin is one thing; one's only daughter quite another.

He spoke harshly to Kate. Her mother spoke harshly to her. Then they spoke kindly, asked her what was troubling her. After that, confident that they had done all they could, they ignored her behavior in the hope that she would return to normal, so that they would not be forced into the difficult and embarrassing position of having to place her in the private wing of Stafford Lawn alongside Cousin Margaret.

One did everything one could before taking such a step, especially with one's only daughter.

Kate didn't even seem to be hungry at midday, although on some Thursdays, when her mother was out at a club meeting, Kate might wander down the back stairs in her green chenille robe and the bunny slippers she had had since her feet had stopped growing; uncombed and uncaring, she would eat whatever the cook set in front of her. Leaning her elbows on the big oak kitchen table, knowing she was interfering with the kitchen staff's routine, she would linger for most of the afternoon over black coffee and silence. Mary Clancy, who had been with the family since before Kate was born, might mutter under her breath but would never say anything critical of a member of the family, certainly not in front of those catch-as-catch-can helpers she had working for her these days. Eventually, before her mother was due to come home, Kate would climb slowly back up to her room, to spend most of the afternoon soaking in a hot tub bath. By dinnertime she had stiffened herself with quite a lot of Southern Comfort (she had become accustomed to it, hadn't bothered to switch when Scotch became available again) and could sit at the table and listen to them all with what she considered perfect equanimity.

Somewhere along the line an unspoken decision had been taken to ignore Kate's glazed eyes and morose disposition. The family was waiting for her to pull herself together; guests were, of course, too polite to notice. There was plenty of bizarre behavior on Beacon Hill, always had been, and there had been that unfortunate marriage, and Kate had been widowed so young, poor dear, of course she would recover herself soon. The hiccups were probably a minor nervous disorder, and the poor girl's shaking hands were more to be pitied than blamed . . . ? No one who dined with them would ever stoop to gossip. Never.

When the house was silent and her parents and the servants had retired for the night, usually by ten o'clock, Kate put on a dress and high-heeled shoes and went out to Scollay Square.

"Hey, here's Gracie, where've ya been, honey? You're late tonight!"

"Hi, Grace, have a drink. We're way ahead of you."

The ladies who gathered at the Good Time Bar and Grill every night were a lot more fun to be with (even Schatzie, who always ended up on a crying jag) than any other females Kate had ever known. Even Rose . . . with Rose, Kate had been shy, even awed, unable to trust their friendship because she had never, in those days, known who she was herself. But with her pals at the Good Time she was no different from anyone else. They were easy laughers and made no judgments on each other. They lived for tonight, every night, and for whoever was sitting alongside them at the bar or in one of the back booths. Their club had one rule only: Drink up. And have a good time at the Good Time. Two rules, then. Rules you could live with. Kate stepped inside the bar every night like Alice down the rabbit hole, but she had no illusions about finding anything wondrous.

Only a few men were in the place; it was still early. The regulars.

"Where's the fleet tonight?" she asked as she hoisted herself up on a stool next to Madge. Not all the boys in blue had gone home after the war.

"In and out, in and out!" Madge answered with a roar of laughter that ended in a bad coughing seizure.

"Give her a drink, Red!" Kate shouted to the bartender. "Can't you see the lady's choking to death?"

"Who's paying?" Red answered laconically. He filled a water tumbler with Kate's drink and slid it down to her.

Before anyone could answer him, before Madge could catch her breath, before Kate had taken her first sip of the booze, two cops came into the bar and strode toward them. Their faces were mean and serious. Madge and Kate looked at each other. The jukebox was playing "I Don't Want to Set the World on Fire," but no one was humming or dancing. All talk stopped in the place.

"All right, ladies, let's go," one of the cops said. He had an Irish tinge to his way of speaking.

Kate was astonished. What had the women done? To which "ladies" was he referring?

"Come on, come on," the other policeman said. They both were tall and broad-shouldered, and one still had the kind of haircut that they give to marines. You couldn't see anything but stiff brush around his cap. Kate took a long sip of her drink, watching them as they came up to Madge, who looked terrified. Her eyes had grown huge and suddenly bloaty under the makeup.

To Kate's surprise, the first cop grabbed Madge's arm rudely and tried to pull her off the barstool. And then her own arm was being yanked! Kate lost her balance and fell into his arms. He stood at least six feet tall, maybe more, and her head came up only to the brass buttons in the middle of his endless chest.

"Let me go!" she demanded, pulling away from him. But the policeman held her fast, and now he was smiling, which was infuriating.

"No ladies allowed unescorted in bars, now. Come quietly, you know the ropes."

"They wasn't doin' nothin'," Red said mildly.

"You want us to close up your joint?" the cop holding onto Kate's arm growled.

Red shook his head and retreated down to the other end of the bar.

They were pushed and shoved into the back door of a windowless vehicle, with hard, narrow seats lining the sides. The policemen laughed at them when they struggled. Billie kicked one of them, aiming high, with the heel of her spike shoes, but the burly young Irishman only laughed more. They slammed the door shut with a tinny clang, and Kate could hear it being locked from the outside. It was totally dark in there. Schatzie was crying. The others were shouting curses or just clinging to each other to keep from being thrown onto the floor as the paddy wagon started off with a jolt.

Kate felt a rising claustrophobic terror deep inside herself. For the very first time in her life she knew that she was helpless, in the total control of forces which were not reasonable, civilized, intelligent, predictable. She had strained all her life against the ties that bound her to Beacon Hill; now she had succeeded in cutting herself free, and there was nothing but darkness and violence, and no one to save her. She held her breath against the smells in the van, against the scream that wanted to burst from her throat.

The terrible ride came to an abrupt end, and the door was opened. The women were pushed and pulled out, shepherded rudely up a flight of broken cement steps. Kate didn't even try to see where they were. Her eyes were on the ground as she tried not to stumble against the woman being hustled ahead of her. Inside, in a small, airless room, a bored policeman sat at a high desk and recorded their names. Then they were taken out in groups of four by a fat woman with a striped uniform and a wispy mustache.

Kate gave her right name. "I want to call my lawyer," she said. Her outrage was stronger than anything she'd felt in years. How dare they treat a Stafford this way? She would have each and every one of them censured, at the very least, if not drummed off the police force and sued for false arrest.

They didn't care that she was a Stafford and that she lived on Beacon Street. They didn't care that she demanded to call her lawyer or her brother Henry Stafford. They thought she was some character.

"Cute when she's mad, ain't she?" one of the arresting officers said lazily, not meaning it, sneering at her. "God, I hate whores."

Kate was stunned into silence. Later, after the hideous humiliation of a delousing bath, supervised by the matron, who obviously enjoyed the sight of all those naked female bodies cringing and trying to hide themselves from her and each other, she was given an unironed gray jumper to wear and led with the others into a large room with bars on the doors and windows. There were bunk beds in rows of three along the walls, with no sheets to cover the ugly stained mattresses. There was one toilet right out in the open with a filthy sink next to it and one grimy towel on a roller that didn't work.

Kate sat on the thin mattress of a lower bunk next to Madge, who seemed to be taking it all in stride. Madge had managed to keep her cigarettes somehow and offered her one, with a light off the end of her own.

"Keep one going, we got no matches," Madge said cheerfully. "Hey, is your name really Stafford? You related to those big millionaires who think they own this town?" She was impressed.

"They won't even let me make a phone call. It's the law, I know it. They have to let you make one phone call."

"Sure, honey, they will. But not till morning."

"You've been here before?"

"A couple of times. It ain't too bad. Look at it this way, it keeps you out of trouble for one night anyway!" She broke into her generous, contagious laughter again and, as always, dissolved into coughing.

"I wonder what my family will do." Kate couldn't help shuddering. There would be endless lectures, talk about disgrace and scandal and weak links in the chain, it would be awful for quite a while. But oh, how she longed for the haven of 4 Beacon Street right now. . . .

"Them Staffords run the whatdoyacallit, the Watch and Ward Society, don't they? Think they can tell everybody how to run their lives. Hey, did you read *Forever Amber,* you know, that book they wouldn't let 'em sell? I got a friend, a fella, who got it for me in New York. I'll lend it to you, it's good. Juicy, if you know what I mean. I got the good parts all underlined," Madge said, smoking and coughing and chattering cozily.

"My father is one of the officers of the Watch and Ward," Kate admitted.

"Hey, no kidding? That's rich! Hey, everybody, listen here! Tell 'em, Gracie, go on, tell 'em, it's rich!"

Kate was mortally embarrassed, but even so, giggles were rising in her throat. She shook her head and blushed furiously in the dim light from the corridor outside the barred door.

"What's funny?" someone shouted glumly.

"Shut up, let me get some sleep, for Christ's sake."

"Hey, Gracie here says her old man's one of them Watch and Warders! Won't he be tickled purple when he finds out where she landed!"

And Kate laughed, and laughed, and laughed with good old Madge, and some of the others joined in, and she felt that she was as low as she could ever sink, so why not enjoy it, and that made her laugh more, and so passed the night, not too badly.

She telephoned Hank in the morning. He came with their elder brother, Edward, to get her out. Before she would go with them, she insisted that they pay the fines for Madge and Schatzie and Billie, her pals.

"Hey, thanks, kiddo. Listen, big brother, you're not so bad-lookin'. Anytime you want a little fun, you know, my pleasure. Gracie knows where to find me. Thanks, Gracie, see you around!"

"Loitering for purposes of prostitution," Edward said through tight white lips. His driver couldn't hear; the window was closed between the front and back seats. Kate stared out the window at the early-morning streets. Between her and Edward, Hank sat with his hands clasped together. He was twisting his class ring around and around and around.

"Where do Mother and Father think you are?" Hank asked finally, not looking at her.

"Well, usually I'm home in bed by dawn. They never ask. Good taste forbids," she snapped. What right had they to be angry with her? It was her life. She had only called them so they could save the precious family reputation, for their own sakes. It didn't mean a damn thing to her. . . .

They drove to Hank's house on Marlborough Street. Edward refused to sit down at the table with her until she had washed all the makeup off her face and changed into one of her sister-in-law's dresses. (Laura was in Milton with the children, happily spared this embarrassing family episode.) The dress she pulled out of the master bedroom closet was a blue shirtwaist with white trim. It hung on Kate's bones. There were no shoes in the closet that could possibly fit; Hank's wife seemed to have the traditional size nine proper-Bostonian feet. Kate kicked off her own spike heels and came down to the breakfast room barefooted. Her brothers pretended not to notice. Only the serving girl stared.

Hank had called home to tell their parents not to worry about Kate. She hadn't been able to sleep, he said, and had taken a taxi to Marlborough Street late last night; they had sat up talking, and she had stayed the night.

Now the lecturing began.

The maddening thing was that they were trying to "understand" her, not that either of them ever could. There was a thin, grim white line along each side of Edward's mouth, indicating that something like anger might be fighting to get out, but emotions never had a chance in that sterile ground. Christian, charitable, and, above all, controlled.

Edward was saying, over steaming silver serving platters of omelet and toast, that it was her inherited streak of independence. He actually said he envied that, wished he were more like that himself instead of the dependable, stalwart, and undoubtedly boring old stick he was. Now the problem was to keep it out of the newspapers and, of course, for it never to happen again. Which he was certain it would not. Nevertheless, he would feel more reassured if he were to have his sister's word on it.

She was furious and frustrated at their kindness. She wanted to tell them that the charge of prostitution hadn't been far off the mark, and in fact, their sister was as close to being a whore as a girl could get without charging for it. She must have had—oh, a hundred, maybe— men whose names she didn't know . . . but she didn't have the guts to say it.

Staffords always stuck together, no matter what. She had been desperately trying to get unstuck. But whom had she called with her one legally permitted telephone call? Dear Hank, of course. There he sat, his kind eyes avoiding hers. It was infuriating.

Suddenly she turned on them, on their forgiveness and understanding. She was shouting, and she didn't care. She didn't even care if Hank's servants heard her.

"You two, sitting there like stuffed birds, putting morsels of egg in your beaks and nodding your silly heads! You're extinct, don't you know that? Useless, anachronisms, that's what you are, what we all are. Staffords think they own the city, still loyal to the goddamned king, for Christ's sake, if anybody knew the truth! You think you run everything and everyone, you think you're superior because you're rich and proud and charitable and cultured—oh, yes, and kind, so kind, always . . . but you're not! None of us are! We're boring, boring; we're war profiteers and capitalist imperialists; we're goody-goodies and moral monsters, telling other people what to do and never criticizing our own because we're above criticism, we're special, we're Staffords! I hate it, and I hate you, both of you, and I hate . . . I hate myself worst of all!''

They stared at her exactly like two giant birds in spotless collars and neat neckties, bits of food perched close to their mouths but forgotten in the shock of their sister's extraordinary outburst.

Hank was the first to recover. He put his fork down and nodded solemnly. "You're right, of course. All of the above. It's true.''

Edward smiled grimly (when he grew very old, those two lines would be carved into his face like deep cracks in stone). He shook his head, as if impatient with a child who is insufferably slow to learn.

"It's all true," Hank went on gently, kindly, "but don't you see, Kate, we're what we are? We can't change that, can we?"

"And as it happens, in this strange world we live in," Edward took up the refrain, "we are the best there is. It may be wrong, we may be heading for obsolescence, and that might be a good thing for the rest of the world; but the fact is, Kate, Staffords just now are the best that there is. What would you rather be? You've seen enough of the world to know—you don't really want to give up one single privilege you despise so vehemently. Now eat your omelet or you'll hurt Cook's feelings."

"Anyway, Katie, we have to stick together because who else would have us?" Hank said with a wry smile. "Haven't you proved with your young life so far that there's nowhere else for us to go, nothing for it but to stay where we belong, forever, and do the best we can with it?"

"Until we dry up and blow away like Great-great-grandmother's China fan," Kate said slowly, thoughtfully. "We'll sit in a glass case in a museum no one ever goes to, thinking we're still the center of the universe, the hub. . . . Boston is a laughingstock to the whole world, do you know that? Banning books and arresting women because they don't have escorts . . . we're dead, and we don't know it."

"Oh, don't we?" Hank said sadly. He dug into a forkful of omelet and chewed it longer than any omelet needs.

Kate was exhausted. She was suddenly drained of her anger and in need of sleep.

"May I crawl into one of your guest rooms?" she asked Hank in a small voice. "I'm very tired."

"Take the little blue room," he said. "It faces north, and the sun won't wake you."

"Why don't you get heavier curtains?" she said, smiling wanly, feeding her brother the straight line for an old tired, boring family joke.

"Because guests are not usually expected to sleep past sunrise," he answered. "Go on, happy dreams, I won't let anyone wake you."

She stood up on unexpectedly wobbly legs and left the table. At the door she hesitated. It was hard to say what she had to, even to her own dear brothers.

"Hey . . . thanks for everything," she managed.

"Hey? Hey? What's that? Slang! Shocking!" Hank mocked with his old grin.

" 'Thank you' is not inappropriate, Henry," Edward commented calmly. "It's been damned inconvenient, and I've missed an important meeting this morning with this nonsense."

"I do thank you, Edward," Kate said, impulsively coming over to him, leaning down to kiss his smooth cheek. Two thoughts occurred to her: He had taken the time to shave before coming to her rescue, and she wondered if he'd ever been kissed by a whore before.

"And you, darling," she said to Hank, going around the table to kiss him in turn.

"What's all this sudden show of emotion?" Edward wanted to know.

"If I didn't think it would embarrass you to death, I'd tell you that I love you both," Kate said. She started to leave the room. Then she turned back and blurted, to their astonished faces, "For . . . being there, and loving me . . . for being family." Then she turned and shut the door between herself and them. Her own cheeks were burning with the extraordinary effort of the words.

Part FOUR

Chapter Twenty

1948-1950: KATE

Was anything so defeating as a tolerant family? All you could possibly do was to finally stop struggling. You could bang your head against the wall forever, and it wouldn't make a dent, neither on the wall nor on your head. They had it padded; no one could hear you cry.

A columnist wrote an oblique reference to one of the prominent members of a prominent family's being arrested in a low bar in Scollay Square. That was all. Kate's parents said nothing to her. What was there to say? It all seemed self-evident, obvious. One did not do the sort of things she was doing; therefore, those things were not being done. If one's daughter was committing suicide before one's eyes in a most obscene, lingering manner, one must pretend to be quite absorbed by what one sees elsewhere.

But Kate never went back to the bars again. There really wasn't any point. She had not enjoyed the sex with strangers; drinking too much made her sick every morning; she had nothing in common with the women who'd been her overnight cellmates. What had they ever found to talk about all those nights in the bar anyway? She couldn't remember.

Her father died of a heart attack. He was sixty-nine years old. Kate couldn't cry for him very much.

One afternoon she took down the album with its stuffing of news-

paper clippings and photographs she had never gotten around to pasting in. She sat for hours turning over the memories: a picture of
Patrick, head defiantly high, wrists in handcuffs behind his back,
being taken to jail during the clash with the Italians who had marched
for Mussolini that brave and terrible summer of '36 (could it really
be so long ago now . . . nearly twelve years?); snapshots taken on
their wedding day, laughing, laughing, Rose and Marco and Patrick
and a thin, gawky young girl who must have been herself, clinging
to Patrick Casey's arm for dear life; a photograph of him when he
was an altar boy, angelic and desperately sincere in a white lace
collar; faded sepia-toned photographs in the old style, of Patrick's
long-dead parents and his favorite aunt; more news clippings of strikes
and meetings and riots and demonstrations and speeches and rallies;
a handmade valentine. . . . Kate turned over the dead things, the
dry, crackly, yellowing papers, the faded photographs of people she
had never known, the picture of herself he had carried to war, and
after a long time, when the light was gone, she got up from the chair,
and feeling her joints stiff and aching, she laid a fire in the nursery
fireplace. When it was nicely burning, with a cheerful crackle and
glow, she fed the photographs and clippings, one by one, to the fire.
It was all gone in just a minute or two.

She supposed she'd live the rest of her life in this house and die
here, eventually. All her efforts to get out had come to this, but now
she felt free enough to set and light a fire without permission, in her
own room. She understood full well what that meant—resignation
and acceptance. No more running away from her fate. Might as well
be cozy.

She began to see her mother more objectively, not as the ogre who
kept her captive in the tower, but as a victim herself, one of the links
in the inexorable chain. The two of them were links, one following
the other, not much difference between them. It made her wince and
then laugh to see that. When she saw that she and her mother were
no different from each other, she knew that she had discovered one
of life's most ironic and terrible truths and that she had reached maturity. In a way, it was a relief to be resigned to one's fate, to come
in out of the buffeting winds.

She found herself almost staring at her mother sometimes as if in a distorting mirror. Do we look for ourselves in those "fun house" reflections or for reassurance that it's not really us at all?

Her mother: wearing corsets with laces and bones and sensible walking shoes with dark print dresses, never doubting for a moment how things should be, oblivious of anything negative or unpleasant, refusing to acknowledge that the world was a changing and illusory place. Nothing did change inside 4 Beacon Street. There were fewer servants now; some of the furniture was showing its shabbiness, but there was no thought of replacing it. Craftsmanship was not what it had been when the furniture was originally commissioned to be made, when the carpets were brought by clippers and Stafford schooners from China and India and Constantinople. Fewer of Anne's contemporaries came to call now, but even death was no threat; it had always existed and therefore was acceptable. The world which Anne Stafford inhabited was perfect; since the perfection had been achieved before her own lifetime, it was clearly her duty to maintain things as they had always been. What on earth could anyone possibly want that was not right here in this house, on this street, in this city?

It never occurred to either Anne or Kate that they had anything to communicate to each other beyond polite table conversation now and then, perhaps an occasional exchange about a relative or acquaintance who had become engaged or had died. In company they had much to say; alone together, either because they understood each other or because they did not, they wasted no words.

Her mother would die someday; Kate would take her place. Perhaps she would marry her cousin Charles, perhaps not. It wouldn't matter to the house. She would go on living there, becoming as peculiar and as antique as her mother. She found, in all this, an unexpected well of sympathy—was it love?—for her mother after all.

Kate no longer drank Southern Comfort, but only an occasional Scotch or sherry. She took care with her appearance, disguising herself every day as the proper, well-brought-up young woman of gentility and breeding that everyone else had always known she was. A Brahmin of Boston, to whom style was ephemeral and therefore of no interest, and to whom taste was a matter of tradition and therefore not to be questioned. Without any real effort Kate slid into the role which had been awaiting her return from the aberrations of youth.

(God was so smug, she thought once, He must be a Bostonian. He knew she would return to the fold; everyone had always known it, except herself for a little while. She wondered if Patrick had known it, too.)

It occurred to her that even her debaucheries were part of the tradition; there was no escape. And so she made her peace with it. Her cousin Charles was kind and attentive, if boring. Absolutely predictable and malleable in many ways, Charles could be teased and used and dismissed and taken lightly; still, he came around, steadfast and smiling. He said he loved her.

"Oh, look, Charles, that little boy over there, on the huge sled. He reminds me of you when you were nine or ten."

"Which one? Oh. The poor little tyke being pulled by his nanny? Why does he remind you of me, Kate? I didn't still have a nanny by that age!"

"But just look at him. He's very unhappy. I'll bet it's because he wears glasses, and he's fat, too, poor thing. The other kids won't play with him; that's why he needs his nursemaid. I'll bet he still sucks his thumb."

"Don't be cruel."

"Want to bet? Let's ask him."

"Kate! You wouldn't!"

"Well . . . we can ask the nanny. She'd tell."

"I still don't see why he reminds you of me. Don't walk so fast; it's too cold to keep up. I'm out of breath trying to keep up with you. What's the hurry?"

"Come on, Charles."

"You're not really going to ask? Let's go over to the Ritz and have some hot chocolate. It's too cold to be out today."

"All right. Want to go to a movie?"

"In the afternoon? What an idea! Well, all right, if you really want to."

"Charles, do you know that Sundays in Boston are famous all over the world for being so boring? Do you know that in New York the bars are open on Sundays, and the theaters, too, and restaurants serve mixed drinks, and . . ."

"Really?" He was huffing and gasping, trying to keep up with her, and his high round cheeks were bright scarlet with the effort. But he was smiling. He always smiled.

She took pity on him. "All right, Charles, I won't insist on the movies. There's nothing good playing anyway. And somebody might see you going in. It wouldn't do your law practice much good if word got out that you did frivolous things on Sundays, would it?"

"That's true. Good of you to think of it," he puffed.

"What do you want to do then?" she asked him.

"Get inside someplace where it's warm," he answered fervently. "How about the Parker House? I'm bored with the Ritz."

"It's a long walk," Charles said dubiously.

"We could run," she suggested, not at all serious. Poor Charles would have a heart attack.

"We could go back to your house," he suggested.

"No, thanks."

"Then lets just cross the Garden and pop into the Ritz, okay?"

"Okay," she relented.

Over hot chocolate, no whipped cream, he proposed again. She hadn't been saying no; she just hadn't said much of anything.

Maybe it was the invigorating below-zero temperature; maybe it was the crystalline snow covering the world on this bright Sunday, making familiar territory look new, wiping out old tracks. Kate gazed down from the second-floor windows of the hotel, seeing the Public Garden and the Common from a different angle, seeing her house with snow decorating it exactly as it had appeared in *Architectural Forum* magazine of January 1901.

Maybe it was the snow. Maybe it was wondering where her best years had gone. Maybe it was Charles himself, thawing across the table from her, his glasses steaming from the hot chocolate and his eyes pleading with her as if she were capable of feeling something. Something sparked an old mischief deep inside her, and she leaned across to answer him in a low, conspiratorial murmur.

"Charles, I'll tell you what. I'll marry you on one condition."

"You will? But that's wonderful, Kate, wonderful! I accept your condition, whatever it is. Oh, Kate, you've made me the—"

"You'd better hear me out first," she interrupted him, already regretting her whimsical decision. But what difference would it make? She'd just as soon sleep with Charles as alone.

"Dear Kate, darling . . . go ahead. What's the condition?"

She whispered across the heavy white damask tablecloth set with massive silver and crystal and gleaming sunlight. "You'll have to make me pregnant first," she said.

"Kate!" He looked around to make sure no one had overheard. Then he tried to see the joke, staring into her eyes for the sparkle that would reassure him it was another of her games.

"I'm serious," she said calmly. She leaned back and stared out the window. There was ice on the pond, and some rowdy boys were daring each other to test it.

"You can't be serious," Charles said. He was very sure there was a joke in it somewhere, and she could almost see the calculations going on behind the thoughtful blue eyes.

She just waited, not saying anything at all. Charles was shockable, but he wasn't stupid. He'd catch on that she was serious; she just had to give him time.

"You mean it."

"Uh-huh," she agreed.

"Oh, my God."

"Come on, Charles, this is 1948. They don't burn you at the stake for it anymore. Don't you want to have children? I mean, what if I'm too old or something? I'm thirty-two after all. Don't you want to make sure—no point in getting married, is there, if we're not going to have children?"

"But . . ." He was silent, playing with his heavy silver knife, making nervous little taps with it on the tablecloth.

"Don't you want a son to carry on your name and all that stuff?"

"Well, of course, but . . . Kate, you have to admit you're suggesting a very unorthodox way of going about it. Why can't we just get married in the normal way and then . . . well, see what happens?"

She just shook her head, slowly, and shrugged.

Charles stared at her. Deep vertical trenches lined themselves up on his forehead, between his eyebrows.

"Okay, forget it," she said. "It was a silly idea."

"Then you'll marry me without . . . uh, without . . . that?"

She shook her head no. She took a sip of hot cocoa.

He reached across for her hand. She let him take it. Hers didn't have much life in it.

"All right," he said in a near whisper. "If that's what you want. Just give me time to get used to the idea, okay?"

She nodded.

"What will your mother say, your father, and mine for that matter? Everybody will know. . . ."

"Oh, we'll just have a fine, healthy, bouncing, seven-month premature child, that's all. It's happened before."

"I wouldn't want them to think—"

"Please stop saying that," Kate said wearily. "Let's forget it. It was a lousy idea. Listen, I'm suddenly hungry. May I have a scone?"

Charles wagged two fingers without lifting his hand, and the waiter was at their table in seconds.

"Yes sir?"

"The lady will have scones, please."

"Yes, sir. Anything else, sir?"

"No, thank you."

Kate smiled. "I thought you were going to say, 'The lady will have a baby, please,' " she whispered.

"Didn't I? Are you sure I didn't?" Charles answered with an embarrassed grin. "Oh, Kate, if that's what you really want, but . . . I still think you're teasing me. But will you marry me, please?"

"With the condition?"

"Yes."

"Then I will."

He did something completely out of character. Right there in the second-floor dining room of the Ritz Hotel, where anyone might see, he raised her hand to his lips and kissed her palm, then held it to his cheek with his eyes closed. He really did love her.

"Shall we tell your family?" he said after the waiter had brought the hot scones in a basket covered with thick layers of white damask napkin.

"Tell them what?" Pretending not to understand what he meant. Why did he have to be so—so—so much like everyone else?

"Why, that we're engaged."

"Come on, Charles. I meant what I said."

"Well . . . how . . . I mean, where . . . I'm willing to go along, Kate . . . darling . . . but I don't quite see how . . . I mean, I don't live alone, and neither do you. Do you mean a hotel room somewhere? I'm sorry to be dense about this, but I've never . . ."

"Why, Charles . . . are you a virgin?"

He blushed. He avoided her eyes. "No, of course not. For heaven's sake, Kate! It's just that . . . well, you know."

"Charles, look at me, come on . . . we've known each other all our lives. You know everything about me. I've been married before. I've had lots of lovers. Some whose names I didn't even know. I've been arrested with some . . . ladies of the night, friends of mine, drinking buddies, in a sleazy bar and held overnight in the drunk tank as a whore. Charles, you know all that. Are you sure you want to marry me? Aren't you afraid I might give you syphilis or something? Come on, Charles. You'd better say it before it's too late. I know you; once you make a commitment, you won't back out. But I'm giving you the chance now. Charles? Go on, it's okay. Back out. Back out, I want you to."

"You want me to? You've changed your mind?" He looked stricken, more by the fear she would change her mind than anything else she had said.

"No, I haven't changed my mind. In fact, I like you more now than I did a half hour ago. Don't ask me why. Maybe it's because you've got a little thin brown mustache of cocoa on your upper lip— no! don't wipe it off. It's very sexy."

"Kate, don't embarrass me. You seem to enjoy embarrassing me."

"I want to know, very seriously, Charles. I'm covering up with jokes, don't you see that? I want to know if my having been a whore makes any dif—"

"Don't ever say that again. Not ever."

"It's got to make a difference. Does it excite you, Charles? Does it make me more attractive to you? Or does it disgust you? I need to know."

"I've always loved you, I guess. It—I don't think it makes any difference what you've done. You've been unhappy. So've I, Kate.

Maybe we could make each other a little less unhappy. Maybe we could even make each other . . . happy.'' He could hardly look at her as he spoke, and she knew it was the nearest he had ever come to expressing emotions. She was touched.

"Then . . . let's get a room. Right now. A suite, for our honeymoon. Today, this afternoon,'' she said quietly.

"In the afternoon? Today? Here? In this hotel? The Ritz?''

"Yes, in the broad daylight, on a Sunday. Wouldn't the people in New York be shocked if they knew what went on in Boston on Sunday afternoons? I dare you, Charles. Can you get us a room?''

"I . . . why, I suppose . . . but, Kate . . .?''

"What?'' She was already bending over to pull on her overshoes, impatient to be out of here and get on with it.

"Can't we go to the Parker House instead?''

She grinned. "Yes, Charles,'' she said meekly.

Charles was a hesitant lover, but he surprised her with his willingness to be led. His body was too round, too soft, but his love was a comfort and so different from Patrick's that the comparison she had feared in any new relationship never really occurred to her. It was comfortable with Charles and, once in a while, passionate. He took a little flat on the third floor of a house on Commonwealth Avenue, and they spent long pleasant evenings and weekends there, playing at domesticity and love.

To her great surprise, she conceived very quickly. She had never been pregnant before; never having been "caught,'' she had come to believe herself barren. Her bravado did not extend to visiting the family's doctor or any other doctor in Boston; as an unmarried woman in need of a gynecological consultation, she called a friend who lived in New York. All the Boston ladies had at least one friend living in New York who could supply the name of a good doctor there when the need arose. The doctor confirmed what she could hardly bring herself to believe.

As she went home on the train, her feelings were wildly stirred. Did she really want a child? Was she willing now to give over her carefully insulated heart to another human being, one who would be totally dependent on her and force her to care again?

The capitulation was utter and complete. Now she would marry her cousin Charles Stafford and live with him for the rest of her life in predictable days and nights, doing what she was expected to do, had always been expected to do.

But . . . a child! Her own child . . . suddenly she knew how very much she wanted it, wanted the life to stir inside her. Looking out the train window, she remembered being eleven years old and running away from home, taking this same train to New York, to throw herself at Charles Lindbergh and be his love. She saw her own face, faintly lined now, smiling sadly, reflecting back at her against the whirling industrial landscape where lights were beginning to go on against the twilight. Twenty-one years ago. And finally she was taking the train home, giving up the adventure, accepting her fate.

Well, at least you tried, she told herself. I don't know whether you're smart or stupid, taking more than twenty years to learn that there's no way out. You sure gave it the old college try, though.

Charles was delighted, if not surprised. That was what she had wanted, wasn't it, and what one must expect if one carried on as they had been doing? He said they must announce their engagement immediately and proceed with the wedding without seeming unduly quick about it. It would be embarrassing for the family when the baby was born two months or more "prematurely," but he supposed they could live it down. Why on earth had she insisted on this absurd way of doing things, not that he cared for himself what people would say, but their son might carry a stigma all his life? Wasn't she a bit sorry now that she had wanted to defy convention? After all, every rule had its reason. Yes, she admitted, she was in fact a bit sorry about it now.

The wedding was the first really grand social occasion in Boston society since the war, and despite Kate's secret feeling that she herself was the fatted calf, she was a beautiful bride and quite enjoyed being the focus of everyone's approving attention.

They went to Bermuda on their wedding trip, and when they returned after six weeks, Charles enrolled his unborn son in Deerfield Academy, class of 1966, and Harvard, class of 1970.

Charles's father, Kate's Uncle George, gave them a house in Milton for a wedding gift, and Kate's mother gave them a house on Joy Street. While they waited for the renovations and furnishing to be completed, they were at home at 4 Beacon Street, where Kate tried to cope with the novelty of being a settled young matron. She was so bored that she found herself playing old games from her childhood, trying to make the time go faster.

"If I count every rose in this carpet, including the little ones around the border, then it will be four o'clock and almost time to change for dinner . . . if I concentrate on listening for the church bell, I won't hear the grandfather clock ticking and a whole hour will have passed without my even knowing it . . . if I breathe exactly as Charles does, in and out with the same rhythm, I'll fall asleep, too. . . ."

She took to wandering the house again, as she had done as a child, in the middle of the nights. Wandering alone, one hand on her swelling stomach, she missed Hank and wondered if he still walked restlessly at night, too. She waited and listened for her baby to begin stirring. She began to drink brandy, late at night, with a book on her lap and a series of cigarettes, lit one from another, and her thoughts blank. Sometimes she was surprised to find tears rolling down her cheeks.

In her fifth month, which her mother thought was her third, Kate began to bleed. After four days and nights of terrible pain and fear, they took the dead baby from her. It would have been a boy.

Charles cried, in the privacy of their rooms, and she consoled him.

"We'll have another child," she promised, holding him in her arms. She thought: Maybe I do love him.

She stopped teasing him after that and saw in her husband qualities she could honestly respect. Without passion, without pain, without highs or lows of any kind, their marriage grew strong and solid. They conceived again, and in August 1950 Kate gave birth to a healthy little girl. They named her Emily Grey Stafford, after the very first of their line, the fisherman's daughter who had borne her first child at the age of seventeen aboard a schooner bound from Liverpool to Boston.

Chapter Twenty-One

1952: KATE

"Hello, is this Rose? Rose Mallory?"

The voice on the other end of the line was wary, less warm than Kate remembered. "Who is this?"

"Rose, it's Kate Stafford. I know it's been a long time, but please don't say you've forgotten me!"

"Kate? Well, what a surprise! Nobody's called me by my maiden name for nearly twenty years. I'm Rose McCall now, you know. Mrs. Alvin McCall."

"Yes, I know."

"Well."

"I . . . I read about your troubles, Rose. It's horrible. It's a nightmare. Is there . . . anything I can do?"

There was a long silence at the other end. Then a sigh. Rose sounded older—but of course, they both were.

"I don't know . . . is there anything anybody can do?" Rose asked rhetorically. "It's nice of you to call, Kate. But you could get in trouble. My phone's tapped, you know." The matter-of-fact way she said it was chilling.

"Rose, I'd like so much to see you again. Can we get together, maybe have lunch?" Kate asked.

"Oh, I don't think we'd better. You'd only get in trouble."

"Rose, you mustn't worry about me. It's just a question of . . .

well, I'm not sure you want to see me after all this time." Funny, Kate was usually so sure of herself these days. Self-confidence came automatically with being properly married and settled. But just now she realized she sounded as tentative as she had the day she'd first met Rose. Rose had been the self-assured one then.

"Will you meet me tomorrow—say, at Locke-Ober's, one o'clock?" Kate asked.

"Oh, well, Kate, it's kind of you, but . . . no. No, I couldn't. Thanks all the same, though. I appreciate—"

"You don't want to see me."

"It's not that, Kate. But things are . . . different. And anyway, Locke-Ober's . . . I don't have the clothes to wear to a place like that!" Rose was reaching for the old lightness, but there was no lilt in it, not now. So many years . . . so much had happened. . . .

"Please, Rose, we can go wherever you say. How about . . . oh, any place, it doesn't matter. Let's go to Jake Wirth's, we can sit and talk over a knackwurst and beer as long as we want to, and it won't matter what you wear. Unless you really don't want to. Of course, I'll understand if you feel . . . that you'd rather not. After all these years . . ."

"Well, I would like seeing you again, at that. But you shouldn't, Kate. You really should be careful who you associate with. I read about you in the papers, too, you know. The society page, not the news. You wouldn't want to make the news, believe me. And you might if you get mixed up with me."

"One o'clock tomorrow, at Wirth's. I'll make the reservation. I do look forward to seeing you again, Rose. It's been much too long."

"I'll be there. But if you change your mind and decide not to show up, I'll understand. I mean it. It'll be okay."

"I'll be there. It's been much too long. We'll make up for it. See you tomorrow, Rose."

"Say good-bye to the FBI before you hang up. They get so bored listening to my conversations."

"So long, Rose."

"Bye."

It was a warm spring day, but Kate was shivering when she hung up the phone. Startled to find her hand too shaky to light a cigarette, she went upstairs to get her old gray wool cardigan and stayed huddled in it all the rest of the day, trying to shake off the chill of foreboding and sadness that Rose's resigned and unexpectedly calm and lifeless voice had thrust through her. Kate's hands were jammed deep into the pockets of the sweater, clutching convulsively at little knotted wads of Kleenex, as she watched the hearings on the little television set all the rest of the day. She couldn't sit in one place for long. Standing up, pacing back and forth, she couldn't stop watching and listening to the rantings of Senator McCarthy as the grim inquisition went on and on.

She was sure that she would be called. They were making lists of all those who had ever been involved in any way with the party, calling them to Washington to appear before the committee, forcing loyalty oaths on them, blackmailing them with illegal threats of incarceration and worse if they didn't list all the names of everyone they knew or even suspected to have been members or sympathizers. On television it was the Army that was being investigated for "subversives" who might be lurking there; in private hearings, hundreds of citizens—maybe thousands, before it was somehow going to be over—were being called up, their right to political free thought denied, their jobs and their lives threatened by the mere calling of their names.

"You'll ruin your eyes watching that thing all day," Charles complained mildly when he came home to find her curled up on a sofa in front of the flickering gray screen. ("Point of order! Point of order!" Joseph McCarthy was shouting.) It was exactly what her mother would have said, but Anne was in Dedham visiting a cousin.

She got up and walked over to the television, bent down to turn it off. The abrupt silence wrapped her with relief so profound it was almost suffocating; how easy it was, still, for her to shut the grotesque man and his ugly threats out of her house, out of her life . . . . so far. "Yes, of course, you're right," she murmured. She shrugged, feeling cold despite the heavy sweater.

"Didn't you go to the Wednesday Club today?" he asked.

"No. It seems suddenly ridiculously irrelevant. Charles, don't you think I ought to talk to Hank about preparing some kind of statement?"

"Statement? For what? How is Emily, and where is she by the way?"

"I think Miss Pruitt took her out. I heard them on the stairs a little while ago."

"Kate, I do like to see the baby when I come home in the evening. I wish you would ask the nursemaid not to take her out at this hour."

"All right. Charles, what do you think?"

"About what, dear? Come along upstairs with me. We can keep the doors open between the rooms and talk while we change for dinner. You're really letting this Un-American Activities thing get the better of you. What's happening to the schedule around here? I really don't understand why the whole house has to fall into disorganization because of Senator McCarthy." He turned from the sitting room and started up the stairs. Kate followed him.

"Charles, I just don't think you understand how serious this is. I was a Communist, you know, I really was, even though you and the family would like to forget it. I'm in jeopardy, don't you see? It's not just a television show after all."

He turned into his room. She stopped in the hall, and finally he turned back to look at her. "Darling, you really don't need to worry about all that. I can promise you, nothing is going to happen to you. Or to any of us. If there are really subversives in the Army and other places of influence, like the movie business, then I'm sure you'd have to agree that it could be dangerous for this country. No one is going to bother about well-meaning solid citizens who once believed in something and then saw the light in time. Believe me, Kate. I do know something about these things. There is absolutely no reason for you to become paranoid. No one is after you. Now you go put on something pretty and I'll just shave and shower, and—"

"Sometimes you make me furious, Charles. You really do."

"You think I'm not taking you seriously. But I am, dear. I assure you I take it very, very seriously. You have my word on this, Kate, I've looked into it already . . . I'm way ahead of you, dear. Of course, your past is a serious matter, and naturally I'm concerned about its coming back to haunt you. I've discussed this with your brothers at some length—there, you see, everyone does indeed take you seriously—and I can truthfully assure you that you're perfectly

safe and will remain so. Now will you stop worrying about this thing
and get on with your normal life? Wear your blue dinner dress for
me, will you? I like what it does''—he came over to her, put his
hands on her arms, spoke in a near whisper—''what it does for your
bosom,'' he finished with a nice smile. Then he dropped his hands
and gave her shoulder a little pat to send her toward her room.

Kate took a long hot shower and toweled her body vigorously until
her skin was raw and bright pink. Then she covered herself in white
cotton underwear, nylon stockings, a long peach-colored half slip,
and the blue dress Charles had requested. It had long sleeves and a
soft-falling skirt down to her shoe tops. She buckled her medium-
sized pearls around her neck, brushed her hair, and rubbed her lips
with a dab of Vaseline. She never put on lipstick before dinner, even
when there were guests. Why soil the linen and give trouble to the
laundress; why paint it on when one would only be wiping it off
shortly? Her annoyance with Charles had abated completely by the
time she came out into the hallway again. Dwelling on such things
only led to poor digestion; Charles meant well, and she was, after
all, very fortunate to have him. One could do worse; some of the
marriages she knew of were appalling. And, she mused as she descended the stairs, he did take her seriously. He said so, and she
believed him. Yes, she could certainly count herself lucky. It wasn't
easy for a man like Charles, with his deep sense of family, to take
such a chance on the wild and radical girl she had been, actually to
marry her, not knowing when she might revert. Of course, he wouldn't
have gambled if she hadn't been—well, of the royal blood, too, so
to speak, but still . . . He had never once brought up her sordid
past; he had forgiven her completely, generously. A dear, good man
and probably better than she deserved, although of course, she had
turned out to be the perfect wife for him, hadn't she? They were
happy together, a good match. One mustn't dwell on ephemeral pleasures, making love and finding a special intimacy no one else in the
world could know. . . . It was futile and inappropriate and nonpro-
ductive to think about such things when one had a good, solid marriage. It was enough, more than most people had, if one was to believe
what one read everywhere.

The next day, she arrived early at Wirth's and settled at one of the big round tables to wait. To her own surprise, she felt a little nervous. She wondered how Rose would look, if she would seem old and worn and poor. Kate wondered how she would find the tact to offer help, financial if needed or any other kind she could give. She wondered, too, if her motive in seeing this friend from her past was truly charitable, if perhaps it was a mistake to dredge up things best left dormant. If she herself was not in danger, was it really wise to become involved? She was horrified and revolted at herself for such thoughts. Rose was late now, maybe not coming at all. . . .

And then there she was, standing beside the table, looking shy and beautiful, smiling down with genuine pleasure at her old friend. What a perfect place to meet, Kate thought irrelevantly—Rose's sturdy, robust beauty was so perfectly framed by the simple, rich dark wood paneling of the landmark tavern; there was something of the Madonna about her, a glorious painting celebrating God and flesh blended into one timeless woman's face.

The conceit was gone as quickly as it entered Kate's mind when Rose slid into the chair opposite her. Instead of meeting her eyes, Rose was looking furtively back, glancing around the room with suspicious eyes at the lunchtime crowd. Looking, Kate realized with a stab of shock, for someone following her, spying on this innocent reunion, an informer, a government agent, the unidentifiable enemy. In Boston! It was horrible, and it was really happening. She waited, not smiling, until Rose finally turned to her.

"You look beautiful," she said, meaning it. "I'm very glad to see you again, Rose. Are you all right?"

"Oh, sure. Right as can be. Can I have a beer, do you think?"

The waiter brought a brimming pitcher and two heavy steins, which he filled till the foam spilled over onto the tabletop. Kate asked for another tonic water and weathered his frown.

"How did you find me?" Rose asked.

"The newspaper story about your husband's arrest. It mentioned you, and . . . Marco. You didn't see it?"

Rose just shook her head, sipped slowly at her beer. Then she shrugged, and her mouth tried to smile, not successfully. Now Kate could see that Rose was terribly tired; her face had lines that shouldn't have been there. Not yet. "Marco, huh? Poor old Marco. So now they're even dredging up the dead, huh? What did they say about him?''

"That he was a party member.''

Rose laughed, a short and humorless, almost ugly sound. "Well, that's really something, you know. Marco was never in the party. He hated any kind of organized anything. What he was, he was an illegal alien, did they say that?''

"No.''

"Well, I suppose they'll find it out if they're really looking for the goods on Al. Maybe they'll deport me to Italy. I've never been there, might be nice to have a free trip. Do they pay for your passage when they deport you?''

"They can't do that, Rose. You're an American citizen; you were born right here in Boston!''

"They can't do a lot of things, but they're doing them. They put Alvin in jail, didn't they? He's a sweet man, Kate; you'd like him. Never did any harm to a living soul. They put handcuffs on him. Handcuffs!''

"Was he in the party?''

It was an innocent question, thoughtless but without malice. Kate was stunned to see Rose react with narrowed eyes and an involuntary physical withdrawal, her back pressing against the rounded chair-back. Rose stared at her like a cornered stray, fearful, unsure. "Who told you to ask me that?'' she whispered. "How come you called me all of a sudden like this, Kate—or should I say Mrs. Stafford? What's this all about anyway? Not that I think you'd tell me.'' She downed the rest of the stein and scowled angrily at nothing in particular.

"Rose!''

"Kind of suspicious when somebody you haven't seen in all these years suddenly calls you up and wants to have lunch, just the day after your husband gets his name in the papers for refusing to rat on people. And handcuffed and hauled away to a goddamned federal penitentiary. I'm sorry, Kate, but I don't trust you. I can't figure out what you want from me. Talk about old times? Naming all our old comrades so somebody can pick it up with a tape recorder from the next table? Jesus, you don't know what it's like. If I'm wrong, I apologize. But I don't trust anybody anymore. My husband is in jail!

And you . . . why, you're one of the Boston Staffords, all for law and order and—you probably voted for Senator McCarthy, for all I know. I mean, I don't know you anymore, do I?''

"For heaven's sake, Rose, he's from Wisconsin, for one thing!''

Unexpectedly the tension was broken, and they were able to laugh. A little, not much, but it made everything all right between them, if only for an instant or two. Kate reached out her hand to touch her friend's, found it cold and taut, clutching the thick stem of the empty glass. She took her hand away, lifted the heavy pitcher, and poured more into Rose's glass.

"This is a nice place,'' Rose said, "real fake working-class, isn't it?''

"Yes. It's been here since the 1860s.''

"I'm sorry,'' Rose said simply after a moment.

"Oh, Rose . . . it must be so awful for you. I know there's no way anyone could really understand what you're going through—it's a nightmare, and nightmares, like dreams, are so lonely, so unshar-able . . . I know. But dear Rose, please, please let me be your friend.''

Rose nodded, with a little smile, and sipped at her drink.

"How about something to eat? Schnitzel, or knuckles, or knack-wurst . . . anything you want. . . . Oh, Rose, let's remember Marco and—and Patrick, and pretend we're still girls and we're in love, and none of this has happened, could we?''

"How about you, Kate?'' was Rose's answer. She looked directly at Kate. "What's your life like these days? Happily married? I know you've got a little girl of your own, haven't you? How old is she?''

"Two.''

"Terrible time to be born in, isn't it? Oh, I didn't mean that, I'm sorry, what a thing to say! It's just that . . . oh, well, she'll be a Stafford, won't she, and no harm can come to her. I mean that in the best way, Kate, no offense.''

"Rose, is there anything, anything at all, that I can do?''

Rose was fiddling with the stem of her glass, not aware that she was gripping it so tightly her knuckles were white. She shook her head no.

"Have you got enough money?''

"Oh, sure. I've got a good job, you know, if they don't take it into their heads to fire me now on account of . . . I'm a secretary, you know. I never had any kids. Not that I didn't want them; it just didn't turn out that way."

"What about your husband's defense?"

"Defense? It's all over, nothing to be done. There won't be any trial or anything. Contempt of Congress, it's called. No, I don't need any help. Thanks, though. What about you?"

"Me?"

"Sure, what are you going to do if they make you testify? You were a member of the party, everybody knows that, so what if they call you up and tell you to name everybody you can remember who was a member, what're you going to do then?"

"I . . . don't think they're going to call me. My . . . Charles, my husband, told me that they're really not interested in individuals—how did he put it?—well meaning, but misguided, something like that. He said they wouldn't call me. I think he had some inside information, you know, someone close to the committee or something who told him that. Anyway, it sounds right. If they tried to call up everybody who believed in the things we used to, there wouldn't be room for them all in Washington. No, I guess they'll leave me alone."

"Your family really has that much clout?"

"No, Rose, you misunderstand. . . ." The waiter appeared with their luncheon, and she waited until he had set out the huge plates with fat sausages and mouthwatering sauerkraut piled high and the dark bread and potato salad and the bowl of juicy dill pickles between them. "It's really sinful to eat this way in the middle of the day," she said, "but what fun!"

"Sure. Looks great," Rose said.

"No one has any clout with a congressional investigating committee," Kate went on, "but they do know people who know what's going on, judges, I guess, lawyers and senators—oh, not anybody on the committee, of course, but I guess that's how Charles knows they're not after little fish like me."

"All Alvin ever did was sign an antiwar petition, disarmament or something. He hardly even remembers. He never was a member of the party, but he won't give them the satisfaction of saying so."

"Rose!"

"What?"

"You mean he's innocent, and he wouldn't even tell the truth?"

"He wouldn't tell them anything except his name and address," Rose said. "He told them he thought the whole inquiry was unconstitutional, and when he wouldn't take it back, they threw the book at him. Anyway," she went on, taking her fork to the mounds of kraut, "he's got a lot of good company in the pen. Intellectuals and writers and movie directors and—did you know Karl Marx started writing down his ideas while he was locked up in jail someplace?"

"So did Hitler," Kate said.

"Well, Alvin's not in that class. He only wants to be a good teacher. He teaches history, you know, and he's wonderful at it. You should hear him in a classroom full of kids; he really gets them excited about things. He loves teaching . . . they probably won't ever let him do it again, though. Shit. Excuse me."

"Rose, do you think it's funny, I mean funny-odd, not funny-ha-ha, that I probably won't be called?"

Rose hesitated only a flicker of a second before answering; it might have been because she had something in her mouth to chew and swallow first, and then she said, reassuringly, "Aw, no, you can bet your husband knows what he's talking about. There's a lot of ex-party people who won't be bothered, sure."

"In a way," Kate said slowly, "I feel—well, guilty, I guess, and even disappointed, in a peculiar way, about getting off scot-free."

"Why?" Rose said sharply. "Did you do something wrong? You think they're right and people should be punished for what they believe or used to believe?"

"No. I don't think that's what I mean."

"I get it. It's part of that 'let's pretend it's old times again' routine, huh? You want to feel involved again, part of things, am I right?"

Kate looked up, startled. "I wonder," she said slowly. "I wonder."

"Stay where you are; hang on to what you've got now," Rose advised sagely. She wiped her face and hands with the big white napkin and sat back. "You just take care of your little girl and teach her all the things she has to know and forget about the way things used to be. Use your luck, Kate; you've got nothing to feel guilty about. I'm going to go now; I'm past my lunch hour already. Thanks for lunch, and . . . and . . . it was good to see you again, Kate. You're looking really swell.''

"Rose . . .''

Rose was standing, clutching at her worn handbag, clearly anxious to get away. Kate looked up at her, reached out a hand to touch hers.

"Let's see each other again soon?''

"Sure.''

"And you'll let me know if there's ever anything you need?''

"Sure. Bye, Kate. Give your little girl a kiss for me.''

"Good-bye, Rose.''

"Will there be anything else, Mrs. Stafford?'' the waiter asked discreetly. The room had nearly cleared, but she had made no move to leave.

"What? Oh, no, nothing more, thank you.''

The sun on Stuart Street nearly blinded her when she came out of the restaurant. Something did, anyway, making her eyes sting. Guiltily she remembered that there was a dinner party tonight at the Harvard Club. She wouldn't be able to eat a bite. But if Charles noticed and asked what was wrong, she decided not to tell him anything at all about her enormous, ill-advised lunch. She walked briskly all the way home, trying to burn away the calories and the pains around her heart.

Chapter Twenty-Two

1857: GRACE

"Un-American! That's what it is, un-American, by jingo!"

Grace Porter Stafford thought her father was God until she was three and a half. Probably most children do. In Grace's case, her father encouraged the misconception by bellowing and issuing orders from a very high altitude in a voice that literally shook the rafters of the house in Milton, where they lived.

She thought he was president of Harvard, the United States, and the world until she was nearly six, when she discovered that he was all bluff and loud talk. Other people were afraid of him, but she never had been. By the time she was ten she knew why that was so: He had never once, in her memory, looked her in the eye. He hollered at everyone except her. Her big brother came in for a large amount of hollering, and her mother, too, and certainly the servants. Guests got hollered at; they called it debate. But he never, never raised his voice to her. It was sometimes interesting to listen to his opinions, loudly expressed, on every subject in the world. His specialty was patriotism.

"It is un-American!" Ned Stafford would boom out, and that would be the end of any further discussion on the subject, the last word, so to speak. How he had come to be an arbiter of what was "American" and what was "un," no one could say, although it probably had a lot to do with the fact that his grandfather had been Harry Stafford, the Boston Patriot himself.

It had been eighty years since the War for Independence, and of course, Grace's father had not yet been born at the time of Harry Stafford's treasonous acts against the king, which had fortunately turned out victoriously. But as a direct descendant Ned believed he had a right, even a duty, to pass judgment on what was rose-red, snow-white, true-blue American and what was dangerously otherwise. People listened to him, took his word for it without much argument. After all, it didn't hurt anybody. If Ned Stafford said someone was un-American, why, you didn't hire the fellow as a foreman or anything else, and that was the end of it. No harm done. Anyhow, the wine at his table was the best to be had this side of France.

Some things Ned Stafford considered American included: Boston, Massachusetts; Harvard College; railroads; business; and strong young men who headed west to build ranches, farms, churches, and schools.

His list of un-American things was much longer and included: New York City and all of continental Europe; upstart colleges with no traditions; young malcontents who went west to look for gold; warmongers who spoke of the secession; and slavery.

Slavery was the most important issue these days, after the economy, of course, and Ned Stafford was on the right side there. Everyone in Boston who counted for anything was against slavery; as for the economy, Ned Stafford was an industrialist who had been written up all over the English-speaking world for his brilliant and farsighted innovations in industry and manufacturing.

Ned Stafford understood the economy, Americanism, politics, and he believed in the right of all men to be free. What he didn't understand was his female child. She was not at all what he had a right to expect; he wondered what it possibly could have been in his wife's family which had caused this mutation to occur. He was very careful to treat the unattractive little girl kindly and fairly.

Born late, an afterthought, with a brother nearly in his teens, Grace Porter Stafford should have been a china dolly, a pretty little pet for the family. Instead, she was a fat, plain child, constitutionally unable to wear a stocking for ten minutes without a hole mysteriously appearing in it. Her mother's and aunts' constant admonitions to "do try to act more ladylike, Grace, dear,'' seemed to set off an uncontrollable reflex resulting in a broken vase, spilled milk, grass-stained skirts, unsightly scratches. Her fingernails were permanently grimy.

"Our Grace is a remarkably talented artist" became the refrain, through lips bitten in the effort not to scold. There had always been Staffords, in every generation, who stood out from the others in ways that seemed to end either in leadership or in the sanitarium. By the time she was ten it was clear that little Grace was one of "those." It was devoutly hoped that she would develop into one of the talented, rather than one of the touched; tolerance and even pride for such aberrations made the other members of her family feel their own serious responsibility for holding up the traditions. If there had to be eccentrics in the line, it was all the more important for others to flaunt their stability, solidity, and good New England sense.

But the child was a trial. This very day she had upset the tea table, bounding past it on her way to reach the butter cookies. The heirloom silver pot, made by the hand of Paul Revere himself, had been dented, and even now Grace's mother was supervising the efforts of two kitchen girls to remove the tea stains from the Persian rug. Grace had been banished to the garden with her nurse, Mary Murphy. (As for the carpet, the reason it was in the country house instead of still in Boston was that it already had a sinister dark stain that couldn't be taken out; some said it was blood from a family quarrel that had taken place more than a hundred years before.)

"You're so pretty,'' Grace was saying as her chubby fingers moved surely, quickly over her sketchbook, touching here and there to add just the right line, curve, shading which would bring Mary Murphy's likeness to the page.

"Go on!'' the sixteen-year-old immigrant laughed, blushing. She was seated cross-legged on the grass, with her apron covering her limbs. In the deep shade of the willow tree, Mary's frizzled red hair and masses of brown freckles became muted, and she did look almost pretty, like a colorful bird alighted for a brief moment in repose. The child's hand flew swiftly to catch the beauty that she saw, sensing without understanding the fragility and sadness, the impossibility of it. Mary was only a poor Irish immigrant girl, with no future at all, and already her hands were red and chapped from too much soap and water. Soon there would be lines in her face, and Mary would be a woman. But if she could stop the moment, catch it on paper forever . . .

Grace was perspiring through the sleeves and bodice of her French waist; her scuffed boots, one of them unlaced, dangled from the bench that circled the tree. Her thin, limp hair fell over her damp forehead and across her cheeks, but the little girl was oblivious of either the July humidity or the occasional breeze drifting past. All the restless vitality that caused her so much grief when she tried to do ordinary things was focused and controlled when she worked at her drawings; she was content.

"It's hard to sit still so long," Mary Murphy said, not complaining, but stating the fact of it.

Suddenly the child tore the page from her sketchbook and ripped it across. "Not your fault," she muttered. "I'll start again. Tilt your chin a bit, upward, yes, like that. How beautiful. Stay like that, it's perfect."

"You'll make me blush," the girl said. "I'm sure I don't know what to think of all this. Nobody ever accused me of being beautiful before."

"Shhh." For a while they sat, artist and model, in rapt silence except for the movement of the charcoal against the paper.

"There!" Grace said at last. "How do you like it?" She held out the sketchbook for Mary to see.

"Why, Miss Grace! You've caught the likeness this time for sure! It's like lookin' in my own lookin' glass, I swear it is."

"No. I can't catch the movement, the—oh, well, I'll try again later. I suppose we'd better go in now. I want to see that little baby again. Come on!"

Mary stood up, rubbed the back of her aching neck, and smoothed her skirts. "Oh, didn't you know?" she said. "The baby's gone, early this morning, with her mother and the others. Your brother took them out before sunrise, in the wagon. I helped them get ready."

"Damn damn damn!"

"Why, Miss Grace Stafford! If your mother could hear—"

"Oh, I wanted to see that sweet baby again. I never saw such a sweet baby. I never saw any black baby before in my whole life!

What's the good of letting runaways stay in the cellar if you can't even get to play with them?''

"It's a fine thing your mother and dad are doin', and your brother and all, helping those poor darkies to live free. Why, they're takin' the chance of getting hanged for it or shot and worse!''

"Well, don't you think I know that? Come on, let's go climb up in the apple tree and hide. I'll wager you a sticky bun we could stay there till suppertime and they'd never find us.''

"And you'll be havin' me fired if you miss the dancin' school one more time. Though why they want to have it on such a warm day is beyond me. Come on now, be a good girl.''

Grace stuck her tongue out and turned to gather up her book and papers and chalks and charcoals. "I wish I were a boy,'' she said.

"Why, don't they have to go to the dancin' school along with the girls? Sure they do, and wear those stiff collars, too.''

"But they're allowed to climb trees whenever they want to.''

"That's true,'' Mary agreed wistfully. "Back in County Mayo, I used to climb. There was an old fence that ran along the pasture. . . .''

"Did you catch the devil for getting your skirts torn and dirty?'' Grace was seriously interested in the answer and stood waiting to hear.

"Oh, I never wore a skirt in those days,'' Mary said airily. "It was my brother's trousers I wore, for lack of the money, you know. My mother said there'd be time enough to dress fancy when I had to go to work. And it was hand-me-downs then, and didn't I hate it!''

"Trousers? You wore trousers? They let you?''

"Well, there wasn't anybody to care what the little ones were covered with now, was there? It wasn't a fine house we lived in, not like this one, I can tell you. And everyone around as poor as we were. Not like you, Miss Grace, havin' to set the example for other folks. And goin' to fancy places like the dancin' school and tea parties with the whole family dressin' pretty all the time. With a seamstress and a laundress and all . . . not in County Mayo it wasn't!'' She laughed cheerfully at the thought.

"Oh, I'd give anything if I could wear trousers.'' Grace sighed. She heaved herself off the bench and tucked the sketchbook under her arm. They started to walk up the gentle, rolling long slope of the lawn toward the house.

"Boston will never recover," her cousin Henry said at dinner that night, taking up his accustomed refrain from where he'd left off just the night before. "The city is ruined, destroyed by the Papists, thousands of them arriving every day, no jobs, no morals. All they know is to get drunk and have children. Everything we've built in the last two hundred years is turning to slum and saloon. There's no respect for honest labor among them; they think of nothing but having a good time. And voting, for the price of a glass of beer."

"Pas devant la domestique," Grace's mother said in a low voice, referring to the Irish serving girl who was just then handing him a plate of codfish cakes and baked beans.

But servants were not supposed to listen. Their cousin went right on with his obsessive complaint; nobody was going to tell him his manners!

"They couldn't get jobs in their own country because they're ignorant and don't want to learn. Why, most of them can't even read or write—"

"Then it's our duty to teach them," Grace's father said calmly. "And that's exactly what we'll be doing as well as putting them to work at jobs they can respect and be proud of."

"Yes, well, maybe we're being too optimistic about what they can do," Henry Stafford grumbled. He nibbled at his codfish cakes as if they were poisoned.

"Your damned Know-Nothing party has been completely discredited, Henry, and you ought to give up on it. It's been shown up to be un-American. We all were immigrants once, you know."

"How was dancing class today?" Grace's mother asked her, changing the subject with all the subtlety of the soprano's entrance in a Wagner opera.

Grace made a wry face.

"Manners, Grace," her mother said sharply. "Answer my question, if you please."

"I hate dancing class. Mr. Pananti is a dodo. And nobody wants to dance with me because I'm too fat. Some of the boys called Maud Howes and me nasty abolitionists, and we almost had a fistfight."

"Liberalism is being sorely tested these days," Grace's cousin Paul said wryly. As a sophomore at Harvard, Paul was rather famous for his cynicism at meetings of the Hasty Pudding Club.

"A fistfight!" Grace's mother muttered nervously, touching her napkin to her lips.

"Now, Jane, I'm sure Grace is exaggerating greatly. She knows very well that girls never, never fight and certainly not with their fists. She's joking, dear."

But under the tablecloth that draped her lap, Grace's fist was tightly clenched.

"I wonder what old Harry would have to say about the Irish if he were here today," Cousin Henry said. "Even the old Boston Patriot would have some second thoughts if he could see the results of too much open-handed democracy and where it's led us. Why couldn't we have kept the Republic as he gave it to us? Now we've got our hands full, with desperate immigrants who can hardly speak the language, wanting to become citizens and even vote! Your grandfather would turn in his grave—"

"Old Harry would say, 'Put them to work,' Henry; that's what he'd say. He'd see the same golden opportunity that we do, and he'd be the first to cheer our Passmore scheme. I'm sure of it."

"Yes, he'd be proud of you both," Grace's mother said. "Eunice, will you pass the salad around now, please? Paul, do have another helping of baked beans; you're thin as a rail. Grace! That's your third helping!"

"I'm still hungry," the unhappy child protested.

"I don't know where you get that appetite; it's really verging on the tragic, dear. Well, now . . . no more discussion of food at the table!"

"I have something to show you all after dinner," Grace's father said, leaning back in his chair. "I've been saving it as a surprise. The architect has finished the plans for the entire village of Passmore, and I have them in the study. A remarkable piece of work."

"Well, it's a remarkable scheme, Ned," his wife said proudly. "You're a true visionary, just as *Harper's* magazine said."

"I'm still not sure we're not making a fatal mistake, spoiling the workers. An ideal community, indeed! People don't respect what they don't pay for," Henry grumbled.

"You liked the idea well enough when you saw the projection of profits,'' Ned Stafford reminded his cousin. "However, there is still time to withdraw if you want to. I won't have trouble finding another partner, although I did hope to keep it in the family. . . .''

"I'm in, I'm in. If there's a war, such a factory will be sorely needed. I won't let my country down.''

Later they pored over the huge blueprints and maps with the tiny round circles that would soon be real trees. Passmore was Ned Stafford's inventive and daring scheme—a wholly planned community of workers, all under one benevolent and generous employer. Forty-five miles from Boston, Passmore would be much, much more than a center of industry; it would be a humanitarian and utopian place where any who wished to work hard, regardless of education, would have an opportunity to build a good healthy life for himself and his children.

Ned Stafford had hired the best minds in the country, and they had thought of everything: the two modern factories built low and nestled between winding rivers and hills, surrounded by carefully designed buildings, everything the body and soul might require—two churches (Unitarian and Catholic), an elementary school and a high school, a meeting hall where the democratic principles of town meetings could be explained and encouraged to flower, pleasant walks with trees and benches, a central all-purpose dry goods and food store, rows of neat new houses with little individual gardens, and even a social hall for occasional musical and dramatic presentations. Nothing had been overlooked. All the world would sit up and take notice, and other industrialists would begin to follow the Stafford example when they saw how happy the workers would be, how productive the factories, how brilliant the solution to the immigrant problem.

The new factories would be models of modern inventiveness and efficiency, but more than that, they would be the first ever to be designed with the health and contentedness of the workers in mind. There would be windows for even the most menial laborers to be able to look out of, to see the green hills and blue water rolling by as they spun and wove and operated the splendid new machines. There would be indoor facilities for washing one's hands. Green plants would be allowed in some of the offices, and there would be regular times during the workdays for rest periods and luncheon and dinner hours.

It was daring for the employers to provide such distractions, and many of Ned's friends and colleagues said he was going too far this time.

But his rivals were watching the experiment avidly. No Stafford enterprise had ever yet failed to turn a hearty profit. And the family had always had faith in the basic goodness of men and their wish to better themselves if given the opportunity. Passmore would give the Irish a real chance to prove whether they could work as hard as any men and show how they responded to being treated with respect and decency and fair play. Already the applications for employment exceeded the planned need for the work force. Ned was already considering another factory and more houses, although it would mean building on what had originally been planned as parks and greens.

Ned had taken his elder cousin in as a full partner despite his eccentricity and Know-Nothing politics, for the simple reason that Henry Stafford, Jr. was an ingenious inventor who held scores of patents for machines and other timesaving devices for industry. He had made several million dollars before Ned was able to convince him that the inventions should be kept inside the family and not sold to rival firms.

After supper the elder generation played cutthroat poker for pennies and nickels, leaving Grace and her cousin Paul to their own devices. She had a special responsibility to entertain him, with her brother, George, out on a buggy ride with Alice Hamilton tonight.

"Want to play loo or dominoes?" she asked halfheartedly.

"No, thanks. Unless you really want to, of course."

"No. Want to walk in the garden, maybe get a breeze?"

"You don't have to amuse me, Grace. I'll take a book from the library."

"What are you reading at Harvard this year?"

"It's summer holidays, Gracie. I'm resting my mind, resting my mind, that's all. Boring it to death, in fact. Emptying it totally, the better to fill it again next term."

"And you're practicing your lacrosse, aren't you?"

"Oh, of course, every day. I have to stay in good physical condition to stay on the team."

"I wish I could play lacrosse."

Her cousin smiled at her. "Poor Grace, still wishing you could be a boy?"

"Yes," she answered fervently.

He leaned over and whispered wickedly in her ear, "Why don't you just go ahead and be one then? You could if you wanted to, you know."

Grace was only ten years old and not sure what was possible and what wasn't. She tended to believe older people, even if she was starting to learn how often they lied or teased, which was the same thing as long as you believed them. She looked at Paul with her eyes wide; her tongue licked at some residue of raspberry pie that had stuck in the corner of her mouth.

"What do you mean?" she whispered back.

Paul leaned back against the antimacassar his aunt had recently introduced onto every chair that her dashing but greasy-haired nephew might land on. He looked down on his gullible little cousin—Lord, why did she have to be so fat!—amusing himself with the reflection of a kind of worship in her little piglike eyes. What was a bored young man to do on a summer evening stuck out here with nobody but his own family?

"Don't you know what being a Stafford means?" he told her conspiratorially, keeping his voice low enough to be unnoted by their elders off on the other side of the big airy room.

"Well . . . what?" she asked, not sure whether he was teasing or not.

"Well, for heaven's sake, Cousin Grace, a Stafford can be anything he wants to. Hasn't anyone ever told you that?"

"You mean a lawyer or a financier," she said, disappointed. "Not if you're a girl, though. Girls can't be those things. Even Staffords. Especially Staffords," she added as an afterthought.

She started to turn away from him, but Paul thrust out his long, bony fingers to clutch at her sleeve. He dropped it quickly, having encountered a sticky place. What a messy child it was!

But she was listening again, again all ears.

"Grace Stafford, if you want anything at all in this world, you can damn well have it. Go ahead and be a boy if you want to. Who's to stop you?"

Her eyes widened, staring at him, trying to fathom his reasoning. Now she backed off, and Paul's eyes closed as if weary from the effort of imparting this precious, heavy secret.

"I don't believe you," she snorted at him. Paul opened his eyes, but his expression didn't change. He didn't care whether she believed him or not—that was the very best sign that what he said might be true! She'd have to think about it awfully hard. But she knew better than to try to discuss the thrilling possibility with anyone else. Paul wasn't going to bother talking to her anymore; he had picked up a magazine and was thumbing through it.

Grace went over to the table of cardplayers, waited until the hand had been played and her father had swept up all the pennies and stacked them in neat columns next to his ashtray. Then she bobbed a clumsy curtsy. "Good night, Mother, Father, Cousin Henry," she said all in one breath.

"Going to bed? So early?" her mother asked, suspicious of anything unusual in her daughter's behavior.

"And leaving your cousin to fend for himself?" her father added, his eyebrows up but his eyes never leaving the cards as he shuffled them. "Not very hospitable, is it?"

"Paul said he would get a book from the library to read."

"Well, that's very nice of him, to excuse his hostess from her duty," her father said.

"Since we're here every blessed evening of the entire summer, Ned, it won't hurt the boy to amuse himself for once. Let the child go to bed if she wants to, and deal the cards," old Henry said irritably.

"Good night then, Grace . . . dear," her mother said, and the others chimed in, and she was finally free.

After Mary had helped her undress and wash her hands and face and under her arms and her feet, and she was wrapped in the voluminous cotton nightdress and tucked into her bed, she lit the oil lamp and took her sketchbook out from its drawer next to her bed. She drew herself, fat and ugly, dressed in trousers and waistcoat and high stovepipe hat. She tried again and again, and then she tore up the drawings and got out of bed to burn them in the fireplace, this time remembering to open the flue before she lit the match to the papers.

She climbed back on top of the bed and thought for a long moment, and then she drew herself, slim and handsome, in jaunty narrow trousers and a shirt of her own design. One of the drawings was so satisfactory that she hid it at the bottom of her wardrobe in the cigar box with the six strands of rope around it and the warning "DEATH TO ANYONE WHO OPENS THIS BOX!!" with the skull and crossbones dripping blood on it. Then she blew out the lamp and went to sleep.

She dreamed that she was a soldier, with her hair cut short and grown thick under her fine crimson tricorn hat trimmed in gold braid. She rode a huge gray stallion into battle, and all the other soldiers, who were grown men with hair on their faces, took orders from her.

Sometime near dawn she was awakened by the sound of the secret bell. It had been rigged so that when a hidden rope was tugged out in the cow barn, a gentle tinkling would be set off in the cellar of the house. If strangers were on the premises, and the deliverers of the runaways had no way of knowing whether there were or not, the bell could be explained in a lot of different ways. Her mother once told Mrs. Alcorn, who was nosy and suspicious, that it was the laundress calling for the kitchen maid to bring down more lye soap.

But Grace knew what it meant, and she climbed down from her bed quickly. Two loads of blacks in two days, a busy time on the Underground Railroad! She bundled herself into her wrapper and flew down the back stairs without her carpet slippers.

"Where are you going?"

Her mother's disembodied voice spoke out from the dark of the pantry, scaring Grace half to death.

"To see the runaways," she answered in a small voice.

"In your nightclothes? Grace, Grace, what am I to do with you? Go back upstairs. And never, never come out of your room until you are civilly dressed, do you hear me?"

"Yes, ma'am."

"You were going to show yourself to—oh, my dear, is there no hope for you at all?"

"Who went to fetch them, Mama?"

"Your father and your brother."

"In their nightclothes, I'll wager anything."

"Don't be impertinent . . . Grace? What are you doing? Are you taking food from the larder? Don't you know that it's food making you fat, too much food? Don't you care if everyone thinks you're a glutton? It's four o'clock in the morning!"

"I'm hungry. I can't help being hungry."

"Go to bed. In the morning you may help feed those unfortunate
Negroes. You know that everything depends on our keeping calm and
cautious heads now, Grace. The safety of these poor runaways, and
our own as well. We may have the sympathy of everyone in this
commonwealth, but we're breaking the law just the same. These people are someone's property, according to the evil, un-American laws.
. . . Well, anyway, you go on back upstairs and to bed."

"Yes, ma'am."

"Good night, Grace . . . dear."

"Mother?"

"What is it now?"

"Why is it nobody cares if boys get fat, but girls can't ?"

"Well, that's not exactly true, dear. A woman should have a nice
well-rounded figure, and I'm sure you will when you get your growth.
I'm sure you'll be quite attractive after all."

Grace knew that was a lie, but a benign one, and she felt a wave
of love for her mother. She kissed her in the darkness, on the cheek.

"Good heavens, Grace, you've got cookie crumbs all over me!"

In the morning she dressed quickly and went downstairs to help.
Cook was hard at work, grumbling and taking breads from the oven;
her brother, George, and the outside servants were packing baskets
of good-smelling oatmeal mush and back bacon and tomato preserves
in the wagon, topping the loads with hay to cross the lower pasture.
Grace climbed on the buckboard alongside Calvin, the stableboy, and
George jumped on the axle, and in a moment they were rolling, heading for the barn and its secret cellar down below the apple orchard.

Inside the barn, with the wide doors shut, it was chilly and dank
and dark. The cows groaned as they waited their turns for the milk-
ing; several young hands were busily filling pails with the plunk-
plunk squirting sounds of early morning, but Grace refrained from
her usual stolen dipperful of the warm, bubbly milk today. She had
important business, and she followed Calvin to the trapdoor carefully, carrying a heavily laden basket in each hand. She was determined not to trip this time.

Her brother led the way down the ladder into the root cellar, and
they followed him silently. Even Grace had to crouch a little bit,

going through the long tunnels lined with planking. Jars of preserves and jams and jellies and fruits and vegetables and chutneys and chowders were slowly filling the shelves as the summer progressed. There was the ripe smell of potatoes and onions and empty spaces for the squash and pumpkins and apples to come. At the end of the cool dark passageway, a recessed door was opened from within when George rapped. Inside, a few candles flickered in the bit of air from the pipes which were set into the dirt ceiling between the beams. There were cots and washtubs and a long table with benches. One sensed rather than saw the presence of the Negroes: ten or so men and women staring at them with fearful, wary eyes. All was silent, silent as a tomb.

There had been stories, spread by slavery sympathizers, about the runaways suddenly turning on their white hosts with knives and garrotes, attacking viciously and silently, and then looting and burning houses in their wake. Grace's father and the other abolitionists said that was not true, that the stories were made up, that the Negroes were grateful to them and knew they had nothing to fear. But Grace always felt a chill of terror lying just underneath her skin when she was down here, watched by the silent eyes and herself too polite or too scared to turn around and stare at them.

Why shouldn't they be distrustful and filled with hate for all white people? Their whole experience had been one of betrayal, enslavement, and harsh treatment from all the whites they had encountered thus far. Frightened, exhausted from days and nights of running and hiding, desperate or they wouldn't have run in the first place, knowing that if they were caught, they'd be sent back to their owners and beaten or hanged, knowing that they were a danger and a chore to their hosts along the Underground Railroad, how could these sad people believe in pure acts of charity and goodwill, especially from strange, wealthy white men? Perhaps there were one or two who still nursed rage in their hearts that had not been beaten out of them—a man with a knife just waiting for the opportunity to avenge a lost wife or child on the first white back that was turned toward him. . . . Grace was scaring herself to the point of trembling all over. Her hands shook as she helped set out the food on the long, narrow table. She felt the silence and the eyes on all sides. She stayed close to her brother's side as they unpacked the steaming bread and porridges.

But as her eyes adjusted to the dim light, she couldn't resist peeking at them. There was something special, something odd about this bunch. From the corner of her eye she saw a giant flash of orange and blue and purple, and her astonishment overcame her fear. She looked up and stared at the woman.

Well over six feet tall, the giantess stood near the center of the room, the only place where her full height could be tolerated in the cavelike dugout. It was implicitly stated in her proud bearing that this woman could not or would not stoop. She was wrapped in a flowing robe of brilliant colors. She had a turban wrapped around her head, knotted intricately, making her even taller. Huge hoop earrings pounded from a dull glowing metal dangled at both sides of her beautiful, flat, round face.

"Oh, how beautiful!" Grace said before she thought. The richness of colors and the strength in the woman's face made her forget her fear. She had to draw, to try to paint this incredible sight! Instead of lowering her eyes as the woman returned her stare, Grace found to her astonishment that she was speaking directly to the woman. Where had she found such nerve? But she was no longer trembling. Her round mouth formed a tentative smile.

"Grace!" her brother said sharply.

But the giantess raised her hand, palm facing them, as if she were ordering—ordering!—George to be silent. She said nothing; but her magnificent face softened, and she nodded slowly. She had not taken her eyes from Grace's face.

"May I bring my sketchbook and draw you?" Grace heard herself asking.

The woman looked puzzled, and then Grace made motions in the air as if drawing.

Yes, the woman nodded. Now she actually smiled down on Grace.

"Come on, let's go so they can eat their breakfast while it's still warm," George said curtly. He took his sister's fat upper arm in his fingers, pinching her hard, and drew her away.

"Don't you know that you insult their dignity when you do things like that?" he scolded when they were out in the sunlit pasture again.

He had left Calvin behind to do his work, and the two of them were walking back to the house.

"She wasn't insulted. She said I could come and draw her," Grace said stubbornly. "Wasn't she wonderful? Those robes! Where do you think she got them?"

"Why, from Africa, I suppose. She must be newly arrived."

"She was the most beautiful creature I've ever seen," Grace said. Her fingers itched to try capturing that wild face on paper. Could she? Oh, how she longed to have talent . . . and the colors! If only she could bring a suggestion of the glory she had felt in the woman, in her colorful robes, the clash of orange and purple and blue, the jagged patterns woven together in flashing, exploding juxtapositions. . . . Of course, George was right. It was the very exotic jungle itself she had seen, rich and animal, bursting with bits of torrid sunlight and darkness all together.

"You'll have to get Father's permission," George was saying.

After endlessly boring discussion her parents agreed that she could go back to the cellar if Mary Murphy kept her company, and Calvin as well. After lunch she hurried back across the pasture, urging Mary to go faster. Poor Mary was terrified and suggested more than once that perhaps Grace could sketch the newly opened wild flowers on the hill, or herself again, or the house itself, or anything except those savage runaways who might kill them both. And she was afraid of closed-in places under the ground, where one couldn't breathe at all.

But they went into the barn and got Calvin to go down with them, grumbling as he did. When he opened the trapdoor, strange and terrible sounds of drumming greeted them. All three were frightened out of their wits.

"What is it?" Grace whispered, staring down into the darkness as they crouched over the open trapdoor at the back of the cow stalls.

"Holy Mother of God, let's run away from here," Mary Murphy gasped, pulling at Grace's sleeve.

Grace wanted to run, too. The drums had a muffled and insistent sound, palpitating like living things.

The two young servants pulled at Grace to come away, making her aware of her responsibility to be calm and sensible. For a wild leaping moment she had forgotten why she was here, but she still clutched

her sketch pad and pen box, and Mary carried the paints for her; the
memory of that extraordinary vision of the giantess in her glorious
colors came rushing back, fitting curiously with the beating, pulsating
rhythms from below, and she knew she must go down.

"I'm going," she whispered, "and you can follow or not, I don't
care."

Their orders were to go with her, and so they followed through the
food cellar and down to the end of the passageway. The drumming
surged and pulsated as they neared, growing faster and more fevered
until the blood in their bodies pounded with the same gathering excitement.

It was the greatest act of courage she had ever done when Grace
raised her hand to rap on the door. In the time while they waited for
it to be opened from inside, she had to pretend to herself that her feet
were bolted to the dirt floor to stop herself from running back to the
daylight.

"Shhh," they were cautioned by Moses, their freedman who acted
as go-between for the Staffords and their temporary "guests." He
stood aside to let them in.

They stood against the back wall and watched. Men were dancing,
a few steps, raising their knees and setting them down, almost lei-
surely. The tall giantess was standing with the two men who huddled
over elongated homemade drums, pounding them and slapping them
and caressing them and scratching them and tickling them and rubbing them with the flat palms of their open hands. They never lost
the beat, while working intricate patterns for the men to dance to. A
young woman leaped suddenly to her feet, danced around bent over
in a kind of half swoon, and then subsided as the drums lowered
their volume to a sigh and then rose again with renewed life.

"What are they doing?" Grace whispered to Moses.

"Witchery," was his answer.

As her eyes adjusted to the dim, smoky light, Grace opened her
book and reached for a piece of charcoal. She began to draw the
dancers, the drummers, all framed around the space into which she
would set the beautiful woman in her African robes.

Her mind raced as deliberately and freely as her fingers: I don't
want to be a man, I don't care if I wear trousers and fight in battles

or not. I will be what I damn well choose, just as Paul said. Even if he was teasing me, even if everybody in the whole world teases me, I don't care. I never will care. I'm going to be an artist.

Standing beside her, Mary was crossing herself over and over again, whispering prayers to the Virgin and Jesus and the Holy Ghost and all the saints one by one. Calvin had made himself as small as he could against the wall in the darkness. When they begged her to leave off and get away from there, she spat at them, "Go on, get out of here! Stop pulling me, damn it! Leave me alone, or I'll have them put a curse on you, I swear I will!"

Her eyes glinted with a light that frightened both of them, more than the drums, more than the glistening dancers and the smells and the magic. They ran and left her.

The ten-year-old girl went on with her work. It was late that night, hours after she had come into the house and had her supper and gone to bed, that Grace Stafford realized she would probably never be troubled by other people's fears and scruples and silliness ever again. It might have been the magic or just the concentration of working at her drawing, but somehow she had been lifted out of all her worries about being fat and clumsy and a disappointment to everybody. She really didn't care much, and never would, as long as she could work with paper and ink and colors.

Chapter Twenty-Three

1865-1939: GRACE

Something about the President had caught the young girl's imagination; she had worshiped him, finding true style in his manner despite the fact that his background was as different from Back Bay as one could get. She even admired his wife, that rather silly social butterfly—thinking that if *he* cared for her, she must have fine, if hidden, qualities. She was just eighteen when he was assassinated. Somehow she knew, the instant she heard the horrifying news, that the bullet which had penetrated the President's brain would change the world forever.

It was true then; everything turned bitter and sour. The freedom which had been promised to the blacks did not quite materialize the way they had thought and hoped it would; southern whites would not comply with the new laws, and the Negroes themselves either feared to claim their new rights or grabbed them in distressing ways.

The sixties were a time of dreadful upheaval, culminating in the impeachment of President Johnson in '68. Even though he was acquitted, the scandal rocked the country; in Boston men spoke in low voices of their fears that the very foundations on which the Republic had been founded were in jeopardy. The war had severed the Union in two parts; putting it back together again under one flag was a formidable task. It was time for a military man, and General Grant appealed to a large majority of the voters, although not in Massachusetts.

In Wyoming women were given the vote. It was true, nothing would ever be the same again.

Grace Stafford's parents looked on her as strange, exotic, and disturbing proof of the world gone awry; she came to her young womanhood in the sixties, and they simply could not understand her, not even enough to try to change her. She grew in their midst like a flower never before seen by human eyes; they could only observe and wonder. Because she was their daughter, and a Stafford, and because she was impervious to their opinions, they felt a certain pride in her very strangeness, in a curious way, as if her odd clothing and unsocial manner were exactly what they had most desired in a daughter. Of course, it was a great relief when the dean of the Fine Arts Department at Harvard looked at her drawings and proclaimed her a genius.

When the President was shot, Grace gave all her dresses and fancy waists and skirts to the Boston Ladies' Committee for the Poor and Indigent and ordered all new skirts and jackets to be made from coarse black silk and linsey-woolsey.

"Black! It's not appropriate, Grace!" her mother had said. It was one of Jane Stafford's last efforts to effect change in her daughter.

"I am in mourning, and what's more, I shall stay in black for the rest of my life. It's much less trouble and will eliminate the time and energy one has to give to selecting adornments. It suits me perfectly."

"It doesn't suit you at all. You're a young girl, only eighteen, and . . . one only wears mourning for members of one's family, Grace . . . dear."

"I intend never to think about clothes again. What's for luncheon?"

"I don't know how you expect to attract a husband, Grace. Honestly!"

Grace laughed. "I'll take a hamper out to the meadow with me; the light is wonderful this morning," she said, calmly pulling up the drawbridge across the moat that separated her from her mother's concerns.

With a telltale note of hopelessness in her voice, Jane told her husband that very evening, "Someday she's sure to fall in love, and then things may be quite different. She's going through a difficult time."

"You've been saying that about her since she was two," Ned Stafford remarked, not looking up from the *Evening Transcript*.

"And when that happens, she'll begin watching her figure, and caring about her appearance, and . . ." Jane's voice trailed off.

"By God, nothing but dire news in the press these days," her husband grumbled. "Here's an editorial saying Boston's in danger of becoming second to New York as a port. Shocking thing for the *Transcript* to say, shocking!"

"I'm sure it's true," Jane consoled herself aloud. "She'll fall in love like any normal girl and lose all that extra weight and wear pretty dresses again, I'm sure she will."

But she was wrong. Grace didn't fall in love until she was forty-three years old. It was just as well that Ned and Jane Stafford met an untimely and tragic end eleven years before that extraordinary event; neither could have survived the shock of it. It would not have been the fact that Grace fell in love with an actress, but that the object of their daughter's affections was a married woman, with a child; even the most tolerant Victorian heart could forgive only so much. (Boston itself could only gasp and refuse to believe it. The scandal was so salty it was indigestible. Therefore, it did not exist.)

Grace Stafford's work achieved international repute; museums bid against each other for the right to buy her drawings and pastels. She was invited to symposia to discuss art in New York, Philadelphia, and even St. Louis, which had pretensions to culture. She traveled abroad at the expense of the French government and the London Fine Arts Society to be present at exhibitions of her work, and everywhere she went she left behind a marvelous, if wrong, impression of what Boston was like.

Grace and her brother, George, had a serious falling-out over the petty matter of who should inherit the estate when their parents were killed in the collapse of the Tay Bridge in Scotland while touring the British Isles by train. It was 1879; Grace was thirty-two years old and her brother eleven years older. George had his own house on

Beacon Street, a two-year-old son, and a wife who refused to step
foot outside the city for any reason whatsoever. It was an oversight,
Grace told him, that the house and grounds at Milton devolved on
him. Surely it should be hers. She had lived there all her life and
would not live elsewhere. And it would be hers; never would Grace
Porter Stafford live under the protection of any man, not even her
brother.

George refused to grant his sister any part of the land, saying that
women should not inherit, that he would always see that she was well
provided for, and at any rate, her own trust funds were more than
adequate to allow her to buy property and build wherever and whatever she liked.

What he was really thinking, and his sister knew it full well, was
that she was a full-blown crazy and should be incarcerated. Grace's
reputation as a genius cut no ice with him; he found her an embarrassment.

She threatened to take the matter to court. He didn't believe she
would commit such a scandal.

But he decided to outmaneuver her; she was only a woman, after
all, despite the outrageous trousers she had taken to wearing. (Thank
God she didn't attend social functions or the usual women's gatherings! The arty people she associated with didn't seem to find her odd,
but of course they were a peculiar assortment themselves, John Singer
Sargent, Winslow Homer, Mark Twain, and that bunch.) George prevailed on his wife, Helen, to visit his sister and to persuade her, as
only a gentlewomanly sister might do.

"Go to Milton? Certainly not!" was Helen's response. "Let her
come here, and I'll certainly talk to her."

"Helen, my sister is quite capable of causing a public scandal, I
don't believe you understand how serious this is."

"George Stafford, I thought we had determined once and for all
that you would never require me to travel. Before I agreed to marry
you, the issue of a honeymoon trip—"

"Oh, for God's sake! Milton is a half hour's ride, and the house
is quite civilized. It's not as though I'm asking you to explore the
Northwest Passage or accompany Stanley up the darkest Nile!"

"There are insects in the country. I am extremely sensitive to insects. A bee sting once gave me the most frightful fever; I might

have died. And that bee was right in Louisburg Square! I don't know how it was allowed to get in—''

"Helen, you don't seem to realize what is at stake here."

"Invite your sister to have tea with me. Or I shall, I don't mind. She can come to the house, and we can have a nice chat."

"On a Wednesday perhaps? When your musical society is meeting? In her trousers?''

"Well, she could come on another day when no one would be here."

"Helen, I want you to go to Milton and spend a day with her, and that is final."

"A whole day?"

"Yes."

"In the country?"

"That's right."

"You promised me when we were married, you'd never make me leave Boston. You promised."

"Extreme times call for extreme measures."

A long pause.

"Are we really in danger of losing a great deal of money, George?''

"It's not the money, Helen, dear. I certainly do not begrudge my sister anything material. She can have it all. But she is—well, she is—an eccentric person, as you know very well, and for her own good, I cannot allow her full control of her own property . . . no, there might come a day when . . . Helen, I wish you would simply obey me and stop arguing."

Pause.

"Love, honor, and obey."

"Yes, that's it."

A deep sigh.

"Your sister frightens me, George. She's so . . . so . . . strong, so . . . big and strong . . . like a man."

"Well, you've always been able to twist me around your little finger, now, haven't you, dearest? You certainly know how to get around any man . . . and anyway, whatever the appearance of it, Grace is still a female. I believe she will react more readily to another female than to a man. Even to me."

Sigh.

"All right, George. I'll go."

"Good girl."

"And I'm to convince her not to fight the will?"

"Right. You understand perfectly. I knew you would."

"If I get bitten by an insect, I shall never forgive you, George."

"But wouldn't a pretty velvet cape cover such a contingency?"

"The one I admired on that sketch of the queen!"

"The very one. You may order it as soon as you return from your visit."

"You are generous, George. Cruel . . . but generous."

"Now don't get that pretty pout on your little face, or you'll make me late for my lecture."

"I'll write a note to Grace this evening."

"There's my little girl."

"George?"

"Mmm?"

"Do you think red would be too . . . too regal?"

"Red? For what?"

"Oh, my new cape, silly!"

"Oh. Yes, definitely. Not red. Blue, I should think, a subdued, conservative blue."

"Yes, of course. You have good taste, George."

"I like to think so. Good night, dear. I'm off to the club."

When he had left the room, Helen took up a pen to begin making a list of the clothing she would need for a whole day's trip to the country.

"Well, I never expected to see you in Milton! Come to get a tour of your new house, have you? Now that you and your husband own it."

"Why, no, Grace, not at all. I've come to . . . console you on the loss of your dear parents."

"Come on, I'll show you the gardens."

"Oh! I mean . . . must we?"

"Come on."

When she saw the asparagus growing in neat rows ready for the harvest, Helen was truly impressed and astonished. "I always thought Cook braided them in the kitchen," she observed.

She was a bigger ninny than Grace had ever thought, and it just proved what a waste of time and energy one's family could be. A whole afternoon's work time lost.

Over tea Helen began expounding heartily on what a good, generous, thoughtful, considerate, protective, trustworthy man her husband was. Grace caught the gist quickly.

"Oh, he's sent you to sweet-talk me into giving up the lawsuit, has he? Tell him to put it in his hat. Either I get this house and all the land it's on, or I start proceedings Monday next."

"Oh, Grace, you wouldn't!"

Grace stood up. All 250 pounds of her rose from the oversized chair to loom above Helen like the pictures she had seen of Gibraltar standing at the entrance to the Mediterranean, guarding the sea.

"Look at me, Helen."

Helen looked up, smiling nervously.

"I would."

Helen nodded and bit her lip. She set her teacup down very carefully. Then she looked up at her giant sister-in-law again. "May I go home now?" she asked quietly.

It was not only the house in Milton but several millions in cash and some nearly forgotten acreage along the Massachusetts seacoast which Grace demanded and received from her brother. Once the transaction was completed, in the discreet offices of their cousins' law firm, brother and sister strolled forth together onto Park Street and remained for the rest of their lives excellent friends, that closeness being based as much on mutual respect as on mutual parentage.

By the time Grace stunned society into silence with her great love George Stafford had mellowed enough to tell his wife to "shut up" even in the privacy of their bedchamber when she dared raise the subject of his sister's embarrassing behavior.

In the winter of 1890, the eminent artist Miss Grace Porter Stafford attended every single performance of the touring Shakespearean Guild's production of *Romeo and Juliet* during its three-week stay in Boston. She sat in the first box, alone and unsmiling. Discreet glances through one's opera glasses revealed her stern profile gazing down onto the stage, following the graceful figure of Juliet, ignoring Romeo completely. After each performance Miss Stafford waited at the stage entrance in her closed carriage for Miss Jenny Cardozo to join her, and they would be driven off for a private supper to a place or places unknown. The actress's husband, who was also her manager, walked back to the hotel alone every night, appearing jaunty and swinging his stick as he went.

Miss Cardozo retired from the stage and from her marriage at the end of the run. She and her little boy went to live at Miss Stafford's estate in the country. The liaison did not prove to be a problem for society hostesses, since Miss Stafford had declined to attend social functions in Boston ever since the President's assassination in 1865.

Miss Cardozo lived at the house in Milton for nearly twenty years, dying finally of a painful cancer, lovingly tended by Miss Stafford herself. Miss Cardozo's little son, called Peter Stafford, inherited.

Grace Stafford lived to the ripe old age of ninety-two and died in her own bed at Milton. Her mind stayed keen until very near the end, when she began to weep copiously for the dead President for whom she had worn mourning all her life.

Chapter Twenty-Four

1960: KATE AND EMILY

When Emily was ten, she came home from school one afternoon wearing a large shining button on her blazer that said JOHN F. KENNEDY FOR PRESIDENT.

"Well, now where'd you get that?" her mother asked, with some amusement.

"Margaret Alcorn had one, and I said it was pretty, so after school we walked over to Park Street, where they have a whole store full of things like this, and they gave me one, too. May I have a piece of banana cake?"

"You're not too young to start watching your weight, dear. We wouldn't want you to have a problem later. Do you understand what that button says on it, what it means?" The little girl was so solemn, her cherubic cheeks so pink and innocent, that Kate's overwhelming love for her daughter sometimes seemed more than she could bear. She reached out to touch the neat brown pigtails, thin but bravely beribboned, and was rewarded with Emily's shy smile.

"I'm pretty hungry," the child said. "And I can smell the cake all the way from the kitchen. Should I take the button off? I will if you want me to."

"Why, no, dear, it's up to you, if you want to wear it, although your uncle Edward is coming for dinner, and you should be prepared to have him start on a tirade about . . . oh, how Boston is letting

down the country and the pope will soon be taking over this country
. . . you know. You've heard him on the subject of Kennedy before.''

Emily nodded her head. ''Boring,'' she said. Then she watched
her mother for a minute, waiting.

''All right,'' Kate said, knowing she was weak but unable to resist
that sweet round face looking up at her. ''One piece of banana cake,
and that's all,'' she said. ''Come on, I'll go in the kitchen with you.''

''To make sure I don't eat too much?'' Emily asked over her
shoulder as she led the way out of the parlor, through the reception
room, to the passageway running alongside the dining room.

''No, Emily, you know better than that; you know I trust you to
be honest, absolutely and without question. Don't you?''

The child's head nodded up and down yes, but she didn't turn
around or slow her steps toward the back of the house.

''I thought we might talk. I'll have a cup of tea with you. We'll
have a little tea party, just the two of us.''

They opened the door into the wide bright kitchen, immaculate and
in the doldrums of midafternoon; Mary was having her rest. This was
the only time Kate didn't mind being in this part of the house. She
was intimidated by cooks, who always seemed to know how things
fitted together, the absolute rules for browning meat, steaming
asparagus, causing cakes to rise, not allowing lettuce to wilt and
other mysteries of life. But now it was lovely, just the two of them,
mother and daughter, tiptoeing across the well-worn and shining lino-
leum to set their own tea at the big round oak table in the center of the
room.

''Now then, isn't this cozy? Tell me about how things are going
at school.''

''Fine.''

''Your French going all right?''

The child nodded, her round cheeks filled with cake.

Kate's glance kept straying to the political badge so incongruously
perched on Emily's prim school blazer. ''I wonder what your friend
Margaret's grandfather would say if he knew she was wearing a Kennedy button,'' Kate mused aloud. ''Senator Daiken is hardly a liberal, you know.''

"Margaret said that Senator Kennedy went to Harvard, so it's all right to be for him even if he is Irish," Emily said solemnly.

"That sounds like Margaret's father. John Alcorn is an idiot. Kennedy's being Irish has nothing to do with anything, and neither does his having gone to Harvard . . . well, not much anyway."

"Really?" Emily looked politely interested, although she clearly was not. She finished her cake and was busily picking up the last remaining crumbs with the tips of her fingers, popping them into her mouth in a way she well knew would never be permitted in civilized company. Kate said nothing, secretly enjoying the chance to indulge her child in a moment's naughtiness. Emily was in fact expecting a reprimand, and she looked across at her mother in anticipation. But Kate was smiling at her fondly, and Emily grinned back, pushed her sticky fingers down into the napkin on her lap, and left the rest of the cake crumbs on her plate.

They were close, the two of them. Kate worked hard for that; it was terribly important to her. Emily was the most important person in the world to her: her only child. Their relationship would be strong and lifelong, and they would always care for each other, she and her daughter. There would be no estrangement, none of the difficulties she had had with her own mother, the chasms opening up between them that widened every time one or the other tried to cross—none of that with her and Emily, not ever! Wasn't she aware of the pitfalls? She was intelligent and possessed of knowledge of Freud and Spock and the world. Her daughter would grow up unafraid to feel love and even speak of it. Especially her love for her mother.

Emily was a happy child, and they were close, Kate reassured herself over and over. Emily was close to Kate's mother, Anne, too. That was something that Kate had never been able to figure out, although of course, she was delighted about it. Anne would certainly never have permitted the child to put her fingers in her mouth that way, sucking the crumbs off her plate.

"May I be excused?" Emily was asking now. "I have to practice the piano and do my homework."

"Yes, dear, run along. Oh, by the way, dear, of course, I want you to make up your own mind about these things, but . . . just for tonight, I do think it might be best to remove that Kennedy button, simply to avoid what we talked about when your uncle Edward comes?''

"Oh. Sure.'' Her pudgy fingers were fumbling to remove the badge as she left the kitchen.

She takes after Charles, Kate thought, watching Emily's solid back, her firmly set shoulders. And my mother, with clear, untroubled eyes and hardly any chin . . . her knee socks don't even fall down the way mine always did. It's a comfort to know she's such an even-tempered, sweet-natured child. She'll never have to live with the torments of doubt and rebellion that used to rage through me . . . thank God that's done with.

She rose from the table and left the silent, empty kitchen. In the hall on her way to the library, her hand reached out to pass along the smooth edge of the reception table as she walked by, a habit. The table had been made to her great-grandfather's specifications by Thomas Chippendale, Jr. It had stood in this exact spot in this hall for more than a hundred years, ever since the move from Commonwealth Avenue.

Kate and Charles had never lived in their own house on Joy Street after all. Carefully, dutifully furnished with family things gathered from both sides of the Stafford tree, some new pieces added from this or that young furniture designer on Newbury or Park Street, even a special shopping trip to Italy, the house had taken a year or more to be made ready for them to move into. Armoires and sideboards had been stocked with their silver and crystal and china and linens, the windows had been draped, the floors scraped and waxed, the walls papered, furniture polished, carpets laid, but the house remained empty except for the elderly couple pensioned off as caretakers there by Charles's father. The walls of the Joy Street house were hung with five of old Neddy Stafford's paintings, chosen from the storage rooms of the Stafford Archives.

They had planned to move as soon as the baby was old enough, but then, sadly, the baby had never been born. There were some concerned friends and acquaintances who feared that the miscarriage might throw Kate Stafford back into the fearful, uncontrolled grief that had been evidenced after her first husband's death, but there was a collective sigh of relief that must have been audible all the way to

Rockport when, after a reasonable period of bed rest, young Mrs. Charles Stafford went on overseeing the furnishing of her new house in just the sort of brave carrying-on anyone would expect of a woman in her position.

When the house was ready, finally, it seemed so difficult, so troublesome, so alien to move out of 4 Beacon Street to the other slope of the hill three blocks away. There was no decision made; it was simply put off. Charles would go along with anything Kate wished, everyone knew that, it was such an excellent match—and soon enough she was expecting another child. When Emily was born, it seemed to decide the matter forever. Kate's old room became a nursery again; her daughter would grow up there as she had. Anne, of course, stayed in the master suite at the head of the stairs, where she had slept every night since her marriage forty-one years before; Kate and Charles moved into Edward's and Hank's rooms, which opened onto each other through the shared sitting room. The house on Joy Street would pass to Emily when she married, someday. In the meantime, it stood unoccupied, well cared for, a minor curiosity for tourists and parvenus who liked to point out this and that idiosyncrasy of the idle rich. No one on Beacon Hill thought much about it.

The time when she had not lived in this house seemed more and more unreal to Kate as the years went smoothly on. Her first marriage faded to a dim and almost forgotten memory, like a film once movingly experienced as it flickered across a screen. It was a fiction she had once believed in, a phase she had gone through; it was a romantic and vaguely embarrassing dream she had had as a very young girl. If, once in a while, something occurred to remind her of the way she had been, Kate felt only a mild wonder and something she supposed was relief; she had gotten away with it; against high odds she was safe now and forever. Then she'd push it well out of her mind.

Kate had come home to her true self. She had taken her place on the boards and committees of the museums, the hospital, the library, the lecture and exhibition halls, the opera, the symphony, two schools, and a small girls' college. Many of these fundaments of science and culture and society bore her family's name—earlier Staffords had established them for the good of all the people. These trusts were sacred, and solid; they wouldn't change with the political tides. A school, a museum, a library, a hospital—these wouldn't turn on you or let you down. These things were . . . safe.

And there was 4 Beacon Street, officially named a historic landmark now. Her home. Why had she ever left it, even for a little while? She honestly couldn't remember anymore. How she loved it, with its fine, worn furnishings, each thing in its rightful place as it had always been. The shining smooth old brass, and heavy silver, and the delicate porcelains collected by a great-uncle or two; the carpets brought on Stafford ships from India and Persia; the gleaming polished floors cut from trees that had been alive a thousand years ago and more, worn smooth by generations of Stafford feet; the soft leather-bound books written and read by Staffords; the snuffbox and porringer which Paul Revere had made for Harry Stafford after the night of the Boston Tea Party . . . and the money, yes, that was part of it. Kate had come to appreciate how stocks and bonds and unbreakable trust funds made all other things possible. She had come to value her heritage, and she understood that it was her clear and sacred duty to pass this appreciation of duty and privilege along to her child.

If, once in a while, when she glimpsed a man's slight, taut back and sandy hair blowing in the wind, her heartbeat reared and pounded for a startled moment, and if the sight of an Irish face crinkled in an uninhibited grin made her choke back an unexpected catch in her throat, no one knew. She hadn't taken a drink of anything alcoholic since her second pregnancy, nearly eleven years now. She never curled up on the old window seat to look out over the Common anymore, being much too busy with her charities and clubs and caring for her enchanting child and her difficult mother.

Anne was nearly senile. She had several friends as long-lived as herself, and they came regularly to call, or she went to them. They were the grande dames of Boston, and the older they got, the less they seemed to be bound to either this century or any other.

"I'm thinking of keeping a cow," was one of Anne's typical conversation openers one morning at breakfast. "The milk comes in those unhealthy cardboard boxes now, have you seen them? Probably filled with radiation. We have the right, you know. All the original owners of property bordering the Common have the right in perpetuity to pasture our cattle there. There wouldn't be a thing any of your legal agencies could do about it either. Perpetuity, you know. Yes, I think a cow would be just the thing.''

Legally she was right. She was dissuaded only because her sense of pride in the park was as great as her conviction of personal ownership.

Everyone always remarked on what a wonderful character Anne Stafford had become, how clear her mind and strong her bones. Kate alternated between admiration and exasperation. She was certainly a wonderful example for Emily. They went for long walks together nearly every afternoon. What a sight they were—the spry old lady with her thick malacca cane brandishing in the air as she talked, instead of supporting her as it was meant to; and the chubby little girl skipping along at her side to keep up. Watching from behind the parlor draperies, Kate told herself it would be childish and petty and probably neurotic to feel left out. She was glad that her mother and daughter got on so well.

"Good evening, dear."

"Oh, Charles! I didn't hear you come in."

"All alone with the lights unlit? Woolgathering, were you?"

"Oh, no." She leaned down to turn on the table lamp. The days were getting shorter; it was dusk already. "I was watching Emily and my mother setting out on their walk."

"Really? I didn't see them as I came in."

"They went out a while ago."

"I see. Well, I'll go on upstairs and have my little rest before dinner."

"Charles?"

"Yes, dear."

"I've been thinking . . . Emily came home wearing a Kennedy button today, but she doesn't have the vaguest idea of what it's all about. She needs to begin developing a sense of responsibility about these things, don't you agree? She never pays any attention to political talk, and she's not too young to begin. It is an election year; what better opportunity to learn—Charles? Are you listening to me?"

"Of course, dear. Just riffling through the mail, but I'm listening. I'm listening. And yes, I agree with you, of course. Emily should begin to take an interest. Never too young. What did you have in mind?''

"What would you think if I took her to one of those storefront headquarters that seem to be opening all over—even in this neighborhood, I understand—to do some volunteer work? I'm sure there are a lot of young people actively participating in the campaign, and it would be good for her, and—''

"Be careful what you lend our name to, Kate. I'm not at all pleased with some of Nixon's policies . . . and methods. His character seems dubious to me and to a lot of the people whose opinions we respect.''

"Nixon! Never, Charles. That man is loathsome. I'm talking about joining in the Kennedy campaign.''

"Oh! Well, we'll have to think about that. I mean, you must follow your own conscience, of course; but . . . well, you have been swayed by rhetoric and personality before, dear girl, and I think you must be extra-cautious, after all these years, if you intend to . . . well, jump in again, so to speak.''

"Jump into what? Millions of people are becoming involved in this campaign. The Democrats aren't quite the same as the old CP, after all.''

"Has it occurred to you that the senator might not want—since you bring it up—an ex-Communist, no matter how 'ex,' on his staff? Liberals have to be very careful about that sort of thing, you know.''

"Charles, for heaven's sake, I don't want to be on his staff. I simply think it's time we began educating our daughter, and all I want to do is to take her down to the headquarters right over here on Park Street and maybe stuff some envelopes. No one has to know our name, and I doubt if they'll even ask for a loyalty oath.''

"No need to get testy, dear. Of course, you must do exactly as you think best, as you always have. Although there may be some raised eyebrows and some questions asked. But you can count on me, as you know. Whatever you decide to do.''

"Yes. Thank you, Charles.''

"Your brother Edward will be upset, you know.''

"Edward had his chance. Don't you remember when they wanted him to run for the Senate? He said politics had become much too undignified to be a serious man's profession.''

"Yes," Charles murmured. Having delivered himself of everything he had to say on the subject, and having actually tuned in to his wife's comments and opinions for a record number of minutes, he now turned his attention to the mail.

"I know I don't need your permission, but I want it," Kate said, more to herself than to him. He wasn't listening anyway.

Charles came over and kissed her dryly on the forehead. "You do what you think best, dear," he said, and left the parlor to go upstairs for his rest.

Well, she thought to herself, what the hell. One last gesture before I settle down to a graceful middle age. She poured herself a glass of tonic and raised it to the empty twilight-sodden room. Up the rebellion! she mouthed silently. But there was no taste and no color and no kick to it. In some danger of feeling sorry for herself, she went around the parlor, turning on all the lamps, and took a book at random from the glass-cased shelves to read until it was time to dress for dinner.

Chapter Twenty-Five

1960: KATE

"We're going to work in the Kennedy campaign," Kate told her daughter the next day. "What do you think of that?"

"Okay," Emily said, without much interest. "Do I have to go to dancing school anyway?"

"Yes, of course you do." Kate laughed. "Come on then, let's go over to Park Street and present ourselves as volunteers."

"May I have my after-school snack first?"

"You're going to eat yourself into a replica of your great-great-aunt Grace if you're not careful!" Kate heard herself snapping.

Emily giggled. Her rosy little face reminded Kate of one of those impish little putti, the dimpled baby angels that ring the walls and fountains and ceilings of palaces and gardens all through Italy. Mischievous, adorable, even a little sly—but still angelic.

Emily always took things literally. "But I wouldn't wear men's clothes or smoke cigars," she said. She was looking down, carefully skipping to avoid stepping on any cracks in the sidewalk.

"No, I should hope not," Kate agreed. She wondered how much Emily knew about "those things," the family euphemism for Great-aunt Grace's notoriously long and public sex life. She wondered if this was going to be the Big Talk. Children had no sense of timing. When you were prepared and even eager to discuss important things, they couldn't be bothered; suddenly, when you least expected and really couldn't take the time for it, difficult questions popped up, sometimes in disguise. Kate prided herself on being an enlightened modern mother. She had lived—hadn't she?—and she had read Freud and Krafft-Ebing and even the Kinsey Report. She and her child would be able, always, to discuss anything and everything together.

Emily would never have to find out about things—about Great-aunt Grace, for instance—the way Kate had. Of course, she realized it was unfair to blame her own mother. Anne herself was a victim of puritanical-Victorian prudery, unable to discuss "those things" with anyone, especially her own daughter. The entire world knew about Grace Stafford, since she hadn't troubled to hide her idiosyncratic tastes and proclivities. She had been as famous for her blunt honesty and peculiar "personal" life as for her paintings. It was a great and lasting embarrassment to Kate, not that her famous aunt had been a notorious, well—pervert; not that at all, but her own shame at having been well into her thirties before she had understood any of it. It was damned awful to have the facts of life explained to you by your second husband! Her daughter would never be kept in the medieval darkness, Kate intended to make sure of that.

But still, one had to wonder how much a sweet little ten-year-old girl could understand. Maybe it was too early; maybe Emily was still too young; maybe this wouldn't need to be the Big Talk she had been anticipating with mixed dread and determination for years. She did want to get over to the campaign headquarters while there was still time to get some real work done. . . .

"Cousin Martha says the reason Great-great-aunt Grace wore men's clothes was 'cause she was too fat to get into a dress." Emily said this without looking up from her careful perusal of the sidewalk's many pitfalls. All right, Kate thought with a pang of anxiety and the wish that she had a cigarette, so this is the time, very well, then here we go.

"Do you believe that?" she asked casually.

Emily shot her a sidelong glance. "No!" she said. "That's just silly. Great-great-aunt Grace wore those clothes 'cause she was a lesbian, that's all. That's why her mistress's son called her Dad, too. You know who I mean, that man Peter, who lives in Gracefree? That used to be Great-great-aunt Grace's house, and she left it to him 'cause she adopted him legally. His mother was her lover. She was a very famous actress till she ran away from the stage and her husband and everything to live with Great-great-aunt Grace. So her son was Peter, and he became Peter Stafford, only no one in the family admits it.''

Through all this, Kate was standing like a statue in the middle of the sidewalk in front of the Park Street Church, staring at her cherubic little girl as if the child had just stepped off a little green saucer that had come from another planet to land in the Old Granary Burying Ground right next door to the church.

"Where on earth . . . who told you all that?'' she managed to gasp, finally.

"Gram told me,'' Emily said. Her innocent eyes began to narrow, imperceptibly. She pulled back from her mother's incredulous staring. No, don't run from me! Kate needed to say, this is all wrong! But she couldn't say anything at all, and the moment passed, and there was a new distance between them that might never go away, and somehow Kate blamed her own mother for this estrangement, this turning upside down of the mother-daughter-mother, daughter-mother-daughter thing. It hurt to see Emily pull back; there was nothing she could say or do to stop it.

Some people passed them and stared as they went by. Emily blushed heartily and stared at her shoes, but Kate still seemed paralyzed, permanently rooted to the middle of the sidewalk in front of the Park Street Church.

"What?'' Kate asked her finally. "What did you say?''

"Gram told me,'' Emily repeated, sounding frightened. Her face was round, and her eyes were apprehensive; she knew she had said something bad or rude, but she didn't understand what or why. "I'm sorry, Mama,'' she mumbled. "Are you mad at me?''

"No . . . of course not. Not at all. Why on earth would I be angry, dear?'' Kate said. She turned and continued on past the Burying Ground toward the bustle of Tremont Street and the storefront whose red, white, and blue paper streamers could be seen from here, fluttering in the wind.

"Gram tells me all 'those things,' anything I don't understand, like about sex and stuff,'' Emily explained helpfully. She had to skip now, just to keep up with her mother's long, purposeful strides.

"She never told me 'those things,' " Kate couldn't help remarking.

"I know," Emily agreed sympathetically.

"What do you mean, 'I know'?" Kate demanded sharply.

Out of breath now from trying to keep up, the poor child was practically panting. Kate suddenly felt a wash of love and sorrow welling up inside her, and she slowed her step, reached for her daughter's hand. One doesn't apologize to a child, of course, but there are ways of letting a little girl know you didn't mean to take it out on her. She squeezed her daughter's hand, a private sign. Emily's hand neither responded nor pulled away. "What did you mean?" she repeated, more gently.

"Well . . . Gram says that you were much too emotional and curious when you were my age. She couldn't talk to you about sensitive things, Gram says, but she says I'm a different type. She says I'll never go off half-cocked."

"Half-cocked . . . did she really put it that way?"

Emily nodded, clearly growing more uncomfortable by the minute. Her hand lay in her mother's palm like an oyster on the half shell.

"Your grandmother's getting senile," Kate said with finality. "Well, here we are! My, it looks crowded and busy in there, doesn't it? This is going to be fun, Emily, isn't it?"

"Yes, Mama," Emily agreed in a suddenly quiet, shy voice. She followed her mother into the bustling, cheerful chaos of the headquarters.

A robust young Radcliffe girl signed them on and led them across the room to a long table where other women and young people faced each other in two rows of an efficient and amiable assembly line. They were folding a campaign brochure, passing it along to be put in envelopes, which were then moistened, sealed, and sorted for the postage meter machine. The busy, chattering workers made room for Kate and Emily; almost instantly they felt part of the inner circle of dedicated zealots. It was a good feeling, although there was no one there whom Kate recognized.

Only a few minutes had passed when the door of an inner office opened and a harried young man rushed out, looked over at the volunteer table, and headed through the crowd toward them. He went directly to Kate, leaned down to speak quietly in her ear, asking if she would mind, please, coming with him for a moment. Inside the little office, adorned with posters of the senator and large maps of Boston, the commonwealth, and the entire country, the young man asked her to sit down. He called her by name.

"We're awfully glad to have you aboard, Mrs. Stafford," he said.

"Aboard? Oh, yes, well, thank you. Glad to be aboard."

"Naturally you'll be doing really important work in the campaign. I'm sure that when the senator hears you've volunteered, he'll be—"

"I'm here anonymously, Mr. . . ?"

"Oh, but Mrs. Stafford, you could do so much to influence votes in this neighborhood—among your friends and the other really important Brahmins—"

"No."

"Ma'am?"

"I'm not here to offer the Stafford name. I'm here as an individual, just another volunteer. And I find the term 'Brahmins' outdated and a bit insulting. It was Oliver Wendell Holmes who coined it, and he did not mean it as a compliment."

"I am sorry. I'm really sorry. I'm terribly sor—"

"Maybe I'd better forget the whole idea." She got up from the chair; but the young man was distraught, and she unexpectedly felt sorry for him. She was beginning to be that way sometimes; never meaning to, she sounded like her mother. She sat back down again.

"It's okay," he said nervously. "Of course, we're glad to have you serve in any capacity you want to. Please. I didn't mean anything pejorative, honestly, I didn't."

He had a nice smile, and suddenly she felt like a mean old lady. How had she turned into that? It was the atmosphere of this place, the excitement, the camaraderie of the devout working together, sharing their belief in some dream of a better world. It made her remember things she didn't want to remember, made her miss herself as she once was . . . dangerous, treacherous ground.

"I'm sorry, young man," she said wearily, "I didn't mean to frighten you. Of course, you meant well, I can see that. You believe in what you're doing . . . I do understand that."

"Thank you, Mrs. Stafford. I'm sorry if I overstepped—"

"It's quite all right. You're only doing your job, and anyhow, I'm

quite accustomed to people and causes wanting to exploit my name."
She wanted to sound friendly, understanding, somehow to communicate across the newfangled generation gap to this young man that
they were not so different after all, that she had once been a fire-
eater like him . . . but it came out sounding pinched and mean
somehow.

The young man was relieved, if not happy. He had probably thought
she was going to put him in the stocks and have him publicly whipped
or something.

"Uh . . . oh, yes, I see," he said. "Well, thank you for coming
in, and thank you very much for being so understanding about my
gaffe, Mrs. Stafford."

She nodded and left his little windowless office to return to the
long communal table with all the other cheerful, anonymous volunteers. She was delighted to see that her daughter was listening attentively to a discussion at her end of the table about the candidate's
proposal for something called a Peace Corps. The young people
seemed very excited about that; their hands flew in rhythmic tedium,
folding, stuffing, folding, stuffing . . . but their minds were racing
ahead with all the hopes of the future.

Walking home in the early twilight, Emily could hardly contain
her excitement. She actually bounced, quoting everything she had
heard and describing what she'd seen; she could hardly wait to tell it
all to Gram when they got home. She ran directly upstairs to knock
at Anne's sitting-room door, not even stopping to wash her hands
and face or ask about a snack. Kate watched the pigtails bobbing up
the stairs. She shrugged out of her coat and went up, too, for a quiet
bath and a bit of a rest before dinner.

She had dozed off. Emily was tugging at her arm. The bedroom
was mostly dark, except for the light beamed in through the open
door to the hallway. Emily was calling her over and over, urgently,
sounding frightened.

"Mama, please wake up, Mama, Mama, please, please, Mama
. . ."

"For heaven's sake, Emily! I'm awake, dear. What is it? Is something wrong?"

"Something funny's happened to Gram. I'm scared, Mama."

Kate sat up, threw her feet over the side of the bed, and reached for the lamp pull. "What is it, Emily? Tell me calmly and sensibly now."

But the child's face was contorted with fear, and tears bubbled up over her round red cheeks. Kate had never seen her child so out of control before; cold apprehension slithered across her skin. She moved quickly, sliding her feet into her leather slippers, wrapping herself in the robe that was always within reach when she napped. Emily ran ahead of her, through the hall and directly into Anne's sitting room.

Kate heard her mother's rasping breaths. She went quickly to the settee where Anne sat, feet still firmly on the ground but with her head uncharacteristically leaning to one side. Her mouth was open; she looked more vulnerable and frail than Kate could bear to see.

"Tell Mary to call Dr. Franklin right away. He must come here at once, do you understand?" she told her daughter. Emily's eyes were wide with terror, and she backed away, nodding, then turned and ran from the room.

"Mother? Mother, dear, can you hear me? It's Kate . . . Mama?"

She thought she should help Anne lie down, and yet she felt too respectful of her mother's body to actually touch it, to lift those dry, spindly legs that had so much remarkable strength in them, to set her mother's head at a more comfortable angle, to smooth the formidable knot of gray hair, to loosen the pearl buttons of the blouse that seemed to constrict the air that painfully retched up through her mother's throat. All she could do was to lean over Anne and murmur to her.

"Mother . . . I'm here, dear . . . the doctor is coming, you'll be all right . . . are you in pain, Mother? Is there something I can do?"

Anne's eyes fluttered and opened and stared at Kate for a moment.

"Mother, Mama . . . I'm here, I'm here. . . ."

Her mother's dry, puckered lips were twisting and making an effort to speak. The old woman's tongue flickered at the edge of her mouth, and then she said very clearly, "You have always been a great disappointment to me," and she died.

Part
FIVE

Chapter Twenty-Six

1968: EMILY

The whole world was in bloody shreds out there, but everybody's parents acted as though the news hadn't reached Boston yet. Emily's friend Hermione Jones (Ham Bones, of course, since first grade) said that the people on Beacon Hill wouldn't believe the news from any other medium but lanterns in a steeple. Then they'd send somebody out on a horse to make sure.

"In the meantime," Ham said dourly, with a smile she thought was ironic and a deep, long drag on some good Acapulco Gold, "in the meantime, wear your clean white gloves, dance the gavotte, and remember Boston is the Hub of the Universe. Everyone is watching us, my dear, to learn how to conduct themselves."

With that, both girls succumbed to the ho-hos, rolling on the carpet, abandoning themselves to whoops of giggles and the giddy tears that come from too much laughing. They were in Emily's room. Her mother thought they were studying, not that she'd mind hearing a bit of girlish laughter coming from her daughter's direction. Kate always told Emily she was "too solemn."

Now there was hypocrisy for you. At Emily's age her mother had run off with an Irish Catholic Communist (impossible to imagine her proper, matronly mother lusting after sex so uncontrollably that she'd defied the family and gone off to live in furnished rooms and cheap hotels, fucking her head off from here to Omaha!), but what a fit

she'd have if I tried a number like that, she thought. Actually it was
probably very romantic in those days; how silly and—well, young—
it sounds now. Hard to imagine anybody bothering . . . and anyway,
look where it got old Kate, right back to square one. Not much per-
centage in all that sweat, was there? What was the point?

Emily reached for the cigarette papers, took out a judicious portion
of grass from the little plastic Baggie, and began pushing the leaves
through the tea strainer so that a fine powder fell onto the clean white
tissue, ready to be rolled.

"Whew! It must really stink in here. Maybe we'd better burn some
incense. You got any?" Ham asked, waving her arms around in the
air.

"Oh, it doesn't matter. Nobody in this house would know what
they were smelling anyway," Emily said, with a shrug. "You could
put an inch of grass on top of my father's Cream of Wheat for breakfast, and he wouldn't even notice. He'd just eat it, get stoned out of
his mind, and go right on acting exactly the way he always does,
which is, come to think of it, actually pretty stoned."

That should have struck them as funny, but it didn't. They sat
glumly, cross-legged, watching Emily's pudgy fingers expertly rolling the paper around the dollop of sifted grass, smoothing the joint,
running it past the tip of her tongue to seal it, twisting the ends. She
lit a match and inhaled, holding the smoke in, and passed it to Ham.

"I used to actually get out of bed and stand up, all alone in my
room, if I heard 'The Star-Spangled Banner' over the radio, you know
that?"

Emily spoke out of a long, compatible silence. She was lying on
her back, gazing up at the carved moldings along the ceiling. They
were painted white, and the rest of the room was painted pale yellow,
and she'd never noticed before, but each little flower and curve of
the design stood out clearly in its separate dimensions. The moldings
had been carved when the house was built, a thousand years ago or
so, and she'd lived in this room all her life, and she'd never noticed
how complicated and ingenious the designs were. As she stared at
the molding, tracing it with her eyes around and around the rectangle
of the ceiling, it occurred to her to wonder why anybody had gone to
all that trouble. She wondered if her own mother, who had lived in

this room until she got married and had her own child had ever bothered to notice how alive and truly beautiful the molding was. There
had been a time when she would have asked Kate a dumb question
like that. . . . "Huh?" she said lazily, aware that her friend had
said something, maybe a long time before.

Ham was sitting up, picking at her bare toenails through the leather
thong sandals. "I said all kids do that, so what?" she repeated.

"So then they killed Jack Kennedy, and then they killed Martin
Luther King, and now they've killed Bobby Kennedy, and I don't
feel like standing up for 'The Star-Spangled Banana' anymore, that's
all."

"I don't see what that's got to do with anything," Ham said plac-
idly. "I saw some green nail polish at Filene's, but I didn't have the
nerve to buy it. Would you?"

"I'd have the nerve but not the bad taste," Emily commented dryly.
"Hey, save the roach."

"I'm still smoking it."

"Oh. Sorry. I thought you let it go out."

"No."

"Okay."

They were silent for a while, again, and then Emily said, dreamily,
"I used to like Jackie Kennedy, even though my mother said she was
vulgar. Did you?"

"Oh, sort of. She was okay."

"I thought she was special," Emily went on. "I thought he was
some kind of god or something, I really did. I worked in his campaign, you know. My mother and I both did."

"Wow."

"I thought they were special. Hell, what did I know? I was ten
years old."

"Do you remember where you were when you heard he got shot?"
Hermione asked.

Emily reached for the joint. It was getting very small. Her roach
holder was in her bedroom, and she didn't feel like getting up and
going all the way across the sitting room and into the other room and
going to the trouble of opening a drawer and poking around under
her underwear for it. She held the smoldering damp end of the joint

with her two index fingers. She took the last drag, snuffed it out carefully, saving it for later, and then she said, "Sure I do. They say everybody does. That it's the kind of thing you remember all your life; your memory gets frozen, like in shock or something, forever. I remember what I thought, too. I thought about the word 'assassination.' I had always thought it meant Abraham Lincoln, and I remember thinking: Why are they using such an old-fashioned word? and then I thought—oh-oh, nothing's ever going to be like it used to be. And I was right. And I was only twelve years old."

"Thirteen."

"Huh?"

"Emily, I was thirteen in 1963, so you must have been, too. November twenty-second, 1963. I was in Miss Larkin's English class, and she told us, and some of the girls cried."

"How proper of them."

"Well, gosh, Em, lots of people cried. Didn't you?"

Emily raised herself up on her elbows. Her blouse was all twisted, and an expanse of soft white underbelly rolled up over the cramped waistband of her jeans. She stared with something like disgust at her friend. "Are you kidding?" she said indignantly. "I never cry."

"Oh, come on, you must cry sometimes!"

"Never."

"You mean never in public."

"Well, of course, never in public! But never in private either."

"Emily Stafford, I don't believe you. That's just not humanly possible."

It was true, though. Emily laced her fingers through her long, straight hair. It was her best feature, by far, and of course, her mother was always after her to cut it off.

She had been watching Bobby Kennedy a minute before it happened, just last night. It had been boring, the same old crap. He'd won the primary in California and made the usual speech—who cared?—and she was about to turn off the television and read herself to sleep when there was a terrible commotion and someone calling for a doctor on the screen, and it wasn't a dramatization or a commercial, and there were a series of horrified faces and then they said the candidate's been shot, Bobby's been shot, and she'd turned off the set, and the silence had been almost worse. She'd sat and trembled physically, shaking all over and feeling cold, and then she'd smoked two joints of Gold all by herself and zonked out till morning. But the face of one woman kept coming back into her mind, nobody in particular, just one of the people at the headquarters out in California, one of the faces on camera showing horror. . . .

"I'll bet you cry plenty when you want to," old Ham Bones was sniffing haughtily, sort of to herself, sort of to Emily.

"Oh, put a sock in it!" Em retorted. She had heard that in a British movie.

Ham looked as if she were going to break out crying herself, but just then there was a knock on the door. Em's mother.

Scrambling to her feet, Emily felt like a huge, beached whale trying to get up on end. She stuffed the makings under the cushion of the sofa and motioned to Ham to do something with the ashtray, quickly. Ham was absolutely in a panic. She was terrified of parents, other people's as much as her own.

"Emily? May I come in?"

"We're studying, Mother." Waiting to see if Kate would buy it, Emily stared at the panels of the door between them. Her face revealed a flash of emotion, quickly thrown off.

"I'm waiting, Emily." Kate's voice was as imperious as Anne's had ever been. Of the two, Emily had preferred her grandmother, who at least had taken the long view. Anne Stafford had lived long enough to know that you couldn't expect perfection in anyone, least of all a young girl. Emily missed her. Her grandmother had never once said she was fat, or that her manners needed improvement, or that she had (loathful phrase) the wrong attitude. Anne Stafford had just assumed her grandchild to be perfect, simply because she was her grandchild, and consequently never looked for or saw any flaws.

Oh, well, everybody died sooner or later. You had to be pretty stupid to let it take you by surprise or to let yourself miss anyone. . . .

"Open the window," she mouthed at Ham, who leaped up and ran to oblige. There was a June storm whistling outside, and a rush of cool air cut the fumes a bit. Emily called out, sounding near death from boredom, "Come in, Mother."

"You know, my mother never knocked when she came into this room, when I was young. She always assumed she had the right, that privacy didn't exist for young people. I've always been very careful to—it smells like a locker room in here!" With that, Kate crossed past her daughter and her daughter's friend, who stood awkwardly, just watching her, and leaned across the window seat to pull down the sash against the rain that was starting to dampen the cushions.

"You ought to know," Emily muttered under her breath.

"What was that?" Kate turned and eyed her daughter sharply.

"Nothing."

"Hello, Hermione. You two look very guilty. For heaven's sake, what have you been up to? Studying, indeed!"

"We were talking about Senator Kennedy, Mrs. Stafford," Ham answered politely.

Kate's face softened. "Isn't it terrible? So much violence everywhere. It's particularly hard when you're young, I know, to understand—"

"Understand!" her daughter snorted. It was something between derision and disgust. She turned her back on Kate and stared out the window at the rain.

"Yes, I guess you're right," Kate said quietly to her daughter's plump and eloquent backside. "There is no sense to it. No sense at all. Maybe that's exactly why it's so important to maintain one's sense of balance, keep life going on as usual, when terrible things happen in the world. I don't know whether you understand what I'm saying?"

No answer from Emily. Hermione was uncomfortable; she nodded nervously in affirmation of Kate's point.

"Maybe it's exactly at times like this when having family and continuity in one's life is most important," Kate went on. No response. Angering, she went on coldly. "I suggest you do get at your homework now. If you want to solve the problems of the world, it might be a reasonable idea to graduate from high school first. Your final exams are not going to be canceled because of this, you know. The world does go on."

"Right," Emily murmured, without turning around.

Kate waited just a beat; long acquaintance with teen-aged hostility had not given her any clues to penetrating it, and she left the room without even a sigh. When the door had closed behind her, Emily turned from the window and slumped down heavily onto the floor. She leaned against the record cabinet. Her friend perched tentatively on the arm of the wing chair.

"God, she really pisses me off," Emily said. " 'The world does go on.' God!"

"Mothers are impossible," Ham agreed.

"Especially that one."

"How come you hate her so much?"

Emily shifted herself over to reach under the cushions of the sofa for the packet of grass. She pulled it out and began to roll another joint. "I don't hate her," she said. "She's just another hypocrite like all the rest of them."

"Yeah, but you said 'especially' her."

"Well, you see . . ." Emily lit the twist and dragged the smoke deep into her lungs as if nearly desperate for it. She waited till she could hold her breath no longer, let the pressure out, and then went on to say, "Our Kate was once a fire-eating liberal. More than that, I mean, a real honest-to-God card-carrying Communist. She and her first husband were, like, organizers, traveling around and getting people to sign up for the party. Well," she amended guiltily, "not for the party itself, but for the unions, which was pretty much the same thing. But all she ever does these days is preach to me about—oh, you know! All the usual shit."

Ham nodded sympathetically. "You going to have a coming-out party?" she asked. "I have to."

"I suppose." Emily yawned. "I hope it doesn't have to be in a tent, though. I look like a tent in a long white dress as it is; it would be a tent within a tent." She snickered and then dissolved into the only thing she ever really felt anymore—total silliness.

Instantly Ham was laughing, too. Whatever had seemed so important and desolating had been banished again.

When her telephone rang, Emily rolled over onto her belly and reached for it, still giggling. "Secret agent oh-nine-five, licensed to kill," she announced.

"Hi, Emily. Are you going to the demonstration?"

"I dunno. Just a minute." She put her hand over the mouthpiece and told Ham loudly, "It's Margaret Alcorn, wanting to know if we're going to the demonstration."

"What demonstration?" asked Hermione reasonably.

"What demonstration?" Emily asked into the phone.

"Oh, for God's sake, don't you two dilettantes know what's happening outside your own little world? Are you guys stoned? Sounds like it. Somebody shot Bobby Kennedy last night. And now he's dead. Oh, God, it's so sad! Anyway everyone's really upset, and all the kids are going to join this big demonstration over in Cambridge. I thought maybe I could get a ride with you if you're going."

"She wants a ride. You want to take your sports car to a demonstration? She wants to go in style."

"Sure, might as well. What time?"

"What time?" Emily asked.

"I don't know, about two, I guess. I couldn't go before that anyway; I've got to go to church with my parents first."

"Okay, pick you up around two." Emily managed to get the phone back on its hook and slumped back down prone on the carpet. "It's sure to be depressing. But what the hell, we might as well go."

"Maybe we'll meet some boys this time," Ham said hopefully.

"That's as good a reason to go to a demonstration as any other." Emily shrugged. "What should we wear?"

"I'm not going to change. If I went home first, my mother would never let me out again, especially for something like that, are you kidding?"

Sunday strollers on Commonwealth Avenue smiled to see the young girls driving past, three of them crowded into the two-seater open-top MG, with their innocent laughter and their banners of thick, shining, long, straight hair flying out behind them. They seemed to be the affirmation of life, on this mournful, horrified, tragic day of one murder too many. Boston's Kennedys had been Boston's hope; now they were gone . . . but look, there go some flowers of Boston aristocracy, we'd forgotten, for a minute, about our own power to endure. There they go, laughing and beautiful, young inheritors of all the best we ever had or ever will have . . . maybe . . . the Irish came and went; the Brahmins endure.

They parked the car on a side street six blocks from the main entrance to Harvard Yard; there were already great crowds of people walking toward Massachusetts Avenue from every direction. Mostly students, of all sizes, shapes, and ages, and young mothers with babies in arms or strollers, older people with gray hair and serious faces, the Hare Krishnas and the Jesus freaks with their costumes and pamphlets, young kids looking unnaturally solemn. But everything was solemn; it was different from the antiwar demonstrations. Everyone was subdued, sad. No one shouted, no jeerers standing on the sidelines. The cops had little to do. Some students were handing out black armbands.

"Oh, God, I knew this would be a downer," Ham murmured in Emily's ear.

And then, suddenly, there were shouts behind them. The three girls were in the middle of the street, surrounded on all sides by people, and it was impossible to see behind them; but the anguish rippled quickly through the crowd, and suddenly it was a mob, a pushing, shoving force of elbows and shoulders. Emily lost her balance; she would have fallen and been crushed, but there was no room to fall; she was carried along like a rag doll, and if she screamed, she didn't even hear it herself in the howling rage that had overtaken the mourners.

"Grab my hand!" she shouted to Ham, reaching out and reaching with her other hand for Margaret's. "We've got to get out of here!" She didn't know whether they heard her or not, but she had someone's hands to hold, and she began pushing, hard, winnowing her way through the pressing mob.

She was almost at the iron fence, still holding onto her friends, when they were gassed. It might have been Mace, for crowd control, it might have been tear gas, as the radical student papers would claim; but it didn't matter then. Emily heard Ham shriek; her hand tore loose from her friend's; she saw Ham gesturing wildly, rubbing her eyes; her mouth was open, and she was screaming, "I'm blind! I'm blind! I can't see!" and then she was gone.

Emily retched violently and vomited, stumbling to her knees in the sudden agony of sick cramps. She put her head down on the fringe of grass along the Yard fence, but the dizziness would not leave her;

all around her other people were falling down, retching and groaning and clutching at themselves, sick and scared.

Someone grabbed her, pulled her up. One of her shoes came off, and as a weird kaleidoscope of colors, sounds, jagged shards of feelings whirled past her, she thought crazily of how her mother hated those sandals and would be glad they were gone. Suddenly it was dark, and her head was banged, hard, on the ground—no, a floor— she was inside a van. Other people were there, moaning and retching and sobbing, too. It smelled vile. There was no way out. The door clanged shut, and in the terrible darkness someone groped for her hand, found it, and held it in a friendly way. She was grateful. The spinning began to slow down inside her head. Clutching the stranger on her left, she reached out her right hand blindly, found a hand that was trembling and clammy, and held it as her own was being held. In a moment the stranger's trembling stopped, and Emily felt a kind of pride in herself. She wondered what had happened to Ham and Margaret. When the van stopped and the door was opened to the glare of light, people let go of each other and filed out into the street. There was no one she recognized. She didn't even know for certain whose hands she had been holding.

The police just took names and addresses, and everyone was crowded into big holding cells and rooms with unsmiling guards watching them from the locked doorways. After only a couple of hours her uncle Edward came to bail her out. He was just sitting there, ramrod-straight in his funny old-fashioned stiff pinstriped suit and white straw hat, waiting for her in the anteroom of the station when she came out.

"Hi," she said.

"Emily," he acknowledged, wrinkling his nose.

She was embarrassed. "I guess I really smell bad, huh?"

"Well," he said in one of his peculiar attempts at humor, "it's not exactly Evening in Paris, is it?"

"What's that?"

"It's the only perfume name I can think of. Ladies used to wear it, not nice ladies, of course. I haven't the foggiest notion what ladies wear now. But not, I think, the particular scent you have on."

She laughed. She kind of liked old Uncle Edward; he was all right.

"Shall we get out of here?" He took her arm as though escorting her into dinner at the Harvard Club. They walked outside. It was raining, but the car was waiting right at the curb. Other people were straggling out of the station house and going off into the dark drizzly streets of Cambridge.

"Funny," she mused out loud, "it rained all morning, and then the sun came out when we left for the demonstration, like a sign or something; but it was just another wrong clue."

"What's that?" he asked. They settled into the back seat of the car, and it pulled away from the curb.

"Nothing," Emily muttered, sinking down into herself. She didn't even want to talk until they had crossed the river again and were nearing home. Then she asked, more out of idle curiosity than really caring, "How come you came for me, instead of Dad?"

"Oh, well, I am a lawyer after all. They're very much worried about you, of course. They wanted to come, but at the time we agreed it might be best not to cause any more of a scene than had already been brought to the attention of the newspapers. Your uncle Henry usually handles these things; but he's in Europe just now, and so it fell to me."

"I suppose Mother is waiting with a candle in the window and a few well-chosen words of wisdom for me."

"No, in fact, she had to go chair a meeting of the Historical Society. She wanted to give that up in order to be with you—the reports on the radio were fearful, you know—but your father and I managed to assure her that you'd be all right. I called them as soon as I spoke to the captain, so they know I'm bringing you home safely."

"It must have really upset Mother to think of her darling daughter in the slammer."

Uncle Edward was oddly silent. She peered at him in the passing lights.

"Actually," her uncle said slowly, "your mother herself spent a night in the—what did you call it?—the slammer. A very long time ago."

"Really? No kidding! Mother! What'd she do? Come on, tell! Probably committed a public nuisance by wearing the wrong kind of hat to a meeting of the Opera Guild committee."

"Well, actually . . . it was a case of mistaken identity. The police thought your mother was . . . she had wandered into the wrong kind of place. Accidentally, of course. The whole thing was a ridiculous mistake. You needn't mention to her that I told you at all. But maybe you should know that your mother is human after all."

It wasn't a pleasant thing to hear about one's own mother. It was okay somehow when it was yourself, and there were lots of other people in the same boat, even some of your school friends; but to think about your own mother in jail was . . . it wasn't anything the same. It was kind of sickening, in fact, although Emily wasn't sure why. But she felt suddenly kind of sick.

"What did she do?" she heard herself asking her uncle in a small and girlish voice. Her throat was tight; it was probably still the effects of the tear gas.

She thought of her grandmother, saying, "Skeletons in one's closet belong exactly there. Now let me see how your needlework is progressing," whenever Emily had asked about her mother's Commie days; it had been the one subject Anne wouldn't discuss with her. It had given her a nightmare, she remembered it now, a dream of Kate turned into a skeleton, nothing but bones and a grinning empty skull hiding behind neat rows of her dark silk dresses beyond a closet door, in the dark.

Her uncle hadn't answered her. She repeated the question. "What did my mother do to get sent to jail?"

"Perhaps I shouldn't have mentioned it," he said.

"Now let's see how your needlework is progressing," Emily muttered to herself, grinning at her own reflection in the window, seeing her own skull outlined and nothing particularly interesting about it.

"What's that?"

"Doesn't matter, forget it," she said. Her finger traced the outline of her initial on the glass.

Just before they pulled up in front of the house, she burst out, "Was it because she was a Communist?" She turned to look at her uncle, waiting for his reply, refusing to let him off the hook again. His elderly, distinguished profile was outlined against the trees that lined the sidewalk. He didn't turn to look at her, but he did answer, finally, slowly.

"Your mother was never a Communist," he said.

"Are you kidding?"

"She was a very young girl when it all happened, and she thought she was in love. A young girl in love does foolish things sometimes. That's all there was to it."

Emily didn't move to get out of the car, even though they had stopped and the driver had opened the door on her side. She just sat there and stared at her uncle's carved-stone profile.

"But . . . but she's always telling me how terrifically sincere she was, how she thought she was saving the world and all that stuff—"

"It's all in the records. Your mother's political past was thoroughly examined, and depositions were given to what was once called the House Committee for the Investigation of Un-American Activities. A fine body, watchdogs of our freedom, so little understood by the public that . . . ah, well, water under the dam now. But you must never believe that your own mother was a subversive, Emily, no matter how she tends to look back on it now. It's all in the records."

"You mean . . . it's all a lie?"

"Not at all, Emily." He was looking at her now; but it was dark, and the light from the streetlamp fell on her, not him. She listened and tried to understand. "She may try to romanticize it all now. Looking back, one tends to do so, especially a woman, one whose lover was killed in the war . . . such a romantic way to die, noble, too . . . a woman will enshrine such a memory forever, and everything will always stay the way she wanted it to and never grow old or dangerous. . . ." He trailed off.

"Uncle Edward, what do you mean, dangerous? I don't understand. I'm terribly confused."

"What? Dangerous? Did I say 'dangerous'? Well . . . well, I must have meant . . . Communists, of course. Communists, revolutionaries, wanting to overthrow the government, they're very, very dangerous. Must stay always on our guard against revolutionaries. I'm old enough to have been alive when the czar was murdered, and his whole family, too. . . ."

Emily sighed loudly, but her uncle paid no attention. There would be no further sense made from him tonight; he was off on his favorite topic. "Good night, Uncle Edward," she said dutifully. "Thanks for bailing me out."

She climbed out of the car. The driver helped her. As she started up the walk to the house, her uncle called out softly in the darkness, "Good night, Emily. You're very welcome, but don't let it happen again."

And the door slammed and the car drove away. Emily went inside the empty house. Her mother was out, and her father would be in his study with the door closed. Or maybe the door would be open, meaning he was waiting to talk to her. It didn't matter either way.

Chapter Twenty-Seven

1968: KATE

"You're not the first person in this family to be involved in a street riot, you know. You needn't feel proud about it."

"I'm not proud of it, Dad. It was hardly the Boston Tea Party, you know. Nothing that might go down in history or anything. Just a bunch of kids getting gassed by the pigs."

"Colorful language," Charles observed acerbically. He turned his attention to the newspaper, folding it carefully, lining up the corners just so, arranging it in its place at the left of his oatmeal bowl. "I expect you picked that up on the street. If you're hoping to be mis-understood, that's exactly the way to go about it."

Emily didn't answer. Charles dismissed—or rather tabled—his daughter then, with the flat statement that they would meet in the library at five thirty that evening. He did not look up from his paper again until he excused himself from the table after his second half cup of coffee.

Kate had said nothing. Breakfast was always a quiet time; the din-ing-room drapes had to be kept drawn against the corrosive east light that would fade the original Alice blue of the chairs, and the shadowy room was simply too large and solemn for morning talk. Echoes of great dinner parties hovered in the shadows of this room, brilliant discourses by some of the most important and influential minds of the last hundred years. One could hardly chatter about daily distractions or even private family matters in this room. For years Kate had been considering an alteration to the house, converting the cold-storage pantry into a cheerful, sunlit, plant-filled breakfasting room, but changes were pleasanter to contemplate than to act on.

She sipped her coffee slowly, glancing across the wide table at her daughter, who was evidently (for the first time in her life) not hungry. She was proud and excited about Emily this morning and longed to tell her so. This child, this fat little girl who had always seemed passive and bored, was suddenly charged with the same passionate fires that had illuminated Kate's own youth; she was glad for her daughter, thrilled and terrified for her, too. This new creature, this young woman across the table, had hidden depths after all—there was so much they had to say to each other! But the dining room, with Charles presiding over breakfast, was the last place in the world for that. The renewal of their bond, mother and daughter, would wait. It had already waited for so very long.

Sipping her coffee, watching her daughter's nervous fingers picking at crumbs of untouched toast, Kate indulged herself for a moment in her little fantasy in which the two of them (someday in the future) were settled into a warm, comfortable intimacy. She had imagined herself and Emily, sitting on the west lawn of the Milton house, under a tree (with dappled sunlight, of course; if it's a fantasy, why not have it all?) chatting and confiding in each other easily. They had so many secrets to share, nothing was kept back, their mutual love and trust were a kind of miracle to other people; to them it was natural, spontaneous . . . Kate didn't realize she had sighed aloud until she sensed her daughter's quickly averted glance across the wide table. She smiled quickly, but Emily didn't get the signal; her eyes were downcast again as though fascinated by the minute crumbs of the uneaten toast.

"Why, Emily, dear, you're not eating a thing," she said, and added quickly, to paint over her surprise with the brighter colors of concern, "Do you feel all right?"

"Yes, fine. I'm just not hungry this morning."

"I think that's the first time I've ever known you to refuse food, and I do believe that means you're really growing up at last! When we can control our appetites, we can begin to control our own lives

. . . .'' She trailed off, stopped talking, and took a bite of her own toast, which crunched loudly, having been allowed to cool until it was like cardboard painted with cold butter. Neither her husband nor her daughter responded (to either her words or the irony of her munching); she might as well have saved her breath. Charles, of course, was absorbed in his newspaper; he loathed morning conversations. And Emily seemed so far away . . .

Charles dabbed his lips, excused himself, and left the dining room. Before Kate could say anything to establish the rapport she so achingly longed for, Emily was asking to be excused.

"But . . . I hoped we could have a talk," Kate said. "Would you like an orange, dear, or some nice fresh hot toast?"

"I'm really not hungry, Mother, thank you. Please excuse me now, or I'll be late for school."

Kate only nodded. Disappointment stuck in her throat like a small sharp bone, but she swallowed and even managed to digest it and told herself there would be other times more suitable for herself and her daughter to have that talk, that first of a lifelong series of warm, intimate, cozy confidences. . . .

She had to leave the New England Historical Landmark Protection Society meeting before it concluded its business of the day, turning the gavel over to Hortense Hobson in order to be home by five thirty. She left her dripping umbrella in the rack. Her husband's umbrella was not in its place as yet. She hung her Burberry on its hook inside the closet door, alongside Emily's rubber poncho. She must have been sweltering under all those folds of rubber on such a warm, if wet, June day, but Emily's choice of clothing had been a contentious subject for too long in this house; if she hadn't learned the value of style over fashion by now, then she would simply have to live her life as an eccentric. The child was nearly eighteen after all. Nearly the age Kate had been when she had left home . . . never mind that; it was her daughter's turn now.

She found Emily alone in the library, curled up in one of the Queen Anne chairs next to the unlit fire. Her paint-splattered jeans contrasted joltingly with the pale green brocade of the chair. Emily seemed to be thinking; one must draw that conclusion since there was no book on her lap or on the table alongside her chair.

"Hello, dear. I was so afraid I'd be late, and your father isn't even here yet, I suppose I needn't have rushed after all."

"Miss Coe called to say he'd be twenty minutes late," Emily said.

"Oh, good . . . I mean, that gives us a chance to talk—doesn't it?—before . . . well, on some subjects your father and I have different opinions, of course, and . . . I'd like you to know how I feel before he . . . not that I know what he'll want to say to you, but—Emily, could you just stop twisting your hair like that for a moment? It's so distracting, thank you, dear. . . . What I want to say is this: Whatever your father, or any one else, says, and I'm sure you have the sense to weigh all advice very carefully, I want you to know that I'm behind you a hundred percent; in fact, I'm very, very proud of you."

"Well, I don't know what there is to be proud of, Mother. I don't think I know what you mean. I didn't do anything except throw up and get myself arrested."

"But you took part! Your generation is on the march, the way mine was in my time. I was always a bit afraid that you were—unpolitical, not really concerned about the world outside your own little center." She stopped. Emily was doing that irritating thing of twisting a strand of her long, thin hair between two fingers, around and around and around. She did it almost all the time, and all her friends did it, too. It seemed to have taken the place of nail biting, which was what Kate and her contemporaries had done as teen-agers. "Do stop twisting, dear," she said.

Emily stopped. She began turning the little silver rings that she wore on every finger, around and around and around, first one fleshy hand and then the other.

"I want you to know that whether I personally agree with you or not, I'll always be behind you and supporting your right to work on behalf of any cause you feel is just and—"

"Mom."

"Yes, dear."

"I don't have any 'cause.' I told you, I don't even know what that was all about yesterday. I don't care anything about politics. I think all those kids out there yelling, 'Stop the war,' and stuff like that are just asking for trouble. I wasn't, and look what happened, I got it anyway!"

"Emily! How can you be . . . how can you *not care*? I thought
. . ."

"Oh, Mother! The only time I ever cared about anything like that
was when you and I worked together on the Kennedy campaign—I
mean, the other one, you know, John—I really liked that okay, but
well, I was just a little kid then. By the time I was really conscious
of anything he was suddenly dead. So there didn't seem to be any
point. . . ."

"But . . . but how did you get mixed up in that demonstration in
Cambridge yesterday?"

"I don't know. Nothing else to do, I guess."

Kate stared at her daughter.

The dappled sunlight of her fond fantasy didn't exist; instead, there
was the cold, familiar library hearth with its neat dry pile of last
winter's ashes stretching for miles between them. We're parallel lines,
she thought sadly, Emily and I; there's an illusion of them meeting,
somewhere off in the far distance, beyond the eye's perspective, but
parallel lines never can meet, never. She was silent for so long that
Emily finally looked over at her with something like concern. Then
she said, not really meaning anything by it, "I suppose you'd rather
have me be a Commie, like you back in the good old days?"

Kate picked up her needlepoint, which she kept in a large antique
Chinese basket next to her chair. She studied the work as she spread
it out on her lap. A touch of dark green might do to outline the lighter
green tree. . . .

Charles was more than twenty minutes late already. It wasn't like
him at all to keep them waiting like this.

Emily was waiting for her to say something. Children have no
sense of timing. When you want to talk, they don't, and then unexpectedly they catch you off guard and you have to answer somehow,
ready or not. It isn't fair. She remembered thinking those same
thoughts before, long ago, when the child had been at the age for
asking other kinds of questions. The facts of life had been a breeze
compared to this, she thought. Then she remembered: It had been her
mother who explained the facts of life to Emily. Behind her back.

"If you really want to know about my—my past—I'll be very glad
to tell you," she said finally. "But you must respect what I say. I
mean, well, lately—in the last few years, I haven't felt your respect,

dear. It's been hard to be myself with you. I've been sad about that. But . . . I want to tell you, I want very much for you to understand. I'll be glad to tell you exactly how it was if you really want to hear. You have a tendency to become bored with me sometimes, I know, and this is a rather longish story. Are you sure?''

"I've always been kind of curious. Actually, it's kind of weird having a mother who was a Communist. People just think it's well . . . weird. You know.''

"I know what people think, and that doesn't interest me in the slightest, as you should be well aware, Emily. But I would like to know what you think. Yes. That interests me.''

"Oh, I don't know, I guess I never really thought about it much, to tell you the truth. But if you want to talk about it, I'll be glad to listen. I mean, you know, I'd like to hear about it, and . . . well . . . if you want to tell me.''

"You're not just being polite?''

Emily shook her head no. She stopped twisting her rings and began on a long single strand of hair again. The telephone rang, and Emily scrambled to the desk to pick it up. It was Charles, saying there was a meeting which would keep him another fifteen minutes or so.

"Go ahead, Mother,'' she said as she settled back into the high-backed chair facing Kate.

"Yes, well . . . I was . . . that is to say, it was a time when people really thought the world could change. There was a terrible depression, you know about that, of course, and fascism was rising in Spain and in Europe, people were dying. Yes, then, too. Things haven't changed very much after all. Your generation doesn't exactly have an exclusive on violence. But we had illusions in those days, ideals and principles. It was possible to believe that we could change things. If we cared enough, worked hard enough, refused to compromise . . .''

"You and Patrick Casey,'' Emily murmured.

"Yes . . . and others, lots of others. All over the country, all over the world, people were getting together to fight against oppression and exploitation and . . . well, those were the catchwords anyway. It all seemed pretty clear, back then, the difference between right and wrong. I wasn't the only naïve one, believe me.''

Emily nodded. "Go on, Mother."

"Well, I guess there isn't that much more to tell, after all. Funny . . . I've never talked about it, not in all these years, and now when I want you to understand, there just doesn't seem to be any real way to make you see. I was very . . . different then."

"Well, what changed you?"

"Changed me?"

"Yes. I mean, how come you gave up all the ideals and stuff and came back to Boston and married Dad and decided to be a capitalist after all?"

"Emily, are you . . . no, it's a legitimate question; of course, you have the right to ask me that. I guess it was mostly the war. The whole world was fighting, the issues were different . . . and afterward it was all suddenly complicated, not clear anymore. . . ."

"And your lover got killed."

"My what!?!?"

"Patrick Casey."

"He was my husband, Emily! Yes, he was killed . . . a lot of people were killed. But it was much more complicated than that, even—"

"Was it?"

"Yes, of course. What do you mean?"

"Well, I don't see why you couldn't have gone on with what you were doing, I mean, if you really believed in it."

"Of course, I really believed in it, but—well, it just got complicated. Stalin turned out to be—insupportable, and the unions became almost too strong, and the lines between the good side and the bad side weren't quite so clear anymore."

"And then you had to save your own skin. I mean, that comes first after all—doesn't it?—when all the ideals and principles are really put to the test. I'm sorry, Mother, but it's just awfully hard to sit here and listen to all that crap. It's not you personally, I guess, but your generation sure seems—well, hypocritical. You're lying to yourself, and that's your business; but it makes me just feel sick and bad when you tell me how noble it all was, and you want me to believe it."

"Emily, I don't know what you mean." Something heavy, huge,

and painful was forming itself inside Kate's chest; it was suddenly hard to breathe normally. This is what civilized people learn to avoid, she thought, this kind of hurt. Talking did it. Talking about important, personal things—emotions. My mother was right, damn it, and all her generation and the women before us knew it, too, and I should teach Emily not to hurt me, never to let herself be—

"I mean, old Senator McCarthy and all that, I guess you forgot about that. When you said you'd never been a Communist, when you swore that you were just a rattled, emotional young girl in love. Just a foolish, giddy girl too swept off her feet to know what she was doing. You had it both ways, didn't you, Mother? Oh, hell, I don't blame you. I don't even care. Only don't come at me with that holier-than-thou shit, okay? Excuse me for swearing."

The needlepoint slipped from her lap onto the carpet, unnoticed, as Kate lurched to her feet. She was standing over Emily, grasping her shoulders hard in both hands.

"I don't know what you mean!" she cried. "I don't . . . know . . . what you mean!" To her horror, she was shaking her daughter, hard; her tears blurred the sight of Emily's terrified face. Physical violence was abhorrent to her; she sat on the board of the League to Cease the Abuse of Children, yet she could not stop shaking her own child, hard, with the intent to hurt, hurt deeply. Her fingers dug into Emily's soft, yielding flesh. Emily's head was thrust back against the chair, then jerked forward with the force of her mother's pain.

"Stop it!"

Charles was suddenly there, shutting the library door quickly behind him, striding toward them, loosening Kate's vise grip on the terrified girl's shoulders. He guided Kate to her chair, which exactly matched the one where Emily sat blotchy and quietly blubbering.

"I never expected to see such a thing in this house," Charles said. He went around the desk that formed the major piece of furnishing in this small room and sat down in the huge leather chair that had belonged to Kate's father.

My father's chair is much too big for him, Kate thought irrelevantly. There was something else, something odd and unexpected— wave after wave of queasy fear, almost like old friends, so familiar was the feeling and the setting: the anticipation of terrible concentrated parental attention to be centered upon herself, in this very room. Do qualms and fears linger in a room for years and years, settling back inside one's guts the instant one is vulnerable again?

But Charles was her husband, her cousin—not, certainly, her father. And this room was her own sanctuary now, forever purged of her father's sickening cigar fumes and her own embarrassing fears. There was her needlework, in the basket she had chosen, there was her chair (which had been her mother's), there was her writing paper in her father's desk drawer and her own check stubs and bank statements and invitations and engagement books, and there was her husband sitting there, looking at her as if she had committed a crime. Their daughter had stopped sniveling, and the room was dead silent except for the ticking of the pendulum clock.

"I don't know what caused you to do what you were doing when I came in, Kate, and I shan't ask. If either of you wants to tell me, of course, I'll hear you out, but it's my impression that whatever happened in this room before I came home was between the two of you and must be resolved between you. I do want to discuss the matter of your involvement with the police, however, Emily."

"Yes, Daddy."

"Don't call me that, for heaven's sake, Emily. That's a very childish name, and you're a grown woman. People will think you're slow."

"Okay. Dad."

"Kate?"

"Hmm? What is it, Charles? Oh, oh, are you waiting for me? It's all right. I'm quite calm now. Go ahead and talk. I'm quite all right, thank you."

"Emily? Tell us, please, what that was all about then."

"Well, I was telling Mother. It wasn't about anything as far as I was concerned. Mother thinks everybody has to have a big cause they're willing to die for; well, I just don't, that's all."

"Emily, that's very unfair. You're misrepresenting me, and you know it."

"You were the one who was hitting."

"No, I was shaking you, not hitting you. Let's get that straight, please. I've never hit you, although now I think possibly I should have."

"Kate! I'm really shocked at this!"

"Oh, Charles, please try not to be such a stuffed shirt. Hasn't it occurred to you that I wouldn't be shaking Emily if I hadn't been very badly shaken up myself? You walked into the middle of serious, unfinished business here. Emily and I are both very upset—"

"I'm not upset. Not anymore."

"Emily, you're really asking for it, you know that? Deliberately trying to get my goat—"

"Ladies, please! I never expected to hear such—"

"Oh, shut up, Charles!"

"I think you'd better leave the room, Kate, until you're feeling a little calmer, more in control of yourself. We'll excuse you, won't we, Emily?"

"Sure."

"Charles, are you out of your mind? I am this child's mother. You are her father. I think the two of us should be able to talk with her. Why are you treating me like the child here?"

"Because you are acting like the child here, Kate, and an exceedingly wrought-up emotional child at that. When you calm down, we will be more than willing to talk to you."

Kate stood up slowly. She looked down at her daughter and then across her father's desk at her husband. They were looking back at her with intelligent concern.

"All right," she said slowly. "Yes, I think I'd like to get out of here. You're quite right, Charles. I will leave you two to talk things out, and—" She was at the door, her hand on the knob. She turned. Without inflecting her tone, she added, "You can both go fuck yourselves."

He was obviously right. She was not only childish and emotional but totally around the bend, she thought to herself as she turned to ascend the stairs. And good, she thought, for me.

Chapter Twenty-Eight

1968: EMILY

Once in her room, Kate realized she could not bear to stay in the house; she grabbed a scarf and her warm gray cardigan sweater from the closet and almost ran down the back stairs. Mary, seeing her heading toward the carriage entrance, thought to ask about the planned chops for dinner, what with the price shot up so since last week, but something kept her from opening her mouth, her mistress looked that distracted. When she saw Miss Kate backing out of the garage in the old black Ford two-seater, Mary assumed there was something to be attended to in Milton, probably having to do with the new gardener and the roses. She made the decision on her own, then: scrod and boiled potatoes instead of the chops, prices being what they were.

It never occurred to Kate to pay attention to where she was going, hadn't for years. A lifetime of walking on her own streets in areas where there were not likely to be any surprises had given her an arrogant confidence which would have dismayed her had she been aware of it; she walked exactly as her mother had done. And in a car, either someone else was driving, or the old Ford seemed to know where she was heading without conscious direction. On an early summer afternoon one drove to Milton, of course; the automobiles from the Hill in May and June formed an irregular, discreet southerly parade, taking favorite furnishings, supplies of canned goods from S. S.

Pierce, fresh tennis balls, and chambermaids to Milton, to ready the houses for the warm months.

Rather than taking a firm direction, in fact, Kate's thoughts just then were uncharacteristically awash in a kind of vague, uncertain self-pity. Things she didn't want to think about were trying to surface; she was angry and had indulged in a childish, emotional outburst directed at her husband and, oh, God, her child. Her eyes were clear, but she wasn't really seeing the parameters of Commonwealth Avenue as she turned the corner.

The faithful Ford reared suddenly at an unfamiliar intersection, probably confused by the grotesque new structure that loomed up, rising triumphantly on widespread concrete pylons to straddle the ruins of fine old historic neighborhoods. Startled, Kate tried to turn, in any direction, but was forced by the other cars to drive onto the monstrous new expressway itself. The jaunty old black coupe meandered onto one of the speed lanes, to the ill-contained annoyance of other motorists. Horns honked at her, and some drivers seemed to be leaning from their windows to shout at Kate as they passed. One man in particular seemed to be gesturing at her, at her car; he actually slowed down and gestured for her attention. She rolled her window down a few inches to catch his meaning.

"Get a goddamned horse, why doncha, insteada that creepy antique!"

With that, he stepped on his gas pedal and screeched past her, in his scratched red hunk of tin that wouldn't last two years. She had no doubt she would pass him along the way sooner or later, either with a blown-out tire or horribly killed in an accident of his own making. She devoutly hoped so.

When the stench of exhaust and acrid smog blew off, an unexpected fragrance wafted in through the open window, taking her so by surprise that she gasped. It was fresh sea air, salty and evocative of summer, of childhood afternoons on the beach, and she was overcome by an atavistic, inexplicable longing for the sight of fishing boats, men in dories rowing home with their catch in the dying light of the early spring day. . . . Kate leaned her head out to gulp in the tang of salt air, but now it was gone, and her lungs filled with motor fumes and city staleness.

The old Ford must have known, better than she herself—it wasn't Milton she wanted; it wasn't anything familiar or dutiful. It was the sea and being alone with unlimited horizons to stare out at: the soothing and somehow exciting surf breaking irregularly, regularly, roughly, calmly, bringing up new treasures, stones and shells and bits of colored glass that had been buried in the deep water for years and years and only uncovered now, this minute, this wave, for her eyes alone to discover. . . . she had never realized before how very deeply she loved the sea. Suddenly it became an urgent matter for her to drive onward, passing under green signs that advised turning off to Winthrop, Chelsea, Revere, Everett, Medford, Malden, Saugus, Lynn, East Lynn, Nahant, Swampscott . . .

Yes, why not? I'm free, freer this minute than I've ever been. I can go where I like. North instead of south, the beach instead of the country, Nahant instead of Milton, all the way to Maine if I like. I can go where I want to. We'll follow our noses, this old Ford and I, people can laugh at us all they like; we're going to see the sea.

Maybe I'll go to Marblehead or one of the smaller fishing villages near there. Yes, that would be lovely. I'll walk on the beach, just to breathe the good fresh air and watch for things no human eye has ever seen before, rocks or shells or living creatures brought up on the tide, on a wave, for me to see and fall in love with for one ephemeral instant before the sea takes it back again. . . .

How maudlin, worse—sentimental. If that's what thoughts of the sea brings out in me, I'd damn well better stay far away from the real thing! But even as she scoffed at herself, she was thinking how she longed to stand and wait for the fishermen to come home at sundown with their catch.

I am fifty-two years old. I never thought I'd live this long. My neck is wrinkled, and my eyes, too, and my hair is half-gray, and no man has smiled at me with delight in twenty years or more. I miss that very, very much, she admitted to herself. My daughter is gone from me; I've lost her, maybe forever. She feels . . . contempt for me. More than I ever did for my mother. Or worse . . . she feels nothing.

Driving alone freed one's thoughts in the most extraordinary way. She had even begun to stop loathing the expressway; ugly and destructive as it was, there was a certain exhilaration one felt, soaring above the city streets like this, with no need to stop for anything, nothing at all in her way, no cross traffic, no pedestrians. Only the other cars with their idiotic drivers turning to stare at her. One young man, with an absurd mustache, leered at her from his ugly little Volkswagen as he passed. Impulsively she pushed on her horn. It did have a funny sound, an old heehaw, reminding her suddenly of her father's Model T that had gone—how was it?—ah-oo-ga, ah-oo-ga. Kate found herself laughing aloud, all by herself. Her sensible brogan pressed the gas pedal down; she was doing almost fifty, but still the other cars passed as if in some kind of race.

The overhead sign read Salem; it appealed to her. She turned the car into the right-hand lane in order to take the upcoming exit. It was an odd thing to do; she couldn't have explained it to herself, much less to the frantic and outraged motorists scrambling to get out of her slow and lethally erratic path.

Once off the highway, the exit ramp turned one out onto a smaller but no less noxious boulevard. At the first traffic light she realized that she never should have allowed the Ford its head; she would soon be depressed if she stayed on this straightaway lined on both sides with hamburger stands and used car lots. Waiting for the light to change, she peered out at the signpost of the intersection. She was on Paradise Road, and if that were not in itself sufficiently ironic, the cross street was called Stafford's Pond Lane.

The light changed just as she veered over to take the turn, and the driver behind her was not quick enough to avoid rudely smashing into her taillight. She would have stopped and exchanged attorneys' names with him, but the man gunned his motor and drove away. She rounded the corner onto the lane and then stopped the car and got out to inspect the damage. She took out her pen and notebook and jotted down the man's license plate number. He would have to pay for the repair, of course, and she might consider suing him for leaving the scene of an accident as well. Then she got back behind the driver's wheel and sat quietly, without turning the key again, to collect her thoughts, which were scattery, to say the least.

I'm on a toot, she thought with the same indulgent amusement (oh, well, she's harmless) that she and other people had allowed in the case of her eccentric mother when she was in her last years and dotty as a field of daisies. It's true, I have probably become a full-blown eccentric, but I see now that by the time that happens it doesn't matter a damn bit. I really don't care one way or another whether I'm odd or not, or what the world thinks, or Charles . . . or Emily, if it's come to that.

But for myself . . . now what am I doing in Salem? This road was named after my great-great-great-great-uncle. Maybe even greater, more generations than I can count now. Charles Stafford, the rigid Puritan, the witch burner—no, must be fair. Witch hanger. The righteous judge, the man who sentenced women to die and drove his own wife mad.

And with the slow certainty of revelation that cannot be explained in terms yet understood, with the shock of a rational mind confronted with absolute evidence of communication across centuries and the hint that perhaps there is meaning in all things after all, Kate realized that something had drawn her to Salem, and it was connected to the thing that had drawn Emily Stafford here 276 years before.

When she stared at the signpost again, she couldn't read it; the spring day had lengthened into twilight and darkness without her noticing. There was a chill in the air. Kate reached for her cardigan and slowly put it on. Then she started the motor, turned on the headlights, and began to drive slowly up Stafford's Pond Lane. She knew it would pass by the place which had once been known as Gibbet Hill, and she expected to recognize it, even though it had been converted into neat little rows of prefabricated houses, its past distorted for reasons of profit—too choice a piece of real estate to give up to ghosts. The tourists were told lies about where the hangings had taken place; it was more convenient to have them stand about the little square in front of the "Witches' House," down the street from Hawthorne's House of Seven Gables, and the souvenir concessionaires, where maps of old Salem and booklets about the events of 1692 were sold. But the real Gibbet Hill, where the real women had been hanged to death to pay for men's fears, that place was unmarked now.

How she knew, she did not know. But with absolute certainty she drove up and stopped in front of a little house with aluminum siding painted green and a statue of a drunk leaning against a lamppost on the lawn. She sat in the black Ford coupe and stared at the neat, defoliated half acre plots. Against the little streetlights that were deliberately dim, Kate could see dark-shawled bodies hanging lifeless from three solitary crosstrees. She could almost hear the low sounds of someone mourning for them. She sat huddled in the inadequate warmth of her gray cardigan sweater, and tears filled her eyes.

"You need some help, ma'am?"

She tried to see the face that hovered outside her car, but her vision was teary. She did not wish to open the window. She shook her head no and tried to smile a polite thank-you, hoping the well-intentioned man would go away and leave her to collect herself. Oh, she wanted to be away from there, and she would go quickly, as soon as she collected herself.

"You lost?" he persisted.

She shook her head. For heaven's sake, did she look like a burglar, if that's what he was afraid of? She had better speak with him after all. She rolled down the window one inch.

"I know exactly where I am, thank you. Good night," she said pleasantly enough. She rolled the window up again. The man did not budge.

"I know everybody on this hill if you're looking for someone?" he persisted, raising his voice to be heard through the glass. She ignored him. "It's private property?" he went on, evidently unable to state anything straight out without a question mark at the end of it.

Kate sighed and opened the window again. "Yes, I know," she said. "What do you call this place these days?"

"These days we call it the same thing we always called it. Thought you knew where you were?"

"I suppose you think I'm trespassing."

"Yes, ma'am. It is private property, and seeing your car just parked here, and you not getting out, makes people a little uneasy? We haven't had much crime in this neighborhood, and we hope to keep it that way."

"I think you've had a great deal of crime in this neighborhood," Kate murmured, but under her breath, and the man didn't make out the words, which was just as well.

"What was that, ma'am?"

"I said I was just leaving. I won't bother to thank you for your hospitality."

"There's plenty people in this town who make a good living off gawkers. Whyn't you go on down to the town square and see about that?" the man said.

She had nothing further to say to him, and nothing he could possibly say would interest her. The car started right up at the first turn of the ignition, and suddenly she felt that she couldn't get away fast enough or far enough. She saw him in the rearview mirror, standing in the middle of the winding street that led to the top of the hill; for an instant she feared to see him raise his fist at her, but she turned the Ford down the hill, and the man disappeared from sight.

Once again on Paradise Road, she turned into a filling station. While the attendant was putting in gas, she made a telephone call from the booth attached to the outside wall next to the unusably filthy rest room.

"Hello, Anna, this is Miss Kate, will you put my brother on, please? I am calling long distance."

"Yes, ma'am. Wait, please."

She waited. Anna was very old, and one must try to be patient, although why Hank and Laura didn't send the poor thing out to pasture in Milton, she really couldn't—

"Kate? Is that you?"

"Yes, Henry. Now listen, dear, please, I don't have any more change, so I can't repeat myself. I'm in Salem, and I want you to meet me here as soon as you can. You can be here in a hour or less. Take the highway."

"Salem!"

"Yes, that's right. I'll wait for you someplace; there must be an inn. . . ."

"Charles telephoned. Seems to have no idea where you are. He sounded almost worried, Kate. What's going on?"

"Oh . . ." Her voice became soft and rather sad. "I guess it's . . . a trace of the old insomnia, Hank. Remember?"

There was a pause at the other end of the line, and she heard Hank mulling aloud, "It's damned inconvenient," and she waited, and there was a clicking sound on the line, and then he said quickly, "I'll be there," and hung up.

Dear Hank. He saved me twenty cents, but he has no idea where to meet me. Ah, well, there will certainly be an inn at the center of town, and it will have low ceilings with imitation beams and a fire going in the hearth, long tables with initials carved in them and good sturdy chairs and decent simple food. I'll find it, and so will Hank.

Only after she had found it, and was hungrily attacking the thick slice of rare roast beef, did it occur to Kate how odd it was to have envisioned this place so exactly. She must have been brought here as a child. No child could grow up in Boston without having been taken to the historic houses, battlefields, burying grounds, meeting places, churches, state houses, old and new, and sites of massacres, revolutionary parleys, literary inspirations, insurrections, and witch-hunts which surrounded them on all sides. This inn was no older than she was, and weathering its years less well at that. Nothing authentic about it (certainly the original Emily could not have been here at least!), but somehow she had known it would be here, looking exactly as it did. Hank would find it as easily and naturally as she had; he could probably tell her exactly when they had been here before, too.

As for the other, the thing that had happened to her on that awful little suburban hillside, she understood now that she was hoping Hank would explain that away, too, when he came. Although she wasn't at all sure she would tell him about it; no sense giving the family more reason to pack you away to the funny farm than they could manage to ignore. See which way the wind lay, once Hank got here. She was impatient, but it had been less than an hour since their phone conversation when her brother walked into the main public room of the inn.

He was handsome, better-looking now nearing his sixties than he had ever been. He had escaped the slow rounding of the shoulders which had so diminished their father in his later years and made him seem to disappear before their eyes. Edward had inherited that unfortunate tendency to slump and looked as resigned and old as any Stafford in the portraits; but when Hank strode through the low door of the inn, he had to duck his head, and when he came across the room to her, everyone in the place turned to look at the tall, distinguished, clearly important gentleman from Boston.

"You're a very satisfying brother," she said in a low voice as he sat down beside her.

"Well, I'm glad to hear that, after canceling a bridge game and driving all this way in the middle of the night," he said pleasantly enough, in the nothing-to-fear, calm, authoritative tone he must use with his law clients. The waitress came over. Hank ordered a pot of coffee, was told all they had was "instant," and he smiled and said that would be fine. Nothing more was said until the young woman had brought the order and retreated.

"Now what's this all about?" he asked quietly. "Charles is terribly upset, and—you haven't done anything like this since you were a rebellious kid. And why Salem, for heaven's sake? You'd better tell me all about it, Kate."

She sipped the awful powdered coffee and tried to think where to begin.

"You know, no matter how deeply I retreated into the way of life that was expected of me, the easy and comfortable and conventional ways . . . no matter how much I sold out . . . no, don't interrupt me, Hank. Let me say what I have to; you're the only person I can talk to about this. It's very hard. . . ."

"Go on."

"Well, I always had the knowledge, in the back of my mind, that once—once I had done something because I believed in it, something of my own deciding. . . . I had dared and defied traditional wisdom—the family, I guess, is what I'm trying to say—oh, well. That once in my life I had been unafraid. I guess that's what I'm trying to say. Can you understand, Hank? Please?"

"I think so. I'm trying to. I think I know what you're referring to, but why has it come up now?"

"Emily . . . Emily told me that you . . . that Edward said my having been"—unthinkingly Kate lowered her voice, although no one was near enough to their table to overhear any of their conversation—"a Communist was not something I had done honestly, but because I was . . . in love, and that was all there was to it. Emily accused me of saving my neck during the McCarthy time by denying that I was ever political at all, but that I was merely a silly girl in love. I think that was Emily's exact phrase.''

"Is that all?''

"All, Hank? Yes, it's all. It's my whole life or, rather, the only part of it I ever respected. You can't see that?''

He was silent. He sat thoughtfully for a long moment, and then he reached out to pat her hand. He smiled a bit sadly. "Yes, I guess I see. Poor Kate. I do see, dear. You want it both ways, though, you know. Communist and capitalist, safe and risky—Patrick and Charles. But not all at the same time, you know; that really is asking a bit too much. As a matter of fact, Edward and I, with Charles concurring, arranged for you not to have to testify in the House Un-American Activities investigation—''

"Arranged it? Arranged it? You pulled strings and used all the family influence to keep me safe? Without my knowledge, behind my back—''

"You never would have agreed—''

"Of course not! Agreed to deny everything Patrick and I stood for, fought for . . . how could you do that to me!''

"All right, Kate. We're the culprits who took away your integrity, if you want to look at it that way. But we also saved you from public embarrassment, possibly even jail. You see, Kate, it always was a game for you, even though you didn't know it. You would not have understood how serious it might have become. The family could have survived it, but—''

"The family . . . oh, Hank, can't you see that the family—you— took away from me the only self-respect I'll ever have? Oh . . . why did Patrick have to die?''

"Are you going to cry?''

"Certainly not.''

"Did you hear yourself just then, Kate? Talking about your self-respect, saying—and believing, I have no doubt at all—that you wanted to be judged on your own. And in the same breath, calling for the man who led you into all of it, a man who's been dead for more than twenty years, Kate . . . I think we should finish this talk in private if you're finished with your coffee.''

"Yes, all right.'' She felt confused, even distraught by what Hank had implied; it needed thinking out. She went to the ladies' room and splashed some water on her face, only to discover that there were no clean towels and she had to blot it as best she could with toilet paper. She stared into the mirror at herself—middle-aged, plenty of character lines, although no sags or pouches that she could see, not yet. I don't want to be old, she thought, I'm not ready yet. She smoothed down her skirt, straightened her hair as best she could, and went back out to rejoin her brother, who was too old, too.

"By the way, is your car all right? I saw it parked outside here, which is how I knew where to find you. Did you know you had hung up before telling me? If it's running, maybe it would be kinder to send Tom back to Boston with my car and you and I can drive together."

"Yes, yes, fine . . ."

"Well, then," he said when he was behind the wheel of the Ford, "back to Boston?"

"No, not just yet, Hank, if you don't mind. Could you—could we drive around Salem a bit first?"

"It's a very dreary town, Kate, and it is nighttime, you know. Won't be able to see anything—was there something in particular you had in mind? Why did you come here anyway?"

"I don't know . . . maybe the association, you know, with witch-hunts. Isn't that what we all called the McCarthy hearings, witch-hunts? I don't know, maybe that's it. Unconscious associations? Didn't we have an ancestor or two who lived around here?"

"Of course we did, you know that. The original old Charles and his two sons, before they ran away from him. You don't have to ask me that."

"Do you think we could find where they lived?"

"Now? In the dark? But we haven't any idea where it was, have we? Not that there would be any traces anyway, even if we knew the exact spot . . ."

"But you're interested, aren't you, Hank? Remember how we used to unearth all the family skeletons and look for scandals in the Archives—oh, the old Ark, we did have fun, didn't we?"

"We thought we were discovering things no one else knew," Hank agreed as he shifted gears. The Ford lurched forward and up the little street. "It was exactly what they wanted us to do, of course. My kids did it, too; didn't Emily?"

"No. Emily has always been a child of the present; she doesn't seem interested in the past at all. Emily is a great disappointment to m—oh, my God. Oh, I didn't mean to say that, I didn't . . . Emily is fine. More like Charles than me . . . turn left here."

"Here? Hold on. Now then, where the hell are we, and more to the point, why? Will you please explain this, Kate?"

"Can you see the name of the street?"

"I'll slow up at the next signpost . . . there it is . . . let's see, hard to read . . . Buffum's Lane . . . and the other one is Cemetery Road. What's this about, Kate? I'm too old to be out this late hunting down wild mysterious geese."

"Well, you see, I was on a road before called Stafford's Pond Lane. I thought this was it. I guess I'm a bit turned around."

"Damn!" Hank turned off the ignition and folded his arms across his chest. He waited with elaborate patience for her to explain this extraordinary scene he found himself party to.

Hank swore only when he was upset. It made her nervous. She reached past him and pulled out the button for the headlights.

"What are we looking for, Kate? This is a dreary little place, and all its proper burghers are in their proper beds at this hour, as we should be. What are we doing prowling about like thieves in the night? I really must insist on making some sense out of this now."

"I thought we might be able to find the route our ancestor took on her famous ride. Silly, I guess. No one marked it; old Charles's house was burned to the ground after he died. It's probably a supermarket now."

"How about giving some thought to young Charles, Kate?"

"Who?"

"Your husband. Have you any idea how anxious he is? You're behaving rather erratically, you know."

"Didn't you tell him where I am, and that you were coming to meet me?"

"Yes, of course I did, but still—"

"I'm sure Charles is waiting very comfortably, with a fire going if it's chilly, and a brandy, and a book to keep him company. A good light to read by, and maybe a Haydn quartet on the phonograph."

"Well, I fail to see what that has to do with anything, really, Kate—"

"No, of course not, except, well, it just occurs to me that I don't really need to worry about Charles at all. Even if he's anxious, as you say, I know he's very comfortable, and I don't need to worry about him, that's all. He's really on a very even keel, always will be, no matter what happens to other people around him. Charles has some kind of inner balancing wheel; nothing can ever really disturb his equilibrium. Nothing. He'll be just fine, no matter what."

"What on earth are you talking about?"

Kate shivered, suddenly impatient to be away from that quiet crossroads. "Sorry, Hank, dear. It must be this godforsaken place. I always was suggestible; isn't that how Mother used to put it?"

Her brother nodded, and with a smile that was half sigh of relief, he turned his attention to getting the car in gear and moving forward. He hated to drive, which accounted for his keeping a chauffeur—an extravagance many people didn't understand. Kate was touched to see him struggling with her eccentric old Ford—the crank or whatever it was finally caught, and he concentrated all his attention on the streets ahead of them.

Something about the movement, the solid comfort of her big brother at the wheel, and the darkness, the strange coexistence of mundane and melodramatic in this place—all combined to free Kate's heart, to let the words flow as they had not done since the long-ago nights when she and Hank were the only people in the world. She leaned her head back against the high seat and told her brother all the things she had been keeping from herself.

"You were always my best friend, my best listener, Hank. I never even talked to Patrick the way I could talk to you; he wouldn't have had the foggiest notion of some of the things . . . oh, well. Dead twenty years! What would he think of me now, I wonder? He'd be disappointed, too."

"Too?"

"Mother's last words, didn't you know? Long after I had given in, stopped fighting, after my pathetic attempts to lead a rebellious, meaningful life . . . after Patrick . . . and of course, my famous drunk act . . . I was trying to do it her way. Your way. The family's righteous way. And here I am, an insipid imitation of Mother, living in her house, living exactly the way she did, even sounding like her sometimes. And dear old Anne left me with her dying curse, so that as long as I live, I'll know I can't measure up to her. All of a sudden it occurs to me, Hank—maybe I don't have to try anymore.''

"Did she really say that? What were her words exactly?''

"Dear Hank, always the lawyer. 'You have always been a great disappointment to me.' Quote unquote. Nine words, engraved on my soul. Tattooed on my forehead, like the mark of Cain. But guess what? They have plastic surgery now that can remove tattoos, even engravings. How about that, Hank? Maybe I don't have to keep trying to get Mother's seal of approval for the rest of my life. I mean, after all, she's dead, and—hey, guess what? I'm not!''

"Don't quite follow you,'' he said carefully. He turned the car onto the highway, keeping the needle at a precise, unwavering thirty-five miles per hour. The drivers who passed them did not, Kate noted, laugh or jeer. This was Henry Stafford IV at the wheel; his dignity and his fine, strong, regal profile instilled respect even in strangers fleeting past in the dark night. He was impressive, solid, and wise.

"Let me think it through, out loud,'' she said. He drove, looking straight ahead and listening to her, bless him.

"Most of my life,'' she went on slowly, choosing her words as carefully as he guided the Ford, "most of my life I've resented—wrongly—the fact that being a Stafford meant I'd always have a safety net under me, whether I wanted it or not. When I was young, I wanted to do wonderful tricks, soar through the air and take chances, show what I could do on my own. But the net was always there. There was no way to do my high-wire act without that safety, that insurance, spoiling my act, keeping me from really proving something. So finally I just said, 'The hell with it,' and let myself get caught.

"For the past twenty years I've just let the old net hold me safely. I hardly even squirmed, did I? But suddenly—Hank, suddenly I see that I can simply walk out of the arena. I don't need to do stunts. I don't have to prove anything, not to myself or anyone else.''

"Well, of course not!'' Hank said, gamely trying to understand.

She felt the physical rush of excitement revving up her blood; she had forgotten how good it felt to become excited. The ideas were tumbling over one another like fireballs erupting from a long-dormant, seemingly dead pile of rock.

"It just never occurred to me that there might be another way of being a Stafford, neither rebelling nor capitulating, but using the inheritance—and I don't mean just the money, but all the generations that have gone to make me who I am—to make something out of myself according to my own standards. Not yours and not Patrick Casey's and not anybody else's. I wonder what mine might be. . . . I'm sure I have some, good ones, too. It might be interesting as hell to find out."

"You're not going to become a Red again, are you?" Hank asked. She thought he might be making a feeble attempt at a joke, but she saw the veins on his hand swell in the moonlight as he gripped the wheel.

"Now what would be the point in that?" she reassured him, surprising them both with a short but genuine burst of laughter. "That may be where I end up, but it's hardly a starting point, is it? No, Hank, whatever political integrity I end up with this time will be my own. Not some wonderful young man's, and not yours, and certainly not anything the family will be able to save me from. Without my knowledge," she had to add, from the residual bitterness that still lingered there.

"I've got a lot of thinking to do," she said. "I'm going to think about my fifty-two years of living and see if I can add them up so they make some kind of sense for the rest of my life." She took a deep, long breath, catching the smell of the sea beyond the motor fumes.

"But your life makes perfect sense, Kate. You have a fine life, productive and useful, and—well, what about Emily?"

"Emily is grown now, Hank. She's the age I was when I left home, remember? And . . . God! What if she feels about me . . . the way I do . . . did . . . about Mother? I couldn't bear it. Oh, Hank, I can't depend on Emily for my own salvation. I care too much for her."

"Nonsense. You know Emily loves you. Of course, she does. You're her mother."

"Oh, Hank!"

He was silent then, concentrating on driving down the straight road toward home. The lights of Boston were ahead of them now.

"I think you need a rest," Hank said gently, without taking his eyes from the road. "Why don't you talk to Charles about opening the house in Milton a bit early this year?"

"Yes, that's a nice idea," she answered.

They drove home in companionable silence. The thoughts tumbling in her head were like bits of shell and stones which had lain deep in dark waters for aeons; they were her private treasures, tossed by the waves onshore this night for her alone to see with sudden, lucid clarity.

Children on a beach run to their mothers, their nannies, their brothers, and their friends with their discoveries: "Look, look what I found, look what the wave tossed up, share my wonder!" But no one understood; people didn't even really care. Kate's find was for her eyes alone; she was too grown-up to hope that anyone, even dear Hank, could see the promise of it, too.

Chapter Twenty-Nine

1970: KATE

Emily dropped out of Radcliffe halfway through her first semester. She was living with some friends in Cambridge; she refused to allow her parents or anyone in the family to visit there. Kate, who did a lot of reading, thought it was because the place was filled with army deserters and hippies lying around passed out from drugs; Charles expressed the opinion that their daughter was a chip off the old (maternal) block and would soon come to her senses; the reason they were not welcome was simply that the child was having a fling at independence; it would pass. Charles said that along with the rest of her generation, Emily was not neat, and the flat was probably messy, and the child was probably embarrassed to have them see—he knew how it was; she could be sure that was all there was to it, nothing to worry about. Their Emily would be home one of these days and wiser for the experience out on her own; that's how it was these days, different from when they were young. Have to keep up with the times, Charles liked to say. As for the roommates, it never occurred to him that they might not all be female and white and well brought up.

Kate knew better because she had spied on Emily. It was the day after four students at a college in the Midwest had been gunned down on their own bucolic campus, having gathered in sorrow and protest at the bombing of Cambodia. Kate had been deeply upset by the news. Until that moment she had not let the war in Vietnam enter her conscience as it had so many others'—some of her friends were out there marching and protesting all the time, going to Washington for a redress of their grievances, setting up underground railroad stations for the young boys who refused to fight an unjust war and had to flee to Canada or Sweden. But Kate had remained aloof from it. Then the gentle people of Cambodia were bombed. And children in Ohio were shot.

Suddenly she feared for her daughter. She tried to phone her. The telephone in the flat Emily shared with an indeterminate number of other dropouts and students had been disconnected. In a panic she could not explain, Kate drove to Cambridge, not knowing what she would do when she got there.

It was only by chance that she knew the address. On one of her infrequent visits to Beacon Street, Emily had carried a huge floppy cut-velvet bag on a ribbon over her shoulder. She had rummaged deep inside the bag for something—a cigarette—and a casual collection of clutter had spilled over; Kate, sitting next to her daughter on one of the parlor sofas, leaned deliberately to look at the front of an envelope with exotic stamps and an airmail border. It was from India, addressed to Miss Emily Stafford and Mr. Joe McGrath at an address on Webster Avenue in Cambridge. Kate had made a note of the number. Emily was still her only daughter after all, even though everything else between them had somehow died.

It shocked Kate to be reduced to reading her daughter's mail (even the outside of an envelope) and spying. But a few weeks later there she was—hiding in her car outside the awful tumbledown brownstone rooming house, waiting for a glimpse of Emily. When her daughter did come out of the house, Kate's first thought was dismay at how thin she was.

Emily was dressed in the outlandish costumes all the young girls affected those days, rather pretty, soft lines and wild jumbles of color, a long skirt and layers of blouses and T-shirts and vests. Kate's throat filled with love words she could never have articulated. Emily was turning away, sauntering down the street. She hadn't seen her mother parked there like a private detective in a B movie, and if she had, it would have only widened the distance between them.

Kate took a pen from her handbag and wrote on a page of the little notebook she always carried: "Come for dinner tonight." She folded it, and then an afterthought made her unfold the page and add: "Bring a friend if you wish." She waited until her daughter was out of sight, around a corner, and then she got out of the car and went up to the door of the rooming house. It opened to her touch. There was a row of mailboxes in the vestibule. No Stafford. But she found McGrath. There was no lock on the mailbox. She opened it, put the note inside, and left. She walked back to the car and drove to Somerville, where she was very late for a meeting of the hospital board.

Emily had left home, dropped out of school, refused to tell them her address or introduce them to her friends; but it never dawned on her to refuse an imperial command to her mother's table, nor had it occurred to Kate that such a possibility existed. Emily and her young man, Joe McGrath, presented themselves at the front door promptly at half-past six. The boy, in his very early twenties, looked exactly like every other young man of his sort, with yellowish facial hair, wire-rimmed glasses, dirty blue jeans, and a too-thin body which had not been deodorized.

Charles served the fifty-year-old sherry and seemed genuinely interested in the opinions of their guest. Emily sat immersed in her usual passivity. Neither Emily nor Kate spoke much at first. Not like strangers; there might be many areas to be touched on and discussed between strangers. Kate sipped her tonic, listened to her husband's civilized conversation and the ugly boy's condescending answers. She wondered if Charles knew that this unkempt boy in torn and ragged tennis shoes was probably sleeping with their daughter every night.

Emily leaned forward, set her glass down on the table, and said casually, "Since we're here, I guess we'd better tell you our plans. I mean, I was going to wait till . . . but you might as well know now. Joe and I are going to India."

Kate was acutely aware of the clock ticking out in the hall. It was she who finally broke the strained silence because she could not bear the grin on Joe McGrath's face.

"I thought the time for that silliness was over," she said. "I know that it was very stylish to follow the Beatles in search of drugs and gurus and all that nonsense a few years ago, but I had thought it was passé by now. I should have thought you'd come up with something a bit more . . . well, inventive. Why India, for heaven's sake?"

"India is eternal," said Joe McGrath.

What an ass.

"India is full of starvation and disease, flies and filth, and American children have been known to go there and never be heard from again," Kate said sharply.

Emily murmured something that sounded suspiciously like *tant pis*. Kate didn't look at her. She looked at Charles instead, waiting. It was the father's duty, surely, to issue the final edict. Why was he hesitating, what was he thinking?

"Well, in my day—before my day, actually—students used to go on what was called the Grand Tour. In those times it meant the usual places, you know, Paris and London and Venice and Florence, Rome and the centers of antiquity. I never went myself, but I suppose this is your generation's version of the Grand Tour. Looking for exotic foreign places, well, that's not such a bad thing, I suppose. Matter of fact, I rather envy you. . . ."

"Charles!"

"Hey, far out," was Mr. McGrath's comment.

"Oh, Daddy, I'm so glad you understand," Emily burst out, and then regained the distant, cool demeanor she had let slip for a moment. "Not that you could have stopped us anyway," she concluded cruelly.

The clock chimed the half hour.

"Shall we go in to dinner?" Kate suggested. She led them into the dining room, averting her face to keep private her sudden battle with a hard rock of pain that seemed to have struck deep in her chest.

The conversation at dinner that night could have been taking place among the ruins at the foot of the Tower of Babel. Charles spoke in his language, advising the young people which sights to see, based on his reading of Kipling and other romanticists of British rule. Joe McGrath, who came from God knew where, wolfed down the roast beef and Yorkshire pudding as if he hadn't dined in weeks, not really listening to Charles but nodding between mouthfuls as if he understood. Emily toyed with her food and gave no sign of hearing anything except some inner voice which occasionally made her smile for no reason at all.

And Kate, unable to swallow, filled with unknowable, unnameable fears for her child, wanting to slap this boy's dirty hands for having dared to touch her, wanting to say something that would reawaken her sleeping daughter, but having no words at all. No words, not in any language.

"More broccoli, Mr. McGrath?" she suggested.

When they had left, finally, Kate asked Charles how he could be so goddamned calm about it.

"Why, I thought you were calm yourself," he said with mild surprise. "Had no idea you disapproved. You know, young Peter Barrows went off on one of these hegiras a year or so ago, and when he came home, his father arranged for him to present the Tuesday Club with a talk. He showed us some really interesting slides and seemed to have acquired an extraordinary knowledge of that part of the world. It was very interesting. Monasteries in Tibet and that sort of thing, good education for the young these days, I think. Should do our Emily a world of good. I don't quite see your objection."

"You really don't mind her going halfway around the world with that . . . twerp? Sharing a sleeping bag, and God knows what else—"

"For heaven's sake, Kate, must you see sex in everything? I'm sure it's all very innocent. They're just friends, surely. Young people do these things differently than we did. They don't have the same attitudes about, well, sex and such that we did. You really should try to keep up with things. We don't want to be old fuddy-duddies, do we? Besides," he said, finally looking at her, "you and I both know that Emily would turn her back on us if we raised any serious objections. It's your fault, you know. You have been so afraid of losing her that you've failed her in every way. When was the last time she ever gave you a gift? Birthday, Christmas, ever? You give and give and give to her, it's embarrassing. She has nothing but contempt for you."

She looked at him. I am in a world of strangers, she thought. I think I will leave now.

"Good night, Charles," she said.

"Good night, dear."

The insomnia was like an old and trusted friend. She looked out her window down onto the Common, thinking of her mother's plan to keep a cow there. There were people strolling under the lamplights, talking. I'd like someone to talk with, she thought. That would be very nice. A young couple stopped at a bench; from her window they looked very much like Emily and her young man. They seemed to have lots to talk about, and they laughed and touched each other. Then they stood up and put their arms around each other and kissed, and then they walked on away from where she stood, behind her window, looking on.

Then there was no one in the park at all; it was past midnight, and hers was probably the only lighted window on Beacon Street. She thought of New York. There was always someone awake, and there were always lights on there. She smiled to herself, remembering when she had run away from Boston to find Lindbergh, the Lone Eagle. It occurred to her now that she had not been silly to do that. She had only been too young. The illusion, the faith and sure knowledge that wonderful things could happen to her—that had not been silly or wrong. That had been beautiful. Dead now, was it? No more illusions, dreams, no more faith? Nothing ever again to look forward to . . . was it possible? Could she bear it?

But the trains still left from Back Bay Station. They flew through the dark countryside with wonderful going-someplace noises that she could hear in her memory. They took one away from Boston and into the world of exhilarating possibilities.

She had tried, all her life, to live either in opposition or in capitulation to what others expected of her. Now she was free to begin living for herself.

She went to her desk and lit the lamp, put a blank piece of paper in her typewriter. The list of things that must be done before she left was not long at all. And she would take very little baggage with her.